PRAISE FOR

The Princess Beard

"A rollicking adventure about friendship and finding one's place in the world . . . [a] fantastic series finale. Dawson and Hearne crown their trifecta of tempestuous hilarity with enough puns and fairy tale spoofs to tickle anyone's funny bone."

—*Booklist* (starred review)

"Challenge[s] gender roles in fantasy and skewer[s] social trends . . . This is a clever send-up of fantasy tropes and modern culture."

—*Publishers Weekly*

"As fun as the first two [books in The Tales of Pell] . . . a crazy story of questionable meat products, an unusual pirate captain (a parrot), and a motley crew of recruits including a muscle-bound centaur who can conjure delicious teatime treats, a dryad who wants to be a lawyer, and an elf who's tired of working for his uncle. Naturally hilarity ensues."

—*Elitist Book Reviews*

PRAISE FOR

Kill the Farm Boy

"A rollicking fantasy adventure that upends numerous genre tropes in audacious style, the first installment of Dawson and Hearne's Tales of Pell series is a laugh-out-loud-funny fusion of Monty Python–esque humor and whimsy à la Terry Pratchett's Disc-world."

—*Kirkus Reviews*

"Dawson and Hearne's reimagining of a traditional fairy tale is reminiscent of William Goldman's *The Princess Bride* and William Steig's *Shrek!* Irreverent, funny, and full of entertaining wordplay, this will keep readers guessing until the end."

—*Library Journal*

"The hilarious parody novel by *New York Times* best-selling authors Delilah Dawson and Kevin Hearne is one of the brightest reading selections of the summer, and its deliriously fun tone and satirical embrace will have you laughing out loud until strangers begin to look at you oddly."

—*SyFy*

"*Kill the Farm Boy* is a smart comedy, not only because it skewers modern tropes with a deft but direct hand, provides twists and turns to what should be a classic quest, or has representation in sorely needed ways, but because Dawson and Hearne know exactly when to dole out the humor amidst all this deconstruction of nar-rative. . . . Nuanced, complicated, and human."

—*Tor.com*

"Take every fantasy trope, every dungeon crawl, every fairytale stereotype and put them in a bag, smash the bag with a hammer, then dump out the pieces and you get *Kill the Farm Boy.* It's a romp of a book, with clever turns of phrase, goofy characters, a quest they don't realize they're on, all while poking fun at every fantasy book you've ever read. Terry Pratchett would be proud. . . . Simply fun to read."

—*Elitist Book Reviews*

"*Kill the Farm Boy* is a delight for any lover of puns and fairy tales. . . . With a fabulous and unexpected ending, and magic enough to delight even the grumpiest of Dark Lords, *Kill the Farm Boy* brings together two authors and their creative vision in the pages of a simply delicious novel."

—*The Skiffy and Fanty Show*

The Princess Beard

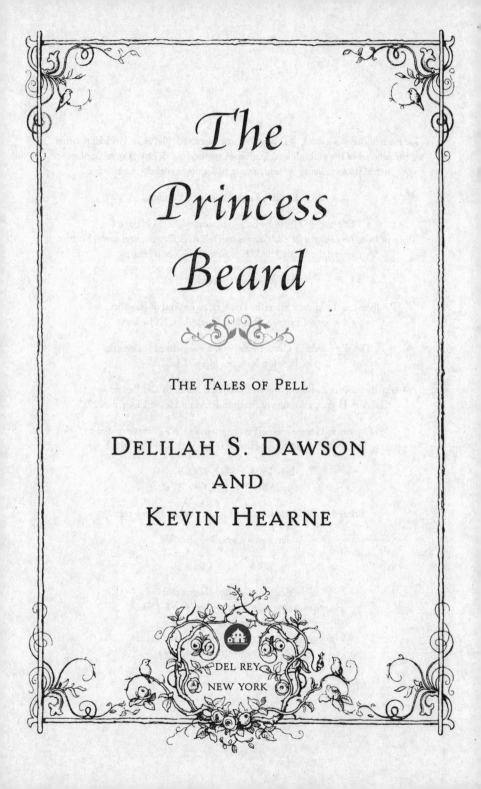

The Princess Beard

THE TALES OF PELL

DELILAH S. DAWSON
AND
KEVIN HEARNE

DEL REY

NEW YORK

2020 Del Rey Trade Paperback Edition

Copyright © 2019 by D.S. Dawson and Kevin Hearne
Excerpt from *No Country for Old Gnomes* by Delilah S. Dawson and Kevin Hearne copyright © 2019 by D.S. Dawson and Kevin Hearne

Published in the United States by Del Rey, an imprint of Random House, a division of Penguin Random House LLC, New York.

DEL REY and the CIRCLE colophon are registered trademarks of Penguin Random House LLC.

Originally published in hardcover in the United States by Del Rey, an imprint of Random House, a division of Penguin Random House LLC, in 2019.

Map by Kevin Hearne was originally published in *Kill the Farm Boy* by D.S. Dawson and Kevin Hearne (New York: Del Rey, 2018)

ISBN 978-1-5247-9782-9
Ebook ISBN 978-1-5247-9781-2

Printed in the United States of America on acid-free paper

randomhousebooks.com

2 4 6 8 9 7 5 3 1

Book design by Caroline Cunningham
Frontispiece otter illustration: iStock/Andrii-Oliinyk
Title page border: iStock/jcrosemann
Title page and chapter opener ornament: Vecteezy.com
Space break ornament: iStock/mxtama

To our readers,

with love and tea and cake.

A foul vole, ye owl!

CONTENTS

The
Princess
Beard

1.

ATOP AN IVORY TOWER CRAMMED PERILOUSLY CLOSE WITH FOINE BOOKS

Call me Itchmael.

But do not call me late to brunch.

For I am the mouthpiece of the god Pellanus, and it is a tiring job, and I am an old elf in possession of dodgy knees and a distaste for mimosas. I was once a carefree elfling sprig, enjoying the heady pleasures of the Morningwood, but then I received the Call. It was as if the double-headed god spoke directly to me with both mouths.

"Itchie," the god boomed, a male and female tone merging.

"Yes, hello?" I said, because that is called conversation.

"You are to be the next Sn'archivist," the god continued.

"Oh, really?"

"Yes, really."

"Ah."

And then there was a long and awkward pause, and I suppose Pellanus felt as confused about the whole thing as I did, because every time I tried to speak, so did they.

"You—"

"I really think—"

"Itchmael, shut up."

And thus I did shut up, because Pellanus is a capricious god, and spontaneous combustion is real.

"Itchmael, you are to go to the Siren Sn'archipelago. There you will find a tower, and within, you will find a very dead skeleton."

"Aren't all skeletons dead?"

The god paused. "Sure. If you say so. You see, the last Sn'archivist is but a ghost, and you will replace her."

"As a ghost?"

"No, Itchmael. As the next Sn'archivist."

I took a moment to consider it.

"Forgive me, O Pellanus, but that does not sound like a good job offer," said I.

"It is not an offer!" the god boomed, both voices ripe with fury. "It is a holy order! This is the Call. Not like a regular call, but the Call, with a capital *C*!"

"Ah," I said again, because I was quite determined to become a door-to-door sales elf. "Are the benefits good?"

"Er, yes?" the god said. "Super good."

And with that, I told King Glosstangle of my sacred duty, was roundly laughed out of the Morningwood, and found the fastest ship to the Siren Sn'archipelago. There, just as Pellanus promised, I found a tower. Within that tower, I found a corpse, which was very dead, as Pellanus had also promised. I also found a fleet of helpful monks dedicated to my care; the benefits were indeed good. The first thing I did was to ask the monks to remove the skeleton as well as the ruined rug beneath it. The next thing I did was to request a new rug, plus a citrus salad, a journal, and a quill.

For Pellanus had just begun to speak to me, and I had much to record.

Now I have a purpose.

And that purpose is driven by schedule.

Oh? Yes? What?

Pellanus has just informed me that proper Fantasy books are always written in third person past tense, and so I will switch. Are you ready? Because, you see, I will no longer speak as I, Itchmael, but will begin telling a different story about other people, mostly. Still, when you see the Sn'archivist, that's me. I mean him. I mean, I am him.

Bother.

Ahem.

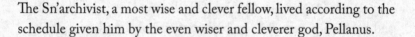

The Sn'archivist, a most wise and clever fellow, lived according to the schedule given him by the even wiser and cleverer god, Pellanus.

The schedule was simple but sacrosanct. The schedule, at this point, was as much of a biological imperative for the Sn'archivist as eating, sleeping, or visiting the boom-boom room. And after waking, and blatting a sonorous blort on the tower boghorn, and quaffing three cups of kuffee and a rasher of boar bacon, it was time for him to write, without fail—and generally without variation.

For uncounted years he had written tirelessly about the same subject. A vital subject, to be sure, for it was the secret source of joy throughout Pell, but he'd begun to wonder in recent months about whether he was accomplishing anything, since he'd filled floors of bookshelves with volumes on the subject but no one ever came to read them. What was the point of possessing such knowledge if it was never shared? He often read aloud to his shining gnomeric construct, Reginald the Affirmation Gecko, but that didn't count. Reginald never retained anything he heard. He only spouted one of his many thousands of affirmations whenever the Sn'archivist required a response and, when lacking the proper affirmation, congratulated the Sn'archivist on continuing to exist. *Your wit is a shining beacon of hope in a dark world!* the gecko might say, or simply, *Wow! Nice elbows, pal!*

The location of his tower might have had something to do with the poor distribution of his work, the Sn'archivist mused. Perched on the eastern precipice of an island in the Sn'archipelago, his home was hardly convenient to the populace of Pell, and he was not entirely sure they knew of his existence. He was supplied and fortified by the Sn'archdruid and a handful of monkish Sn'acolytes who looked after gardens of produce and herds of livestock, but they never asked to read his tomes. They sat around their campfire at night and listened to the Sn'archdruid tell them stories and sing them bawdy ballads about the early, earthier days, when Pellanus had been but a young and gawky god, but whenever the Sn'archivist tried to join them and sing songs of his knowledge, they fell silent and looked at their shoes and soon made excuses to go back to their holy hovels.

Ah, well. No matter. He'd always known that following the Call would isolate him socially as well as geographically. He had his work and his gecko, and that would have to be enough. The Sn'archivist had just finished another volume yesterday and shelved it lovingly on the tenth-floor anteroom. This morning he would start a new book, putting quill to paper and letting the knowledge of years and the enlightenment of Pellanus pour out of him. But after his first cup of kuffee he didn't feel like frying up the usual rasher of boar bacon. Instead, he wanted something different. He wanted . . . oatmeal! With fresh fruit! Fiber, by Pellanus! And vitamins! He rummaged in his pantry, searching for the oats, already feeling that something extraordinary was about to happen. He was about to deviate from the schedule. Indeed, he already had! Whether this would prove to be the beginning of something remarkably fine or remarkably tragic he did not know, but the prospect of variety was like a siren's call, irresistible and alluring.

Soon enough he sat before a bowl of oats topped with raspberries, blueberries, slivered almonds, and brown sugar. And when he sampled his first spoonful—oh, what splendid magnificence! An explosion of taste with a muted subtext of circulatory health benefits!

"Reginald," he declared, "this oatmeal is delicious."

The gold-and-silver affirmation gecko blinked and cocked his head, tiny gears turning audibly in his skull as he considered a reply. "Think of how happy you're making your colon right now!" Reginald said. "You're just a super dude!"

The Sn'archivist grunted happily and continued eating. And then, halfway through his breakfast, after his second cup of kuffee but before his third, a voice spoke into either ear, except it was two voices: A woman's in his left ear and a man's on his right. Identical tones and inflections, but octaves apart.

"Today, you will write a different book," the voice intoned, and the Sn'archivist froze, not wanting to miss a single word. It was the voice of the great two-faced god Pellanus, gracing him with divine inspiration, as it once had so long ago, when he'd received the Call. He was to write a single book on a new subject, display it in a place of honor, and then point it out to whoever next came to call on him in the tower.

And then the double voice told him the subject of the new book.

The Sn'archivist dropped his spoon, oatmeal forgotten, and gulped down his last cup of kuffee. He rushed downstairs to the third floor, where his writing desk was, and ran his thin fingers over the stack of blank books waiting in a crate beside it. He pulled them all out and inspected them, wishing to choose the most flawless specimen for what was to be a truly special work. Several had small tears on the corners of the pages. Others had tiny scuffs on the cover. But eventually he picked one that seemed closest to perfection, with crisp ivory sheets and a rich ruby cover, and he placed it reverently on his desk.

Today was different because today he would *write* something different. Something important! The oatmeal had been a herald of the divine! He was a conduit for powers far beyond those of most mortals! He dabbed his quill in the inkpot, paused briefly over the paper to savor the moment, and then he scratched out two words, pregnant with meaning, on the first page:

Otter balls.

Yes. That was it! That was it *exactly*. He didn't know exactly what *it* was, only that those two words were most definitely, exactly, it. He could feel that he had written something vital. Something crucial. Words with the power to save lives.

But he rather hoped no one asked him to explain how.

2.

SURROUNDED BY LUSH LOCKS OF HAIR NOT ENTIRELY UNLIKE SPUN SILK

Elsewhere, a hirsute lady slept in a tower covered in thorns.

And then, quite suddenly, she didn't.

The Lady Harkovrita blinked and coughed. It was fusty in this room. Or musty. Moldy? Rusty. Roadkilly? Something unpleasant to her nose, anyway, even if she couldn't pin down the precise word for it. She was groggy, which she felt was intensely unfair since she did not remember consuming any grog. In fact, she did not remember going to sleep at all. The last thing she remembered was being given a rose by a sweet little slip of a girl shortly after her father, the Earl of Borix, had decreed that roses should be entirely eliminated from Tennebruss. Something about preventing a curse.

A gift of contraband, she'd thought as she took the rose from the girl's hand—what was her name? Argabella! That was it. The girl was going to bard school or something boring like that, but her willingness to defy the earl's decree regarding roses forced Harkovrita to admit she might need to reevaluate whether or not Argabella herself was boring. "How thoughtful," she'd said to the girl. "And exciting." And then nothing after that, until now.

The blinking did little to clear her vision. She was gummed up pretty well with a remarkable case of eye boogers, so she raised a hand to knuckle them away and discovered that someone had done something horrifying to her fingers. They were heavy and unwieldy and most of all nightmarish, because the fingernails were perhaps a foot long and curled in yellow loops and twined together.

Harkovrita nearly screamed, especially when she realized it was the same with her other hand: Her fingertips had all decided to nail one another. But she choked it back because she realized someone must be pranking her. She would not give them the satisfaction of a reaction. She would just quietly get up, remove these horrors from her hands, and go about her business, which was the business of being a supremely bored and sheltered lady of Borix at the dubious mercy of her noble father. At least this prank was a change in routine, and she did appreciate that. A little shivering body horror was occasionally a good thing. She didn't feel groggy anymore.

Rising to a sitting position took greater effort than it should have. As with her hands, her head weighed far more than it was supposed to, especially at the base of her skull. Looking down to either side, she saw thick braids of hair coiled like massive yellow snakes with a lustrous coat of fur instead of scaly skin. The braids disappeared behind her, and as there was no one else in the room, she had to assume that this massive amount of hair was actually hers. Or, rather, not hers but surely fakes attached to her as part of the same prank as the fingernails. But then there was the fine downy hair that draped down her front and tickled the top of her chest: How had the prankster passed up the opportunity of braiding that? And why wasn't it in her eyes?

She started to raise a hand to brush it away but realized her fingernails would make pretty much everything but walking impossible until she got rid of them. Those had to go first. She should have some clippers in her bureau, if she could get it open. Or handle the clippers. This was such a strange prank to pull on her. Why would anyone go to such trouble?

Punishment. It had to be. She'd refused to accept the marriage her father had arranged with some lord's brat in Taynt, a kid named Vendel Vas Deference, and in response the earl had decreed that next month Harkovrita would go to the Lovely Ladies Ultimate Finisher School in Songlen and then marry Vendel anyway, by Pellanus.

Well, by Pellanus, she would exit the stage before that particular play ever began.

She took a deep breath and exhaled, examining her room. It was a bit different. No tapestry on the wall, which was strange. She'd loved that woven vision of unicorns disemboweling young squires while maids giggled into their hands. And no mirror on her bureau. None of her model ships were in evidence either. Was this even her room? Yes, the shape of it was the same, the light from the window behind her bed the same, and this was indeed her bed, and that was her wardrobe and bureau made from well-polished Morningwood. There were simply some things missing and some . . . extra things in their place. The hair brushing against her chest and neck was very strange, though, and had only become more so as she turned her head from side to side. It shouldn't be down there without passing in front of her eyes first. Unless . . .

Harkovrita's nostrils flared and her breath came in quick gasps. She needed to check on something. Carefully, awkwardly, she brought her hands up to her face, but with her fingers pointing away at first, until she tilted them up and placed her palms flat on her cheeks and rubbed. There was hair there. And it was attached. To her jaw.

"I have a sharting *beard*?" she said into the silence. Her voice sounded high and panicked and she didn't like it.

Harkovrita gave serious consideration to letting loose with a scream after all. But on the cusp of belting out a bloodcurdling holler o' horror, she stopped: A scream would bring people running. And then they would see her like this, with too much hair everywhere and fingernails as twisted and yellow as an old goat's horns.

"No, no, no, no, no," she said.

She needed to be where other people were not. Probably forever. Because it was becoming clear that this was no prank but her actual condition. She had been asleep or unconscious for so long that she had grown out her hair and fingernails like this—and a beard!—and they had let her. Her parents, the castle denizens—they'd all neglected her completely. The curse that her father had been so worried about had obviously come to pass, foisted on her by an innocent bard with a verboten rose.

She didn't want to linger in a cursed tower any longer. Nor did she want to be kept, patronized, sheltered, the subject of mocking songs or the butt of jokes, or given away as a prize to Lord Vas Deference. She just wanted out, which was a feeling she'd had before but never intensely enough to leave comfort and privilege and pie behind—the pastry chef made such an amazing strawberry rhubarb pie! But now she felt as if she couldn't get out of the castle fast enough. Practical matters would need to be handled first, however. She quietly spoke a list aloud:

"Fingernails. Chamber pot. Different clothes."

How long had she been asleep? Her bladder felt ready to burst. But emptying it would require functioning hands just to deal with the massively poofy dress her parents always forced her to wear.

She swung her legs over the side of the bed and tested them. No tingling, no problems. She stood and tested her weight. That was all fine. And then she took a step—or tried to.

Harkovrita tripped on her twisted toenails and flailed a bit and clacked her long nails together. The sound was so gross that she felt the gorge rising in her throat. The nails were thick but seemed brittle.

"Time to break a nail," she said in a low voice barely above a whisper.

Sitting down with her rear on the floor, she placed both hands in front of her, with the monstrosities curling up and away. She raised her right leg, cocked a knee, and slammed the heel of her foot down on the nails, just beyond the tips of her fingers. There was a sickening crunch and crackle and a large portion of the nails fell away, luckily with very little to no pain. A couple more strikes and her hands were freed from the bulk of their weight. The nails were jagged, ugly things and still too long, but they were at least manageable. She rose with a shudder of revulsion and hobbled over to her bureau, quietly cursing the weight of her braided hair and feeling it drag through the mess of twisted fingernails behind her. And then it brought her up short; while she had enough slack to reach the edges of the room, it was only just enough, since the rest trailed out the window and obviously snagged on something out there. She was on a leash and would need to free herself of that as well as everything else.

Harkovrita yanked open the top drawer to find it rearranged since the last time she'd opened it, which was for her that morning but in reality had been who knew how long. She must have slept for years. She didn't think she could grow this much excess keratin in a couple of months. Maybe the arranged marriage was off now, but no matter: She didn't want to be given away to anyone, ever, and as long as she was under her father's roof, he'd assume he could dispose of her as he wished.

It took some searching, but she found her nail scissors and went to work, first on her crusty toenails and then on what remained of her fingernails. She might have clipped them too aggressively; on a couple of fingers she damaged the cuticles in her desire to be rid of them. No matter; she was relieved. And now needed to relieve herself.

As she squatted over the chamber pot, she wondered over other practical matters. Had she had her menses while she slept? Had she wet the bed? Why wasn't she wearing a diaper and a hospital gown covered in hideous ducklings? How had she kept hydrated and fed? Were her teeth entirely mossy, or had some servant diligently brushed the plaque away? And if all that had happened, who had tended to her? She was so mortally embarrassed by the mere *thought* of what it would take to keep her alive and well all that time that she resolved never to see anyone in Tennebruss again. Farewell, Mother and Father! Farewell, courtiers and guards! Farewell, itinerant gnomeric pudding merchant with the extra-chunky pistachio pudding! The thought of never tasting that treat again, or the pastry chef's pies, nearly made her reconsider, but she shook her head.

"No. I've been given a chance at a new life, so there's no use living the old one," she said into the quiet. "It is time for strange new puddings and fantastic adventures in pie."

Finished with her bodily needs and done speaking dramatically to no one, she untied the stays of her formal velvet dress and stepped out of it and the petticoats beneath it, striding to her wardrobe to find more appropriate clothing for the road: breeches, tunic, and belt, which she'd worn during her training sessions with the master-at-arms. These items were hidden in the back so her mother wouldn't find them. She even had some brown leather boots that would serve well for hikes. As she buttoned up the tunic and belted it, she considered the tug of the long braids anchored to her scalp and running through a hole in her bed and out the window. She wanted to cut it all but had never actually cut her hair before and wasn't quite ready to take that step.

She pulled out her blue traveling cloak next and checked the secret pockets sewn into the lining: Yes, her funds were still there, hoarded coins from birthdays and other holidays. She would be well supplied with fickels for a short while. She noticed that two of her plainer cloaks were missing—ones she used for sneaking about—and that the closet smelled like a corpse.

What else to take? She rummaged in her wardrobe and found the gift from her uncle, a hempen gunnysack emblazoned with the name of Chekkoff's, a fabled market in Cape Gannet near the Seven Toe Islands. She'd always wanted to go there. Well, why not now? Might as well have a destination in mind.

She shoved some extra clothes into the Chekkoff's gunnysack, as well as a gnomeric firebird a pyromaniac cousin had given her for her sixteenth birthday. She added a rapier, a mace, some brass knuckles, a beret, a gryphon's quill, a saltshaker, a flower press, a grimoire, and a porcelain unicorn. Surely something in there would come in handy at some later moment of great import.

From her bureau, she pulled out a pair of shears and then moved to the window behind her bed, peering out and down to assess the ridiculous length of her hair dangling down past a discomfitingly overgrown thatch of roses. She might not have quite enough braid for what she hoped to accomplish, but it would be close. Taking the stairs, she knew, would be a mistake. There was no way she could exit without being seen, except out her tower window. And the longer she waited, the more likely it became that she would be discovered by someone tasked to look after her. No time to waste.

The first thing she did felt utterly delicious: She used her shears to hack off both braids at the nape of her neck, leaving her hair just long enough to brush her shoulders and fit in a stubby nubbin of a pony-tail. She stowed the shears in her bag and tied both braids together, using a double-fisherman knot she'd been practicing from her favorite knot book, then secured the braids to one of the heavy posts of her bed. As she tested the knot and found it strong, she felt a little frisson of excitement. Her mother had encouraged her to give up knots and take up tatting instead, and she was pleased to see evidence that she'd chosen wisely. Tatting wouldn't save her now.

Holding on to her braided-hair rope, gunnysack over her shoulder, she straddled her tower window. She had been warned all her life to stay far away from this window, lest she fall out or be attacked by a squirrel, but now she drank in the clear air and noted the dense perfume of roses riding the fair breeze. She hooked the rope around her thigh and began rappelling down, boots pressed against the brick. The braid held, and soon she stopped worriedly staring up at the window and quickened her descent—until she ran out of hair rope, perhaps ten feet above ground. Surrounded by a troubling number of what appeared to be halfling skeletons trapped among the thorns, she dangled from the end of the rope for a moment, let the sack fall first, then let go. Her feet sent prickles of pain up her spine as she landed, and it stung when she stood to walk, but she picked up her sack and headed straight for the nearest road. She'd decided to head south, out of Tennebruss and toward the busy port city of Sullenne. Finding passage on a ship would get her out of Borix quicker than anything else.

No one stopped her. No shout went up from the tower. She pulled up the hood of her cloak and limped along the road, looking nothing like the Lady Harkovrita but more, she hoped, like a wild young man in need of a razor and a destiny. For the moment, the beard was exactly the disguise she needed, for all that it dangled past her belt and kept getting caught on the buttons of her tunic.

Her boots, while very fine, proved to be a bit uncomfortable after a couple of miles. She could feel blisters forming on the backs of her heels. Her muscles ached and her back cracked, but not unpleasantly; she felt the exhaustion of that long sleep lift as her body woke up. She began to wonder where she would spend the night as the sun crept toward the horizon, shining in her eyes. She did not have a portable shelter, and for all her reading on maritime life, she had never slept a single day outside. She might be able to fend off a determined groundhog with her shears, but a pack of wolves or a wandering band of rogues would be much more problematic. "Highwaymen," her father called them, right before damning them. That was, in fact, all she knew about them, because the sum total of what her father said in her hearing was an irritated snort, followed by "Highwaymen. Damn them!" Then again, he said the same thing about goats, children, and bunions, so perhaps her father's reactions did not adequately reflect the real world.

The sound of creaking wood, hooves on hard-packed ruts, and the low murmur of a man's voice caused her to turn around. There was a wagon coming along, pulled by an old brown horse, a single man holding the reins.

Harkovrita slid over to one side of the road and waited. He might be kind or cruel, but either way he was going to catch up to her. Might as well be prepared.

He was not a nobleman or even a merchant, judging by his dress. He was most likely a farmer taking a load of vegetables to the coast, since he wore a muck-covered jerkin over mud-splattered pants tucked into boots begrimed with manure. His jaw was strong and clean-shaven, his thick dark eyebrows and hair framing a warm tan face bereft of guile. A stalk of hay, complete with fuzzy seed bundle at the end, bobbed up and down between his teeth. He nodded once at Harkovrita from far off, acknowledging that awkward moment when it was too far to shout greetings, and she nodded back, adding in a wave. He waited until he was closer and then politely asked his horse to halt.

"Pleasant afternoon, sir," he said, and Harkovrita almost took insult but then remembered that she was dressed as a man and currently had a beard. She really needed to shave that off. But in the meantime, best to play along. She pitched her voice low to sound like a man's.

"Afternoon," she replied. "Don't suppose you'd let me ride along?"

He cocked his head at her. "Well, I sure wouldn't mind the company, no, sir, but I'm not sure you'd like paying the price."

"Why? What is it?"

"You'd have to listen to me talk the whole dang way."

Harkovrita blinked. "That's it?"

"That's plenty. I've been informed on more than one occasion that I talk too much and the best thing I could possibly do is shut up. I'm a fearful affliction to ears, it seems, to hear other people tell it, not that the animals seem to mind a ding-dang bit. And I like to talk about boring stuff."

"Stuff like what?"

"Jam and cows. Other barnyard animals too, but mostly them cows and their heckin' moos."

"I like jam and cows."

He grinned. "Then I reckon you might survive the journey without me doin' any damage to your sanity. Hop on up." He scooted over on the seat and jerked his chin at the space he'd made for her. She climbed up and settled back with a sigh, grateful to give her feet a rest.

"My name's Morvin," the man said. "What's yours?"

Harkovrita gaped. She hadn't thought at all about what she would tell people. She couldn't say she was the Lady Harkovrita, recently escaped from the tower at Tennebruss. If she gave him a man's name now, it wouldn't hold up well once she shaved her beard. She flailed for a moment, then decided to do something no courtier in the castle had ever done: express genuine vulnerability.

"I'm not particularly fond of my current name and I'm thinking I'd like to choose a new one. Have you ever felt that way?"

A small crease appeared between Morvin's eyes. "Cor, I reckon I haven't, although once I named a cow Mr. Mutton on accident and tried to get him to change it over to Robbie, and he wouldn't have none of it. But I can understand well enough that sometimes a body needs a good ol' redo. I just decided to choose a new life meself, so here I am."

Harkovrita grinned at him. "Me too!"

"Hey, no kidding?"

"I jest not!"

"That's fancy talk, jesting is. Bit like jousting but more bells and less havin' holes put in you by lances 'n' such. You should have a fancy name to go with it, eh?"

"What sort of name do you think would suit me?"

"Huh. Well." Morvin examined her face closely. "That is a mighty unusual beard, if you don't mind me saying, sir."

"No, I don't mind. Unusual how?"

"Well, it ain't all scraggly and coarse like most beards you see. That's like really fine baby hair, all silky, you know, and I ain't never seen the like. And underneath that, well, you got some features that might almost be, uh . . ." He stopped talking and looked down.

"Almost what? Be honest with me, Morvin. I promise not to take offense."

"Well, I surely don't mean none, so I hope you'll remember that promise. But you have some features that might look a bit like . . . a woman's. But I figure you don't really fit in either camp, and if someone gave me two boxes and told me to check one for you, I'd make a mark somewhere in the middle."

Harkovrita beamed at him. "I agree. That's quite perceptive of you. So what sort of name should I choose?"

Morvin shrugged. "One that's neither here nor there. All sorts of folks in the world that don't fit in one or two boxes, and they have all sorts of names to suit 'em."

"Hmm. What do you think of Morgan? It's a bit close to your name."

Morvin squinted at her. "I reckon that would fit you mighty fine. It's fancy enough and works for ladies and gents as well. Or sheep, probably."

Harkovrita held out her hand and the farmer took it, albeit awkwardly, as they sat side by side. She pumped it up and down. "My name's Morgan, Morvin. Thanks for giving me a ride. Now let's go, and you can tell me all about jam and cows and why you decided to choose yourself a new life."

Morvin clucked at the horse and shook the reins. The wagon lurched forward and he looked pleased.

"Well, Morgan, you ever heard of invigorated ham jam? It's the most amazin' stuff. Got a load of it in the back of the wagon here. Most folks just put it on toast, but I'm tellin' ya, there's so much more you can do with it."

And so Morgan settled back against the wagon seat with a new name and a new life and dreamt of the many possibilities of ham jam, every single one of which was better than marrying some reeking lump of a bratling lord of Taynt.

3.

FLOODED WITH GALLONS OF STEAMING
FAILURE AND PISTACHIO MACARONS

"Ninety-seven, ninety-eight, ninety-nine, and ... one hundred!" Vic let the barbell fall to the ground with an unnecessary and startling thunk. The gnomes he'd paid to sit on top of the barbell and cheer tumbled off, their hats landing in the dirt. Vic looked around. None of the other centaurs in Ye Olde Krossfitte Gymnasium so much as looked up.

"You sullied my cardigan!" one of the gnomes shouted, which wasn't a cheer at all.

Vic looked down, his eyes roving over acres of his own muscles, both in his human flesh up top and in his horseflesh down below. He was a meaty-man torso stuck on a Clydesdale chassis and bedecked with a yellow crop top, and he'd put a lot of work into his guns, and the gnome should've been more appreciative, considering his wee little spaghetti arms.

"I paid you already," Vic growled. "Now begone before I stomp you to pudding!"

The gnome grabbed his hat and scurried out the door with his friends, shaking his tiny fist and shouting, *"He who sullies another's sweater won't have a day that gets any better!"* in a way suggesting that, despite his false bravado, the gnome would spend the rest of his life hiding from anything with hooves.

Good.

At least someone recognized Vic's latent lethality and obvious swoleness.

He flexed his pecs, one-two, one-two, and considered the other swoleboys currently lifting and grunting around the room. It was like every other gym he'd encountered from the Centaur Pastures to the Bearded Plains to Pyckåbøg, and just like in all those other places, it was cram jam with elf biceps and dwarf glutes and centaur flanks and glistening troll chests peppered with the most masculine sheen of sweat. Vic looked at his hands in their fingerless lifting gloves. Flexing his fingers, he offered up his daily prayer: *Dear Pellanus, Keep these fingers from revealing my secret and let them only be used for swole and manly purposes. Amen.*

A giant hand shoved him aside, almost causing him to trip over a dumbbell. "Oi, My Little Pony." The troll grinned, revealing teeth that looked like stumps. "Quit hogging the mirror. This corner of the gym is for serious lifting only, not flexing your ladyfingers. Or are you a bard? You gonna play a dainty little lute?"

Vic's lips lifted in a snarl as his, yes, somewhat feminine fingers curled into fists.

"You talking to me, Sissy MacTeaparty?"

With the fondness for name-calling that all trolls shared, this one turned on Vic, his eyes alight with pleasure. "That's Fergus MacMurdernuts to you, pony boy. You want to take this fight outside?"

No, actually, Vic did not. He loved lifting, loved being swole, loved cutting a swath through any crowd that valued their toes and didn't like a luxurious black tail flicking at their eyes. But he did not enjoy fighting, especially not with an audience. Fighting tended to bring out . . . well, his worst qualities. Qualities he wanted to keep hidden.

"Love to fight you, bro, but I've got an appointment. To, er . . ." Vic trailed off, trying to think of the most masculine pursuit in the world. "To go fishing in a freezing mountain stream with my bare hands while drinking whiskey and eschewing my father's funeral."

A nearby centaur, a dappled gray Percheron, turned around, scowling. "That's cold, dude. Like, don't you think your father deserved the bare minimum of respect? I hate my dad, but when he kicks it or breaks a leg or whatever, I'm totally heading home to the pastures, at least to support my mom."

Vic almost winced; he'd miscalculated.

"Oh, yeah, well, my mom is dead. So it's just him. Was just him. And he . . . he liked . . . he played with dolls and painted his hooves?"

Another centaur turned around, this one a palomino with flames painted on his plate-sized hooves. He lifted one, pawing the air for emphasis. "You got a problem with painted hooves, bro?"

The troll just sat back, arms crossed, grinning maniacally. As much as trolls loved fighting, they mostly just loved instigating pile-ons of trouble and then eating whoever lost.

"Your hooves look fantastic," Vic said, hoping the other centaur could hear his sincerity, as the dude's sausage fingers were curled in fists, one airbrushed hoof stamping in annoyance.

A third centaur rounded on him, this one a slender but still tough-looking Thoroughbred with a glossy black coat that suggested he supplemented with omega-3s. "I assume you're going to put down braided beards next?" he asked, his chest-length beard wagging. "Or eyeliner? You got a problem with that? Because this is just how we do things in Qul, and I'm not here for your toxic and ignorant viewpoint. I'm here to lift—because it's good for cardiovascular health and also counters later osteoporosis."

"Me too!" Vic said, fully aware that his voice was an octave higher than it had been before three centaurs and a troll had backed him into a corner. "I just want to be swole with my swole bros! No offense meant!"

"Offense taken!" the centaur with the braided beard said, stepping closer.

"Say, what's your name?" the palomino asked.

Vic puffed out his chest and gave an up-nod. "You can call me Vic."

The palomino rolled his eyes. "That's not your name," he growled. "If it is, you're not a centaur, and I can see you are, even if you're a poor excuse for one. What's your full name? I'm Stampeding Triumphant."

Vic gulped. By Pellanus, that was a fantastic name. He had to choke back a compliment and remember that he was on the spot here. Mustering what dignity he could, he lifted his chin and said, "My name is Pissing Victorious."

"Ha!" Stampeding Triumphant barked.

"I would've guessed Sniveling Pathetic," the troll chortled.

"Or maybe Insulting Boorish," the stallion from Qul said with a sniff.

"Or Waxing Insecure," a gnome muttered from just outside the window. He popped out of sight with a squeak before Vic could flick him with his tail.

The gray centaur crossed his arms. "You're not from around here, are you, buddy?"

"He's not," Stampeding confirmed. "He's a rube, fresh from the pastures. Probably hasn't ever been to a big city like Sullenne before or learned to live among and respect other cultures." He stamped a hoof. "Pasture Boy, d'you remember what they do back home to trespassers?"

Vic felt utterly called out. To have his name mocked hit closer to home than he liked. And if Stampeding Triumphant was from the Pastures, then Vic couldn't put on his Tough Guy from the Country routine. Because the palomino could clearly invoke the Even Tougher Guy from the Country routine.

"Well?" the palomino demanded.

"S-s-s-stomp the trespassers to bits and leave them on the edge of the territory in decorative gift bags," Vic whispered.

At that, all three centaurs, the troll, and everyone else in the gym laughed. At him.

"Why's that funny? It's true."

"It's funny because it's so pathetically xenophobic," the Thoroughbred said.

"But mostly 'cause you're so scared you're tap-dancing, mate," the troll said, pointing down.

And it was true. Vic's carefully polished and, yes, ever so slightly tinted hooves were dancing with inelegant clomps, his flanks quivering, his tail twitching. He felt a blush start up his cheeks and spread into the hairline of his mullet.

"I'm just flexing," he muttered. "Uh, working my hocks. It's leg day."

"It should be brain day!" the palomino bellowed. "You trod on my workout bag!"

Vic danced backward, all control of his equine half lost. His hoof slipped on a barbell, and he pinwheeled his arms as he fell heavily on his rump and let out a squealing whinny.

"Did somebody fall down go boom?" the Thoroughbred chortled.

"Gonna live up to your name now, Mr. Pissing? Gonna make a mess?" This from the gray, who was laughing so hard he was partially whinnying, but not in the high-pitched way Vic was.

"Looks like you need a beginner's tap class more than leg day," the gnome observed from the window, more boldly now.

"I can hold my bladder! I'm not dancing! Dancing is for girls!" Vic squeaked as he struggled to muscle his bulk to standing.

The palomino shook his head sadly. "Dancing is for everyone," he said sagely, giving a graceful hop. "What you're doing is a public disturbance. If you would just ask for help—"

"Hey!"

Every head turned toward the burly dwarf who'd just appeared in the door marked Ye Old Employees Onlye, and every swoleboy took a respectful step toward the wall.

"Mr. Kross, sir," the troll said with a slight bow. "What an honor!"

"Shut your piehole, Mac, and back away from the ballerina with four left feet!"

The dwarf had a rope in his hands, and everyone got out of his way as he stormed across the gym, directly toward Vic. Vic could feel his skin shuddering like he was beset by flies, and the fear sweat drying into his bay coat itched something terrible. When the dwarf stopped in front of him, he wanted nothing more than to gallop away and never enter a gym again, but instead, his rear hooves lashed out, putting a hole in the wall and upsetting the cozy home of a family of muscular mice.

"You," the dwarf said, pointing one finger at Vic. "Were you born in a barn?"

". . . Yes?"

The dwarf rubbed the bridge of his nose. "I forget that only works with people who don't have hooves. What I mean to say is, don't you know they make rubberized hoof covers for this sort of nervous condition? You can't just go putting holes in a person's walls. It's nothing to be ashamed of, but it's right there in the rules." He pointed to a hand-painted wooden sign on the wall. Rule 6 read: THOSE WHO LACK SELFE-CONTROL MUST WEAR RUBBERIZED PROPHYLACTIC GARMENTS FOR THE SAKE OF PUBLIC DECENCY AND OUR RATINGS ON YE OLDE YELPE.

"Can we talk about this in private?" Vic squeaked.

"No," Mr. Kross barked. "You ignored the rules and made your problems public."

"This isn't usually an issue for me."

"*Usually* only counts in things that don't involve disrupting the lives of lifestyle coaches and well-behaved mice." The mice squeaked their agreement and flexed in annoyance before scurrying back into the safety of the wooden wall.

Vic realized his human upper half was now fidgeting too, almost wiggling his fingers, and he crossed his arms and tucked those rebellious digits into his manly, sweating, hairy armpits before they could do something even more embarrassing than his horsey half had done.

"I'd be glad to patch it up, sir," he said.

The dwarf nodded thoughtfully. "Know how to do handiwork, eh?"

"Er, well, no, Mr. Kross, sir, I just wanted to . . ."

"Act like you're traditionally masculine and know everything?"

"Yes! Wait. No?"

"You seem fairly confused about personal balance, young buck. Look down."

Vic looked down. He'd been so discombobulated by being yelled at, in public, by a knee-high dwarf, that he'd stumbled into the yoga corner of the gym and deflated several yoga balls. He turned suddenly, and his dancing hooves clattered into a stack of metal weights, sending them skittering and tripping the other gymgoers. That was not how the day was supposed to go. He'd just wanted to stop in at a gym, get his pump on, impress the local swoleboys, find some drinking buddies, and head to the nearest inn for foamy mugs of manly lager and the chance to ogle some fillies and feel like Gulping Glamorous, the famous centaur mascot of the Bushy Beer Company. That's all he ever wanted, but somehow it never worked out. Usually it didn't go this badly—usually he just slunk out of the gym alone, having been utterly unnoticed.

But, as Mr. Kross said, *usually* was for things that didn't involve dancing the can-can and putting muddy hoofprints on a collection of expensive yoga mats.

"Sir, I'd really like a chance to fix this situation," Vic said. "If you'll just give me a . . . thingy, a trowel? I'll, um, spackle the wall, or—"

The dwarf's eyes boggled. "Give a clumsy centaur a sharp object? In my place of business? Are you barmy?"

"No, sir."

"Then simply pay the fracas fee and get out."

"Pay the . . . what?"

The dwarf coolly pointed to another sign, this one reading: FRACAS FEE: FIVE FICKELS. "You start a fracas in my gymnasium, you pay for the trouble you cause me."

Vic dug around in the fanny pack slung around the point where his human torso met his equine lower half.

"I don't have five fickels," he said, very quietly.

The dwarf just shook his head. "Get out of here, kid. And you might as well stop talking. I've got a mess to clean up, and I don't need you to add any more to my load."

With as much dignity and swoleness as he could manage, clenching his biceps and his buttocks, Vic walked out of the gym, his head held high and his magnificent tail flicking over the disastrous yoga-corner carnage. He was followed by the not-so-quiet mutterings of the Krossfitters.

"Poor guy has the self-control of a yearling hopped up on Blue Bull," the palomino complained.

"Can't even talk about his feelings or ask for help," added the gray.

"And he didn't apologize to the mice!" said the scandalized Thoroughbred.

"You're not even worth getting my club out of my locker." This from the troll, who was twirling a barbell on one finger as if it weighed nothing.

Past that gauntlet of shame, Vic stepped out the door and into the near-omnipresent gray drizzle of Sullenne. The dwarf grumbled behind him, his spackling trowel scraping against the wall, as the other centaurs continued to loudly and self-righteously express their pity for Vic's lack of balance and manners. As if they didn't also dance around like prey animals when frightened! No matter what the head told the heart, the heart couldn't always get that message to the equine's hindquarters. Why, it was rumored that even the great Howling Thunderous, Fury of the Five Pastures, had danced a fierce jig during battle!

No good telling the swoleboys that now. They'd just find some other reason to ridicule him.

The problem, Vic assumed, was that he still wasn't buff and manly enough. That he was too soft, too girly, just like his father had always claimed. Perhaps he would have flames painted on his hooves, like the palomino. Or grow his soul patch into a bushy beard, like the Thoroughbred. Or maybe even cut his tail into a club, like the gray had, which only served to make his rump look bigger and more muscular. But to do those things he'd need money, and he wasn't willing to waste coinage on surface problems.

Because he'd lied to the dwarf. He did have fickels—many a fickel, in fact. He'd been saving up to take a ship to the island of Mack Guphinne, where, legend said, a certain ancient temple sat. It was whispered that any supplicant entering the temple and performing the proper rituals would be subjected to a series of tests, their mind and heart probed intimately to measure their worth. And if they were found worthy, their greatest dream might come true.

Vic's greatest dream was to have the softness and sweetness purged from his body and soul, that he might become the stud his father swore was in there, somewhere. And that meant he would finally lose his secret weakness, his shame, that parasite that he couldn't shake, no matter how far he roved from home or how very swole he became. For perhaps dancing hooves were bad, but wiggling fingers were worse.

"He left a butt-shaped sweat blot when he fell!" one of the centaurs howled from inside the gym, and laughter shook the rafters.

"Clydesdale? More like Clydesfail!"

At that, Vic had had enough.

He looked up and down the street, then crept as much as a seventeen-hand Clydesdale with a ripped dude's torso could creep, easing along the alley behind the gym. Finding an open window, Vic slipped his hands inside the room beyond. As he waggled his fingers, feeling the magic build with his rage and shame, he smiled. And waited.

It wasn't long before the screaming started.

"So hot!" someone screamed.

"It burns!" shouted another one. "Like lava!"

"My gym!" Mr. Kross screeched. "It's ruined! Flooded! Oh, gods of Pell, why? Why'd it have to be tea?"

"And is that a pistachio macaron?" someone else asked. "What the Pell?"

Soon the centaurs were cantering out of the gym, their fetlocks red and bare, the hair singed off and smelling slightly of Shih Terrace green tea. The paint ran off the palomino's hooves in ripples, revealing the telltale signs of past laminitis due to binge eating. Elves and dwarves ran out, their shoes fizzling away as if eaten by acid as they screamed. Jerky MacJerkface the troll barreled out, his green feet pink, the toenails boinging off like popcorn as he whimpered. Behind them all came the swirling tide of boiling hot tea, gallons and gallons of it, along with a light curl of cream and a few quickly dissolving sugar cubes.

"My eye! My eye!" The Thoroughbred galloped into the street, both hands over his face. When he pulled them away, a single pistachio macaron fell down, covered in smeary black eyeliner.

Vic withdrew his fingers from the open window and trotted away down the alley. All the swoleboys were too busy whining about second-degree burns to notice him.

It wasn't easy, being afflicted with tea magic. But sometimes, secretly, it had its uses.

Still, he would've traded every drop of magic in his blood to be a normal centaur, who danced only when he danged well meant to.

4.

FLABBERGASTED IN A SMOKE-FILLED TENT

❧❧❧

Tempest was shopping, which was not a thing dryads generally did. She pointed to the garment labeled as a *grey hooded cloak*, which was significantly more attractive somehow than the one next to it described as *gray hooded cloak* but spelled with an *a* instead of an *e*.

"I'll take three of those, if you have them," she said to the merchant, pointing to the grey cloaks. She saw only two at present.

The clothing merchant puffed on his pipe, releasing a cloying odor of tobacco, cloves, and vanilla, and nodded once, chucking a young lad on the shoulder. "Fetch another from the back, boy. The grey with an *e,* now, not the gray with an *a*."

The boy nodded and disappeared behind a thin curtain, and the merchant puffed again before removing the slimed stem from his mouth and pointing it right at Tempest's face. Smoke streamed out of his mouth as he spoke and filtered up through his white mustache, which was stained yellow underneath his nose from years of such exhalations.

"It's the hood ye want, isn't it?" he asked. He wiggled the pipe's stem around at the collection of vibrant vines and narrow-bladed leaves covering Tempest's head, where a human woman's hair would be. "To hide all that foine green foliage."

Tempest looked down, her jaw clenched. "Yes."

"Yer a dryad, is that roight?"

She sighed. "Yes."

"Never thought I'd see a real one. Izzan honor. Why d'ye need three cloaks, then?"

"To hide. People hereabouts have not been kind."

"Oh? Howzat? Noice girl loike you, seems as if the world'd be kinder."

Tempest had barely spoken to any humans—they all seemed more interested in her magic than in her mind. But this old man leaned forward, eyes crinkled up in a kindly way, and it all just came tumbling out.

"We don't want attention at all. Bruding was the first big city we'd ever seen, and everyone who noticed us gasped or whispered or begged to be healed or worse—made lewd suggestions about wood nymphs, based on some terrible Pickleangelo paintings. We even had to fend off a couple of persistent suitors with rather sharp refusals—as in, the sharpened tip of a dagger at their throats."

"Thas terrible, that is!" the old man cried, thumping the table with a gnarled fist.

Tears rose to Tempest's eyes as the quiet darkness of the stall and the old man's heartfelt sympathy unspooled the feelings that had built up inside her.

"So we hurried to Tennebruss, but it's no better. We find the same ignorance everywhere we go. We thought autonomy among idiots would be better than our old life. We were indentured servants to a demigod, Tommy Bombastic. He treated us like something between a maid and a . . . well. The less said, the better. But a passing halfling noticed our hopeless plight and used his legal knowledge to negate Tommy's agreement with our father. So we're free now, but we'd hoped the world beyond Tommy's enchanted forest would be dynamic, cultured, and welcoming."

"An' it ain't?"

She shook her head. "No. We just want to find a place where we won't be seen as creatures to be exploited—but as people. We need to get far from Tommy's forest and away from the stares and the whispers. Stormy and Misty are hiding back at the inn, terrified of showing their faces outside."

When Tempest spoke her sisters' names, true surprise bloomed on the merchant's face, and the abrupt rearrangement of his facial features inspired a fit of coughing that sounded like a serious long-term condition. It was obvious he was doing his best to treat her normally, even if it was a challenge. When he finally subsided, he set down his pipe and peered at her through watery eyes. "Three dryads in Tennebruss? Remarkable, that is. D'ye mind me asking if ye hail from Borix?"

"No, we're from the Skyr. Daughters of the Willowmuck."

"The Willowmuck! I've heard o' him. Been warned, actually, if ye don't mind me saying, because he's one of the most feared willowmaws around right now. Poor lasses!"

Tempest smiled and sniffled. "Father can be frightful, for sure."

What the human didn't know was that willowmaws do not begin life as stationary carnivorous trees. In his willowmaw state, Tempest's father ate most anything that wandered underneath his canopy. But once he'd drunk enough blood to soften his hardened heartwood, he would someday walk the world again as a drynad—not that he was particularly kinder in that form. There were very few of his people left, since edible folks tended to chop them down or set them on fire in their willowmaw forms. Everyone loved dryads and drynads when they lived as slightly leafy humans, looking beautiful and healing folks of any ailment, but no one wanted to tolerate them when they were living the part of their life cycle that required them to be bloodthirsty trees.

"But it seems like everyone is born with the potential to be frightful, doesn't it?" she finished.

The merchant nodded. "Roight you are, miss. That's why we must all go out of our way to be kind." The boy returned with another grey cloak and the merchant waved him on. "Give it to the noice lady; there's a foine lad."

The boy shyly held out the soft grey cloak, and Tempest took it and beamed at him. His mouth dropped open and he looked away, blushing. Her smile tended to have that effect on many beings, and she wound up feeling embarrassed for causing their embarrassment; it was a vicious cycle of blushing. She looked back at the merchant, whose eyes were twinkling as he witnessed the lad's harmless discomfort.

"What do I owe you for these?" She hoped the cost wouldn't drain the meager contents of her purse. They'd had little opportunity to earn money while in Tommy Bombastic's service.

"Bah." The merchant waved his pipe at her, scoffing at the question. "Ye have given me a rare gift just by walking in me tent and talkin' to a lonely old man, that's fer sure. Take 'em, and may they keep ye safe and well and remind ye that there's good in the world."

Tempest froze. "Surely you are jesting with me now." Her eyes flicked to the tent flap, wondering if a watchman was waiting outside. "Is this a trick? If I walk out without paying, I'll be seized for theft or something like that?"

The merchant hastened to reassure her. "No, no, I'm serious. I've done very well for meself and shan't suffer the loss o' three cloaks. Look, I'll write ye a bill of sale, saying they're paid for, and then ye can rest easy." He crammed the pipe in his mouth and puffed as he scrabbled for ink and paper at his table. His quill scratched over a scrap of paper, which he proffered to her. She took it, noted the date, and read:

Three foine grey hooded cloaks sold to bearer, paid in fulle.

Signed,

Cappy Tallist, Esq.

Tempest sighed in relief. "Thank you, Mr. Tallist."

"Ah, call me Cappy, and thank ye fer visitin' me today. What's yer name, if I may?"

"Tempest." She drew closer to him. "Are you sure there is nothing I can give you for these?"

"Nah. I have a story that will last me to the end o' me days. Nobody I know's ever met a dryad before, although a few have been eaten by the odd tree. That's mighty foine. The meeting, I mean, not the bein' eaten." His eyes flew wide, and he went into a fit of wet, hacking coughs that required a grubby handkerchief and ended with a pained wheeze.

"But that cough of yours. Are you well?"

Cappy sighed in patient resignation. "Well enough, aye. I'm old, is all."

"Please, give me your hand, Cappy?" She extended her own, and after a moment he took it and she clasped his thick fingers in her slim ones and shut her eyes. The illness dwelling in his lungs was immediately apparent. Steeling herself against what was to come, she whispered of health and grace and concentrated on the masses of the old man's innards that were blackened or twisted from their natural pink moistness; soon they flourished again and broke up into so much bloody detritus that both she and Cappy began to cough. He tried to pull his hand away, but she held fast to him until he was clear. He finally took a deep, shuddering breath, and then a deeper clear one, tears streaming down his face.

"I don't know what you did, lass, but . . . thank you."

"I renewed your lungs. You would not have lived out the year. If you will take some friendly advice, Cappy, stop smoking that pipe now, so you'll be around to see your grandchildren grow up."

The merchant nodded at her. "I will." His gaze traveled to her arm as she withdrew her hand, and his expression darkened with concern. "What is that? Are you all roight?"

Tempest looked down and saw the smooth brown skin of her forearm marred by a new scaly growth. It was not large, only the size of three peas in a pod, but she knew what it was: willow bark. Healing Cappy had pushed her closer to her time of roots and hardness.

"Oh, it's nothing," she lied. She plastered a fake smile on her face, hoping her fear didn't show. "Don't worry about it. The important thing is that you are well. Thank you again for the cloaks. Good day."

Cappy Tallist made some noises that might have been speech, but she didn't hear anything distinct. She pulled the first cloak over her shoulders and settled the hood to hide her face, then snatched up the other two and exited, hurrying back to the Purple Mushroom Inn, where she'd left Stormy and Misty. She burst into the room and tossed the cloaks at them, ignoring their greetings.

"Do either of you have any bark on your skin?" she asked.

"What? No," Stormy answered indignantly. Poor Misty just looked confused.

"Well, now I do." Tempest pulled back her cloak to show them her arm and saw their eyes widen in alarm.

"Oh, pixie plops, Tempest! What did you do?" Misty asked.

"I healed someone as thanks for these cloaks."

"Why in Pell would you do that? Did you not have enough coin?"

"No, I volunteered."

Stormy snorted. "He probably gave you the cloaks for free, didn't he?"

Tempest only blinked at her in answer, and Stormy's face darkened. "I knew it! He manipulated you! Tempest, we've talked about this!"

"He was so sweet and kind. He needed help, Stormy."

Stormy rolled her eyes. "They *all* need help! But they never help us! They drain us dry until we're wood, and then they burn us to ashes when they can't exploit us anymore! You have to stop."

"I will," Tempest said, looking down. She didn't know if Cappy Tallist had intended to gain her sympathy or not. But she knew that she hadn't felt exploited until just now. She'd felt good about helping him until her sister all but said that she'd been suckered. She was a rube. A sap. A gull. "I won't help anyone else. Anyway, I got us cloaks."

It didn't feel like an accomplishment anymore.

"Thank you, Tempest." Misty stepped forward, and hugged her, and Tempest leaned into her sister's embrace. This was what had gotten them through their years at Tommywood—one another.

"I'm grateful too," Stormy said, arms closed. "I just don't want to see you in the ground before us. I worry about you."

"Well, I'm as worried as you are," Tempest said as Misty let her go. "Because I don't know what we're supposed to do next."

"We were talking while you were gone." Stormy stubbornly stuck out her chin. "We think we could do well if we struck a deal with a dwarvelish bathhouse somewhere. If nothing else, working for Tommy made us amazing servers."

"Yeah," Misty agreed, nodding enthusiastically. "We're thinking we could go to Grundelbård or Sküterlånd at the base of the hills, and we'll make good tips, and when it's time to be trees we'll put down roots in the forest."

"Except you'll eat people."

Misty sniffed delicately. "Except for that, yeah. But look at it this way: plenty of clean food, thanks to dwarvelish bathing customs!"

"We both think it's a good plan," Stormy added.

But Tempest shook her head. "That's fine if you want to do that, but it's not a future I would choose. I don't want to serve anyone ever again. I did it for a hundred years. Now I want to help people."

"By healing them?"

Tempest steeled herself and straightened her spine. "No. I want to do it the way that halfling man helped free us from Tommy's contract: by using the law. I want to become a lawyer."

Her sisters scrunched up their noses in unison and said, "A lawyer? Ew!"

Stormy followed up with "And how are you going to accomplish that?"

Tempest shrugged. "There are law schools all over the place. One of them has to be willing to take me in."

"Okay," Misty said, "but can it be a dwarvelish school near us, at least?"

"Dwarf law is mostly about beard cleanliness and beekeeping. I think I should learn human law, since I look more human than anything else," Tempest said. "And because the humans seem so blasted determined to be in charge of things. Plus, the other peoples might not accept me as easily. I've heard there's a good law school in Bustardo."

"Bustardo? Is that in Kolon?" Stormy asked.

"No, it's in the earldom of Burdell."

"But you'll be so far away!" Misty protested.

"Only for a little while. After I get my degree I can practice wherever I wish. I can move closer to whatever dwarvelish inn you're working at."

"So . . . we're splitting up?" Misty asked.

Normally, Tempest would've made a joke about splitting logs to break up the tension and calm her sisters. But this time, she felt the tears welling in her eyes and nodded, letting them fall. She'd known this moment would arrive almost as soon as they were free. For the first time in her life, she wanted something different from Stormy and Misty. There was a destiny ahead of her that no dryad had ever pursued, and she wanted to be the first to blaze that trail—straight into the courtroom.

"No!" Stormy glared at her. "We have to stay together!"

Tempest looked her pushy older sister in the eye and cleared her throat.

"I object," she said firmly.

Just saying the words for the first time thrilled her, and a new, deep longing arose in her heart—a longing for a leather briefcase and a hefty stack of depositions.

This dryad would soon become part of the judicial branch.

5.

HIGH ABOVE THE RAGING SEA
IN A TURGID EDIFICE OF GREAT RENOWN

It was almost three o'clock, and Alobartalus was ready. He was wearing his shoes with the especially high heels, his spider-silk robe was brushed to a glittering shine, and he'd carefully painted over his freckles with a dwarvelish unguent called Poppi Groppe's No-Spot Dewdrop Glop. He could hear the crowd trundling up the path from the dock, relieved to disembark from their ship and finally see a legend made real: the Proudwood Lighthouse.

He still had a few minutes, he knew—the barkers and hucksters and street musicians would be doing their best to relieve the island's visitors of their coin as they walked the Proud Processional. Here, a human child with pasted-on ear tips danced up and sweetly demanded reciprocity for the Traditional Elven Flower Anklet she'd tied around someone's ankle—the thing was a hideous confection of lurid paper flowers, which no elf would be caught dead in. There, a gnomeric middle-aged woman standing on a box under her flowing robes professed to know the secrets of the spheres and offered to tell fortunes using her Vessel of Elvish Divination—which was really just a painted bucket full of glitter and mistake fortunes from a fortune brownie company in Kolon. And over there, a kilted human with flaxen blond hair plaintively played a pan flute, wiggling the sporran at his waist suggestively in the hope that someone would drop in a copper or two. That, at least, had some merit—many an elven flutist had waggled his sporran at a human lady, doing his duty to follow the king's edict and spread the elven seed. But real elves didn't have hair made of broom straw or sporrans made of deboned badgers, and they would never initiate dalliances without a properly ferny grotto and far-superior manscaping.

Amateurs, the lot of them. But Alobartalus didn't mind. They were fun to hang out with at night, once the crowds had returned to their ships, and they played a mean game of Poop Chutes and Bladders around their campfire. He vastly preferred them to the real elves back home in the Morningwood, who—

Enough of that. The human tourists had fought their way past the vendors and now stood on the threshold, trembling and unsure and filled with awe. After a few moments, one of them got up the courage to pull the golden rope beside the sign on the front doors, which read: YE OF NOBLE HEART MAY RING THE BELL AND ENTER THE REALM OF THE ELVES OF PELL.

A golden chime echoed through the lighthouse, dinging solemnly up the circular stair and donging out the windows on every level, all the way up to the top floor, where an elvish fire burned so ships wouldn't run aground in the sacred magical mists of the Bonnie Strait, which separated the lighthouse island from the Morningwood proper. Somewhere, Alobartalus's uncle, King Thorndwall of the Morningwood, Lord of All Elves and Master of Magic, would hear that sound and think, *Ah, yes. That thunk-headed dimwit of a nephew of mine will be doing his little dance instead of bothering me, and he'd better sell several Enchanted Morningwood Rods to fund my imported-cheese habit and leather jerkin collection, or else.*

Alobartalus looked in the Silver Mirror of Galadriadwenna, consciously relaxed his furrowed brow, turned his frown into a wise and knowing smile, and wished for the millionth time that he looked like a proper elf. He wished his ears were a bit pointier, his legs a little longer, his flesh less freckled and prone to eczema, and his belly a little more like the inside of a spoon and a little less like a barrel of Jyggaly Juice. If only he weren't so elf-conscious and elf-critical! Girding his silk-swaddled loins, he strode to the door, tripping only once as his trailing cloak got caught under his high heels.

Standing before the double doors, he muttered, "C'mon, Al. Think elfy. Really, truly, magically, snottily elfy." He tossed glitter into the air and threw the doors of carved Morningwood open with a dramatic flourish.

"Welcome to Proudwood Lighthouse," he intoned, looking down his nose at the crowd. Or trying to—even with the heels, he was shorter than most of them, so it was more like he tipped his head back and glared into their nostrils. "I am Alobartalus Olivegarten, son of Dampfnudel, sister of King Thorndwall, and—"

"Oi, you!" called a man from the crowd. "No more o' them pasted-on ears like outside. We want a real elf! The brochure says, *You will be greeted by a Real Honest-to-Pellanus Elf,* and so I's want to be!"

Alobartalus took a step back and tried not to panic. "I am a true elf, my human friend, born under the downy fronds of the most secret clefts of the forest, raised—"

"No you're not," a woman cried. "Elves is tall 'n' willowy 'n' pretty, 'n' you look more like me own son, Dordley." At this, she pushed a child forward, and Alobartalus bit his lip as he realized that he did resemble the pudgy boy more than a little, especially had his freckles been uncovered and his curly red hair revealed.

But he wasn't going to admit that.

"Not all elves fit your stereotype, madam, just as not all humans fit the legends told of *your* people." He eyed the man who'd called out first. "Are not all humans noble, broad-chested, and ever ready to help a friend?" The man deflated over his ale belly, and Alobartalus faced down the woman. "Kind, graceful, and birthing strong sons who don't pick their nose and wipe it on priceless artifacts?" The woman wrenched her beloved Dordley away from where he was smearing slime on the Umbrella Rack of Rattlesack the Relevant.

"So, now that we're all clear on the evil of stereotypes, let us continue the tour. As the Morningwood is currently off-limits to humans, dwarves, gnomes, halflings, and anyone not sporting naturally pointed ears and a lineage of seers and sages, Proudwood Lighthouse is your only source of true elven knowledge, artifacts, and souvenirs. Please deposit your fickel in the Enchanted Fickelbox of Fair Fianamalla the Fleet-Footed or be cursed forever."

A granny stepped forward, her mouth bracketed and actively scrunched. "Thought you elves accepted cheese as payment? I brought me a bit of cheese, see." She held up a few crumbles of what appeared to be a very sad Styffy, and Alobartalus thought some rather rude thoughts about his uncle, the king.

"Yes, my fair lady, we elves are, for the most part, quite fond of cheese—complete cheeses, mind, still wrapped in wax and untouched by human hands. But the trading of cheeses in the Morningwood proper is by the king's own command and does not extend to the Proudwood Lighthouse, I'm afraid." He waved a hand at the box. "And, as you can see, the slot is made to fit only fickels, not cheese and pickles."

"Pickles?" the old lady perked up and began pawing through her grimy reticule.

"Alas, madam, we do not accept pickles as payment, and I'm not jerkin' your gherkin."

She stopped pawing and squinted up at him through rheumy eyes. "Yeah, he's a real elf. I met one, once, when I was young and traipsing through a glade. They talk like that, you know. In riddles."

"Euphemisms," Alobartalus corrected.

"Bless you."

Alobartalus closed his eyes and struggled to find his character.

Tall. Imposing. Superior. Otherworldly. Magical. Kind of a prig.

He opened his eyes and spun, tossing out a bit of glitter to rain down behind him. "I trust you will render your fickels and follow me for the official tour of elven wonder," he intoned. "This way to the Room of Erudite Enlightenment!"

When he'd heard the proper number of clanks in the fickel box, he threw open the doors to the room and watched the humans file in one by one, their jaws slack with wonder. A large part of his job, honestly, was about throwing doors open with proper drama and flair. And the Room of Erudite Enlightenment was actually called the Room of Messing with Stupid Humans, and it was just chock-full of enchanted mirrors that made humans get lost for ten minutes, sink into existential fear, confront their greatest weakness, break down crying, and leave feeling as if they'd touched true magic, because they had felt genuine emotions. Alobartalus loved it because he never had to go inside; he could merely wait in the antechamber beyond, listening to the confusion, weeping, and sighs of awe within. And they were so much more pliable afterward.

All this *You're not an elf!* business would be replaced with *Who am I and why am I here, in Pell?* That, in turn, was really good for sales of the Enchanted Elven T-shirts he sold in the gift shop, which were emblazoned with the slogan WELL, WHY NOT?

He sat down on the Tufted Ottoman of Pleased Podiatry and felt the blisters from his high heels fade. But, much to his surprise, someone tapped him on the shoulder. Alobartalus gasped, jumped, and nearly fell off the stool.

"I thought elves were masters of their environment," the boy, Dordley, said, all sullen and suspicious. "Some ranger you are."

Alobartalus looked around to be sure they were alone and leaned in close. "I'll tell you a secret, Dordley. Would you like that?" The boy nodded eagerly, his forelock flapping. "You see, the elves have some ongoing fertility problems. In part because our women are very demanding in bed and our men mostly like to look at themselves admiringly, but also because so many of the women have fled to the west to escape the creeping squalor of the non-elves."

"What's to the west?" Dordley asked, and Alobartalus knew then with complete surety that the boy was one of the worst things the human race had ever invented: a chronic interrupter.

Instead of answering, Alobartalus fetched a fetching hat from a peg on the wall and dropped it on the boy's head. Dordley's mouth popped open, but he said nothing, and he looked very surprised at that occurrence.

"Cliteria's Cap of Censorship," Alobartalus said. "Touch it with those filthy hands, and I'll toss you out of the lighthouse to be eaten by orcas. Now, listen like a good lesser life-form. Ahem."

Dordley utterly failed to interrupt, so Alobartalus continued.

"Every elvish birth is celebrated, for all that it's a messy, violent affair. We've ensorceled chipmunks to scrub the blood off the birches, you know. And one day, a little elf boy was born, and he was so strange that all the elves gathered around to look upon him. He should've been handsome, with a halo of golden hair and clear blue eyes like a summer day. He should've cooed so musically that birds sang back to him and flew in figure eights around his head in blessing. And when his father tossed glitter upon him for the first time, he should've sneezed a perfect, delicate sneeze.

"But this elf child was ugly, red-haired, his skin all blotchy and freckled. His angry cries scared off all the moose they were trying to milk for moose cheese. His eyes were mud brown, his hands were in fists, and when his father threw glitter on him, he shat so hard that it shot out of his silk diaper, up his back, and all over his mother and the king of the elves, who happened to be her brother. And instead of giving the child a name and welcoming him to the Morningwood, the king said, 'This one's going to be a pain in my royal rump.'"

Dordley continued to not interrupt.

"And he was right. I was the least-elvish elf ever born. I was so unelvish that my parents divorced, as my father was quite sure I was half human and my mother had been stepping out with some hideous farmer she'd found shoveling manure. And when I came of age and had done my required service with the Sylvan Rangers, I knelt before my uncle, the king, to be given the gift of a calling and my birthright, and do you know what he did? He exiled me here, to Proudwood Lighthouse, a laughingstock among my own kind."

Alobartalus leaned forward, and Dordley did too.

"I'll tell you another secret, little Dordley: I'm not sorry a bit. I like it here better than I did back home. I like humans—at least, when they're not trying to ruin my day or act like they're better than me. I like the sea better than the Morningwood, and I like seagulls better than enchanted sparrows that crap glitter, and I am *allergic* to *cheese*. So, yes, I am an elf, through and through. But, no, I am not like other elves. And I don't care."

Dordley made a face that suggested that not caring was a very audacious move.

"Most elves crave knowledge and power and cheese and really high cheekbones, but do you know what I want?"

Dordley shrugged.

"I want to sail away from here. Cruise down the Sn'archipelago and meet the Sn'archivist, who resides in his own tower, not unlike this lighthouse. But instead of escorting fools through a tourist trap, do you know what he gets to do? No, you do not. Your tiny human brain can't comprehend it. *He writes.* Legends say the very god Pellanus speaks to him, that birds come to him from all over Pell and tell him stories, and he writes them down. His tower is full of books, all the Tales of Pell, every history ever written. So not only would I be there, nearly alone with plenty of reading material, but I would find out for certain if my father really was a human farmer. Wouldn't that be lovely? To know if I actually share blood ties with someone like you?"

Dordley looked at him, chewing his lip as if he didn't quite believe what he was hearing. With a small sigh of frustration, Alobartalus removed the Cap, and the moment it was off Dordley's head, the boy started yammering.

"So you think yer mam was lyin', and yer da was—"

The cap dropped right back down, and the lad's lips stopped flapping.

"I'm curious, but, honestly, it doesn't matter. I'll never fit in among my kind in the Morningwood, and I've just about had it with standing out from the crowds here. Luckily, even if I was born with less magic than most elves, I still know how to use elven-made magical goods, which means that all I need to do is this . . ."

Reaching into his cloak, Alobartalus withdrew a small drawstring pouch. He took some of the fine, ashy powder inside and blew it into Dordley's face, right before he removed Cliteria's Cap and replaced it on its peg.

"Oi, who're you?" the boy said, backing up until he'd nearly stumbled over the Terribly Taxidermied Tortoise of Tantalos Tippytoes. "Where'm I? Where's me folks?"

Alobartalus smiled his most wise and elven smile. "Why, you're in Proudwood Lighthouse, my dear human, and you've seen such wondrous things!"

"I 'ave?"

"You have! And your parents are in that room, so why don't you scoot along and find them?"

Before Dordley could protest or ask any more grammatically painful questions, Alobartalus opened the door to the Room of Erudite Enlightenment and shoved the boy in, slamming the door behind him.

"Tough crowd," he murmured to himself, pulling a packet of dwarvelish butter biscuits out of his pocket and popping one in his mouth, relishing how it tasted safely of flour and sugar and vanilla and didn't magically expand in his mouth like elven croutons, which he'd always hated.

By the time the humans stumbled back out of the Room of Enlightenment, looking dazed and, in a few cases, embarrassed, he'd changed into his next costume, a copy of King Thorndwall's favorite party cloak and his golden crown with rampant antlers.

"My good humans, did you find enlightenment?" he asked in his most kingish voice.

"Ungh" was all most of them could manage, including Dordley, who'd had a bit of a sick all over his shirt.

"Wonderful! Next we'll marvel at the Portrait Gallery of Very Important Elves, partake in a ceremonial elven-crouton tasting, and walk through the Hall of Most Resplendent and Rampant Rods. After that, I'm sure you'll delight at the chance to purchase your own wand of Morningwood in the souvenir shop, along with a tin of rod grease handcrafted by elf maidens at dawn. Please keep in mind that all purchases support the care of abandoned baby rabbits and elven widows and veterans of the Giant Wars."

The glomp of addlepated humans followed him up the lighthouse stairs to the portrait gallery, as docile as deer who'd wandered into a patch of smoking weed. Young Dordley and his parents seemed especially gobsmacked, but that's how it took terrible people when they looked into those magicked mirrors and saw their true selves. The humans considered it a great gift, a small peek at the sage wisdom elves collected as they lived hundreds and thousands of years in a beautiful forest of peace and harmony.

Little did the humans know it was just another practical joke. Everything in the lighthouse was. If the humans knew what was in that rod grease, they'd *all* have upchuck on their shirts.

Alobartalus felt a bit bad about it sometimes; he didn't think it was fair to take someone's money and then spend two hours playing jokes on them. The portraits were ensorceled to stare back and whisper rude things that sounded like one's inner critic, and the rampant rods were just sticks of pine covered with so much grease that you could barely hold on to one without bonking yourself in the head. And he had to perform the Hurghblurgh Maneuver on at least one choking person during every crouton ceremony, as he was forbidden to tell them beforehand that anything more than a nibble would cause an entire muffin or even loaf to spontaneously spring to life in one's mouth. And the proceeds did not go to benefit anything adorably needy; it simply put more cheese in King Thorndwall's coffers.

But this was Alobartalus's punishment for being who he was: the worst elf, out here on the edge of the world, spreading the worst parts of elven society to gullible tourists.

He was trying to be as elfly as possible for their benefit, and even they didn't believe it.

"'Scuse me, sir."

He looked down to find the old granny tugging gently on his sleeve. A normal elf, a good elf, would've done something terrible and hilarious to punish her for daring to touch his cobweb cloak, but Alobartalus looked into her lined face and felt a wash of sympathy. These humans had such short lives in such broken bodies.

"Yes, my lady?" He bowed gallantly and was rewarded by a giggle and a blush on her withered old cheeks.

"I have this son, see." She gave him a secretive smile and pulled a locket out of the deep recesses of her bosom. "I was traipsing in this forest a long time ago, and I came across this elf fellow, and, well, you know." She giggled again as she recalled some golden moment in the Morningwood forest, and Alobartalus did his best not to roll his eyes and congratulate her. "So my son, Lancelong, is forty but he looks twenty, 'n' he's so handsome 'n' musical that he just can't get along in our little hamlet. I was wondering if you was hiring?"

Alobartalus looked at the lad's portrait and then gazed longingly out the window, yearning to toss the pretty elf's painted image into the sea. This fellow Lancelong looked like he belonged here in the lighthouse, his painting hung on the walls. Slender, with eyes of blue and high, pointed ears poking out of his white-gold hair, his plush lips quirked up in that knowing elven smile that suggested a whoopee cushion was waiting nearby. Alobartalus instantly hated him.

"An' he's accidentally doin' magic all the time, see?" the old lady continued. "The chickens crap glitter, an' the cow gives whipped cream, an' the dog—"

But Alobartalus had heard enough.

"Oh, my fair lady. I am so sorry to inform you that appointments to the Proudwood Lighthouse are available only on a special commendation from King Thorndwall himself." He offered her a sad smile of resignation.

But that only firmed her up. She nodded once and said, "Aye, well, then. I'll send him into the Morningwood to meet the king and see what he says. Foine boy like that, lookin' that elfy, he should fit right in. Don't know why I didn't think of it before."

"Because you're human and an idiot," Alobartalus accidentally muttered.

"What! What? How dare you, you pudgy little dwarfling!" the old woman shrieked.

Out came the drawstring bag of powder again, and then she was sneezing and staring at him in confusion.

"Where am I? Who are you?" she asked.

"You're at the Proudwood Lighthouse, and you've just suggested that you'd like to buy our finest rampant rod," Alobartalus said. "You also mentioned that you needed your son to stay home with you until you die and then visit your grave daily with flowers."

"Such a good boy, my Lancelong," she murmured, following Alobartalus toward the souvenir shop. "So tall 'n' pretty 'n' noble, with such a foine voice and such lovely, pointed ears."

For a moment, Alobartalus let himself pretend the old woman was talking about him.

Then he sold her the most expensive rod in the shop and decided that perhaps he'd told Dordley the truth: He didn't want to work at the Proudwood Lighthouse anymore. Perhaps it was time to finally pursue his dream in the Sn'archipelago. Most bored elves went west, but Alobartalus wanted to go south.

6.

GRIPPED IN THE TALONS OF
AN UNCLEAN AVIAN

Morvin had heard of a decent place in Sullenne to rest their weary bones, and Harkovrita—no, Morgan; she had to remember her new name and use it or else her family would find her—gladly accompanied him there. He wasn't the least bit creepy and he was happy to share snacks, which were pretty big deals in a randomly selected traveling companion.

"The Retchedde Hive ain't fancy, but it ain't full o' cutthroats either," Morvin assured her. "Not the sorta place where you'd run into all sorts of scum 'n' villainy. It's prolly 'cause the criminal element prefers places where they can get drunk and practice their skullduggery . . . or maybe they're kinda scared of bees and cheerful breakfasts, I dunno. I tend to notice how things are, but I'll be a heckin' mess o' giant giblets before I can tell you why they are that way."

Morgan didn't understand Morvin's rambling at first, but she soon discovered that the Retchedde Hive was a small chain of inns owned

by an apiarist in Retchedde that served a breakfast of fresh raw hon-
eycomb and "heckin' good oats."

Morvin was able to secure them both a night's lodging in exchange for a few jars of invigorated ham jam, which must've been
uncommonly good stuff, judging by the crow of victory the manager
let loose.

"At least let me buy you supper," Morgan said once they'd stowed
their gear and seen the horse and wagon situated. "It's the least I can
do."

"Sure, I got me a void that needs fillin'," Morvin allowed.

"Shall we try a Dinny's?"

Morgan had never been to a Dinny's before, but she'd heard exciting stories. As the Lady Harkovrita she'd been fed from the earl's
kitchen, where a team of chefs, sauciers, and puddingsmiths made
sure she was given only the finest victuals for her body's nourishment. An establishment slinging hash and grease and terrible kuffee
was sure to confront her digestive system with new adventures in
gastronomy and perhaps even acute distress. She couldn't wait.

Morvin's lips twitched. "If that's what floats your oats, I reckon."

There was a Dinny's down by the docks, and Morgan smiled at the
competing aromas of burnt toast, fish guts, and salty air as they approached. The night was filled with the susurrus of the tide and the
screeching of seagulls, and she grinned and swung her arms in a way
gowns did not allow. She had never felt so at home.

The interior of the Dinny's was a riot of half-shouted conversations, loud slurps of kuffee, halfling hiccups, and the scrape of cheap
silverware on low-grade porcelain. Morgan regarded it all with wonder, but Morvin looked less than pleased.

"What's the matter?" she asked him.

"Aw, nothin'. What they got here technically qualifies as food. But
the man I used to work for, m'Lord Toby, had a habit of eatin' very
well and I got to partake of his leftovers, often as not. Kinda spoiled
me, I think, what with his delicacies and gourmet doodads. But he's
dead now, so Dinny's it is. The halflings eat it right often, and they

seem a vigorous sort o' people, not droppin' dead from the grease burps or nothin'."

Morgan did not tell him she was used to gourmet fare at her own father's castle; for all of Morvin's comfortably cheerful chattering, Morgan herself had said very little, revealing nothing of her past.

They were greeted by a smiling but tired halfling hostess, and she asked them to follow her. She carried menus that were practically as tall as she was. On the way to their booth, they passed a collection of four beefy, unshaven men who were paying keen attention to a red-and-yellow parrot. The parrot wore an eye patch, and Morgan thought she heard it say *trrrreasurrrre* as she passed. No wonder the men were interested.

Once at their booth she asked for directions to the boom-boom room and sanitation station and immediately excused herself to wash up. Said station was back by the entrance to the kitchen, and there she saw some singularly strange cylinders—drums, really—that had an oily gray substance oozing out from under their puffed-up tops.

EATUM, the drums said in tall black letters, but there was additional, smaller text above and below that word, which turned out to be an acronym. She stepped closer to read. The words *Extraordinarily Affordable, Tasty, & Ubiquitous Meat* explained the acronym. Below that was the line *An MMA Product,* plus a warning to refrigerate the contents of the drum after opening. There were no ingredients listed, however, which was curious and also a bit disturbing. Morgan had never heard of EATUM before, but this Dinny's had enough to feed her father's entire earldom for a month. And, even more disturbing, since when did meat come in drums? It certainly didn't seem fresh, much less sanitary. Even Morvin's ham jam had included an expiration date.

She was curious now to read the menu and see what other strange new foods she'd been missing out on all these years. She washed up quickly in the sanitation station and returned to her seat, where Morvin was frowning at said menu.

"They only have one heckin' kind of gravy, and it ain't my favorite kind," he muttered. "And there's a whole lotta stuff you can put in your hash browns, which makes me suspicious of said taters."

"Why is that?"

"Well, why are they so eager to have you put all that heckin' stuff in there? Ain't the taters good all by their lonesome? Why they gotta distract your tongue with cheese and onions and whatnot? Skittered, encumbered, smoothered, 'n' chonked. They're tryin' to cover up a secret, that's why, and the secret is them taters ain't no good."

"You may have a point there," Morgan said, but she privately doubted that Dinny's had built its vast empire of eateries around a potato conspiracy. It was, after all, pretty hard to mess up a potato.

She scanned the menu and was surprised to discover that breakfast was served all day, which felt like a great rebellion. It appeared that most every dish came with a free side of EATUM—unless one wished to opt for fresh sausage or bacon for a hefty up-charge.

"Morvin, do you know what EATUM is?"

"It's cheap meat," he said. She waited, sure that he would continue at length, but he said nothing else.

"As in it comes from the halfling city of Cheapmeat in the Skyr?"

"Huh? Naw. As in it's just affordable. Pretty tasty and you don't get sick from it, which is really why you wanna avoid oysters, because wow: I seen things. Felt things! Things that was once inside me and then suddenly—horribly, at high velocity—wasn't."

"Okay, so scratch oysters for breakfast. But what *is* EATUM? What kind of meat?"

Morvin shrugged. "That's tough to say. It's really its own thing, because it's marinated in summa them spices they grow down in the islands—I mean savory spices, not the super-hot kind. Tastes kinda like if you crossed snake nuggets with a badger loin."

"I've not had either one of those, so that doesn't help."

"Well, try some EATUM if you wanna know. It don't cost you nothin' extra."

Or, Morgan thought, *I could just ask our server,* who was approaching their table with a brilliant smile pasted on her face. She was a human woman with warm beige skin. The name tag on her tunic said COURTKNEE in capital letters, and underneath that was the revelation that she hailed from Fapsworth in the earldom of Grunting.

"Hellooo!" she cooed at them. "My name is Shoobie and I'll be taking care of you today. Can I get you some kuffee or a Dewdrop Fizzy?"

"You're not Courtknee?" Morgan asked, gesturing at the name tag.

"Oh! No, I forgot my badge at home, but the manager said I have to wear one anyway. You know how it is," she said.

Morgan was unsettled by this news. The management appeared willing to lie to its customers. "Well, kuffee for sure, thanks."

"Me too," Morvin said.

"Scream cream, goat milk, or oat milk?" Shoobie asked.

They both asked for oat milk and then Morgan asked, "Shoobie, can you tell me what EATUM is made of?"

"Pure deliciousness," she replied smoothly, and punctuated that with another brilliant smile. Morvin went so far as to opine that it was pure *heckin'* deliciousness, and they shared a laugh about that because delicious things were hilarious, apparently. Morgan waited for them to subside before replying.

"I appreciate your enthusiastic review. But I wish to know specifically from which animal's flesh it derives. Can you tell me that?"

Shoobie's smile melted away like springtime snow, transforming to the frustrated grimace of someone who saw her tip dwindling. "No, I'm sorry, I don't know."

"Well, who does?"

Shoobie tapped her pencil against her order pad. "Nobody does."

"You mean nobody here?"

"I mean nobody, anywhere, so far as I can tell. It's just cheap, delicious meat. And meat's meat, after all."

"Where does EATUM come from, then?"

Shoobie shrugged. "I don't know. We just receive our shipments and serve it up."

"And you're fine eating something when you don't know what it is?"

"Well, I know it tastes good and doesn't make me sick. Oysters, though—"

"Right?" Morvin said.

"Exactly!" Shoobie cried, pointing at him in triumph. "You know what I mean!"

"I do!" The two of them bonded for a while over a shared history of disastrous sea snot, then Shoobie departed to fetch their kuffee, and Morgan was left none the wiser.

"Doesn't this mystery meat worry you?" she asked Morvin.

"Why should it? If it tastes good and I don't die, then there ain't nothin' to worry about, is there?"

"But what if it's kitten meat or something like that?"

"Cor, that would take a lot of kittens!"

Morgan tried to rein in her frustration. "But what if?"

"So what if it is? Something's gotta eat it."

"I beg your pardon? Nobody's got to eat kittens!"

Morvin leaned forward. "I mean, workin' on a farm like I do, a fella gets used to seein' stuff get eaten. Everything eats something else. There are critters out there that actually eat the boom-boom of other critters. Even predators get eaten by bugs and vultures and worms once they die. It's the carbuncle of life."

"You mean the circle of life?"

"Yeah, that too."

Morgan tried a different tack. "But don't you worry about the lack of transparency? A business that won't tell you what it's serving could be hiding anything. Or mistreating its workers. Or misleading its shareholders."

Morvin nodded, looking crafty.

"So you think maybe EATUM is made up of shareholders 'n' bad workers? An' that it should be see-through?"

Morgan flailed emotionally. Her fingers fluttered in the air, a frenzied dance of digits. "No! But I still want to know what I'm eating!"

"Stuff that tastes good and sends your innards outward, hopefully. Ever since I made them my words to live by, I've found that meals sure are relaxing and enjoyable. I mean, unless I'm in a place where they are committin' all sorts o' *blatant tater crimes*!" His voice rose alarmingly at the end as he looked around for an employee who might hear his criticism and abruptly change their menu just to please him, but Morgan's widened eyes let him know that perhaps he had given his passion a bit too much emphasis.

"Sorry," he mumbled. "I guess I'm kind of a . . . tater enthusiast. The kind that objects to unnecessary dressing of the starches."

"It's all right," Morgan assured him. "I happen to be uncommonly passionate about the evils of patriarchy."

Shoobie returned with their kuffee and took their orders. Morgan was very careful to order a bacon and mushroom frittata and said, "That's just fine!" when Shoobie warned her there would be an additional charge for bacon. Morvin asked for a huge plate of hash browns, "with no funny stuff added in or on top or hidden underneath, because I will be inspecting it most close-like, I do assure you."

"Nothing else?" Shoobie asked.

"Nothin' else but a side of EATUM. I'm gonna make sure at least some taters die with honor in this place."

"How can a potato—" Shoobie blinked. "Okay."

The frittata came out fairly burned and the mushrooms weren't terribly fresh, but Morgan enjoyed digging in regardless. This meal was a hint at what life would be like outside the shelter of her parents' demesne, and it wasn't bad at all. There was just something comforting about extraneous grease.

"Parrrrdon me," a raspy voice said. Morgan looked up from her plate and saw that the red-and-yellow parrot she'd spied earlier was now perched on the back of the booth, just behind Morvin's right shoulder. It wore an eye patch, and its head was cocked so that its good eye was fixed on them, though the head made continual tiny jerking movements as it switched back and forth. "I don't suppose eitherrr of you gentlemen is looking for worrrrrk? Maybe a way to trrrravel south?"

"I am," Morgan said. "What kind of work?"

"The acquisition and subsequent spending of trrrreasurrrre."

Morgan smiled. So that's what she'd heard earlier. This parrot was pitching everyone in the restaurant. "I'm listening," she said. "Though I should tell you that most folks would consider me a woman. I just happen to have a beard. Does that matter to you?"

"Not at all! Not a bit. All hairrrr is equally incidental to me." The parrot paused, making eye contact with Morvin. "Good sirrrr, may I perrrrch on your shoulderrrr if I prrrromise to be gentle?"

"Sure, make yourself at home," Morvin said. "It'll save me from lookin' up and back. That kinda thing is heckin' tough on a guy's neck."

The bird hopped down to Morvin's shoulder and gingerly stepped around. It whistled and trilled with pleasure.

"Awww! This is a verrrry fine shoulderrrr! How did you get such muscles?"

"Workin' on a farm all me life, mostly."

"Excellent! Would you like to hearrrr about my offerrrrr of employment?"

"I'll listen, sure."

"Good good good good good!" the parrot said in rapid fire, its head bobbing up and down each time. "My name is Filthy Lucrrrrrre. On the seas, I am known as the Clean Pirrrrate Luc."

"Hold on a heckin' minute," Morvin said. "Are you filthy or clean?"

"Oh, I assurrrre you I am a most dirrrrty birrrrdie," Luc said, and whistled in amusement. "But people like little jokes, you know. You have hearrrrd about the Nice Pirrrrate Chuck? The Sweet Pirrrrate Crrrraig?"

"No."

"Well, neitherrr of them is nice orrrr sweet," Luc said, "and my featherrrrs be the only clean thing about me."

"So you're a pirate captain recruiting a new crew?" Morgan asked.

"That's rrrright. I know wherrrre the trrrreasurrrre is. It's hidden on one of the Severrrral Macks. You worrrrk on my ship, you eat ship's biscuits and drrrrink grrrrog, and then you get a sharrrre, and therrrre will be plenty."

Morgan watched as Morvin polished off his large dish of EATUM, noting that it looked a bit like cat food. "You won't be serving us EATUM on the ship, will you?"

The parrot blinked and shuddered. "Neverrrr! I don't even know what's in that stuff."

"Right?"

"Exactly!" Luc whistled in triumph and pointed a wing at her. "You know what I mean!"

"Hold on a minute," Morvin said. "If the treasure is in the Several Macks, why are you way up here in Borix?"

Filthy Lucre squawked and ruffled his feathers. "Loooong storrrry! I lost my shoulderrrr, though. Verrrry sad."

"Your shoulder? Do parrots even have shoulders? You don't look all lopsided, if you don't mind my sayin' so."

Luc bobbed his head sadly. "I mean my perrrrch! My human. My firrrrst mate. You have such a good good good shoulderrrr, though. Would you like to be my new firrrrst mate? Therrrre would be a bonus sharrre of gold forrrr you."

"Oh, that's mighty kind of you, Luc, but I'm not much of a seafarin' man. Matter o' fact, only time I ever got on a ship I was yarkin' the whole heckin' time and I ruined a load of tuna, which didn't please anyone. Naw, I reckon I'll stay here and see if the Sullenne Sanctuary for Sulky Critters could use a man o' my particular skills. Critters tend to like me for some reason, which is why I was pretty good around the farm."

"Awwww," Filthy Lucre said, and everything about him drooped, even his feathers. He looked so sad that Morgan teared up a bit herself.

"I'll be your perch if you like," she said, trying to cheer him up. Luc peered at her with a gimlet eye and considered.

"Nope! Too bony. I can tell from herrrre. But you arrrre welcome to join my crrrrew."

"I've never been a pirate before. Do I need experience?"

He shook his head, his feathers ruffling. "I have crrrrew memberrrrs who can show you the rrrropes. Can you fight?"

As the Lady Harkovrita, she had been schooled for years by her father's master-at-arms. "I have some training with the rapier," she said, though she'd trained with more than that. In fact, she had more than that in her Chekkoff's gunnysack, just waiting for the right moment to be of use.

"Fine. If ye like, be on the docks at high tide tomorrrrow. Rrrreporrrrt to my ship, *The Puffy Peach*."

"*The Puffy Peach*? That doesn't sound very threatening."

"Well, neitherrrr does the Clean Pirrrrate Luc! That's the point! Misdirrrrection!"

"Okay." Morgan nodded at him. "Tomorrow, then."

"Good good good good good," Luc said, and turned his head to Morvin. "If you change yourrrr mind, you would be most welcome."

Morvin nodded once at the parrot. "Thank you, Luc. You're the best parrot I've ever met. I hope to see you again someday. Until then, I wish you well."

"Awwww," Luc said, and minced about sadly on Morvin's shoulder, knowing it was time for him to leave but not wanting to. They waited patiently—especially Morvin, as those talons digging into his shoulder couldn't be very comfortable—and eventually Filthy Lucre took wing and flew over Morgan's head to visit the folks a couple of booths away.

"Parrrrdon me," they heard him say, and then they grinned at each other the way people do when they've shared an unusual experience and they know it.

"You know what, Morvin? That never would've happened to me if I'd stayed home."

"Cabbages and clams, Morgan, I reckon not! Ain't every day you meet a bird like that what has a peachy plan to plunder the Several Macks."

"Thanks for bringing me here."

"My pleasure."

Morgan dabbed at her beard with her napkin, dislodging a bit of mushroom and tasting the winds of change on her lips.

"What next?" she asked. "I have shopping to do—I know that much." For pirate fashion insisted upon stripes, torn hems, and thoughtful combinations of navy, burgundy, and a color that swore it had once been white.

"And you'll want to see the barber, you said."

At that, Morgan bristled—figuratively and literally.

Did she want to shave?

She looked around the restaurant. The human men she could see appeared to be in a fight to the death over who could grow the most facial and body hair, and some of them obviously cultivated their look with ferocity and painstaking attention. She saw chops, sideburns, soul patches, spade beards, intricate braids, and beard rings. Mustaches were curled into loops, waxed to stand straight up, or left to hang down like spaghetti. On the other hand, all the women looked as if they spent an equal amount of time *removing* their hair. Their cheeks and chins were as smooth as babies' bottoms, their unibrows ripped into separate, carefully trimmed caterpillars that made them look constantly surprised. Any ankle peeking out beneath a belled skirt was as bald as a naked mole rat but far less wrinkly.

Hairless, pretty, clean, strapped into gowns so tight they could barely breathe.

That's what her parents would be looking for: a Lady with a capital *L*.

And Morgan didn't want to be found, so it made sense not to be one.

Oh, sure, she'd still be a lady with a lowercase *l*. But she'd keep the beard, oil it, trim it, maybe braid the silky sides and invest in some pretty ribbons. And she'd wear pants and a loose tunic and perhaps a jaunty hat. And possibly some black eyeliner, because she was going to be a pirate.

Heck, she could be whatever she wanted to be.

"Forget the barber," she said. "Just help me find one of those dwarvelish beard rings."

Morvin shrugged. "As you wish," he said.

7.

SCRUNCHED IN BY THE MOST
MISOGYNISTIC OF HINDQUARTERS

T empest woke before dawn, silently stretched her limbs, and
walked out the door. She'd gone to bed after her sisters, which
was just the normal way of things; she was a night owl, after all. But
she'd worn her cloak to bed and placed her pack by the door, which
meant that by the time Stormy and Misty shook the tangles and
ladybugs out of their hair, she would be well on her way to Sullenne.
That's where the innkeeper said anyone needing a boat might find it,
as the river met the sea there, bringing together merchants, pirates,
fishermen, and fishwives, although she still wasn't sure if these were
the wives of fish, or half-fish women who were married to men, or
something more quotidian. Dryads knew little of the sea, after all,
except that it was awfully salty and not as terrifying when one was
made out of buoyant wood.

Silently shutting the door, she hurried outside and slunk to the
edge of the city, her cloak pulled down tight. With the money she'd

saved at Cappy's, she stopped to purchase a weapon for self-defense on the road, but the shopkeeper proved most annoying.

"I'd like a sword, please," she said, standing before the rough wooden counter with her back straight and her chin up. "Or maybe two, if there's some sort of a buy-one-get-one-free deal going on."

"Don't sell swords to women," the man said, somehow grunting the entire sentence. "Oy'll sell you a Li'l Miss Dagger or a Betty Club, which is like a Billy Club but pink and weighing naught but two pounds. It even has a little mirror on the end, see, so you can check yer lipstick." He held up the objects in question, and Tempest felt her sap rising.

The Betty Club was indeed pink and looked like it couldn't concuss a chipmunk, and the dagger was lavender with glitter and had a rubber blade and the words *Princess Stabby* painted on the hilt.

"See here," she said, but instead of a growl, it got a bit shrill. "I have a right to buy any weapon I can afford, and—"

The shopkeeper pointed to a sign on the wall that read, MOY SHOPPE, MOY ROOLS, with idiosyncratic spelling.

Tempest huffed in annoyance. "Those aren't even words."

"Moy shoppe, moy words," the man said. "I make the rools. Door's right there if ye don't loike it."

Tempest held her shoulders back just a little more and looked him in the eye as she made quotation marks with her fingers. "Fine. Your 'shoppe,' your 'rools,' but please know that I'm on my way to law school, and when I get my degree, the first thing I intend to do is sue you."

He winked. "Dunno what suing is, but if you do it with yer lips, you can come on back to see me anytime."

With a cry of disgust, she marched out, slamming the door despite the laughably misspelled DOO NOTT SLAMME DOOOR sign.

Outside, she was pleased to pay 15 percent more to the creepy halfling who sidled up with an open cloak dripping with daggers, none of which were pink. Her new weapon wasn't the sharpest or the newest, and she was pretty sure the stains were blood and not chocolate fondue, as the seller swore, but she did name it Mr. Stabby, with full knowledge that if she ever had to use it, she would be thinking of the shopkeeper who'd tried to sell her a Betty Club.

She hadn't wanted to take any supplies from her sisters, so she stopped at carts and shops to buy fresh fruit and vegetables, bread and cheese. In their mobile stage, dryads were vegetarians, but they weren't all up in your face about it; in their woody phase, they were carnivores and not only in your face about it but also eating your face. She worried about Misty but knew Stormy would take care of their younger, sweeter sapling of a sister. For everything that he'd done wrong, their father had named them all appropriately. Tempest wasn't a problem most of the time, but when she was . . . well, it was best to take cover. At least, that was who she'd been before Tommy Bombastic and that was who she was going back to being now that she was free.

The road was well traveled and not at all a fetid mire like some country lanes, but Tempest felt more comfortable walking in the grass along the edge. Her feet could almost taste the soil that she would one day root in—and sooner rather than later, if she wasn't more careful around people like Cappy. She kept her hood down always over her face and hair, praying no one would see her for what she was and make unfair demands or try to trick her again. She would have to harden her heart to keep from hardening her body, even if it meant she had to keep walking when a cart horse went lame on the road with a piteous whinny or a small child got scratched by an old dwarf's pet raccoon and screamed melodramatically. After a full day of walking at her quick pace, unencumbered by her sisters but weighed down by her heavy heart, she decided to sleep during the day and walk at night.

It was faster that way, and as much as the sun energized her, the moon had its own power. She met a tinker once and bought a small and out-of-date halfling law book from him, and she read a chapter every dawn and every dusk, hoping to brush up her vocabulary and possibly learn how to better threaten sexist shopkeepers.

"*Mens rea,*" she would say out loud as she walked, enjoying the words. "Sidebar. Circumstantial evidence."

"Who?" an owl once asked back.

"The defense rests!" she replied, feeling like the book was truly sinking in.

The owl flew away, which meant she'd won.

Finally she stood before the city gates of Sullenne, just after dawn one day. It was quiet and almost beautiful if you squinted, and it didn't smell too much like garbage if you held your nose, which was all one could say about Sullenne on the best of days, really. She kept her hood down as she paid her fickel to enter, and the sleepy guard didn't ask her to reveal her face, thank goodness. Apparently people in cities valued their anonymity as much as she did.

Sullene itself wasn't much to see through the constant drizzle, but Tempest felt wonderful. For the first time, she'd chosen her own destiny, set forth, and made it happen. She hadn't been tricked or forced into healing anyone, and no birds had tried to nest in her hair, and Mr. Stabby hadn't left her belt unless she had to cut up an apple. And she was still flying high from her first courtroom victory over that owl.

Tempest spent her day sightseeing, which was a tad difficult when one had to keep covered by a deep hood and regard said sights through rain that was dirty and gray with an *a*, unlike cleaner forest rain, which was grey with an *e*. At dinnertime, she followed a pair of halflings to a brightly lit restaurant, assuming that if their stomachs were grumbling that loudly and they were that hungry, the food had to be decent.

As soon as the waitress seated her, she knew her assumptions were wrong.

The scent of greasy meat hung on the air, and the walls glinted with splattered fat and halfling fingerprints. The sticky menu felt like the inside of someone else's nose. Said menu told Tempest that this place, called Dinny's, was part of a chain that bragged it was open twenty-five hours a day, 366 days a year, which meant that they had to be so busy feeding halflings that they never had a moment to stop and swab everything off with a lemony-smelling enzymatic cleaner. Still, it seemed like she was the only person who wasn't eagerly anticipating her meal, as the dining room was crowded and loud with happy chatter and the sound of bilious halflings releasing their various gases into air that was, unfortunately, already pretty beefy.

She couldn't do this. Even the vegetarian options on the menu came with a side of some sort of meat lovingly called EATUM. The salad came with meat dressing, meat croutons, and olives, which was the last straw. She had to get out and find a nice soup buffet.

As Tempest abruptly pushed her chair back to stand, it thunked into something big. Something heavy. Something that grunted and muttered, "Who the forelock do you think you are, huh?"

She twisted in her chair and found herself staring at glossy brown legs, the only things visible in the limited field of her hood. When she looked up, she saw the man riding the horse—inside a building? Good groves, city people were strange.

No. It was a centaur. She'd never met a centaur before and she'd heard they were violent and bad-tempered and mostly stayed in their fields, where they always had plenty of room to maneuver and bash one another with maces.

But here was a centaur, in the Sullenne Dinny's, being very cross with her indeed.

"I'm so sorry," she said, keeping her voice low. "I didn't see you there."

"Oh, really?" the centaur said, pawing a hoof. "You managed to miss a person who weighs as much as a wagon full of watermelons and could crush your little head like one?"

"Well, yes," she said, aiming for honesty. "It's a very busy Dinny's."

She wanted to scoot her chair back and stand to prepare to run away, but she realized with a jolt of fear that the giant angry centaur had blocked her in with his body. She couldn't move her chair without slamming his forelegs, and judging by the precise flames painted on his hooves, he wasn't going to like that one bit.

"Oh, so now I'm not a person?" the centaur said.

"That's a completely inaccurate conclusion to draw based on what I said," Tempest muttered, trying not to panic. "I was lost in my own thoughts. Having a rough day. Just wanted to leave. And my hood is kind of hard to see around."

"So pull back your hood and look me in the face, bro," the centaur said.

Tempest didn't want to, but she didn't want to make him any angrier, so she did it.

The centaur's face so high above changed dramatically from aggressive anger to . . .

"How you doin', pretty thing?" he said, waggling his eyebrows.

Tempest sighed. "Not that great, honestly. Would you mind if I stood up?"

The centaur stepped aside, and she was able to scoot her chair away from the table and stand. When she looked up, she saw his belly button, which was deeply uncomfortable for her but seemed to amuse him. He had more lint in there than she would've expected.

"My name is Vic," the centaur said, puffing out his chest, not that it needed puffing. "Short for Pissing Victorious."

"You're doing what?" Tempest recoiled, staring down at her bare feet.

The centaur stomped a hoof in annoyance.

"I'm not—I mean—not right now," he growled. "It's a name. Centaur names work like that, you know—a gerund followed by an adjective. What's your name, little filly?"

Tempest tried to edge around him, but he moved his hindquarters and flicked his tail, boxing her in. Her instinct was to bow her head, make herself small, and try to get through the evening without causing any drama. But then she recalled her years with Tommy Bombastic, and her will coalesced. Never again would she let some man make her feel small, tell her where she could go and when. She pulled her dagger and put the point against his equine belly.

"I'm not a filly, and I'm not telling you my name, but I will tell you that my dagger is named Mr. Stabby and that's definitely not chocolate on the blade. Now, you are going to stop blocking my path or—or—or . . . I am going to turn your eight-pack into a leaky keg."

For a moment he didn't move. She added some pressure on the dagger, just the tiniest bit, so that it was on the verge of drawing blood. It made him squeak and Tempest marveled at the feeling of power that gave her.

Finally backing off and giving her room to pass, the centaur grumbled, "Nobody was blocking you, honey. You don't have to be such a mare about it. You're not even that pretty."

Instead of arguing, Tempest darted around him into the safety of the room at large. All around them, conversations had continued as halflings, dwarves, and humans alike shoveled greasy food into their mouths and went to great lengths to avoid getting involved. If anyone had noticed her distress, they'd done nothing about it. And no one would meet her eye now.

It was a world that definitely needed more lawyers, and Tempest was getting to like the taste of arguing. She spun around and pointed at the centaur.

"You were blocking me and now you're gaslighting me about it, and I don't owe you nice or pretty," she barked before walking with as much dignity as she could toward the door. "You think you're the centaur of the universe, but you know what else? Nobody likes this tough-guy act. It makes you come off as sad and insecure. So there. I rest my case."

The centaur didn't seem to like that—she could feel him walking behind her, his huge hooves making the boards bow under a little as they clopped down.

"You shouldn't talk to people that way," the centaur said. It almost sounded apologetic, but she didn't look back. "Especially not to people who are bigger than you."

Just then a large party crowded in the door, and Tempest realized she was trapped between Vic the man-horse and thirty hungry dwarves, all hung with Telling Cudgels, which meant they were on some sort of Meadschpringå field trip and would be looking for a fight. If she let that fight start, so many innocent people could be hurt, and then . . . well, they would want healing, and she would know their wounds were her fault.

Desperate now, she scanned the dining room for any kind of succor—or a sucker, whatever would give her an out. But the first person she found meeting her eyes was a man with a lush golden beard and the most sympathetic eyes she'd ever seen.

"Are you okay?" the man mouthed. "Need help?"

It only took her a moment to make her choice. She nodded and hurried to his booth.

"Hey, where are you going?" Vic called.

"To sit with my friends, and they're allergic to horses."

She wasn't watching him, but she sensed him deflate. Well, too bad. He had terrible manners, and she was already halfway to a better situation. The man with the beard slid over and patted the bench in a way that could've been creepy but wasn't, and Tempest sat down.

"Thanks for that," she said. "That guy wouldn't take no for an answer."

"Yeah, I know a guy like that too."

Tempest gawped at the bearded man and realized . . . *she* was a bearded *woman*. Or something along those lines. In any case, *they* didn't appear dangerous and hadn't yet blocked her into the booth. The other person in the booth, sitting across from Tempest's bearded savior, appeared to be a man, and probably not a smart one. He had paused in chewing, meat spilling out of his mouth, and there was a waterfall of white bird plops down the front of his shirt.

"By gallbladder," he whispered. "Issa dryad!"

Tempest immediately pulled her hood back into place. "Quiet. Please. And before you ask, no, I won't heal you. Or do anything else. I'm not that kind of dryad."

The poor fellow looked scandalized at the very idea. "Cor, no, miss! It's just that I used to work for a dark lord, see, but not that dark, more crepuscular really, and he was forever trying to find magical creatures—not that you're a creature, as you're obviously a person, although your hair might be termed a houseplant, if I might be so bold. But he was always looking for a dryad or drynad, as you will, an' he told me what to look for if I was out 'n' about an' the trees started talking, but not in the magic-mushroomy way, an' you look like that."

The bearded person tensed and clutched a dagger under the table as the centaur walked by, giving them all the evil eye. But Vic kept going, and the bearded person relaxed, and Tempest realized that she had also gone tense and needed to chill.

"So I'm Tempest," she started.

"I'm Morgan," the bearded person said. "And before you ask, I'm a woman. She/her. I just woke up like this one day. I may have been given a cursed rose that put me to sleep or—anyway, it got weird. Long story. And this is Morvin—he's harmless." Morgan exhaled and put away her dagger. "So was that guy an old boyfriend or something?"

Tempest scoffed. "Uh, no. That was a random stranger who decided he could push me around. I'm actually running away from another dude just like that. Also a long story, and although I know travelers in restaurants like this generally retell their adventures, I'll spare you. Do you know anything about how to buy passage on a ship?"

Morgan grinned, and she had a very pretty grin, which the beard only served to accent. "As a matter of fact, we know a captain who's hiring. His ship leaves in the morning. I'm sure he'd take you on."

Tempest felt the flutter of hope. "Is the ship going to Bustardo?"

"Why Bustardo?"

"Um." Tempest realized that even if she'd been wrong about Cappy, she had to trust someone, and she liked Morgan better than anyone else she'd met so far. "I want to be a lawyer, and there's a school there."

Morgan was nodding. "Yes, I've heard about it. Bogtorts School of Law and Order. Bustardo is quite near the Mack Islands, where the ship is going, so I'm sure that would be a reasonable port to stop at."

"But I don't know anything about sailing," Tempest protested.

"Neither do she," Morvin said, pointing a thumb at Morgan. "Ain't stoppin' her. I reckon nothing does."

"You're not going, Morvin?"

Morvin wagged his head. "Naw. I ain't fond of seas, because of the monsters in it, you know, but also I realized one day that the whole dang thing is a huge fish toilet—"

"Enough about toilets," Morgan said. "We've just finished our meal—well, I have—and we're all paid up. So let's go talk to Luc and see if he needs more crew." She gave a very girly hair toss, and Tempest supposed she'd only recently cut much-longer hair. "To tell the truth, it'll be so nice to have another girl on the ship, you know? I've been really lonely—I mean, it's been so long since I had girlfriends."

Tempest thought about the sisters she'd left behind and struggled to smile. "I'd like that too."

They stood, and Morgan led Tempest over to a round table full of rough, pirate-looking types. Tempest picked out the biggest, meanest one of all, assuming he was the captain, and smiled at him in an expectant and competent way, then added on a *yarrrr* for good measure, just to seem like a joiner.

"Yarrrr?" the big man said back, looking perplexed and a little dumb.

"Overrrr this-a-way, miss."

Tempest turned to focus on a colorful yellow-and-red parrot that was giving her a beady eye.

"That's a mighty fine shoulderrrr you have there, if you don't mind my saying so."

Tempest froze. "I've had quite enough sexist compliments for one night, thanks."

The parrot fluffed up in annoyance. "I don't mean it in a human way, aye? No featherrrrs, no netherrrrs, that's my policy. I mean your shoulderrrr looks woody and solid and I'd like to perrrrch on it. If you don't mind? I've never met a drrrryad beforrrrre."

The bird cocked its head, and Morgan said, "It doesn't hurt," and Morvin added, "It's pretty nice, actually, aside from the dollops."

"Okay," Tempest said, and the bird fluttered to her shoulder and settled down, making little grunts as it scooched from side to side.

"A decent-enough perrrrch, but not the perrrrfect one. Why have ye come to see me, Lady Willow?"

"My name is Tempest, and I need passage to Bustardo."

"Bustarrrrrdo." The bird lingered on the *R*s more than usual, in a wistful sort of way. "Aye, and I can take ye therrrre, if you'rrrre willing to learrrrrn a bit about sailing."

Tempest finally smiled. "I'd like that."

The quartermaster—an old woman with rough dimpled skin like beef jerky, whom the parrot introduced as Milly Dread—passed around a piece of parchment and a quill, as everyone had to sign a release form as well as a contract before they could set foot on the ship. From what Tempest could tell, the contract was a solid one that respected the rights of both parties, which was heartening. She should've been more surprised that the captain was a parrot, but honestly, when your father was a carnivorous tree who'd sold you to a demigod, you couldn't really complain about unusual arrangements. Morgan signed first, then passed the quill to Tempest, who noticed that Morgan's signature was both very ornate and very unsure, as if she had aced calligraphy class but had never actually signed her name before.

The parrot fluttered off her shoulder and landed in the center of the table.

"Therrrre we arrrre, then. A full crrrrew. We'rrrre almost rrrrready to go. Just waiting on the last new rrrrecruit."

Tempest looked around the restaurant, trying to figure out who their final companion might be.

"Ah! Therrrre he be," the parrot said, pointing with a wing.

And Tempest was somehow not surprised to see Vic the centaur swaggering toward them and flexing his pecs.

As the daughter of the Willowmuck, it was just her luck. There was, after all, a reason they were called weeping willows.

8.

UNDER DOUBTFUL SAIL IN DORF BAY

It was good, Filthy Lucre mused, that parrot expressions weren't as readable as the elastic, taffy-like faces of humans and the other wingless bipeds that made up his crew. Otherwise they would know how deeply disappointed he was in them. They might be able to note the signs he broadcast through the fluffing or preening of his plumage, but they probably couldn't understand nuance there. He needed a crew of very salty dogs that could (with time and the absence of fresh vegetables) someday become scurvy dogs, but instead all he'd been able to scrounge up was a crew of rubbery, land-lubbery—in one case, almost shrubbery—well-nourished, low-sodium dogs.

None of whom were actual dogs, but it was customary for pirate captains to call their crews dogs, as it was a far more convenient catchall term than *Get to work, you humans and dwarves and also you, centaur swoleboy with the unfortunate name, and you, Pell's first pirate dryad!*

Luc tootled a small hoot of derision. Centaurs didn't belong on ships! Vic couldn't navigate the ladder that led belowdecks, so he stayed up top and had a bit of sail canvas to drape over himself when it rained. He slept with his legs folded underneath him and his body leaned forward like a lightning-struck tree stump, and he often drooled, a line of it descending slowly and swinging like a pendulum with the rocking of the ship before it finally broke and splatted on the deck. The captain knew this because the crew had watched and quietly made bets on whether the rope of drool would make it all the way down without breaking. Luc had lost a fickel on that once. But the centaur had privately claimed he was a wizard of some kind, although he wouldn't prove it, suggesting his magic was far too powerful to waste on parlor tricks. Still, Luc felt the low-grade hum of magic deep in his pinfeathers and promised he'd find a place for this swoleboy called Pissing Victorious. He would take all the magic he could get for this venture. He'd long ago decided that acceptance meant acceptance of everyone, even those of very strange physiognomy.

And he had to admit he'd taken on the dryad for the goofy novelty of it, even though she claimed she would never heal anyone, knew nothing about sailing, and had no experience fighting. He was mostly hoping she'd get cold enough at some point to set her teeth chattering and say, *Shiver me timbers*, since she was basically a walking, talking tree.

The girl he'd found in Dinny's, Morgan, had a solid knowledge of knots and had already proved that she was an able fighter—perhaps a very fine one—when some stevedore at the docks made a lewd comment within her hearing. Morgan had pulled out a mace from her gunnysack, administered two swift blows, and left him unconscious in a pile of crabs.

"I could've done that," the centaur said, and both Morgan and the dryad had rolled their eyes but made no comment. The women, Luc noted, did their best to avoid the centaur. Ah, well. Luc knew plenty about whether a biped would follow his orders or not, but in other matters he had never fully understood the ways of people with opposable thumbs.

Luc deeply regretted that Morgan's companion, Morvin, had not elected to join them. His shoulder would have made a very fine perch, and Luc felt instinctively that Morvin was trustworthy.

The same could not be said for the first mate he'd had to settle on, Feng Zhu Ye. Not that he thought Feng was plotting against him yet; nor were any of the other lads who'd signed on with him. They were all foine sailors and would serve *The Puffy Peach* admirably; Luc had a sort of avian sixth sense about such things and had never once had to suppress a mutiny, as long as one didn't count the occasional loudmouth he made an example of. It was simply that Feng's shoulder was not quite so luxurious and expansive as Morvin's or as—well, certain shoulders from Luc's past that he didn't really want to think about. Feng was guarded and kept his cards close to his chest. He rarely smiled but rarely frowned. His black hair was neatly trimmed and styled and possessed the remarkable ability to stay still in the wind. His nose was broad and flat, his skin a cool beige, and a golden hoop earring dangled from his left lobe. All of which didn't matter so much as whether he'd be loyal to his captain or not.

It pointed to an utterly mercenary heart, Luc decided, which was a different kind of dependable: trustworthy only so long as he felt certain he'd be paid, and almost certainly mutinous the moment he felt there was no treasure to be had. There would never be any personal loyalty from Feng—unless Luc could contrive some way to put him in debt. He'd have to ponder that soon while working his slow, luxurious way through a ration of roasted sunflower seeds. In the meantime, Feng inspired instant respect from the crew—an important quality in a first mate but not the salty attitude a pirate needed to survive.

Fortunately, Luc trusted his more seasoned sailors to get the new crew properly salty. Two people, in particular, had sailed with him forever: his quartermaster and cook, Milly Dread, and his notable boatswain from Qul, Qurt Qobayne.

Qobayne was the silent, brooding sort except when he had to shout orders, but he had his mercenary side too. It was not abstract riches he was after, and unlike most humans, he was willing to wait for his dream to come true, which Luc appreciated. Qobayne truly loved the sea and seemed to relish a life of rum and poor nutrition. He'd confided in Luc a few adventures ago after a little too much grog that someday he hoped to save enough money to buy the rare set of Waolphware porcelain dishes featuring scenes of frolicsome llamataurs—a deeply disturbing contradiction—painted by the renowned Waolphish artist, Knob Ross, and when that day came, why, he'd leave the life of piracy and join a legitimate mercantile concern with lower but steady paydays and a fully stocked larder. Until then, Luc knew, Qobayne would be utterly competent and reliable, even when he'd poured flagons of grog down his throat the night before and shed a few tears over the beauty of painted llamataurs.

From his perch on Feng's shoulder, Luc watched the brown-skinned Qobayne holler at the crew, trying to get them into shape as they crossed Dorf Bay from Sullenne to the dwarvelish city of Lårpendrånk. They would take on some dwarvelish crew there to help them fight off the monsters that lurked in the south, but even with the added help, they'd stand a poor chance of survival if they couldn't learn their roles.

Qobayne instructed the new folk how to raise and lower sails and how to man battle stations on the gun deck. He covered the delicate etiquette of the poop deck and the concomitant communal reading material. Theft of the vintage *Rolling Bone* collection or the back issues of *Playgnome, Reader's Digestive,* or *Spurts Illustrated* would earn them a long walk off a short piece of lumber. He also took the time to demonstrate how to properly swab the deck, because few people realized that there was a huge difference between scrubbing and swabbing, and *The Puffy Peach* required a thorough swabbing, by Pellanus.

Thanks to his years of piracy and keen observation of the human body, Luc knew the exact moment when his crew began to question whether any of Qobayne's instruction was worthwhile. He ruffled his feathers and cleared his throat, and Feng stepped forward on his cue.

"Rrrright now, some of you arrre thinking," Luc called out, "*Do I rrrreally need to pay attention to this or trrrry to become a competent sailorrrr? What's the point of swabbing?* Well, the point is, when boarrrded by another ship, you don't want slipperrrry footing in the midst of a battle! You need to know each aspect of a functioning ship to defend it and to attack others like it prrrroperrrrly! And after we sail south of dwarrrrvelish lands, the Dolorrrrous Ocean becomes quite dangerrrrous! Many seas full of many monsterrrrs with too many teeth! Not to mention elvish warrrrships arrrrmed with heinous glitterrrr bombs! So I need you to pay attention to the boatswain! What Qobayne is teaching you will save yourrrr lives!"

For a while, anyway, that focused them. But it was not even an hour before the centaur slipped on the deck during a yardarm exercise and slid into the dryad, bowling her over with his flanks. She cried out, "Watch it, horsemeat!"—perhaps not the most diplomatic reaction—but then he reacted poorly. He flexed at her.

"Can't help being this swole. You should learn to stay out of my way. And be grateful I'm here too, because when it comes time to clobber some noggins, I'll keep yours from being clobbered."

Morgan smoothly stepped in front of Tempest, brandishing that mace she'd used so well at the docks. "No, Vic, it's you who needs to stay out of our way, or else the clobbering will begin with your own noggin. Or whatever I can reach."

"Get in therrrre," Luc told Feng, and the first mate waved to his three human friends, who'd been recruited at the same time. They were a strange trio of pale men who probably only had a trio of good teeth between them, but they moved forward on command to insert themselves between the centaur and the affronted women. They faced Vic together, backs to Tempest and Morgan, and as a unit they must have looked more swole than Vic liked. He shifted nervously, his hooves clopping on the deck, almost as if he were tap-dancing, yet another human custom Luc didn't understand.

"'Sup, bros? Who are you?"

Luc paid attention to the answers, because they were quite new and he was a still little unclear on which was which.

"I'm Frij," the first one said. He had yellow hair, a golden sprout of whiskers on his chin, and eyes like a dead fish.

"I'm Mort," the second one said. His clothing appeared to be a collection of brown stains, and he had eyes and a mustache to match.

"And I'm Queefqueg." This last one was orange-haired and freckled and wore a green waistcoat with no shirt underneath it. His arms were turning red in the sun.

"They're all mates of mine," Feng said. "Frij and Mort sailed with me in Teabring. Spent a lot of time raiding in the Seven Toes. Queefqueg grew up in Burdell, but he's been afloat with us for years."

Vic shrugged. "So?"

"So this is obviously your first trip and we're all concerned about your behavior. Aren't we, Captain?"

"That's rrrrright, Feng. We can all see that you arrrre swole, Vic. But we cannot see that you know how to sail. Just now I watched you slip on the deck, slam into Tempest, and fail to execute the maneuverrrr you werrrre instrrrructed to perform by the boatswain. Rrrrather than apologize, you claimed that it was Tempest's fault for getting knocked down. You will own yourrrr mistakes and be civil to the crrrrew orrrr I will dismiss you when we get to Lårrrrpendrrrrånk—and I seem to rrrrecall that dwarrrrves and centaurrrrs do not get along. Which will it be?"

Vic blinked and looked around at the assembled crew, all staring at him with hard expressions. Luc watched Vic's eyes and mouth carefully as the centaur tallied up the score against him. He clenched his fists, and Luc wondered if they might all be subjected to some sort of magical attack in the next moment, but then the swoleboy let his hands hang loose as his shoulders fell.

He sighed, lips spluttering like a horse, and his eyes found Tempest. "Sorry for my clumsiness. I hope you weren't hurt by my muscles."

Filthy Lucre swiveled his head around to see how the dryad responded. She searched the centaur's face for sincerity and nodded once when she found it. "I'm fine, thank you. I'm sorry for calling you a name."

"Good good good good good," Luc declared, bobbing his head. "Now back to trrrraining with the boatswain! Qobayne, prrrroceed."

No blood spilled, no hard feelings. It was a good start. They threw themselves back into the work and Luc ordered Feng to walk him to his quarters, for the episode did throw into sharp relief—for Luc, at least—where the true power dynamic of this new crew was centered: on Feng. Any mutiny against him would require Feng's approval, and that was what all captains, to say nothing of this salty parrot, needed to know. This first visit to his cabin was therefore vital to the success of the entire voyage. Feng needed to understand why Luc was running this ship and why he couldn't simply take over for himself.

Luc always enjoyed the moment when new crew members first experienced his cabin. Instead of the usual desk, there was only the captain's log—a tall piece of driftwood affixed firmly to the floor and furnished with many wooden perches in a variety of diameters. He had no bunk, but there was a chair—nailed in place, of course, for ships were slippery places—so that a guest might sit and enjoy a glass of port or a crew member might get screeched at for disobedience. The walls were lined with shelves, the shelves crowded with books and scrolls and bric-a-brac from Luc's many years of travels, not to mention a few ornate perches. Luc flew to a perch on the shelf that was just to the right of the chair's line of sight, and then he pointed with a wing tip at a wine cabinet next to the chair.

"You'll find rrrrum in there, and plenty of otherrrr fine liquorrrrs, if you like. I just thought we might have a chat."

Feng grinned. "Ah, excellent! Thank you."

Yes, human, take the drink, relax a bit, let the informality seep into your bones, then let's get the inevitable interview over with, Luc thought. He waited while Feng poured himself a glass of dwarvelish honey mead and babbled about rare drinks he'd enjoyed in his travels, and it didn't take long for the man to wind down, conclude he'd been polite enough, and begin to probe for information.

"So, Captain, if I may ask," Feng said, "which of the Several Macks contains this treasure? I've visited a few of them and never suspected there were any riches buried there."

Luc whistled in amusement. "Awww, it's a Mack that doesn't appearrrr on many maps. It's little morrrre than a rrrreef. At high tide you can't even see it. It's a verrrry cunning little island called Mack ... well. I must keep some secrrrrets, mustn't I?"

Feng nodded along, as he was intended to. "And what will we find in this mysterious place?"

"Enough trrrreasurrrre to let us all rrrretirrrre in luxurrrry," Luc assured him.

Feng blinked and briefly looked irritated but then smiled. "Of course. But at least tell me who buried this treasure, and why haven't they come back for it?"

"The perrrrson who burrrried the trrrreasurrrre is dead," Filthy Lucre said. "And I know that because I killed him. He asked too many questions."

This was another moment Luc enjoyed. If Feng asked *how* Luc had killed someone—or, indeed, anything else—Luc would have to demonstrate, because at that point Feng would have proved he was too stupid to live. But his first mate instead scanned the room, took the hint, and thanked Luc for the drink before excusing himself from the cabin. Perhaps he'd seen the weapons hidden on the shelves and trained on the chair, all of which Luc could trigger from his perch with a squeeze of his talons; perhaps he hadn't. But Feng was observant, Luc was glad to note, and now at least mildly afraid of his captain, which was good. When it came down to it, a parrot couldn't make a human walk the plank, so Luc had to think of other ways to make sure he remained in charge.

Feng and his three pale friends would be useful, and Luc felt a little better about the crew. Between them, Qobayne, Milly Dread, his regular salty dogs, and a new, heavily muscled youth called

Brawny Billy, he doubted anything catastrophic would happen in day-to-day sailing. But he didn't know if the untested crew would ultimately prove useful or disastrous when they ran into trouble, and he relished that uncertainty, the not-knowing if one would be adequately prepared. Sailing directly into trouble was easy and therefore boring; surviving and sailing out again was where all the fun could be had, and Luc was a pirate parrot who liked to have himself a bit of fun.

It was possible he'd talked up the treasure while failing to mention the worst of the obstacles they would face on the way there. Luc laughed to himself. The new crew would either shape up quick or fill the belly of a sea monster. If they didn't like those odds, they shouldn't have been born without wings.

9.

AWASH IN THE SLUDGY SLOSH OF
THE SANGUINE SEAS

Vic was glad to jib the yardarm or yubnub the squidward, or whatever Qobayne was instructing him to do, as it meant he could turn his hindquarters on the grouchy dryad and her murderous bearded friend. He'd thought that the people he met outside the Centaur Pastures would look at him, tally up his size, muscles, and general air of danger, and acknowledge his natural physical superiority, possibly even ask for his autograph. He had not expected to encounter quite so much opposition, especially out of smaller specimens with more noodly arms. It seemed like every time he acted like the lead stallions did back home, he earned derision instead of respect—and got assigned to swabbing duty again. The flames he'd had painted on his hooves had been washed away with salty water within days, and the sea air made his mullet all frizzy and exacerbated his asthma.

Apparently there was a reason more centaurs didn't seek solace on the sea.

"Listen up, landlubbers!" Qobayne shouted. "All apologies for the interruption, but it's time to talk about what's to come. If this short trip across Dorf Bay didn't drain you too much, you can stay on board for the much longer, more tempestuous trip from Lårpendrånk, through the Serpent and Myn Seas, past the Proudwood Lighthouse, across the Urchin Sea, and down to Bustardo. If that sort of extended sea journey gives you an aneurysm, you can walk right off this ship and stay away." He focused on each sailor, and Vic struggled not to quail under the man's sharp gaze. "But if you're a certain breed, ready to dive deep and embrace the sea, Captain Luc invites you to come as you are, land legs and all, and become the sailor you were meant to be." He looked around and leaned forward conspiratorially. "But don't be dumb and call the captain Polly, or you might as well be kissing sharks."

This was not Qobayne's first speech, and as always, as if the man had some sort of inborn magical charisma, Vic found himself nodding along. He could do this. He could become seaworthy. He had to. It was the fastest way to Mack Guphinne and the chance to rid himself of his tea magic. Why, he'd nearly splurted sugar cubes when the dryad had accidentally run into him, and that would've been the end of his time on the crew. They'd start calling him Sugarfingers or Babycakes and he'd be back on land at Lårpendrånk, surrounded by swole, homicidal dwarves and hunting for yet another ship, with possibly a more vicious captain, who demanded fickels instead of a bit of light swabbing as payment for passage. And the land route—well, he'd be forced to journey back through the Centaur Pastures, where he'd dramatically sworn to never set foot again in a massive flounce, or to enter the terrifying Morningwood, peopled by sneaky elves who loved to torture and spook centaurs with snake puppets, or to venture forth into the mountains, where the gryphons were said to despise the centaurs as abominations and screech sonnets at them.

No, it was the sea or nothing, which meant it was the sea.

He kept to himself, did as he was told, spoke to no one, and made it safely to Lårpendrånk. While the rest of the crew went on land to do whatever bipeds did, Vic stayed on board, loudly proclaiming that he would guard the ship. The captain gave him that strange, dead-eyed parrot look but allowed it, leaving Qobayne behind as well, which was fine with Vic. The boatswain was fair if a bit melancholy, and he spent most of his alone time playing dolorous tunes on a ukulele and then smashing the ukulele against a barrel before producing a new ukulele the next day. Vic supposed he must get them wholesale from the same craftsmen who supplied instruments to dwarvelish thrash-uke bands, who broke their ukuleles on the skulls of delighted audience members at the end of every show. (He did not understand why anyone would pay to attend an event where they might leave with a concussion, but centaurs and dwarves had many cultural divides to bridge, starting with the dwarves' insistence that hunting centaurs while on Meadschpringå was a good idea.)

When everyone returned to the ship that night, jolly and tipsy, they brought along a quartet of solid, beefy dwarves, each armed with a murderous-looking stave and a magnificent beard that made Vic very self-conscious of the scraggly goatee he'd managed to cultivate. They hauled on board strange, smallish cannons on wheels and what looked like thickly padded mops, or possibly wooden spears wrapped up in canvas. No one mentioned the odd luggage, so Vic assumed it was something normal for dwarves, perhaps used for beard care or centaur bashing. If there was one thing he knew, it was that showing interest in others and asking personal questions only made him seem less authoritative, so he remained committed to being the strong-but-silent-unless-lightly-bumped-and-then-whoo-boy-look-out type.

The next morning, they set sail on calm seas, the boat cutting the water like room-temperature butter as it billowed toward a sunrise the color of a ripe tomato. It made Vic a bit uneasy, since he'd never really liked butter or tomatoes, and when he looked to the captain, the parrot wore an inscrutable expression that suggested he was thinking dark thoughts or was ravenously hungry for some sunflower seeds. But the boat didn't change course, and if the crew was quieter than usual, that only served to help Vic maintain his own silence and not accidentally produce an éclair while fidgeting nervously.

He was getting used to the ocean and to his place on the ship.

Except . . .

It finally hit him when the fussy dryad lady turned to her disturbingly competent friend and declared, "You know, I've never been out of sight of land before."

And it was true. They were nowhere near land. The ocean went on and on in every direction, deep and blue and vast. And Vic was a heavy centaur. Who couldn't swim.

As this realization hit home, a masculine and musky sweat broke out across his sunburned shoulders and the back of his mullet-protected neck, while a cool chill ran down his spine. His nipples puckered up and his rear sphincter went loose, which seemed like the opposite of what would be useful in a fight. When he'd put together his plan to sail down to the Macks and find his destiny, he hadn't really thought about the weeks he would spend on a creaking wooden ship, barely able to walk without tripping over his own horseshoes and making a fool out of himself—much less what would happen if he somehow fell or was forced off the ship. He'd always gone through life assuming that if any interaction went badly, he could extricate himself through just the right insult, or, barring that, just the right kick to a solar plexus, or, barring *that*, turning his tail, dropping a few apples for emphasis, and sauntering and/or cantering away. He'd never considered that his only options were dealing with the problem at hand or leaping to his death in a briny sea.

Vic's heart began to thunder and clatter, his hooves echoing the sound as they clicked and clacked, dancing against the boards of the ship. He felt his hindquarters bunch up, and without meaning to, he began walking backward in little circles, his front hooves lifting of their own volition, threatening to rear. A dribble of Juicy Jukai tea oozed out of his fingertips.

"Vic? Are you okay?" Morgan asked softly, keeping her distance as the dryad lady raised an eyebrow, her arms crossed.

"Yeah. Totally chill. But, you know. Can't, uh. Can't see the land. Like, at all. But that's fine. I can be a seahorse, right? Heh heh. I'm tough. I can deal. This is not . . . this is not a problem. This is just the chillest thing ever. I am soooo comfortable right now."

Morgan stepped forward and put a hand on his forearm, and he whipped it away right before a shortbread biscuit plopped out of his palm. The girl didn't step back, though. Her voice was so low he could barely hear it over the snap of the sails and the slap of the sea. "Breathe, Vic. Breathe in for a count of four, hold it, breathe out for a count of six. Or you're going to—"

"Oh, don't worry. Centaurs can't barf," he informed her, failing utterly to breathe deeply and starting to wheeze a little.

"I was going to say that you're going to stomp a hole in the deck if you don't chill. Or you could wake up the—"

"I am chill!" he screeched. "Totally very much chill, okay, thank you!"

"Shh!"

"Okay, but you can't just shush me. You're not my mom! Or a librarian! Or my mom's librarian!"

Morgan's teeth clenched, and she looked out at the ocean and snatched his flailing wrist and hissed, "We're on the Myn Seas, Vic. If you keep squealing, you're going to attract the wrong kind of attention."

At that, Vic flooded with defensive aggression, a far more comfortable feeling than fear. "Yeah? And what's the wrong kind of attention?"

The ship heaved to the side, forcing Vic to scramble to avoid bowling over Morgan and her dryad friend, and something broke the surface of the water, rising high overhead.

"That kind of attention!" the dryad wailed.

"Sea serpents?" Vic screeched. "Oh, gods, oh, gods, we're all going to die!"

"Didn't you listen to anything Captain Luc said last night?" the dryad muttered. "Sea serpents in the Myn Seas? How they hate loud noises and being disturbed? How we brought on casks of special chocolate to keep them soothed so they wouldn't attack? Milly Dread's been dropping truffles in our wake for hours."

Vic's horsey half was in a full-on panic now, stamping and jigging willy-nilly. "I wasn't with the captain last night! I was here! I have no idea what you're talking about!"

"Did you not notice the red skies this morning?"

"Sure I noticed! Even centaurs can notice the sky!"

The dryad shook her head in a disappointed sort of way. "That old chestnut—"

Finally, something Vic understood. "My dam was a chestnut!"

"Vic, really, shut up. It goes: *Red skies at night, sailor's delight. Red skies at breakfast, toss chocolate and sail fast.*"

Vic refrained from mentioning that since he found hardtack unbearable, he avoided the breakfast table and usually found a quiet spot where no one else could see him use his magic to produce a nice cup of Baoshu Mist and some protein-based tea cakes. He'd never learned the little ditty about the skies, and he'd never heard anything about sea serpents being actually really real and not just another joke by the elves, who loved to spread false maps and lead unsuspecting travelers into stink holes or overpriced troll toll bridges.

He was about to explain all this to the dryad at length, as he felt it very important that everyone know what was and was not his fault at all times, but Captain Luc shouted, "Code Red!" and the deck went insane, the previous premium on silence utterly forgotten. The captain began flapping his wings and screeching orders that made no sense and contained at least twice the usual amount of *R*s, and Feng and Qobayne scurried all over, translating the captain's commands and putting people to work. No one shouted at Vic to do anything, so he backed up until his rump was against the mizzenmast and watched the terror unfold as some mighty beast thrashed and circled the boat, causing it to sway in a way that made Vic wish he *could* vomit, after all.

Morgan and the dryad ran to where two of the new dwarves were unpacking their contraption. It looked much like a cannon but was on big wheels, which the dwarves blocked with special wedges once the black iron tube was in place and facing the huge, snakelike red beast rearing over the boat. The nearest cannon had AUNT FLO written on one side, and the other one said merely TOM. As Morgan and the dryad aimed their tube, one dwarf stuffed a canvas-wrapped spear into the cannon's mouth and the other set to lighting a candle, which Vic considered a total waste of time, given the current predicament. With red, callused hands, the dwarf rammed the fabric-wrapped end of the spear tightly into the tube and fitted a wicked-looking metal hook over the wooden butt of the spear, then gently eased the ladies out of the way so he could expertly aim the peculiar weapon.

"Light the rags!" the dwarf shouted, and the other dwarf shouted back, "Rags glad and ready!" He held his candle to a short fuse, and both dwarves doubled over, hands over their ears.

"It's gonna get a bit explosive and temperamental, my good friends!" one cried, and everyone nearby covered their ears except for Vic, who needed to prove that he had exceptionally durable eardrums.

The moments ticked by. An enormous head at the end of a long, sinuous neck wavered over the boat. The beast was a dark liver crimson, and its head looked a bit like a weasel crossed with an angry snake. Its eyes were a sick, acid yellow with evil black slits for pupils. Opening its foul mouth to show sharklike rows of teeth, it hissed and spit globs of sticky brown acid at the boat.

"That acid'll eat everrrrything!" Luc shouted. "Keep back!"

Vic was horrified and disgusted, but there was nowhere to run, nowhere to hide, so he stood his ground and stamped like he meant it.

"Your ears, Pony Boy!" a dwarf called, and Vic put his hands over his ears just to shut the dude up. "Things are about to get grouchy."

Boom!

The spear exploded from the cannon, the hook lodging in the beast's neck with a spurt of deep-red blood that colored the dark-blue water below. *A dastardly invention,* Vic thought, just the thing a brilliant man would create.

"A solid hit!" the captain crowed. "Team TOM, light the fuse!"

The other cannon went off, its hook lodging in the monster's cheek and causing it to shriek and thrash. As the hideous head flailed on its scaly neck, it flopped over the side of the ship, sweeping one of the dwarves overboard and causing the other dwarf to shake his fist and shout, not with an incoherent bellow of grief but with ardent poetry, "Maddening beast of the Myn Seas! You have claimed my bosom friend! To the last I grapple with thee; from Pell's heart I stab at thee; for hate's sake I spit my last breath at thee!"

"Everybody's so dramatic during the crimson tide," someone said with an annoyed sigh.

"What are those things?" Vic asked Milly Dread. The little old lady had suddenly appeared at his side, arms crossed as she watched the scene unfold with that sort of experienced curiosity that suggested she had evaded death long enough to hope it had conveniently forgotten her. "Those weapons?"

"Tampoons," she said. "Only thing to control the monsters of the Myn Seas. Them dwarves are specialists, see? They're veteran tampoonists who hire on with ships along this route, bring their cannons, watch the moon's path, and leave gore in their wake."

"But it's so . . . gross," Vic protested.

Milly shrugged. "Doesn't matter what you think about it, kid. It's gonna keep on happening as it always has, whether you like it or not, ain't it? At least we'll eat well tonight."

"We're going to eat sea monster?" Vic cringed. He hated seafood.

"Nah. Sharks; they come to eat the monsters, and we'll have meat to last for days. It's always shark week when we sail the Myn Seas."

Vic pranced to the port side and peered over the rail, where he spied sharp gray fins cutting through the water. Frij and Mort whooped and tossed fishing lines down into the churning waves, and Frij's line jerked the moment it hit.

"I got me one!" he shouted. "Stand back, it's a big'un!"

He began yanking in the line as Mort grumbled by his side, his line ignored by the sharks. Then, in a flash of red as quick as lightning, the sea monster's bleeding head careened around, its jaws snapping into Frij's midsection and drawing him down into the sea, screaming all the while.

"Frij! Nooooo!" Feng wailed, running to the rail and extending an ineffective arm after his chum, who was now literally chum.

Without a word, Mort pulled his line in, sweat dripping down his bald head. "Not in the mood for shark tonight," he muttered. "Weevily biscuit's lookin' pretty foine." Queefqueg snickered nearby, which was mostly what he seemed to do, but this soon proved to be false bravado, as his expression crumbled and he dissolved into sobs, moaning, "Friiiiij. He was me mate, he was!"

Vic shuffled anxiously away, as if feelings and weakness were contagious. But he'd accidentally shuffled toward the dwarves.

"Hey, Knock-Knees!" the nearest dwarf called, and Vic's knees did knock as he realized the dwarf was talking to him.

"Who, me?"

"I need your strong arms over here."

"For what?"

The dwarf's bushy eyebrows drew down. "For standing around, looking swole and uncomfortable. Honestly, kid, use it or lose it. This next tampoon is a super one, I've lost my partner, and I could use your leverage."

Vic couldn't think of a single excuse that didn't exude cowardice, so he stepped forward on sliding hooves. The boat was rocking with the sea monster's flailings; red-stained water sloshed over the wood and mixed with an unfortunate puddle of Khotran sweet tea. He made it to the dwarf's side.

"Pull out the biggest one," the dwarf said, indicating the thickest spear.

Vic nodded, reminding himself that he could do this. His hands closed around the wood, and after a good bit of tugging that showed off his vascularity, it plunked out.

"Now stuff the end in the cannon."

It was calming, actually, to just do what the dwarf said, instead of watching the rest of the crew swipe at the sea serpent with swords and other tiny weapons as its bleeding, furious head snapped and bashed into the ship. Queefqueg was now unconscious, having been knocked into a barrel, and Morgan had a vicious splinter in her arm, while several other crew members had taken minor injuries and were wailing about it. Vic had never seen such a dangerous creature, and he could not have been more grateful that sailing the Myn Seas wasn't generally his lot in life.

It took some work, but he managed to get the super tampoon stuffed into the cannon. The dwarf seemed pleased enough with his work.

"Now stand back and plug your ears," the dwarf instructed as he fit another wicked hook atop the weapon, and Vic was happy to oblige, retreating to Milly Dread's side as the dwarf aimed the tampoon and lit the cannon's fuse.

"Fire in the hole!" the dwarf called, and then, again, that massive *boom!* rattled Vic's bones and gave him a headache.

The super tampoon flew through the air, and its pronged hook lodged in the serpent's eye, making the dwarf shout and pump his fist in victory.

"We got it!" the dwarf shouted. "It's a gusher!"

As if in agreement, the sea monster gave a final surge and fell over backward in a bubbling mass of blood and shark fins. Its shimmering scales sank down below the surface, and the entire crew held their breath as they waited to see if it would rise again for one more unwelcome splurt. It died with gurgling shrieks and a boil of splashing red, and a mighty cheer arose.

"Quiet, fools!" the captain cawed. "Do ye want to arrrrouse anotherrrr monsterrrr?"

The ship went silent, and Feng and Qobayne went from person to person, whispering orders, though Feng was still a tearful mess at the loss of his friend Frij. Vic was not surprised to be ordered to swab the deck. That's all they seemed to think his massive guns were good for—endless swabbing.

"Good job, friend," the dwarf said, slapping him lightly on the foreleg in a manly way. "It takes at least two dwarves to stuff the cannon, and you got it in one go!"

Earned pride was a new feeling for Vic, and he felt a wide smile spread across his features. "Hey, I did, didn't I?"

"One might almost forget that it was your shouting that brought down the wrath of the beast," the dryad said dryly.

"I wasn't shouting." It was almost a screech, but Vic caught himself, cleared his throat, and turned it into more of an angry grumble.

"Hey, it's okay to make mistakes," Morgan said, stopping as she rolled a barrel along the deck. "And it's okay to be scared. I'm scared too. I've never been this far away from home. And . . . we just fought a sea monster. I lit a cannon." A grin broke out on her face. "We're really part of the crew. We helped out. We didn't mess up. And it feels amazing!"

Much to Vic's surprise, she spontaneously hugged him, her cheek landing right against his horsey chest in a way that was only slightly awkward. In return, he patted her on the back and muttered, "Good game, buddy."

The dwarf by Vic's side was counting his leftover tampoons, and he looked over with a weary sigh. "You all did well, yes. But let's not forget what was lost. Mo was my friend, and he got washed overboard. We've been riding the scarlet seas as a duo for ten years. We were the best around—Team Maxi Rad, we called ourselves. It's easy to forget that the sea is an unforgiving mistress. The smallest lump of chance can be the difference between victory and tragedy." He looked over the railing. "Goodbye, my friend Mo Trynn. You were a valiant fighter. You loved hygiene and a good shave and tea cakes with a dribble of honey mead on a warm summer night. I will carry on, but

I will miss you. And I'll think of you once a month, on this day, for the rest of my life. Chum to chum."

Vic walked to his side and looked over the railing at the sea below. It was calming, the red fading.

"Mo Trynn did a good job. He was a good dude," Vic said in a way that he hoped was kind but also manly. Without really thinking, without looking down, he exerted his magic and held out an exquisitely decorated chocolate tea cake to the dwarf.

The dwarf tore off half the cake and tossed it into the water below, where it sank with a pretty blurble. Then he stuffed the remainder in his mouth. "A fittin' tribute," he said, his words muffled by globs of sugar, flour, and cocoa. "Mo loved chocolate." Once he'd swallowed, he glanced up at Vic, his head cocked. "Say, you and me might make a good team. How'd you like to join up? Use those guns for good? Join Team Maxi Rad? My name is Skånki Jorts."

A shark's fin surfaced and disappeared far below, and Vic shivered. Not only because of the sharks, but because of dwarves. Even if Skånki had never hunted down a centaur personally, he almost certainly had a relative or friend who had, and his culture considered it acceptable. Vic would most likely never feel safe around a dwarf. And lastly, well . . . it was just so icky. Although he knew nature could be strange—he'd once seen two giraffes mating, for Pell's sake—the Myn Seas were simply too disgusting to bear.

"Thanks, Skånki, but no thanks. The Myn Seas are super gross."

The dwarf's response was unexpected and swift. He drew back, looking affronted and angry.

"Life is gross," he said simply. "It's bloody and messy and, yes, sometimes dangerous. If you let fear hold you back—"

"It's not fear! It's just—"

"It *is* fear, son." Skånki sighed and tugged his beard. "You can tell yourself it's disgusting all you like, but the truth is that the sight of blood reminds us that we're mortal. That we can get hurt. That we can die. Blood reminds us that we're all made of meat. If you're not manly enough to face a puddle of blood, how can you ever truly find balance within yourself? How can you ever truly connect with anyone else? Strength comes from vulnerability. Every time I sail these seas, I remember how lucky I am to be alive, even when it's messy."

Vic's throat had tightened, and his hooves were dancing again. He had to change topics before the dwarf really said something uncomfortable. "Well, I already have a destiny waiting for me down in the Several Macks, and I definitely don't want to get Frijjed."

The dwarf raised a bushy eyebrow before turning to his cannon. "If you say so."

But secretly, Vic was pleased at the invitation. Sure, he'd accidentally called down the wrath of a sea serpent and gotten at least two people eaten. But then he'd helped fight the serpent and ostensibly saved lives after he imperiled them. And he'd done so well that he'd gotten a job offer on the spot. He wouldn't think about Skånki's words too much. He just needed a good workout to get him back to feeling normal again instead of . . . well, whatever was making his insides feel like jelly right now. Adrenaline, probably.

Vic didn't know what he'd do after he'd visited Mack Guphinne and gotten rid of his tea magic, but he was certain it wouldn't involve tampoons. Period.

10.

UPON THE COMING OF MANY
EXPERT SEAMEN

❧

Sometimes, Alobartalus thought, *an elf just needs a vacation.* Not from being fabulous or desirable or elvish, of course, but from the monotony of existence. New experiences were necessary! Maybe he should try a Drinks 'n' Diapers Day of Debauchery, a package deal made famous by the resort city of Humptulips in honor of Pell's last king, Benedick, who had spent much of his benevolent reign diapered and slobbering drunk.

Or maybe Alobartalus could check into a dwarvelish spa for a few days and let them turn his muscles into butter with their massages and baths and magical skin-care regimens, which might include actual butter for all he knew.

Or perhaps—just supposing!—he could find a ship willing to sail south along the Siren Sn'archipelago and drop him off at the tower of the Sn'archivist. That would be the absolute best, but he had to admit it wasn't likely. Most ships headed south from Proudwood

Lighthouse hugged the coast of the continent, since the siren grottoes were deadly and there was little else in the archipelago to attract much traffic.

Regardless, Alobartalus was going to go somewhere soon. He'd sent a notice to his uncle that he'd be taking a month off, since he had about ten months of leave accrued, and as such the lighthouse would need a decent docent to stand in during his absence. He was going to lock up the lighthouse behind him, and there would be no steady drip of profits from the sale of Enchanted Morningwood Rods if the king didn't provide some relief.

Until he left, however, Alobartalus was expected to maintain order on the island. As if on cue, a tidy gnomeric pudding chef who worked in the kitchen of one of the island's watering holes, the Grog Bog, knocked smartly upon his door and apologized politely for the interruption. He then announced that there was a pale, disconsolate, weeping human with red hair and freckles stumbling near the lighthouse, scaring all the local gnomes (which was, in fact, only him) and shouting at the puffin colony nesting in the rocks. Alobartalus sighed and followed the pudding chef outside.

"See?" the gnome pointed to a clearly inebriated man swaying on his feet and gesticulating at the puffins, who did not understand why he was there or what he wanted. The man had a dangerously large bottle of something in his hand—Alobartalus guessed it was either terrible rum or excellent rum, because that was how pirates liked it. If something was terrible they could complain and curse, and if it was excellent they could brag and curse, but if it was mediocre it left them nothing to do but grunt. They liked having a reason to curse.

Alobartalus was all for letting people do what they wished, except when it started scaring the pudding chef and threatening their supply of free-range, rock-grown, readily available puffin meat. He felt obliged to intervene. It would not be the first time he'd pulled such duty, nor the last; as a young elf in ranger service, he had encountered plenty of drunk humans while working at the Sylvan Port. The elves were amused to welcome mariners on their shore leave, because they invariably wished to be doused in sticky fluids and glitter and get smashed on elvish flower wine. The humans looked ridiculous and woke up with killer hangovers and no money, because the elves cheerfully robbed them once they passed out. No one ever seemed to mind, however; the humans simply lied to save face, bragging that they had experienced a legendary night of debauchery among a harem of elvish lasses. Which only brought more humans with more cash. This system worked out well for all involved.

Alobartalus sidled up to the human, who was dressed in a green waistcoat and in the midst of a long tirade demanding that the puffins *do* something.

"Ye all jest stand there with your beaks out, doin' *nothin'*, when there's an ongoing crisis jest northa here! Ye could be doin' somethin'! Ye *should!* But, noooo, you're bloody puffins, aren't ye? Think you're *special.* Think ye don't have any *responsibility.*" The human had streaks of tears running down his reddened, freckled face. Alobartalus didn't appreciate how very similar they looked; it was like seeing himself, unelfly and awkward, in the midst of a nervous breakdown. Still, he had to keep the peace, or else the puffins would grow gristly with annoyance.

"Pardon me, good sir, but is there something I can help you with?" Alobartalus asked. "I don't wish to invade your privacy, but I'm concerned for your welfare." *And for the terrified stiffening and chewiness of stressed puffin meat, which we'd all prefer to be soft and atrophied by a lack of responsibility,* he privately added.

"Can ye bring Frij back to *life?*" the pirate practically shouted. "Because that would be a great help. But nobody can help. Because Frij is *dead,* D-E-D!"

Alobartalus opened his mouth to point out the rather egregious spelling error, but the pirate barreled on before he could interrupt.

"He was me friend. But now he's just anudder victim of the crimson tide. Almost got me too, but the tampoo—*urp!*—tampoonist stanched that bloody monster of the Myn Seas first." Aggrieved by intense memories, the sailor began to suck in and exhale deep breaths through his nose, as his chin quivered and his eyes welled with fresh tears. With each exhalation a thin snake of green snot peeked out of his nostril and lounged on his upper lip, until he breathed in again and the snotsnake was sucked back up into his nose. "An' the worst thing is, nobody else seems to care about me friend Frij! 'Bout how he died like that! Actin' like it's jest normal!"

"Oh, no, I'm very sorry to hear that. What ship was this?"

The sailor wobbled on his feet and belched again, a fresh wave of alcohol sloshing through his bloodstream and slaying uncounted brain cells. His speech noticeably deteriorated.

"Wuzza *Puffy Peach*," he slurred.

"*The Puffin Peach*? Is that why you're out here shouting at puffins?"

"No, *The Puffy Peach*. Under Captain Filthy Lucre. Goin' after trezzure."

"Ah! Sailing south along the coast?"

"No, we gonna go through the archipeladough. Archipelatoe?"

"Sn'archipelago."

"Dazzit," the human said, waggling a finger at him. "That thing you said."

"But why not sail down the coast? The Siren Sn'archipelago is dangerous."

"Captain is wanted. He's the Clean Pirate Luc, y'see."

Alobartalus raised an eyebrow. "Oh, I've heard of him! And what's your name?"

"Me? I'm—*urp!*—I'm Queefqueg."

"It's a pleasure. Listen, Queefqueg, could your ship use another experienced sailor?"

"Prolly, I dunno. I mean, yeah! Because we lost Frij!" The man's face flushed again with remembered grief as he bared his teeth and pointed at the puffins. "And they didn't do *anything* to help! Go ahead and join the crew and maybe you'll get Frijjed too, and these dirty birds will sit here and go fishing and not care a smidge."

"Come on. I'll buy you some fresh rum and a raisin pudding, and then we'll go see the captain."

"No, ugh. I hate raisins. Nature's shriveled boogers, they is." Queefqueg abruptly vomited and Alobartalus deftly took a few steps to the right to avoid getting splashed. This was not his first consultation with a drunken pirate.

"Some other pudding, then. The Grog Bog has the best gnomeric pudding chef in the midwest! I promise you'll feel better."

"What about the puffins?"

"Not to worry, my good man: Someone will eat them, sooner rather than later."

"That's good. Solves that porblem. Ye know, you're not bad for an elf."

Alobartalus hid his smile. The man was drunk, sunburned, and covered in vomit, but at least he knew an elf when he saw one. "So I've been told. Shall we?"

Queefqueq allowed himself to be steered a couple of blocks to the Grog Bog, an unusually clean pirate haunt, due to the fastidious natures of its dwarvelish owners and the fussy gnomeric pudding chef. But it did have appropriately dingy lighting, décor of the rusted-anchor variety, an appropriate amount of crusty netting hanging in corners, and wooden benches as likely to give one splinters as to support one's weight. And the clientele was raucous, unshaved, and unwashed but gently sprinkled with antibacterial deodorant spray on their way through the door.

"Is your captain here?" Alobartalus asked as they entered. Queefqueg paused to scan the room.

"Lemme look. Yep! Over there in the corner." He pointed at a youngish man who looked like he might hail from Teabring or the Seven Toe Islands, with a bright-red-and-yellow parrot perched on his shoulder. He wasn't dressed in the trappings of a captain, but Alobartalus had heard that the Clean Pirate Luc was a bit unusual.

Queefqueg wobbled as he escorted Alobartalus to the table and said, "Cap'n, thish elf is innerested in signing on with us."

Alobartalus beamed at the young man and said, "Captain, I understand you might be sailing south?"

The man smiled back wryly. "I'm not the captain. I'm the first mate, Feng Zhu Ye."

"Oh, I beg your pardon. I was misinformed." Alobartalus tried not to blush, although he knew he was going to blush anyway. He glanced around the room, hoping to see a big floppy hat or a hook hand or some other indication of captain-ness.

Feng hooked a thumb at the parrot on his shoulder. "This is Captain Filthy Lucre."

Alobartalus said nothing. He just stood there, slack-jawed, trying to figure out if this was a joke or not. Then the parrot spoke.

"Why arrrre ye interrrrested in wherrrre we sail?" he asked, sounding a lot more amused than a parrot had any right to be.

But Alobartalus was an elf, which meant he'd dealt with plenty of people who had immense power but looked like walking jokes—and the opposite of that as well.

"I'd like to visit the tower of the Sn'archivist and pitch in with ship's duties along the way."

"An elvish pirrrrate?"

"An elvish sailor. I may not look it, but I am an expert seaman of the Morningwood, and I've got a lot of spunk."

"What do ye mean by experrrrt? That ye can swim if needed?"

"Oh, yes, I am an excellent swimmer. Remarkable stamina. Very motile. But I can also tie all the knots you'd care to name, and more than one captain has admired the cut of my jib."

"Have ye any cerrrrtifications, any way I can know ye have competencies without testing ye for hourrrrs? We've just finished trrrrraining up the new crrrrew, ye see."

"Absolutely!" Alobartalus nodded and tried to puff up with pride but instead puffed out in the belly area. "I am a member of the Sylvan Port Expert Rangers of the Morningwood."

Captain Luc blinked at him a couple of times. "Errrr, doesn't that forrrrm an awkwarrrrd acrrrronym?"

Feng snickered, but Alobartalus just shrugged. "I wouldn't know. Elves tend not to enjoy acronyms, so we don't think about them."

The parrot bobbed up and down on his human perch. "Neverrrr mind. You wouldn't enjoy this acrrrronym eitherrrr. Betterrrr out than in, aye? An elvish sea rrrrrangerrrr. That's what we'll call you. Ye hearrrr me, Feng? He's a sea rrrrangerrrr! You are not to tell the crrrrew about the acrrrronym."

"Bwa ha!" the first mate burst out, then regained control of himself and nodded as solemnly as he could, which was not very. "Aye aye, Captain. Simply a fresh seaman, newly wet behind the ears. Hee hee."

Alobartalus remained steadfastly elvish and did not think about what the acronym might be. His uncle might have been proud of him in that moment, but it was unlikely.

"Rrrright. Come along, then, elf. We could use cleverrrr hands on deck. We'll get ye to the Sn'arrrrchivist in exchange for yourrrr laborrrr."

Alobartalus grinned. "Thank you. That's fantastic. I'll just grab a few things."

"Verrrry few! Be at *The Puffy Peach* in an hourrrr. We arrrre only loading more food and frrrresh waterrrr and then we sail."

"Aye, Captain."

Alobartalus saluted and returned to his tourist trap with a light step and a lighter heart. He crammed some personal necessities in a bag, wrote a note for his replacement, and locked up the Proudwood Lighthouse behind him. The lighthouse lantern, after all, was magic and didn't require his upkeep; he'd merely been a rod-and-grease salesman, but now he was free. A month's leave or more began today! He couldn't stop smiling as he made his way down to the docks.

What if the Sn'archivist offered him gainful employment, obviating the need to ever return? What might it be like, living on his mentor's private island—an island bereft of sunburned, pushy tourists—with access to his vast library, which no doubt smelled of ink and glue and dry paper? Would that not be the most spiffing of all destinies? Why, he might excrete glitter in sheer joy, the way the birds in the Morningwood did!

As he mounted the slippery surface of *The Puffy Peach* and inhaled the rank stench of salt, sweat, and fish, he grinned to himself and thought about all his dreams that were going to come true. He would sail across calm, pleasant seas, make friends with the pirates, and meet his hero. What could possibly go wrong?

11.

SURROUNDED ON ALL SIDES BY OSCILLATING MUSTELIDS

When Captain Luc, Feng, and Queefqueg returned from their secretive trip to the lighthouse island, they brought along an annoyingly large box of pre-weeviled hardtack and something Morgan had never seen before: an elf. A real, live elf, although he looked more like a chubby kid in a bad Pelloween costume.

For all that she didn't know much about pirating yet, Morgan was still surprised that the parrot was willing to take on such a wide array of people, most of whom were inexperienced sailors. If what she'd heard about elves was true, the fellow would only cause trouble on the ship with his elvish pranks, snotty attitude, and constant glittery escapades. Yet when the elf approached her, his smile was open and friendly.

"Greetings! I am Alobartalus," the elf said, holding out his hand for a hearty shake.

"Morgan," she replied, glancing down to see if his palm concealed a buzzer or possibly a secret squirt of glitter. "And this is my friend

Tempest. And that centaur over there is Vic. You, um, might want to give him a wide berth."

"Oh, I'm not in charge of bunks," Alobartalus said, looking confused. "Have they not already been assigned? And what kind of hammock could hold those hoss hocks, am I right?"

And that was when Morgan realized he was perhaps the only member of their odd crew with any training for the sea and also that he was pretty likable, for an elf.

They pulled up the anchor and left the lighthouse behind. Under the gimlet eye of Qurt Qobayne, the crew had succeeded in swabbing up most of the blood and chum that had made *The Puffy Peach* so sticky and rank over the past several days. She was good as new and raring to go, and everyone seemed refreshed and relieved to be out of the Myn Seas and sailing into the fair winds of the Urchin Sea. Milly Dread had assured everyone that these waters were known for their delicious sea urchins rather than the city type of urchin, which was known for pickpocketing and the wanton spread of communicable diseases.

"That kind don't taste nearly as good," she said. "Quite stringy." And everyone inched ever so slightly away as the old woman went back to picking her cavernous nose and singing sea shanties as she filleted a pile of fish, carefully bucketing the chum.

As they sailed out into the crystal-blue waters, Morgan climbed up into the crow's nest, taking her turn on watch. Luc made sure his new recruits—at least the ones who weren't gigantic clumsy centaurs—rotated through their duties so they wouldn't be ignorant rats, although he pronounced it "ignorrrrant rrrrats," which sounded like a great name for a dwarvelish thrash-uke band. Morgan had no fear of heights or seagulls and loved her quiet time alone in the nest, looking out through the spyglass for whales, testy sea serpents, and lost, angry gryphons. Just now she was studying a yellowed and dog-eared copy of *Ye Olde Pyrate Manual*, which Captain Luc had lent her with either a wink or an annoyed twitch of his good eye.

The book was small and old, with fascinating scrawlings in the margins and salty pages wrinkled from years at sea. Although Morgan didn't plan on adding either *arrrr* or *yarrrr* to every utterance, as the book suggested, she did enjoy the chapter on naming conventions, as a pirate captain was expected to select a moniker that either struck fear into every heart or made everyone think, *Oh, the Tidy Captain Herbert? He must be rather pleasant!* right before said Herbert and his dark-hearted crew tossed over their grappling hooks and keelhauled everything within an inch of its life.

The longer she spent on the ship, the more she thought about the many attractions of a life at sea in a position of leadership with a proper sort of hat. Her father would never find her here, and that arranged marriage could not be arranged if her address kept moving and her sword arm kept growing stronger. Pirate clothes felt like pajamas and were far less restrictive than what she'd been expected to wear as a lady. She enjoyed having her shorter hair clubbed back and kept tidy under a kerchief, and she'd grown quite fond of her beard. As a child, she'd been encouraged to brush her long hair fifty strokes every night, and now she spent that time oiling her beard instead, which was far more pleasant. No one made fun of her for keeping her beard or suggested she depilate, nor had anyone made sexist remarks. On the ship, everyone did their job, and nobody gave anybody guff. She was accepted, just as she was.

The pirate life, she realized with an internal *yo ho*, was for her! Now she needed the right name.

As she scanned down the list of appropriate epithets, she thought she might as well try a few on for size.

"The Nice Pirate Morgan," she said to herself.

But she was sick of being nice. Her father had always urged her to be nice and a host of other things marriageable girls were expected to be: sweet, kind, generous, giving, attentive, fecund, silent, still, pretty, *no, please, darling, your mouth is still moving, and it should stop doing that and instead smile.* Thinking about it now, she was fairly certain what her parents really wanted was a goldfish or possibly a vase of fake flowers, not a daughter with a mind of her own.

Perhaps she'd rather go with a more traditional nickname, one to strike fear in the hearts of all who saw her flag and recognized her ship.

"The Vicious Pirate Morgan," she said. "Morgan the Most Murdery."

She smiled. It was good to know there were options, and she didn't miss her old name at all. Who named a child Harkovrita? Honestly? Almost as if someone was trying to make her life horrible on purpose. No one would fear the Dread Pirate Harkovrita. It was good, leaving that name behind as she started her new life.

"The Cordial Captain Morgan," she growled, grimacing properly and squinting one eye, as nearly all pirate captains eventually lost an eye to some threat or other. The full effect pleased her enormously. In that moment she decided she wanted to be the captain of her own ship, although she still wasn't certain what that entailed, as a profession. Was there a pirate university, perhaps, or a correspondence course? To whom would she pay taxes? Could she hire an accountant? They had not yet keelhauled anyone, stormed another ship, or taken anything resembling treasure, but she could deal with grog and fish and biscuits for every meal, which was described in Chapter 3, "Yarrrr, How to Get Scurvy in Only Thirty Dayes."

Putting the spyglass to her eye, she scanned the turquoise waves all around. Behind them, the Proudwood Lighthouse rose stiff and white above the waves, with just the faintest hint of lavender at its tip. A tall elf with golden hair stood on the walk, waving to her in a way that suggested he might need rescuing, and she waved back cheerfully but noncommittally. The tumescent trees of the Morningwood mirrored the lighthouse on the other side of the strait, an explosion of dark bushes hugging the coast, rimed with a sparkle of glitter. She swung the spyglass down and spotted a pretty pod of dolphins skimming along beside the ship, ever hopeful for some bit of fish tossed overboard from Milly's cleaver. Looking ahead, she saw nothing but seemingly endless blue and a sleek ship speeding toward them, black sails billowing.

Wait.

That wasn't right.

Following the instructions in *Ye Olde Pyrate Manual,* she rubbed her eyes comically, jaw dropped, and looked again. The ship was still there, but it was now just a tiny bit closer, which was not what one generally wanted out of a ship bearing Pyrate Flag Number 17, affectionately known as "Exactly What Thy Skull Would Look Lyke wythe Seventeen Swords Stuck yn Yt."

"Ship ho!" she shouted.

All activity on the deck halted; all eyes turned up to her.

"I thought you told me I couldn't use that word?" Vic shouted back.

"No, she means there's a ship coming toward us," Alobartalus said, but not in a dickish way.

"What see you?" Captain Luc cried, in that uncanny way he had of avoiding anything with *R*s when time was of the essence.

"Black ship. Um, fourteen guns and four sails."

"Which flag?" Luc squawked.

"Number seventeen."

"Ah, crrrrackerrrrs. Quickly down, lass. We'll need all available talons to fight this one. Can ye see anything else that might help us?"

Already climbing down, Morgan held up the spyglass once more as she clung to the net. "It's riding low in the water. The captain has a really big hat. And it's covered in brown worms."

"The hat is coverrrred in worrrrms?"

"No, the ship. Probably not worms. Wriggly brown things. It doesn't make any sense."

"So few things do on the sea," Luc called. Morgan blinked as she recognized the aphorism from the manual, where she'd found the list of "10 Cryptic Thinges to Say When You Don't Wante Yer Crew to Know Ye Have a Case of Anxiety Shittes."

But something caught her eye. She wound a leg around the netting, secured her elbow, and held up the spyglass again, leaning into the wind.

"Captain, they're sending a signal! With flags!"

Now she had Luc's attention. "Call it out, then, lass! Let's see if you've been studying yerrrr semaphorrrre."

As the crew hastened to prepare for a skirmish under the orders of Feng and Qobayne, Morgan went on full alert and began calling out letters.

"*N! E! E! D!*" she shouted.

"Yes, yes," Captain Luc peevishly squawked. "Need what?"

"*A! I!* Um . . ."

"Aim? They need to aim? Well, that ain't my prrrroblem! I'd like it if they didn't aim atall!"

"No, Captain. It's hard to read the flags, as there are little brown things crawling up the signaler, and he keeps dancing around. I believe it's *A-I-L*."

"Need *ail*?" Captain Luc considered it. "Gods of Pell! Looks as if these scalawags are boarrrrding us for craft beerrrr when all we have is rrrrum, and they be bad spellers to boot! Well, let 'em come. They can't have me ship's grrrrog, lass, so come on down and help fight 'em off!"

Morgan was too high up to read the parrot's facial expression, and if she was honest, he didn't actually have facial expressions that she could read, but he did seem pretty pleased about the idea of a fight.

By the time Morgan's boots hit the boards, the captain was merrily squawking at everyone to fluff their loins and prepare to fight for their lives and their grog. Morgan was on grappling-hook duty just then, so she went to her assigned spot beside Tempest, who was already twirling a wicked iron hook while she watched the other ship approach. The new elf stood on Morgan's other side, twirling his hook with a maddening speed that suggested he was no stranger to grappling. The hook felt good in Morgan's hand—sturdy and real. It was her first fight with something other than an angry sea serpent, and she'd been studying and was certain she knew what to do. She put a knife between her teeth and grinned, her blood fizzing with salty excitement.

The black ship sliced through the water like a sharp pair of shears through silk, headed straight for them but aimed to pass on the port side, where their cannons could be brought to bear—or, more likely, where they could mount a boarding operation. The figure holding the flags had been swarmed with the wormy brown things and was waving his pennants with no clear message, while the man with the biggest hat—always the captain—was screaming bloody murder.

"Hal! Hal!" he screeched.

"I'm not Hungrrrry Captain Hal!" an insulted Captain Luc squawked back, flapping into the air. "And I don't carrrre if you be thirrrrsty, as we don't have ale!"

The black ship rudely ground itself against the port side of *The Puffy Peach*, and Morgan spread her legs to weather the shuddering wood. Somewhere, the clop and slide of hooves and the splatter of tea suggested Vic wasn't doing quite so well, but Morgan felt alive and was only waiting for her orders.

Finally, Captain Luc shouted, "Grrrrappling hooks! Now, you dogs! Let's grrrrapple!"

Morgan's hook was the first to fly through the air and clank over the other ship's railing, sticking on the first throw. She pulled her line taut as Alobartalus expertly tossed his hook and Tempest missed, her hook clattering down between the ships. *Clank-clank-clank!* The hooks landed all along the rail, the old and new crew helping to yank the invading black barque closer so they could swarm over the side with swords raised. Morgan had expected the other crew to behave likewise, as that's what the manual suggested happened during a dogfight. They were all supposed to meet in a clash of swords and evil laughs and threats. But the other pirates all seemed too busy running around and shrieking as sleek brown forms raced and clambered and squeaked, scurrying between legs and clawing up breeches.

"What are they?" Alobartalus asked.

"Uh, what kind of elf are you that you're not one with nature?" Tempest shot back.

"Not a very good elf, and thanks for the reminder," he said stiffly. "But still, what are they?"

Morgan cocked her head. "Otters?" she said. "Like, really seriously hyped-up otters?"

But she didn't have time to consider that bit of strangeness further.

"Attack while they be incapacitated!" Captain Luc cried, and as one, the crew leapt over the railings and crawled onto the black galleon. The parrot flapped in the air between the ships, just out of reach of any stray cutlasses—not that the invading pirates had the good sense to use them.

They hadn't even shot their cannons once, which didn't jibe with what Morgan had heard about such skirmishes. Perhaps the other captain was hoping to take the ship while it was still in good condition? Her captain, of course, had likewise refrained from putting holes in the black ship, so maybe there was some agreement in place to avoid damaging future goods or blowing up the very ale one craved.

Remembering not to tongue the small dagger between her teeth, Morgan landed on the other ship, sword out, prepared for her very first fight. . . .

But none came. The other pirates were too busy freaking out.

"Who wants a little?" Alobartalus cried in a very unelfly way, but it appeared that no one wanted any.

"Why won't they fight?" Tempest asked. "Mr. Stabby is ready!" When Morgan looked at her friend, she saw the dryad's hair lifting like branches, small leaves shaking as if in a storm.

Confused, Morgan grabbed the nearest pirate by the filthy cravat and pulled him close, putting her cutlass to his throat. "Nrph ner," she growled, before remembering that there was a knife between her teeth. She spat it out and tried again. "You there. What's happening? Why do you want our ale?"

"Ale? Ale?" the man sputtered. "We don' want ale, ye fool! We want aid! *Aid*, as in help! It's the otters! They've gone bonkers!"

"Otters? Bonkers?"

The man gestured to the chaos on deck. Even Captain Luc's crew had joined the pandemonium as sinuous brown otters zipped and rumpused everywhere, climbing up people and reaching paws into the moist caverns of their mouths, searching for shellfish, finding only terrified tongues, and getting a bit bitey when dissatisfied.

The man sighed. "The otters. In the hold. They escaped. They're hungry. And bored, I reckon. Smart things, otters." And then he screamed, as an otter had zipped up the inside of his pants leg and was causing unsightly bulges here and there.

Morgan released him and picked up her knife. "I'm not getting anywhere with this oaf, and I can't fight someone who won't fight back. Where's their captain?"

"There, I think." Alobartalus was pointing at a now-hatless man trying desperately to climb up the nets and getting terribly tangled, due to a magnificent peg leg and a very fancy coat.

Morgan marched over, grabbed the man by the lacy jabot, and dangled him over the boards. He was not a large person, but he kicked and squealed, shouting, "Gerroff! Gettemoff! Blasted weasels! Rabid little stoats!" Morgan snapped her fingers in front of his nose, and he focused on her. His brow first furrowed, then splayed apart and upward in helplessness. "Um . . . avast?"

"Do you surrender?" she barked.

The captain looked taken aback. "Why would I? We're not in a fight. We requested aid, and you're doing a blasted poor job of aiding us!"

"You demanded our ale!" she shouted.

"We requested *aid*! If you can't read semaphore, that would be your own fault. Now, can you help pacify the weasels or shall I set the whole thing ablaze and just take over your ship instead?"

Morgan flicked her eyes at Tempest. "Tie him up, would you?"

As Morgan took hold of the man's lapels, Tempest fumbled with the rope. She clearly hadn't done her knot-tying homework. The captain, of course, wasn't helping but was rather flipping and flopping like a thirsty fish, screeching each time an otter approached. Alobartalus stepped in and deftly trussed up the captain like a roast goose. Morgan placed him gently on the deck and shouted to Luc, "O Captain! My Captain! This puddin' pants surrenders!"

Soon Feng stood before the bound captain, and Luc glared down at him as otter mayhem rampaged adorably across the deck. It was hard to hear anything or take an assertive stance, thanks to the plethora of playful mustelids. Captain Luc kept trying to say authoritative things, but then the other captain would see an otter and scream, frightening everyone.

But Morgan had an idea.

"Milly Dread!" she called, using what she considered her Princess Voice, for although she was a lady, not a princess, she'd been taught to bark authoritatively at people by several governesses.

The old woman put down the otter she'd been brandishing like a weapon and looked up. "Yes, mum?"

"D'you still have that barrel full of fish guts?"

Captain Luc eyed Morgan appreciatively as Milly nodded. "Course I do! Several, in fact! Ye never know when a few dozen buckets of rotten fish guts'll come in handy!"

Morgan grinned. "If you could pop one open, please—a newer one? And feed the otters? Then we could all hear our beloved captain threatening this fool."

"Good good good good good," Luc said, bobbing up and down on Feng's shoulder.

Pleased as punch, Milly Dread used her sword to pop open a barrel, and the otters immediately swarmed toward her on *The Puffy Peach* in a squirmy brown wave, making a chorus of excited squeaks as Milly tossed out bits of chum and cooed at them like they were kittens. Although the smell was nigh intolerable, the noise level went down considerably, and all eyes returned to the two captains.

"Now, as I was sayin', what's all this?" the parrot barked. "Forrrr I am Clean Luc, captain of *The Puffy Peach,* and it would appearrrr I have the advantage of ye."

"I'm Captain Blondbeard," the captain said, drawing up his beardless chin in a failed attempt to look authoritative. "And this whole thing is a terrible misunderstanding. We're not even pirates!"

"Oh, please," Morgan said. "You're flying flag number seventeen, your ship is all black, and you clearly demanded our ale!"

"Untie me, keep the weasels off me, and I'll explain everything," the captain said, sounding as exhausted as anyone Morgan had ever met.

"Do it," Luc said. "But keep yourrrr cutlasses handy."

The deck had gone mostly silent, the sailors of both ships confused and suffering an adrenaline drop and not really spoiling for bloodshed. The otters—for otters they were, no matter what the confused captain called them—were all now sitting around Milly Dread in an orderly sort of way, perked up on their haunches and patiently awaiting gobbets of guts. On Luc's command, Alobartalus deftly untied his knots and tidily stowed his bit of rope, which Morgan found commendably thrifty, although personally she would've cut the man free to make an impression, per Chapter 7 of the manual, "How to Make an Impression by Chopping Things from Ropes to Cabbages to Heads."

Freed, the captain stepped back, rubbing his wrists and looking like he hadn't slept in days. As he spoke, he didn't focus on Luc or even on any of the crew. His eyes perpetually scanned the deck, and he shuddered each time he saw an otter, something Morgan would not have considered possible a few short moments ago, as they were insanely adorable.

"This here ship is *The Morel Turpitude*, and usually we just haul gourmet mushrooms up and down the coast and scare pirates away with our sail. We're really merchants with some pirate trappings, you see. People note the black sails and the peg leg and tend to leave old Captain Blondbeard alone."

"But you don't have a bearrrrd," Luc observed. "And your hairrrr is brrrrown."

Sticking his nose in the air, Blondbeard stuffily muttered, "It's a family name. Anyway. We took on this live cargo in Humptulips. They told me it was ducks. Ducks I can manage, I promise you! I am simply a master of ducks. But as soon as we cleared Truffle Bay, I learned that I literally had no ducks to give. The boxes were solidly built with the normal amount of air holes, and we were given firm coordinates to the island for their delivery. Mack Guyverr they call it, although I've been in and out of the Macks for decades and never heard of it. And there was a barrel of foul-smelling stuff we were supposed to smear on the hull for some reason."

"And what happened then?" Luc nudged.

"It's the otters," Blondbeard whispered. "They escaped. It was madness!"

"They seem pretty chill just now," Tempest said, and they did.

"That's because your lass is feeding them chum. I'm not sure what happened, but as soon as we entered these waters, they went insane. Broke out of their crates, and quite a surprise that was, as they're most definitely not ducks. Squirming up and down anything that held still, scratching with their creepy wee paws. And the squeaking. Pellanus save me from the squeaking!"

Blondbeard abruptly sat down, put his arms around his leg and peg, and stuck his thumb in his mouth.

"So ye didn't seek a fight?" Luc asked.

Blondbeard shook his head but did not remove his thumb from his mouth to speak.

"Aid," one of his sailors said from nearby, where he sat on a barrel, nursing several deep scratch marks and a bruise on his cheek shaped like a seashell. It was the man who'd waved the semaphore flags. "Just aid. I'll be haunted by those wee paws until the day I die. One of 'em threw a clam at me!"

Morgan was watching her captain carefully to see how the parrot handled this peculiar situation, which hadn't been covered in the manual.

"Well, then. My advice to you, lad, is to let the otterrrrs go. Just drrrrop 'em off on the nearrrest island and find a morrrre pleasant carrrrgo."

"But we won't be paid if we don't deliver!" Blondbeard whined.

"Ye won't be sane if ye continue. Look at ye, sittin' about suckin' yerrrr appendage."

With that, Luc directed Feng back toward *The Puffy Peach*, leaving his crew to pick up their weapons, help their victims to their feet, and wipe the otter plops off their boots. But Morgan still had questions, and there was nothing in the manual against interrogating idiots who were simply bad at otter management.

"Why would anyone ship several hundred otters?" she asked.

Captain Blondbeard stood, straightened his coat, and shrugged. "It's best not to ask. People have peculiar ideas about fads. I'll never forget the summer of pet rocks."

"Who hired you?"

The captain gave her a more appraising look. "And why should I tell you?"

With a huff of annoyance, Morgan picked up the nearest otter and aimed it at the captain, holding it under its armpits. The otter made a charming clicking noise and flapped its feet. In response, the captain screeched and ducked, his face hidden under his arms.

"Tell me who hired you, or I'll . . . I'll . . ." Utterly at a loss, she poked the otter's nose into Blondbeard's hair, making the man scream bloody murder. Frightened by this reaction, the otter clambered up Morgan's shirt and curled around her neck in a pleasant sort of way. It was almost like wearing a helpful if somewhat oily scarf.

"All I know is that the ducks—which turned out to be otters— were supposed to go to the Mutae Mercantile Association on Mack Guyverr."

"What was that first thing?" Morgan asked. "How is it spelled?"

"M-u-t-a-e," Blondbeard replied. "Family name, I guess. Not that we can ask them anytime soon, because we're not only off course now; we're headed in the wrong direction. Otters have no sense of direction. You know what? I'm out. If you'd like to take my cargo, be my guest. They're already mostly aboard your ship anyway. I'm going straight back to Humptulips and taking on something easy, like a conference of squabbling academics or a nice load of bricks. Or even pet rocks or troll dolls, at this point." He flapped a hand at her and turned away, trudging toward what had to be the captain's quarters.

Morgan, Tempest, and Alobartalus seemed alone in a bubble of understanding, surrounded by chaos and wounded soldiers bearing otter bites and clam-shaped bruises. Morgan looked from the dryad to the elf, her hand stealing up to stroke the purring otter around her neck.

"Do you know what that means?" she said as everything clicked.

"That we won our first fight?" Tempest said, flexing an arm.

"That that guy's going to have a heck of a phobia for the rest of his life?" Alobartalus said.

"More than that." Morgan looked at the swarm of otters surrounding Milly Dread, horror and revelation fighting for supremacy on her face, for she was very fond of word puzzles. A certain problem had been bothering her ever since that greasy visit to Dinny's, and she'd finally found the missing puzzle pieces. "He said this shipment was for the Mutae Mercantile Association. The MMA. And Mutae is EATUM spelled backward."

Tempest's jaw dropped, and Alobartalus shook his head in horror as Morgan continued.

"EATUM is otters. *EATUM is made of otters!*"

12.

WITHIN EARSHOT OF A MOST
ALLURING SONG

Flightless creatures such as humans and dwarves, Luc observed, always indulged in some heavy breathing after near-death experiences. They also breathed heavily during near-sex experiences, he'd noticed, and often when they were confronted with an attractive cheese plate with assorted crackers and fine mustards. But the breathing after a near-death experience was always Luc's favorite, because it was a prelude to some colorful complaints and imaginative promises of what the bipeds would do the *next time* they were confronted with mortal peril. Usually these threats of future violence involved the stuffing of limbs, vegetables, and/or small animals into orifices they had no business spelunking, but occasionally they involved biochemistry and a healthy dose of outrage. They hadn't exactly been threatened with death by boarding Blondbeard's ship, but they had *thought* they were going to be, so their bodies reacted as if they had. They were all panting fantastically, and Luc hooted in amusement.

"If I ever meet whoever's behind this otter business," Feng ground out between gasps, "I'm going to shove an exploding seed pod covered in the toxic secretions of a bog frog so far up his—"

"I'm going to force-feed him fermented cabbage!" Skånki Jorts shouted as he shook a meaty fist at the southern sky, mistakenly thinking that consuming the cruciferous vegetable would be fatal for all species and not just dwarves. "His intestines will explode and liquefy his abdominal cavity into a slurry of blood and excrement!"

"I'm, um, going to tie him up in the front row of a hardcore yodel-polka joint in Grunting," Morgan vowed, and shrugged when everyone looked at her with blank stares. "What? I've heard that's a terrible way to die." The otter perched on Morgan's shoulder made a startled *meep* sound when she shrugged, and Morgan apologized to it. "I really need to come up with a name for you, don't I?"

"Neverrrr mind that now," Luc called, and then, once their attention swiveled to him, pointed a wing tip at the retreating merchant ship. "Look therrrre, me salty dogs—that's rrrright, you'rrrre salty now! Ye see how harrrrd Blondbearrrrd is tacking to the east? He wants to get back to the safety of the coast just as we want to make it to the safety of the islands. But they won't make it, no they won't: That I can tell."

"What's so unsafe, Captain?" Morgan asked.

"We drrrrifted into deep waterrrrs while we trrrrransferrrred the otterrrrs to our hold."

"And thank you again for that, Captain Luc," Morgan said.

The full-bellied otters were much more tractable, and Milly Dread was confident that she could keep them fed and happy until they reached the tower of the Sn'archivist. There they would set the otters free to form a new colony, since the Sn'archipelago would be home to plenty of delicious sea urchins and other shellfish. Captain Luc had no more wish to see the otters ground up into EATUM than Morgan did, and several of the crew members had turned a bit green, realizing that they had enjoyed EATUM in the past.

"Yes, yes, well, I hope ye didn't become too attached to Captain Blondbearrrrd therrrre. He's still in the kill zone, ye see, floating above his own death, which may be stirrrring even now in the depths of the Urrrrchin Sea! I know we arrrre headed for dangerrrr as well, but taking a chance on the sirrrrens is saferrrr—especially when ye sail with me! But the only way ye can pass safely in deep waterrrr is if the huge, hungrrrry thing beneath the waves is sleeping—orrrr alrrrready full."

"What thing?" Vic asked.

"A monsterrrr—but not like the ones we've faced! No tampoon can kill it. They call it the cavemouth. It can swallow a ship whole, me hearrrrties, and that's no lie. Therrrre is no stopping it, no escape—look!"

The sea foamed and bubbled around Blondbeard's ship. Its crew panicked, some of them leaping overboard in a desperate attempt to escape, but it was no use: They and the entire ship disappeared into the maw of the most massive creature on Pell, the cavemouth whale, as it erupted from the dark waters.

Various exclamations of wonder and horror escaped from Luc's crew as what appeared to be a mobile island rose up past the crow's nest of *The Morel Turpitude,* closed its mouth at the zenith of its surge, then crashed back into the sea. Only Tempest seemed unimpressed with it.

"Huh. Its skin is gray with an *a.* How sad," she said. Luc saw Morgan's eyes go round and wide as she stroked the otter around her neck.

"I'm sure glad we got you and your buddies off there," she murmured.

"Meep," the otter agreed.

"Ye see?" Luc called. "Ate the whole ship, and it has rrrroom for morrrre, I guarrrrantee. That's why we'll hug the shorrrres, wherrrre the bottom is shallow enough that it can't get beneath us, and hope we don't lose too many bodies to the sirrrrens."

"Too many?" Tempest said. "Don't you mean *any?*"

Luc fluttered his wings. "What, ye mean save each one of ye from being lurrrred to yourrrr doom? I suppose it is possible if irrrregular. But only if ye do exactly as I say!"

"We'll do it," Morgan said, and the others all chorused their agreement.

Filthy Lucre craned his head around to look at the sea ahead and then turned back to them. "Fine. Now listen. Sirrrrens arrre not human women, or dwarrrrf women, or any kind of women on top with fish tails on the bottom."

"They're not?" Skånki cried. "That's not what my last captain said."

"Same here. How do you know?" Feng asked.

Luc cawed. "I know because I've seen them! Theirrrr song doesn't worrrrk on me. They don't want to seduce a one-eyed parrrrot to his doom. I've flown to theirrrr islands and I've seen them in theirrrr grrrrottoes and I'm telling you, they'rrrre not fishy at all. How that myth got starrrrted and why it's perrrrsisted I cannot fathom. But the fact is they be birrrrds, like me. Except not. Bloody huge, they be, with human heads and faces and vocal corrrrds, and with dirrrrty brrrrown plumage. And if you don't drrrrown trrrrying to swim to them, they will eat you."

"Eat me?" Feng said.

"Eat you. Talons will rrrrip open that belly and pluck out the spleen as an appetizerrrr, and then they'll nibble yourrrr liverrrr while you'rrrre still alive. I've seen them do it! They asked me if I wanted a bite of one of my own salty dogs! And despite me tellin' ye this, when ye hearrrr them sing, ye won't hesitate. Ye will jump in afterrrr them, gladly, lurrrred by those sweet magical voices singing some completely awful lyrrrrics."

"Will their song affect me?" Tempest asked.

"It affects all bipeds, so farrrr as I know," Luc said. "Though I admit I have neverrrr seen the rrrreaction of a drrrryad beforrrre. Do you want to rrrrisk it?"

"No," Tempest said, shaking her head. "Tell us what to do."

"We have a limited amount of rrrrope belowdecks. Tie yourrrrself up to a crate if ye can and coverrrr yourrrr earrrrs until someone tells you it's safe. That will be me orrrr Vic."

Tempest flinched. "Why him?"

"He's not a biped."

Tempest glanced at Vic and he winked at her. "I'd prefer it be you, Captain."

Luc whistled and continued. "This is vital: Do not uncoverrrr yourrrr earrrrs out of currrriosity orrrr to check if we be past! As soon as you do, you will be lost! A single note frrrrom theirrrr song will ensnarrrre you! Be patient and live!"

Feng frowned. "What happens if we are ensnared?"

"Then Vic and I will do ourrrr best to make surrrre ye don't plunge to yourrrr death. But the best chance to surrrrvive is to be patient as we pass! Sing yourrrr own songs if ye must! Anything to keep the sirrrrens out of yourrrr head!" Luc checked their position again. "We arrrre getting close. Go below now. Boatswain Qobayne will get you situated. I know it will be a couple of crrrrowded hourrrrs with the otterrrrs, but ye have endurrrred worrrrse. Good luck."

They filed down the stairs into the hold, with Qobayne shouting orders at them. Luc flew to the wheel, lashed into place for the time being, and perched on it with an air of foreboding.

"Where do you want me, Captain?" Vic asked once the hatch was closed and locked behind the last crew member.

"Stand overrrr therrrre, lad; face the hatch, and play catch." Luc gestured with a wing to the starboard rail.

"Catch?"

"Yes. Eventually someone will burrrrst out of the hatch and head forrrr the side. You make surrrre they stay on the ship."

"How do I make sure, Captain?"

"Ye knock them out. With rrrrruthless compassion and fearrrr forrrr theirrrr lives."

Vic snorted and grinned, then let the smile fade away as it dawned on him that it wasn't a joke. "You're serious?"

"Only way to keep them safe," Luc replied.

"All right!" Vic exclaimed. "I like this duty already!"

"Good good good good good!" Luc said. "Now we wait."

The noises of the crew settling in below gradually faded as Qobayne and Feng got them tied up, and soon the *The Puffy Peach* continued sailing south in a peculiar silence.

Luc always enjoyed the few spare moments before the beginning of the sirens' song. For that brief window of time it was just him and the ocean; he didn't have to lead, didn't have to fear anything, didn't have to do anything except exist and appreciate it. Having those few minutes, in fact, was why he consistently led his crews past the sirens instead of taking the safer route along the coast of the mainland—plus the fact that the mainland held its own sort of dangers.

Vic wasn't of a mind to fill the silence with conversation either, which Luc appreciated. The centaur flexed a lot and grunted softly as he did so, but these gentle sounds were mostly lost amidst the susurrus of the ocean.

Luc let the tranquility wash over him and swayed slightly on the helm, wishing such peace could last longer than a few minutes. It had been a tumultuous time for him since he'd lost his perch, and this small space of personal calm was much needed.

But then their course drew them close to rocky islands cut with caves and grottoes, and gleaming eyes saw their sails from a distance, and a chorus of voices began to sing a beautiful but deadly song, sweet as chiming bells:

<*Come to us, delicious bipeds! We will give you money! Enough to pay off elected officials who will not only grant you giant tax breaks but craft legislation to efficiently exploit your workers!*>

Luc hooted in dismay. Once in a while the sirens rhymed and it was kind of nice, but they weren't even trying this time; nor were they especially keen on establishing lyrical rhythm. It was a free-form tone poem this trip, the sirens depending on the sorcery of their voices rather than compelling musicianship to win the day. Nevertheless, some fists began hammering on the underside of the hatch belowdecks, the magical lure of honeyed throats already overpowering the crew. Clearly someone hadn't followed instructions and covered their ears.

<And we will give you fame! So much that people will invade your privacy and care about your shoes! Plus you'll get a free puppy!>

The intensity of the hammering increased.

<Tapioca pudding! Just huge bowls of it, big enough to swim in, so much pudding!>

Luc could see the boards of the hatch shudder and warp. There was real urgency, because money, fame, puppies, and pudding—those were compelling lures. Many folks had thrown away their lives for less, and without magical temptation. But Luc knew the sirens were just getting warmed up and the fragile, foolish two-footers were about to get hit with the main attraction.

"Get rrrready," he told Vic. "The big pitch is coming, and nothing will stop those poorrrr bipeds frrrrom clawing out to seek death. Nothing but you, that is."

Vic raised a hand as if he were in school. "Should I just stand on the hatch, Captain? Wouldn't that prevent them from getting out?"

"Maybe. Orrrr it could brrrreak underrrr the weight and leave you to live out yourrrr life belowdecks. Thing is, they didn't obey my orrrrderrrrs and shut theirrrr earrrrs. They need to pay forrrr that. I'm counting on you to teach them that lesson."

Vic only nodded in reply and fixed his gaze on the bucking hatch. The next verse of the song was louder and more irresistible.

<Hot women with fish tails! You can have them now! No idea why people like the sound of that, but it always works! Come on and grab hold of our slippery, slimy fish tails, you naughty, naughty men with serious issues! Rub yourself on our fish scales! Just think of the oils waiting in our flesh, and—eww, wow, this is so gross. Uh—but not to you, no, sir! Fish tails, guys! Get some!>

The hatch exploded open and Feng rushed out, mad and raving. "I want all the sexy fish tails! Give them to me! Yes, yes, yes!"

"I'm saving your life!" Vic shouted with glee as he drove his fist into Feng's jaw and laid him out flat. The sirens' song continued as Skånki clambered up from the broken hatch.

<*Our fish tails are so hot and so fine you could sell burnt kuffee with them! Put a pair of tails on a sign and men will line up to buy that over-priced kuffee just so they can have a cup with fish tails on it! Why settle for a cup, baby, when you can have the real thing? And why not enjoy a dry scone, too? Swim to us now!*>

"Fish tails and beards!" Skånki hollered. "That's all a dwarf wants! Wait for me, my darlings!"

"I'm punching you because I care!" Vic responded, and knocked out the dwarf with a mighty cross. The centaur seemed to take un-usual pleasure in that particular strike to the noggin.

<*We're the fishwives you've always wanted but could never have until now! So salty, mmm, and full of fatty acids! Slicker than penguin snot on an ice floe but hot like your flesh in our teeth! I mean, uh, not that we would know how hot that is, exactly, or how tasty. We'll just have to see, won't we? Might need seasoning. Come on over, love!*>

Alobartalus popped out of the hatch, one eyebrow cocked over half-lidded eyes and a lopsided smirk on his face. "I'll see your fish tails and raise you a real elvish smolder, mistress!"

He took two steps before Vic's fist hammered him to the deck and the centaur declared, "I provide this service for your protection!"

The song continued, and three more crew members rose from the hold briefly before sprawling into concussed oblivion on the deck, but Luc noted with satisfaction that neither Morgan nor Tempest ever emerged. That was good. They were indeed as smart as he'd thought.

The importunate cries of the sirens eventually faded as *The Puffy Peach* passed beyond their reach, forever denying them at least one meal of gullible bipeds. Filthy Lucre preened and enjoyed the hiss and roar of the ocean for a while, and he noticed that Pissing Victo-rious enjoyed it too: a time of peril braced by bookends of peace. He let the moment linger until Feng groaned and brought a hand to his jaw as he woke up.

"Rrrright," Luc said. "Time to let the rrrrest of them know it's okay to get back to worrrrk. Ye did a foine job, Vic. Qobayne has a rrrreplacement hatch to install—we need a new one each time and buy them by the dozen from Huxley's Hatch Hutch in Humptulips. If ye could help haul it into position, that would be grrrrand."

"Aye, Captain. Glad to help."

Luc fluttered down the hatch and let Qobayne know that it was safe. He'd get the crew in working order soon enough. They'd make it to the tower of the Sn'archivist sometime this week and Luc had no idea what horrors or joys awaited them there. He'd never had a real reason to stop at the island until now, but he imagined the crew could use a break, and the otters could use a safe place to live out their natural lives. And besides, the Sn'archives were rumored to possess invaluable knowledge—the secrets to happiness and so on. He'd like to know some of those secrets, because ever since he'd lost his last perch, he'd felt a great many emotions but nothing like joy. He'd give up this treasure hunt now if he knew where to find such joy again.

And he knew that the real treasure would not be the friends he made along the way, because that was the kind of metaphorical crap that clogged up a cloaca. Real treasure was real treasure, metaphors were metaphors, and joy was a comfortable shoulder to perch on. He would find one to sail the seas with him again, or die trying.

13.

ENSCONCED IN A TOWER OF BROKEN DREAMS AND CRACKER CRUMBS

Alobartalus woke up lying on the deck, feeling flaccid and enervated. And, if he was honest, a bit blue. He had a bone to pick with the centaur, who had seemed all too happy to punch him, probably so he could have all the gorgeous, intelligent, fish-tailed elf ladies for himself.

Wait. No.

Shaking his head, Alobartalus muttered, "They weren't real. It was just magic. And magic is all about lies."

"What's that?" Morgan stopped and held out a hand. He took it, and she pulled him to standing. She had no new bruises, so she must've chosen to plug up her ears.

Alobartalus sighed and rearranged his pants, which had twisted underneath him as he fell.

"I just hate magic," he admitted. "I thought that when I left the lighthouse, life would be simpler. Less cruel. That I could trust what

I saw with my eyes. But apparently elves aren't the only ones who use magic to torture people."

Morgan cocked her head. "Very true. A magic rose put me to sleep for most of my twenties, and now I'm not fond of roses or fingernails. I like magic beards, though." She stroked hers for emphasis and grinned. "If that's why you left it behind, then what are you looking for? Because it was my understanding that most elves who leave the Morningwood are either looking for fresh rubes to prank or hoping to get in on the ground floor of exciting new multilevel marketing schemes."

Alobartalus considered it. Part of being out in the world meant that he wasn't going to take the usual elfin route and lie to people about everything. He liked this Morgan person, and she seemed honest and reasonable.

"Well, to tell you the truth, most elves you see out and about have been sent to spread the Morningwood seed among the human population, lest the elves die out."

"Seedschpringå!" Skånki Jorts bellowed as he walked by with a cask of fish bits for the otters. "We dwarves go out to rid ourselves of violence, and the elves go out to make more elves. A Telling Cudgel's a good bit different from a Morningwood rod, ain't it?" He slapped Alobartalus on the back with a meaty paw and kept walking.

Alobartalus's first reaction was typical of an elf: rage at the familiarity and the violent need to slip itching powder into the dwarf's undershorts. But he stopped and took a deep breath and reevaluated. He wanted to be a true part of the crew, and pirate crews did a good bit of roughhousing and backslapping. So this was a good sign. A dwarf touching an elf in goodwill meant that Skånki saw past the general elvish dickishness and instead saw a fellow sailor.

"Oh, to be sure," Alobartalus said to Skånki's receding back. "A Telling Cudgel only gets planted once, but a Morningwood rod gets dipped in oil repeatedly every morning."

The dwarf laughed heartily, and Alobartalus smiled, and Morgan looked slightly confused. "You guys seem really wound up about your wood."

Alobartalus grinned. "If you think that's bad, wait until you hear about our ball-bag competitions. Elvish moose-cheese balls and dwarvelish yak-cheese balls are kind of a big deal."

Morgan grimaced. "I'll have to take your word for it."

"Oh, but you asked where I'm going, didn't you?" Alobartalus looked around, his hands on his hips. "I don't really fit in with the elves, you see. So they sent me out to the lighthouse, where I could at least pretend to be elvish to fool the silly tourists, who didn't know any better. But I wasn't really great at that either, and all I could think about was how I'd always wanted to visit the Sn'archivist."

"I keep hearing that name, but I don't know who it is."

Alobartalus sighed dreamily. "The Sn'archivist is an elf—the most lofty, pure, and erudite of elves, called to sacred service by Pellanus themself. There have been many Sn'archivists over the years, but the current one began his service during the reign of the Great King Glosstangle centuries ago. He lives in a tower on the Sn'archipelago and is tended by the Sn'archdruid and his Sn'acolytes, who feed him and manage the construction and maintenance of his Sn'archives."

As he talked, Morgan cocked her head like a confused puppy. "I don't understand. You're talking about an *arch*ivist and his *arch*druids and *arch*ives on an *arch*ipelago, right?"

"No! Absolutely not! Oh, my poor ignorant human. The elvish *Sn'* prefix elevates all these things to the level of the divine! Most writers merely write whatever foolish drivel comes into their heads, but the Sn'archivist is taking dictation from the gods themselves!" Warming to his topic, he began to pace and gather a crowd, so he put a little showmanship into it. "The Sn'archives contain the direct words of the two-headed god Pellanus, whispered to the faithful and most hallowed Sn'archivist. Each of his many tomes is handcrafted of the finest gryphon leather, the pages pounded from Morningwood birch and bound with unicorn sinew. His ink is made from the juice of the

Apples of Knowledge mixed with the blood of . . . Well, don't worry too much about that. It dries into a deep, rich purple and that's all you need to know."

With perfect timing and dramatic flair, he flung his arms up just as the mists parted, revealing the gleaming white tower of the Sn'archivist rising up from its rocky promontory over the sea.

"Oooh," the crowd said, as if on cue. "Ahhh!"

"Enough o' that!" Captain Luc broke in, flapping up from Feng's shoulder in annoyance. "Less awe, morrrre all-hands-on-deck. Ain't nobody jibbin' or swabbin'. If I'd wanted ye to listen to unrrrrrealistic drrrreams, I'd have let you out to hearrrr the sirrrrens!"

Alobartalus hung his head, for he hated to be called out by the captain. He wanted to be a good seaman, strong and true with direction and vitality, and did not want to be seen as merely a messy waste. With one last, fond look at the Sn'archivist's tower, he climbed into the rigging to do his job, for all that the view made him want to break out in song.

He was finally here! After all this time. After all those dreams.

He was about to meet his hero and perhaps learn his own truth.

Captain Luc expertly docked the ship, with the entire crew— Alobartalus included—on their best behavior. Most of them, he knew, were anxious to avail themselves of the Sn'archdruid market, where many visiting ships traded their goods and where the Sn'ale was said to quench every thirst and coat the throat all the way down.

"I hear they make Sn'oods that are somewhere between gray with an *a* and grey with an *e* and can hide a person in the mist," Tempest said as they all stood at the rail, looking down at the colorful stalls of the market and the monkish figures bustling about in tidy cassocks.

"Qobayne said the druids made gorgeous bows out of pliant, gleaming Morningwood, and I've been wanting to take up archery," Morgan said, then quickly corrected herself. "Sorry. Sn'archery. How much do you think that sort of thing costs? Is it more because it's, er, holy?"

"I don't know, because all I care about is getting my mitts on a

Sn'orkel," Vic cut in, his tail switching nervously and making the girls edge away from his huge, clattering hooves. "Skånki said it can help you breathe underwater, and that seems, uh, pretty useful. To some people. Not me, probably, because I'm not scared of water, but it might be nice to have around."

As the gangplank clattered against the dock, Alobartalus gave them all a brief salute. "All that sounds great," he called as he jogged down the salt-crusted wooden boards. "Good luck with all that Sn'uff."

The moment his feet hit the sand, Alobartalus felt a lift of hope, as if the very particles of the Sn'archivist's island were magical. He felt stronger, taller, more elvish—he even reached up to touch his ear tips, and he would've sworn they were somehow longer and pointier. As he hurried up the winding stairs to the small door set in the base of the tower, he could feel his dream finally coming true. He would knock, and at first no one would answer. But then, after he'd waited an appropriately long time to prove his dedication, the door would open. He would be put through a series of elaborate tests, which he would fly through, because this is where he was meant to be. He'd told Morgan that his dream was to meet the Sn'archivist, but really, it was to become the *next* Sn'archivist. If anything could impress the naysayers back home, it would be to see the name of Alobartalus listed on a plaque here and spoken only in tones of awe by whatever poor sod took over Proudwood Lighthouse.

Wait. No. Not Alobartalus.

Sn'Alobartalus.

Finally, after walking up the endlessly winding staircase within, Alobartalus would meet his mentor in the top room of the tower, where the ancient but still ethereal Sn'archivist would smile a kindly smile and say something like, *Long have I waited for the son of my heart to take up my pen, and Pellanus has sent thee here. Let us partake of cucumber sandwiches as I teach you the deepest secrets of my Sn'archives that thou might take up the torch of knowledge and be lauded amongst all elves as my chosen successor.*

It didn't have to be exactly that sort of speech, but Alobartalus really hoped it would be. Cucumber sandwiches were great.

With every step, he considered the swayback in the center of each stone stair and thought about the Sn'archivist treading this path every day for years as he walked to the beach and thought about how great it would be if a younger elf with a plucky spirit and excellent penmanship landed and offered up his services, releasing the older elf to a life of repose and light fishing.

As he stood before the wooden door, his fingers soft upon the knocker, which had gone verdigris with age, Alobartalus took a deep breath.

"Here we go," he said.

Knock knock knock.

The island seemed to go quiet around him; even the cackling of the seagulls muted as the knocking echoed over the rocks.

For the longest time, nothing happened. And then, something did.

"That was a really swell knock," said a man's earnest baritone voice. "I bet you have truly excellent knuckles!"

Alobartalus felt a flutter of pleasure; to think—the Sn'archivist was flattering him before they'd even met face-to-face!

"Many thanks for your kind words, great sir," Alobartalus said, trying to match the rich, rounded voice, which sounded like honey mead given tone. "I have long wished to meet you and speak with you regarding your great work."

"Wow, what a speech! Those vocal chords are top-notch. And what a resplendent vocabulary!"

Alobartalus had never felt so good about himself in all his life. He was smiling so hard his face felt like it was going to split open, and his heart was yammering like a hummingbird, and he just wanted to hug someone.

"Might I come in and greet you as friends?" he ventured.

"What a super question!"

Inside, someone fiddled with multiple locks, grumbling a bit, and Alobartalus prepared himself to meet the Sn'archdruid or one of his

Sn'acolytes. He grinned warmly so that his future servants might recognize that he would be a benevolent master. But when the door finally swung inward, he was surprised to see a very short figure, bent over double with a hunched back and clothed in what looked like an old tapestry—possibly a Pickleangelo, but so stained with oatmeal and mustard and cracker crumbs and dandruff that he could barely see the unicorns disemboweling some hateful earl woven into the fabric. A heavy hood hid the man's face.

"Hey, you look like a real person!" the man said.

Alobartalus faltered somewhat; surely the sweetly booming voice couldn't be coming from this aged servant. He looked around the antechamber but didn't spot the ethereal, golden-robed elf he sought—although he did see shelves and shelves filled with the tomes he'd so longed to peruse. There must've been thousands of the leather-bound books, spines curling around and around the inside of the tower, their golden inscriptions glimmering but unreadable in the darkness.

"Boy oh boy, are your eyes ever shiny!" the voice added.

"Thank you?" Alobartalus ventured.

"That's enough, Reginald," the old man said, pulling back his hood to reveal a dry, papery face, wrinkled ears with tufts of hair on their points, and weary eyes. His voice sounded like a spider's death throes, wheezing and dusty.

"What a tremendously phenomenal command! You really know how to tell a guy to shut his piehole!"

Seeking out the baritone voice, Alobartalus was confused to discover a gnomeric construct clinging to the wall. It was shaped like a gecko, with round glass eyes and exquisitely painted scales.

"Is that gecko talking?" Alobartalus asked, pointing at the robotic lizard.

"Man oh man, are you ever adept at pointing! Wowee, what an index finger! Just the right mixture of bony and fleshy—I'd even call it supple!"

The old man grunted and sneered at the golden construct. "His name is Reginald, and he's my affirmation gecko."

"Holy moly, that introduction was both correct *and* succinct!" the gecko enthused.

"And . . . he was the one talking to me through the door?"

The old man's rheumy eyes swiveled to Alobartalus. "Yes, for he is faster than I."

Alobartalus tried to hide his disappointment regarding the enthusiasm of those earlier compliments. He still had to convince someone to take him to the Sn'archivist.

"Well, he seems a very pleasant sort," he admitted, his grin returning. "Now, might I meet your master, the Sn'archivist? For I am—"

"No, I am."

"You are?"

"Yes."

Alobartalus shook his head. "You are what?"

"I am he."

"Whom?"

"Yes."

"Oh, gosh, what a spectacularly nonsensical conversation!" Reginald gushed. "Just a festival of fragments, a concatenation of quizzical queries, a real humdinger of a confusing interaction!"

The old man put a hand on Alobartalus's shoulder for balance, reached down, and removed his own house slipper, which he threw at the gecko. He missed, of course, and the gecko didn't even move as the slipper slapped to the floor.

"Whoa dang, that was the best bad throw I've ever seen! Heck of a windup!"

The old man sighed.

"Come along," he said. "It will be easier to show you."

Leaving his slipper on the floor, the old man began to climb the steps. Normally, Alobartalus would frown at the phrase *began to*, but with someone as old and frail as his host, the climb definitely took quite some time to begin. Each step seemed to take an hour as the old man hauled one foot up, grunted, and then yanked up the other with his clawed, arthritic hands. Alobartalus stayed close behind him, ready to catch him should he fall, and Reginald the Affirmation Gecko trailed them, skittering along the wall and babbling things like "Gee, you can really move that foot!" and "Congratulations on your really thick calluses, and can I get a *whoop-whoop!* for that kingly bunion?"

By the time they reached the top of the stairs, Alobartalus was certain that this must be one of the holy tasks he'd expected. Yes, the Sn'archivist must be testing him. With each circle of the staircase, he passed dozens of books he longed to touch while enduring the old man's seeping stench and the gecko's now truly annoying affirmations. But Alobartalus knew a test when he faced one, yes, he did, so he just smiled and kept on, hoping to show his worthiness through grit and patience. As they edged closer and closer to the glowing light at the top of the tower, he felt sure his idol would be waiting there with open arms and possibly a glass of water, because even for a seaman, Alobartalus was feeling mighty dried out.

"Here we are," the old man said, wobbling into the upper room with a sigh of satisfaction.

"Good call!" Reginald boomed. "That's exactly where we are!"

Alobartalus was the last to step onto the top floor, and it was indeed glowing. But not with fairy lanterns or his idol's halo. No, it was some sort of slimy algae spread upon the walls, scrawled in what looked like words that he couldn't quite make out. It must be another test, another clue.

"Does that say . . ." Alobartalus stepped closer. "Does that say *elf butts*?"

"Hot dog, we have someone literate!" Reginald said. "So, so good at stringing together letters to make syllables!"

"But there's more," the old man said. "Tell me, boy. What do you think of this?"

The old man selected a tome from the shelf and lovingly placed it into Alobartalus's hands, and Alobartalus smiled and felt a deep sense of contentment. This was a holy book from the tower of the Sn'archivist! First he marveled at the weight of the thing, then sniffed the supple binding and ran a finger over the fine gold inlays. Next he cracked the cover and fingered the crisp, creamy paper. Last, and with great reverence, Alobartalus turned the first page.

What he saw written there transformed him.

"Elf butts," he read aloud, and he felt his delighted smile melt away into a frown. "It only says *elf butts*," he muttered. He turned to the next page. "Over and over again. Page after page. Nothing but *elf butts*."

The old man finally smiled and nodded, his hands clasped. "Just so, my young elf. Just so."

Sliding past the old man, Alobartalus dropped the tome on the floor and plucked up another at random. This one, too, was filled with only those two simple words: *elf butts*. Sometimes there was an exclamation point, to shake things up. But not a single verb.

Pages and pages filled with those words: *elf butts*.

In perfect handwriting, in beautiful, luscious burgundy ink, or sometimes other colors like cerulean blue or deep purple, the same words again and again: *elf butts*.

"But what does this mean?" he asked, tears in his eyes.

"Ah. You seek enlightenment."

"Well, yeah. An explanation, at least."

The old man moved in a small cloud of his own dust and dandruff to a table where two volumes were prominently displayed. One looked significantly older than the other and he picked it up, offering it to his guest. "This is the oldest book of my tenure. You will see that in form and structure and, indeed, vocabulary, it is markedly different from the others."

Alobartalus practically snatched it from the old man's hands and flipped to the first page.

Elf butts, it said, and he almost tossed it away, but after that, the text changed.

Toight elf butts. Finely sculpted elf butts. Freshly grown organic elf butts. Unbelievably foine secret agent elf butts.

"You see?" the old man said. "Each sentence is one word longer than the previous one. The adjectives never repeat and the sentences expand until an entire page is filled with one long, glorious paean to the exquisite buttocks of an elf. Then they decrease again until we are back to just the two words. I believe it is a masterpiece. The definitive work on the subject."

"But . . . why?" Alobartalus nearly sobbed.

"I don't have all the answers," the old man grumbled in that really annoying voice old people use when they've forgotten what they're talking about but want to seem wise. "I can't explain the inscrutable. It is only mine to listen and write down what I hear. I am a conduit, you see. A conduit for the mind of Pellanus. And though the great god Pellanus has two faces, he and she have a singular mind. A one-track mind, in fact. They've been thinking about elf butts for most of my life."

Alobartalus dropped that tome on top of the other one with a loud thump that echoed all throughout the tower and made the gecko squawk, "Boy, can you ever take advantage of gravity and silence, kiddo!"

"Are you telling me," Alobartalus said, low and deadly, "that *you* are the Sn'archivist? And this is your Sn'archive?"

Without waiting for an answer, he stalked away toward the shelves and picked out another random tome. He opened it. More elf butts.

And another book. Yet more elf butts.

The old man didn't move to stop him. He didn't say a word. He simply smiled beatifically, as if watching a ritual unfold.

"Are you seriously telling me that the Sn'archives are nothing but elf butts and that you're just a crazy old dude?"

"What an amazing grasp of the obvious!" Reginald said. "Just, gosh!"

"Sometimes Pellanus works in mysterious ways," the old man said, nodding sagely.

"This isn't mysterious! This is stupid!"

"Have you really thought about elf butts, though? There's a lot to them. A lot to unpack inside."

"What? No! Don't tell me that! I *own* an elf butt! I don't want it to be packed or unpacked, classified or codified, idolized or rhapsodized, or even touched without explicit consent, you understand?"

Alobartalus had left a trail of tumbled tomes in his wake, the books tossed higgledy-piggledy on the ground, their pages bent and splayed. He no longer considered them holy. This had to be a joke. Or maybe the final test? A test that he was swiftly failing? He had to keep trying. Whoever this old joker was, the true Sn'archivist would be watching them closely.

Alobartalus whirled back to the table where the two books had been displayed: The second one looked new, and he pointed at it.

"Is that book different too?"

The old man's eyes crinkled with pleasure. "It is! An excellent deduction. Tell him, Reginald."

The affirmation gecko spun in a circle on the wall, excited beyond measure. "Gadzooks, friend! That is a darned impressive melon you have on your shoulders! You've got genius-grade brainmeats hanging out in your skull! When life gives you lemons, you make fancy cocktails and throw those lemons at squirrels!"

"Is it about . . ." Alobartalus made a whirling gesture with his hand, unable to bring himself to say it. "You know."

"It is not! It is an entirely different subject. I just finished it yesterday, and I was told by Pellanus to show it to the first person who visited me afterward, and that's you. See for yourself."

Mistrustful, wary of being burned again, Alobartalus edged toward the book. He picked it up, closed his eyes, took in a deep breath and exhaled before opening it and turning to the first page. He opened his eyes and read. Much to his surprise, it didn't say *elf butts*.

It said *otter balls*.

He dropped the book, shook his head, and started down the stairs.

"What a powerful, climactic ending!" Reginald enthused. "With that kind of professional-grade emoting, you could be an actor!"

"But my child," the old man called, his voice a lonely quaver. "Did you not wish to take up my pen and learn the secrets of these Sn'archives? Is it not your calling to be the next Sn'archivist?"

"Not anymore."

"But I have been waiting! Pellanus told me that one day, some expert seaman would come here and I would finally know relief!"

Alobartalus paused on the stairs, one hand on yet another tome chock full of elf butts.

"Well, it looks like all Pellanus actually says is *elf butts* and *otter balls*."

The old man's face appeared, peering down, desperate and frantic.

"Yes! Yes! That's it! Those are the holy words! Directly from the lips of Pellanus! Those are the words that will save you in your most trying moment! Those are the words you were meant to hear! Don't you see? You are destined for greatness!"

Alobartalus walked and then jogged down the stairs, tears coursing down his unelfly face, wanting nothing more than to get out of the tower, off the Sn'archipelago, and away from the island forever. The Sn'archivist was a lie. Every dream of knowledge and winning the admiration of the Morningwood had disintegrated. He would never be seen as elfly, never earn the king's pride as the scion of the Sn'archivist, never see joy in his mother's eyes as he proved he was a true son of doubly elven parentage. It didn't even matter who or what his father was. He was the same thing as the old fool upstairs: an outright failure of an elf. His tears didn't even shimmer.

As he slammed the door and ran down the stone stairs, he could hear the gecko within shout, "Bro, that was a sincerely tragic flounce, and that exit was incredibly moving. You sure know how to make an old man cry!"

But Alobartalus was done with this place.

He was done with elves. Done with magic. Done with dreams.

Back on the ship, he nearly ran into Morgan, who was holding a slender bow of Morningwood, oiling it proudly.

"Alobartalus, are you okay? Did you find the Sn'archivist?" she asked.

He looked at her, his heart breaking. "No, and yes," he said.

"So you're not staying here?"

Standing not quite tall and wiping away his tears, he said, "No, I'm not. I'm going to help you save the otters. And from now on, you can call me Al."

14.

WRAPPED IN A MALODOROUS AND ANNOYINGLY INSISTENT SCARF

Tempest was glad to know Al would be joining them for the journey to Bustardo instead of staying behind with the Sn'archivist. For all that Captain Luc was a fair and generous host and teacher, and for all that the other sailors were friendly and understanding of her tremendous failure in the realm of knot tying, there was a clear delineation between the sailors paying for their passage through work and the salty dogs Tempest would consider "lifers." Most of the latter were missing a limb or an eye, loved nothing so much as grog and the sea, and favored striped shirts and pants that always seemed to end in ragged hems halfway up their calves. She'd recently realized that Morgan was toying with the idea of becoming a lifer too. Tempest even caught her saying "Yarrrr!" once, and although she assured Tempest that she was merely trying to fit in, Tempest knew Morgan wouldn't be making the effort to swallow all those *R*s if she didn't want to stick with it.

But Al was good company, quite unlike all the boisterous elves who'd come to stay at Tommywood with Tommy Bombastic. Quiet, thoughtful, respectful, and he hadn't put a whoopee cushion under anyone yet. And the otters loved him, which was quickly becoming important on the ship. It was clear within hours that the wriggling things could escape the hold easily, and so in the coming days it fell to the newest crew members to wrangle the oily critters while the lifers clambered up into the nets, muttering about the stench of fish and the harm an excited otter could do to a nicely turned peg leg.

"Almost there," Morgan said several days later, appearing at the rail beside Tempest to watch a long, rocky island emerge from the mist ahead of the ship.

The otters had taken one look at the Sn'archivist's island and refused to set paw on the gangplank; it wasn't the right sort of place for otters, apparently. Not enough clams, perhaps, or maybe they could smell the variety of skins drying outside the leather tannery in the market. On the advice of the Sn'archdruid, *The Puffy Peach* had kept her wriggling cargo and set course for Otter Island, which had to be a better fit, judging by the name. After that, they would cross the Urchin Sea to get to the mainland, being almost directly across from the first and biggest of the Seven Toes. For the time being, Morgan's pet otter—or, more accurately, the otter that had adopted her almost against her will, now named Otto—remained wound around her neck like a fur stole.

"So this should be a relatively easy delivery. The captain says the otters should just playfully gambol down the gangplank and take up residence," Al said, joining them.

"And then we move on to Bustardo," Tempest sighed.

Morgan turned to look at her, concern in her eyes.

"Are you scared?" she asked.

Tempest chuckled. "Of law school? Of course not. I know I'm smart."

"Not of law school. Of the . . . other lawyers."

Al shuddered. "Law school? That's where you're going? Aren't there enough sharks in the sea already?"

Tempest whirled on him. "Oh, so you're one of those people who think all lawyers are terrible and bloodthirsty and only want riches and fancy carriages?"

"Um." Al's lips twitched. "Is that not true? We didn't have any lawyers in the Morningwood, but we had tons of lawyer jokes in case one ever showed up. Which they never did. Because we also have bouncers for that sort of thing, and the king has them all firmly bounced."

With a nod of understanding, Tempest said, "Well, my father is a sentient, meat-eating tree who sold me to a demigod, and after a few hundred years of washing his socks, I was released through a single conversation with a lawyer. No fancy carriage, no piles of gold, and he wouldn't even accept payment. He was just a halfling who hated injustice. If not for his kindness, I would still be in a tree house in the Pruneshute Forest, carrying platters of bratwurst for Phlatulense and Skrophula, the pixies who rented a branch."

"I'm glad to know people like that exist," Morgan said. "The halfling—not the pixies."

"We still write letters, Faucon and I. Or we did, when I was on land. He's now a politician in the Skyr, if you can believe it." She lowered her voice. "A little too obsessed with pigeons—and I mean literal pigeons, not in the sense of the slang term—but a very kind halfling. Oh! We're here." She leaned over the railing and shielded her eyes from the sun. But there was something very wrong.

"Um, shouldn't there be otters here?" Al asked. "Isn't that the whole point?"

But Morgan being Morgan, she was already clattering down the gangplank, the first to set foot on Otter Island. Or, as it appeared currently, Paucity of Otters Island.

"We have otter-sign down here. There are empty clamshells every-where, and all the rocks are oily," Morgan called from the shore. "But there is indeed a distinct dearth of otters."

As if on cue, there was a great purring sound from the hold, and a veritable tide of wriggling brown bodies busted through the trapdoor and galumphed sinuously onto the deck. The romp of otters lived up to its name as they wiggled and chittered and scurried down the gangplank and onto the rocky isle, swarming around Morgan and picking up clamshells as if inspecting a new house they were thinking about buying.

"Could ye not stop them?" Captain Luc wailed. "If therrrre be no otterrrrrs on Otterrrr Island, maybe dangerrrr still lurrrrrks about?"

Old Milly Dread lurched up from the hold, covered in otter paw prints and looking even more bedraggled than usual. "Couldn't stop 'em, Cap'n!" she wheezed. "They gone wild! The churls have gone wild!"

Feng stepped beside Tempest, and Luc fluffed his feathers in annoyance. "Can't help things as don't wish to be helped," he grumbled.

"Well, some creatures are pure instinct," Tempest reminded him. "They know home when they see it, I suppose." And the otters did indeed look very at home as they gamboled in the surf, diving and splashing and flapping their feet as they floated on their backs while holding hands.

"Speakin' o' home, and seein' as how therrrre's no way to get the silly beasts back on the ship, we'll be shoving off to Bustarrrrdo next, lass. And you'll be leaving us?"

Tempest was gratified by the disappointed tone in his voice, and she smiled; it was nice to be wanted, even if she was terrible with knots. "That's the plan," she said. "Although it's been a lovely trip, and I'm so glad I got to play at being a pirate for a while."

At that, Luc's feathers went to max ruffle, and he flapped his wide wings and pinned her with a vicious glare. "You've not been playing at being one o' us! If you do yourrrr job on the pirrrrate ship, you'rrrre a pirrrrate thrrrrough and thrrrrough! It's a mindset, not a carrrreerrrr! And you've got the potential!"

The captain cawed, settled down, and softly apologized to Feng for accidentally whapping him upside the head with his wings. He then returned his one eye to Tempest.

"What I mean to say, lass, is that you'll always be welcome to rrrride on *The Puffy Peach*."

Overcome with feeling and unable to hug a parrot of authority, Tempest could only nod and look down, one finger absentmindedly rubbing the spot of bark she'd earned healing old Cappy. Since she'd been on the ship, no one had made any reference to her healing skills, and she wasn't sure if it was because they didn't know much about dryads, because they assumed she was a human with an insane wig collection, or because Luc had threatened their lives, the crusty sweetheart.

"Thank you for everything," she finally said. "It'll definitely be hard to leave."

With a grunt, Luc steered Feng away, right as Morgan bounded back onto the ship with Otto still wrapped around her neck.

"Well, the otters seem settled, although Otto refuses to leave me. I kept putting him on the ground, and he would just claw his way up again." She patted the otter absentmindedly, and he purred. "They certainly don't sense any danger here. But I found this."

The object Morgan held up looked a bit like a battered old hat that several otters had tried to either kill or mate with. It was full of holes, scratched near to death, and very moist. A tiny patch inside read only ANG.

"What do you think it is?" Tempest asked.

"A hat that several otters have tried to either kill or mate with. But with everything else we've learned, I can only assume ... that the Mutae Mercantile Association otternapped them to turn them into EATUM. And one of those MMA agents left his hat behind."

"Then we can't leave our otters here! What if the MMA comes back? The poor things!"

Morgan tossed the scrap of a hat overboard, and they watched several otters give it come-hither looks.

"We can't make them leave. This is their home. We just have to get to Mack Guyverr and stop whoever's in charge, so the otters can safely live out their lives here, where they belong." She cocked her head. "And maybe we should get them a few more hats. They, uh, really seem to like hats. I don't know if it's the soaked-up scalp sweat or the hair grease or what."

The crew pulled up the gangplank, and Tempest and Morgan watched Otter Island, once again replete with otters, recede into the distance. The otters did indeed look much happier than they had been while trapped on the ship, frolicking and fishing and selecting their clamshells with infinite care. That task over, Tempest went to the ship's prow and squinted. There was an expanse they had to cross, and parts of it were deep enough to allow cavemouths to swim up underneath them. But Captain Luc said it was rare for ships to be eaten in the southern reaches of the sea and that the cavemouths liked to feed up by the Proudwood Lighthouse since it was more of a bottleneck and the traffic was more reliable. That did not prevent the entire crew from clenching every sphincter they possessed for several days of sailing until Captain Luc declared them safe. They could see the coastline up ahead, and with it, Bustardo. Tempest just knew that she would feel at home there, as the otters did on their island, although she didn't know that there was anything she liked as much as they liked old hats.

"Are you sure you have everything you need?" Morgan asked the next morning at dawn.

Tempest looked out at the bustling city of Bustardo and took a deep breath.

"I don't have much. And the town will have everything else. Luc gave me my wages. He didn't have to, but he did." She jingled the fickels in her coin pouch. "Although he did dock me half a fickel for tying bad knots. He said I was the least knotty nymph he everrrr knew." Her smile started to wobble into tears, and Morgan put a hand on her shoulder.

"You're going to do great," she said, every word full of conviction. "You're going to make great friends, live in a cool dorm room, study amazing subjects, ace your tests, and become the best lawyer in Pell."

Tempest looked past the busy docks to the twisty old city. On the other side of those crooked buildings was the ferry station that provided transportation across a wide lake, taking students to the enormously grand castle that housed the Bogtorts School of Law and Order.

"I *am* going to do great!" Tempest felt hope lift in her chest. "I'm going to be a great lawyer."

"Don't forget to write!"

"Oh, I'm pretty sure you have to write, if you want to be a lawyer. Writs and things?"

Morgan grinned. "I mean to us. To me. We'll want to know how you're getting on."

"Of course." Tempest felt tears welling up again. "I hear Bustardo is known for their mail flamingos. They're enchanted to deliver mail anywhere in Pell." Her brow scrunched down. "Although you'd think that that would be preferable to the Pellican Postale Service, if it worked well. I mean, after you buy a flamingo, you don't need to buy stamps, just shrimps. But I guess people need jobs more than flamingos do? Ah, well. I'll find out soon enough and hopefully send you progress reports."

They had another clinging hug, and then Alobartalus was pumping her hand and wishing her well, and Vic was nervously handing her a folded piece of paper and a teacup and clopping to the other side of the deck to swab something with his rump turned.

She walked down the gangplank, shoulders back, and felt the now-familiar pudding-like quiver of sea legs meeting solid ground. Once she was out of view of the ship, she unfolded the paper Vic had given her.

Good lucke, it read in beautiful calligraphy. *We will be rooting for ye! XO, Vic.*

Tempest cocked her head. Had the centaur asked someone else to write it for him? It definitely didn't seem his style. And the teacup, painted with willow leaves and quills, held a beautiful tea cake decorated with a dainty briefcase made of modeling chocolate. When she turned to look at the ship, she saw the prow of *The Puffy Peach* but no sign of the centaur or any of her friends. They'd be shoving off later that night, and then she'd have to depend on some random flamingo to find them again.

The cobblestoned streets of Bustardo proper were charmingly uneven and labyrinthine, with tall, colorful buildings and each new street or alley promising all sorts of wonderful things Tempest had never seen before. The Grey & Gray Cloak Cabinet called to her, and she wished she had the time to stop in at Bark Polishers Anonymous or taste the jiggling confections at the Lords and Ladles House of Aspic. Darling pushcarts sold flowers and churros and silver cups of punch, while gap-toothed waifs offered violets, matchsticks, or whispered directions to the nearest tooty bar. But before Tempest could commit to shopping, a flamingo swooped down low enough to fwap her in the back of the head with its gangling legs, and she hit the ground on her belly with a startled "Oof," her hands flying up to protect her face. When she opened her eyes again, she found a sharp cream-colored envelope lying on the cobbles. In superlative calligraphy and a rich navy-blue ink, it read:

Tempest Willow
Halfway Down Blue Booby Ave.
Lying on the Ground, Looking Silly and Unlawyerly

She picked it up and stood, pulling her hood back over her hair and finding a shadowy alley to hide in while she figured out what was happening. Was someone playing a joke on her? Were the flamingos in Bustardo especially aggressive? Or was this just how mail worked here?

Tempest cracked open the wax seal and read the letter inside.

RE: TEMPEST WILLOW

It is understood herewith that you expect to enroll at the Bogtorts School of Law and Order. Pursuant to Edict 179, you will require:

- One (1) set of school robes (all black, no tassels)
- Beginner's package of textbooks from Quibble & Quarrel's Booke Shoppe
- One of the following: Mail Flamingo (can be male or female); Emotional-Support Horse (max 36", must wear diapers); Singing Crayfish (no pop music)

Report to Dock 76.4 at exactly 12:21 P.M. today or you will be counted *in absentia*.

Tempest looked at the sun and realized she would have to hurry. Slipping the letter into her cloak pocket, she walked up the street in a purposeful, lawyerly, unsilly way.

As if the school administration had known the exact route she would take, she first encountered Madam Merkin's House of Jerkins, where she was led to an orange crate sitting before a three-way mirror. An old halfling woman bumbled around her, measuring all sorts of things that had nothing to do with robes, such as the length of her nose and her ability to do a backbend.

"A dryad," someone said in very rude tones. "Bogtorts will let in anyone these days." Tempest looked over to find that the next mirror station was taken up by a human woman who had pale skin, beautiful blond hair, and ice-blue eyes. She, too, was being measured for her robes.

"Law is about equality, and I'm just as equal as you are," Tempest said, holding up her chin.

"Sure, until you get old and try to eat someone. So clever, how the law includes statutes protecting the rights of cannibalistic trees. Back home in Dower, we chop down willows before they can do anyone harm."

"That's funny. Where I come from, we chop down nasty racists before they can do anyone harm."

With a mighty flounce, the woman hopped off her box and stuck her nose in the air, showcasing a wide array of pitch-black nose hairs, suggesting that the blond hair on her head was colored with magic or possibly several hours in a salon.

"I'll see you at school, then, I suppose," the woman said. "If the Sifting Scarf even lets you in."

Before Tempest could ask what a Sifting Scarf was, the woman was gone, and Madam Merkin was handing her a heavy box tied with twine.

The very next store was Quibble & Quarrel's Booke Shoppe. Pushing through the door, Tempest found a bustling business with quaintly uneven wooden floors and bookshelves stretching up to the ceiling, which was hung with dozens of brass measuring scales. Inquiring at the front desk, she was given a large bundle of leather-bound books with gilt-edged pages, and Mr. Quarrel promised he'd have them sent directly to her room at the university.

"But how will you know where my room is?" she asked.

"Magic!" he warbled.

"Really?"

"No. We use indentured goblin servants."

Tempest deflated a bit and decided to carry her own books. It felt wrong, going to law school to help people while expecting someone else to carry her goods for her without getting paid.

Now weighed down by two heavy boxes tied with yet more twine, she huffed and puffed uphill toward the last thing on her list. Pervin's Pet Shoppe was intriguing to say the least, with wide windows cram-jammed with birds of all colors and sizes. Stepping within, Tempest was overcome with the dire stench of literal tons of animal excreta, plus the equally horrific odors of their various foods and unchanged water bowls. She passed a seething, muddy vat of crayfish, each singing its heart out and making her wish she'd bought the Easy-Hear No-Fear Earmuffs that Madam Merkin had urged on her for a ridiculous upcharge. She didn't even venture toward the corner where the miniature horses waited, knee-deep in emotional-support plops.

No, she went straight to a display of flamingos, anxious to feel that heart tug that would suggest she'd found the flamingo meant just for her. From far away, the flamingos were a shifting panorama of shivering pink, but up close, they were a mess of neuroses. Feathers plucked here and there, eyes emitting green gunk, beaks rimmed with gummed specks of paper and rogue stamps. She stretched out her hand to the most healthy- and friendly-looking flamingo, and it bit her finger hard enough to draw blood.

Her stomach churning, Tempest read through her letter again and was disturbed to notice that the wording had changed. It now said:

- One of the following *is required of all students, because only weirdos don't want pets:* Mail Flamingo (can be male or female); Emotional-Support Horse (max 36", must wear diapers); Singing Crayfish (no pop music)

Tempest swallowed hard. If she couldn't even pet the flamingo in the pet shop, how was she supposed to keep it as a pet? Did they sell flamingo cages? Should flamingos be kept in cages at all? Could flamingos perhaps be crate-trained? But she was determined to go to school and to fit in there, so she walked out of the shop ten minutes later leading the beautiful but angsty flamingo on an expensive rhinestone-bedecked leash and carrying another twine-tied box of various flamingo foods, treats, water softeners, vitamins, and feather unguents. She was starting to get a twine rash.

It took some time, tugging her recalcitrant flamingo through the heavy crowds and up the street to the ferry station. She ended up using up all her flamingo treats, and the darned thing, which she'd named Mingo, did insist on pecking her with its pointy beak every time it decided it required another treat. The ferry station was even more heavily crowded than the streets, and Tempest was more tired than she'd been in months and couldn't wait to sit down. School shopping, she realized, was a hundred times harder than being a pirate.

"This is worse than a Tommywood rager," she told Mingo, who aimed a peck at her eye.

Walking up and down the ferry docks, she grew increasingly frustrated. Where was Dock 76.4? And why would anyone name a dock that? The lake wasn't even that big; it seemed to exist only to get students to and from the school, which was an activity that should happen only a few times a year and not require its own dock. And yet, as she walked up and down the space between Docks 76 and 77, tugging her angry flamingo, she couldn't find her goal.

"Ol' Dock 76.4," someone said. "Crowded as all bleedin' get-out with tourists every year. Can't take a step without crushin' a crayfish or gettin' pecked by a giant chicken or emotionally antagonized by a pony."

Tempest whirled around, finding an old man standing there with a nervous redheaded woman in her thirties and her sleeping flamingo.

"Did you say Dock 76.4?" Tempest asked. "I can't find it."

The old man's face split in a kind grin. "Oh, it's easy, lass. You just got to jump off into the space between Docks 76 and 77."

"Really? Because that makes no sense."

The old man winked at her, and the younger woman with him gave Tempest an encouraging smile.

"It makes sense to lawyers," the man said. "It's all about being fearless, ye see."

So Tempest grabbed hold of her boxes and her flamingo leash, took a deep breath, and jumped.

They were laughing before she hit the water with a splash, tugged down by her boxes. As she spluttered and struggled, the flamingo trying to crawl on her head and chase shrimp at the same time, the old man yelled, "It was a joke, fool. You just got to wait until the Bogtorts ferry pulls up to Dock 76. The .4 is a funny old typo."

It took a good twenty minutes for Tempest to swim to the shore, drag her sodden bags and boxes and flamingo up the rocks, and return to her place on the dock. The old man and the redhead were gone, and as the ferry pulled up, a handsome man in a poet's blouse and a hat shaped like a lion turned to her with a smile.

"I'm Tempest," she said, hoping to make a friend.

"You're a right dummy," the man said. "D'you jump off a dock every time someone tells you to? Ain't gonner make it long at Bogtorts."

When it was her turn to board, Tempest watched where the blouse-wearing man went and chose a seat in the opposite direction.

The ferry was the biggest boat Tempest had ever seen, big enough to have two decks and an indoor toilet. She was the only person in her row in back, but at least she had the window to herself. As the ferry laboriously chugged toward the looming school, Tempest looked around the boat. The redheaded woman and the man in the poet's blouse were talking to the blond woman from Madam Merkin's, as their flamingos pointedly ignored each other. Two men with soul patches were engaged in an attempt to set fire to the tail of a halfling man's emotional-support horse. There was a flamingo fight ring going on in one corner, and something noisy in the loo suggested either a mugging or athletic coitus.

Taking a deep, cleansing breath, Tempest closed her eyes and struggled for control. She was going to school to become a lawyer so that she could help people and pay it forward. She wasn't here to make friends, although she very much wished to do so. Nor was she here to party or cause mischief; she was here to learn. Thanks to her sisters and to Luc's generosity, she had everything she needed, even if it was all a bit wet and bedraggled. She could do this.

The ferry docked, and a series of gnomeric-automaton-driven carriages pulled up to deliver the new students through the dark forest and up to the school. Tempest hopped into one but wondered what was the point of making it so difficult to get to the university itself; surely they could've easily taken the road like normal people? Was it to impress upon them the intense journey they'd be undergoing as they became lawyers? Was it to test their patience and commitment?

"No, they're just jerks who think it's funny."

Tempest was rudely awakened from her reverie and had to stare at the strange man facing her across the gnomeric carriage. He wore funny wire-rimmed glasses and had half his hair singed off; a huge red scar slashed through one milky eye.

"Did you just read my mind?" she asked.

"No. You were talking out loud. It was weird."

The man's emotional-support horse snorted in agreement. They were alone in the carriage, the last one in the line.

"The current headmaster is an elf, you see," he went on. "Got expelled from the Morningwood for being a lawyer. Loves pranks. Makes the staircases move and plants venomous snakes in the desks for jollies. You get used to it." She cocked her head at him. "Oh, I'm Gary, by the way. Gary Motter. Around here, they call me the Chosen One."

"I'm Tempest." She thought about offering to shake hands, but Gary's hands were covered in horse dander. "Um, what were you chosen for?"

Gary laughed. "No, like *the* Chosen One, capital *C* and *O*. See, when I was a baby, the world's most evil wizard—"

The carriage, luckily, rolled to a halt in front of the grand door to the university just then, and the driver blared, "Let's all get out without a shout!" in a cheerful robotic voice.

Tempest jumped down and hurried to put as much space between her and Gary as possible. He sounded like a total nutter, and probably the only reason they'd had the carriage to themselves was that they were already the biggest pariahs in the school. An old man in heavy velvet robes with a stuffed owl on his hat waited in the grand foyer to welcome them, but Tempest was too busy looking around to listen to anything he said. Surely there would be an orientation, or a student peer group, or some kind of pamphlet she could read?

The décor was fascinating and strange, and she couldn't stop staring. The rugs had statutes and writs woven into them and the tapestries were clearly Pickleangelos, most of which involved judges in curly white wigs getting defenestrated. But what really caught and held her attention—and made her gorge partially rise—were the recurring motifs seen in various sculptures, pennants, and ceiling frescoes. Roaches, worms, mosquitoes, and ticks covered almost every surface and had no business on wallpaper, as far as Tempest was concerned.

The group was led into a huge hall and seated at the first of five long wooden picnic tables, the hard seats of which immediately made everyone over thirty shift about in abject discomfort. Although the new students' table had been empty, the other four tables were full of upperclassmen, already in their uniform robes. They watched the newcomers, snickering. The old man in the owl hat shuffled to a sort of stage in the front of the room and held up a ragged garment that looked like it had been found in the garbage.

"And now you will be called one by one in a random order, and I will place the Sifting Scarf over your nose and mouth," the old man said tiredly.

"*Wait, what?*" Tempest barked, but everyone else was too excited to care.

"Evilyn Evilla," the old man yelled, and the blond woman from the robe shop proudly sashayed onto the stage beside him. He wrapped the scarf around her face, and she just stood there, not breathing, and after five seconds the scarf yelled, "Mosquitopuff!"

Evilyn grinned and hopped down to sit with a bunch of people wearing red scarves and making concerted buzzing noises like some kind of cheer.

"Uh, what is happening?" Tempest asked Gary, who had appeared by her side, despite the fact that her flamingo kept poking at his crotch.

"You see, the Sifting Scarf is an ancient magical object spelled to place each student in the correct Bogtorts Box. So you'll live in that dorm, eat with that group, be friends with only those people, wear only that group's colors—"

"But I'm an adult with free will," she said, increasingly uncomfortable.

"Not once you've been sifted."

"Tempest Willow!" the old man boomed.

Leaving her wet boxes and angry flamingo by Gary, and noting that she was currently the only student still bogged down with possessions and not wearing her school robes, Tempest walked up the stone steps and took her place on the dais. The old man wrapped the scarf around her mouth, and she struggled not to vomit. It smelled like a hundred years of bad perfume, onion and cabbage breath, and fear burps.

"Let's see, let's see. Where to stuff you?" a voice whispered in her ear. "Wormidor is for those who can wriggle off the hook and bounce back twice as hard when destroyed. Roachcraw is for those who can outlast anything, who can hide the truth, who can drop from the ceiling and surprise the jury. Slithertick is for the students who will dig in their pincers and suck their opponent dry, leaving them weak and diseased. And Mosquitopuff is for those who are stealthy but annoying, who will keep their enemies awake all night and leave them itchy, who can suck the blood out of any stone."

"None of those sound at all like me," Tempest protested in a whisper.

"But where to put you!" the scarf went on. "You're pretty smart, so Roachcraw might be nice. Do you like to skitter?"

"No. I don't feel like I connect with any of those . . . boxes."

"Wormidor could work."

"No."

"Slithertick?"

"Ugh. Gods. That's even worse. Like, slithering *and* ticks? No thanks."

"Then it must be Mosquitopuff," the scarf suggested.

"Not if that Evilyn woman is in there. She's awful."

"But the Mosquitopuff swarm can help you on your way!"

"I honestly hate all four choices, Scarf-guy. Like, I just want to become a lawyer. I don't want to be divided up according to stupid artificial lines and be sectioned off with a bunch of randos. I'm a serious student, and—"

"Ah, my dear," the scarf crooned. "Perhaps you are that rare creature. A divergent. Someone who fits in all four boxes equally well and equally badly."

Tempest exhaled in relief. "Yes. Yes, that sounds exactly like me."

"Kidding!" the scarf chortled. "Everyone fits in a box. We just have to find the right box and cram you in there. Sometimes it can help if you have a preference. Hmm?"

The scarf paused, and Tempest realized that whatever she chose now would influence the next four years of her life—and everything that came after that. This decision would determine her friends, her classes, her specialty, which law firm she interned at, where she would eventually make partner. She had to make the right choice in this precise moment, or her entire life would fall apart like a squashed roach underfoot.

"I choose . . ."

"Yes?"

"To leave this insane so-called school."

Reaching up, she unwrapped the scarf from her face, took a welcome breath of unfunky air, threw the scarf on the ground, and bolted. She left the sodden box of robes under Gary's pony but took her books and dragged her idiotic mail flamingo along behind her. For once, it obeyed, awkwardly trotting by her side and letting out weird little *awk-awk* noises, like it, too, was glad to be far away from Gary Motter's crotch.

Bolting out the front door and into the glaring sun of late afternoon, Tempest considered the automaton carriages lined up along the road to the ferry dock. Instead, she took the perfectly normal road, hailed a real carriage with a real driver, and was back in Bustardo in about fifteen minutes.

Flamingo in tow, she ran for the docks, hoping she wasn't too late. Hoping *The Puffy Peach* hadn't left yet.

She'd made her choice.

15.

AMIDST A HAIL OF
GLUTINOUS ARTILLERY

It was widely considered unsafe for centaurs to be wandering alone outside the Centaur Pastures. Gryphons, trolls, giants, and half-lings wanted to eat them; dwarves on Meadschpringå wanted to kill them; elves took them hostage and held them for ridiculous cheese ransoms; but humans were the worst. Every centaur foal learned the six-line teaching song:

> *Never trot in human cities*
> *Because they'll try to take your kidneys!*
> *If you do go, see what I mean*
> *When you wake up missing your spleen.*
> *They'll draw the marrow from your bones*
> *And make a tonic from your gallstones.*

Such songs, of course, were designed to encourage questions from foals, and Vic had fired some at his revered dam, Barfing August:

Why do they want our kidneys?

Because we have two sets of them leading to a single bladder and they think we don't need them all, and furthermore, they believe they're entitled to take them.

Why do they feel entitled?

Humans look upon us as animals, son, and they feel entitled to do anything they want to animals.

But aren't we part human too?

Yes, but humans always tend to focus on the part that doesn't look just like them.

What the heck is a gallstone?

Gallstones accumulate in your gallbladder over many years. They're basically nuggets of hardened cholesterol. The humans grind them into powder and put them in fruity drinks because they think it will make them perform well during mating season.

What's mating season?

Let's talk about that some other night.

Does the drink work?

No. Unless by working you mean it eventually kills them. Then it works great.

Then why do they think it's great for mating season?

Because humans are stupid, son. Stupid and deadly. Don't go into their cities.

As a result of that conversation, Vic had always suspected himself to be half stupidly deadly. But he was all hungry at the moment, and the captain's decision to grant his crew an afternoon of shore leave in the human port city of Bustardo gave Vic the perfect chance to find enough food to fill both of his stomachs for the first time in weeks.

Ship's biscuits weren't sufficient; he needed a lot of calories to keep his body going, and he'd secretly been conjuring cupcakes and fruitcake during the voyage and scarfing them down when no one was looking; as a result, he was looking a bit less cut and ripped. So despite the warnings he'd received in his youth, he felt it worth the risk to venture into a strange city so he could feel full again. And besides, nothing bad had happened to him while he'd been staying in Sullenne—he'd had more trouble from other centaurs at the gym than he'd had from humans. That was one of the many benefits of being swole, or at least slabby: Nobody wanted to risk being pounded into jelly by his fists, much less his hooves.

His best bet, according to Qobayne, was to find a diner that served breakfast all day, which might provide gallons of steel-cut oatmeal to go with his bacon and eggs. His second stomach was not a true horse stomach, because he didn't have to digest grass; it was designed more along human lines but was very efficient at the processing of grains and fruits, and it dumped its load, so to speak, into a bowel that merged with the one from the human stomach and led to a "common rectum," which was terminology that Vic despised. He thought he had an extraordinary rectum.

As Vic trotted down the gangplank to the docks, humans uttered startled exclamations of surprise at his approach and sometimes squeaked in fear. They didn't get too many centaurs around here, apparently. Their fear was delicious but not nutritious. Vic needed victuals. His stomachs were growling. The other crew members were going off in groups and clumps on other errands and Vic was left alone to find his own way.

"You there." He pointed at a slim man cowering against the wall of a kuffee shop. "Tell me where I can find a diner with plenty of good food." Captain Luc had paid them each a small purse of fickels for their work aboard ship so far, and he was anxious to spend it.

"Th-th-the Knacker Barrel has great f-f-food. And large booths."

Vic took a couple of menacing steps forward. "Knacker Barrel? Are you saying that because of my equine posterior?"

"No, no, all manner of beings eat there! Plenty of centaurs!"

"Where is it?"

The man pointed a quivering finger. "Three blocks that way, on your left."

"Thank you." Vic clopped down the main street of Bustardo, glaring at humans who dared to make eye contact with him. He wanted them to think about losing organs if they messed with him instead of plotting how they could take his. At least the humans on the ship didn't seem particularly interested in his innards; he'd never once awakened to find someone poking his gut to assess the tenderness of his filets.

Spotting the Knacker Barrel, he noted a long row of rocking chairs out front, which made him feel a bit left out. But this was a human city—of course they weren't thinking about the needs of other species. The door was extra wide and tall, at least, and his hooves clattered on the wooden floorboards as he entered a claustrophobic sort of gift shop full of aged and dusty tchotchkes. The walls were covered in old signs and garbage, not to mention several offensive harnesses, saddles, and bridles. Vic almost turned around, but then he smelled grease, and his stomach growled. Politely elbowing his way to the counter, he requested a table and was quickly ushered to a spacious high-top in a corner. That, at least, was just his size. His waiter appeared, greeting him with a welcome enthusiasm, and he ordered a dozen scrambled eggs, a steak cooked medium, five orders of hash browns with onions, and all the oatmeal they had, with plenty of brown sugar, cinnamon, and apples—hold the raisins.

"*All* the oatmeal?" his server asked. He was a diminutive person who sweated a lot. The kitchen must be hot, or perhaps the man really liked his meat.

"All of the oatmeal," Vic confirmed.

"That would be, like, twenty bowls or something."

"Bring it here now, sir. My horse half hungers for nourishment."

"Do you, uh . . . have money?"

Vic understood that this question came up because he possessed no pockets and his fanny pack did not look nearly so swole as the rest of him. He jiggled the coins within, allowing the fickels to clink around, and leaned down toward the server. "All the oatmeal," he whispered.

"Y-yes. Right away."

He stood proudly at his table, one hoof cocked, and glowered at anyone who dared to look in his direction. He didn't want them checking out his torso and estimating where his kidneys might be. Perhaps it was time to eschew the crop-top trend.

The oatmeal started coming, and he shoveled it in as fast as they could bring it out, switching his esophageal valve to close off his human stomach and thereby shunting the oats down the long esophagus to his second stomach. He would savor the steak and eggs later; oatmeal was fuel, and he just wanted to get it in there as fast as he could swallow, in case he had to gallop away from a rogue spleen-snatching gang.

It turned out to be twenty bowls, as promised, and then the steak and eggs arrived with the hash browns. He poured hot sauce on the eggs and shifted his valve over to close off his horse stomach. The proteins and taters were bound for the human stomach.

He took his time cutting up the steak, a perfect pink in the middle, and enjoyed two bites before his eyelids unaccountably began to droop.

Why was he so tired all of a sudden?

His knees buckled a bit and he staggered to the left, knocking over a rake that had been badly nailed to the wall. He blinked furiously. That was embarrassing, and more than a little weird. Oatmeal didn't usually have such a soporific effect.

A human man dressed in a stained white apron emerged from the direction of the kitchen. He had a poufy hat on too. Probably the chef. Maybe the oatmeal chef?

"Heyyuh. Dish ohmeal. Ohmeal? Ohhhhmeal! Whereza T? Suppozed be a T in that word. Ohmeal ish funny. Summin . . . wrong. Widdit." He pointed at the stack of empty bowls with what he thought was a single finger, but somehow he saw three. How was that possible?

"I know, I know," the chef said. "Sometimes people have that reaction. We can fix it. Can you walk?"

"I kin awk. Walk. Yeah."

"Follow me? I can fix you right up."

Vic tried to follow him and walk straight, but tables kept jumping in his path and getting knocked over. The ground wasn't steady.

"Summin wrong," he said again.

"I know, but don't you worry," the man said. "We'll get you all settled. I'm very sorry about this."

Vic staggered into the kitchen, his hooves sounding very loud on the tile and not hitting in any rhythm he found comforting. They were nervous footfalls.

"Muzza." Vic's mouth was so very dry, and he smacked his lips and tried to generate some saliva in there. He was going to say something profound. What was it? Oh, yeah. "Muzza bin summin I ate."

What had he eaten? Vic's thoughts were thick and sludgy, like lumpy oatmeal. That was it! Oatmeal! He'd eaten a lot of it. At this place.

The man in the apron fetched a long boning knife out of a wooden block and faced him.

"You're suffering toxic shock," he said. "I can help you and you'll feel instantly better. Would that be okay?"

"Yeah. Do it."

The chef looked over at the server and several others in the kitchen. "You heard him say I should do it," he said. "He gave me permission to remove one of his kidneys. To save his life, of course."

"Hole on now, hole on," Vic said. "Wuh wuzzat? Kinneys? No kinneys."

"You're having a bad reaction to the food, sir. Just relax. Lock your knees and go to sleep. I know you must be tired."

"No, izza ohmeal. Frumma place. Thish place! Hey! Yourra guy who made a ohhhmeal. *You* did thish to me!"

"No, sir, you're confused."

"Yourra guy my dam tol' me about! You canna have mah kinney!"

The chef took a step back and his eyes flicked to the left. "We miscalculated the dose. Hit him with the extra shot," he said, and that is when Vic realized that his dam's warnings weren't just stories to scare him straight but were actually about real things that happened to real centaurs and it was really about to happen to him. They'd knock him out, and if he ever woke up at all, it would be in a very large ice bath with missing organs and hide-marring scars.

But he *liked* his kidneys. Especially when he could pronounce them correctly.

Many times over the years, Pissing Victorious had wished for the ability to call down lightning on his foes, but *this* was the one time he truly, desperately needed it: to smite the evil human who wanted to steal his kidney. And not just for his own sake—to smite him for *all* centaurs, so that humans would know what dire fate befell those who tried to snaffle centaur body parts. But all he could summon was tea and cake.

Or maybe a pastry? A dire pastry. A scone!

Yes, a day-old scone with expired raisins in it, dense and dry and angry that its ingredients had not been used to bake something more winsome and moist and altogether delicious. A furious scone, an unwanted scone, passed over by hundreds of customers in the kuffee-shop pastry case, the Scorned Scone of Dry and Crumby Death!

With this thought, Vic raised his swole arms and clenched his fists at the chef. In his head he said something victorious and cutting and clever, but what came out was "Gyyyauuughh!" as he poured all his will into a desperate scone-summoning. The chef shortly ceased to exist as a single contiguous unit.

Blood sprayed behind what was left of the chef, and his eyes widened in surprise as a large portion of his abdomen was blown out by a deadly high-velocity scone, which had appeared in the air, rocketed forward, and disintegrated into crumbs even as it destroyed, leaving a visible hole clear through the man's torso.

A gasp from his left drew Vic's gaze, and he saw his server standing there agog as the chef collapsed and the knife clattered on the floor. The server held a small tube that probably contained a blow dart; he sucked in a big breath and prepared to blow.

"Gyyyauuughh!" Vic said again, and another scone missile obliterated his server's head. Vic hoped he'd remember later how he did this, because the results were every bit as good as lightning. Maybe even better.

Other people in the kitchen, however, noticed that two of their co-workers had just been exploded by a vengeful centaur wizard. Some of them screamed and ran, which Vic appreciated. Some of them grabbed knives and shouted, advancing on him, which he did not appreciate at all.

"You don' wanna come ammee, bros," Vic said, backing up until his rear hit a wall. He waggled his fifteen thousand fingers at the scone-peppered bodies as he made his case and staggered slightly to his right. "They wuz tryna take mah kinney. Whuh wuzzeye sposed ta do? Leddum havvit? Well, I *did* leddum havvit, hurr hurr. Lemme go, jus' geddoudda daway, an' nobuddy getzurt." Vic belched. "I mean besides dose guys, who are dead 'cause they're *kinney thieves!*"

An overweight dishwasher, seeing his chance for promotion, erupted with a battle cry as he approached Vic with a cleaver. Vic made a slashing motion with his right hand and shouted, "Yaaah!" and a high-pressure stream of scalding tea splashed in the man's face. He screamed, dropping the cleaver and clutching his burning cheeks. That gave the others pause, and Vic seized on it.

"Jus' lemme go. Jus' step aside. Don' threaten me an' I won' hurcha." Vic hastened toward the back door and the people in his way drew aside, flattening themselves against the walls and hiding behind barrels of mayonnaise and eatum. He had a clear path to the exit, but he was incapable of walking a straight line to it. He swayed and weaved on unsteady hooves down the length of the kitchen, shouting at everyone as he went. "Drop your knives! If you havva knife I'll make you hate cake, I swear!"

Someone promised he would pay for this. They'd get the city watch and call the local battle wizard. He was a dead centaur trotting!

Vic didn't like the sound of that. He didn't want to face a real battle wizard, one who could summon actual lightning. His only hope was to get back to *The Puffy Peach.*

Outside in the alley, Vic got tangled in rocking chairs and tried to move faster, hooves scrabbling on cobblestones, knocking over garbage bins along his way. But he did manage to miss the last one. He hoped that meant he was shaking off the effects of the poison and it wasn't just luck. He turned right, sending a couple of people sprawling in the street as he passed by the front entrance of the Knacker Barrel. Someone burst out of the door and pointed at him.

"Stop that centaur! He just murdered two people!"

There were some gasps and most folks screamed and ran away, giving him a clear path down the street.

"Iwwuz self-defense!" he hollered, both his shouting and the mad clopping of his hooves warning people that a fast horse was incoming. He hadn't known before today that he could summon scones capable of mortal blows, and it wasn't fair to cast him as the villain here. "They woulda stole mah kinneys!" he added, but he didn't think the current witnesses were understanding of his position. While most folks just let him pass with a blank stare, he saw some men and dwarves set their mouths in grim lines and flex, and when he risked a glance over his shoulder—which caused him to drift to his right and knock over a fishwife in a slippery tumble of salmon and petticoats—he saw that people were starting to chase after him.

He hoped Captain Luc would be ready to set sail and that they could actually get away without being blown out of the harbor by the inevitable battle wizard.

He should have listened to his dam and never trotted into this human city.

16.

IN AN OLEAGINOUS OFFICE
HARBORING SECRETS MOSTE FOULE

Morgan felt incredibly giddy. Here she was, stepping off a pirate ship and onto some creaky wooden docks that smelled like years of bad decisions, and it was great. Because it wasn't her sheltered life back in Borix. It wasn't on anyone's orders. She wouldn't be measured for a single froofy dress, and she might even pick up some of those dashing pirate pants with the ragged hems. She was in Bustardo and could do anything she wanted; she could go debauch herself with the other pirates, or shop for striped shirts and kerchiefs, or maybe even bathe! But instead she wanted to team up with an unelfly elf and investigate the sinister Mutae Mercantile Association. Because otters.

"What's the plan?" Alobartalus asked.

"First, we need some distance between us and the sea lions around here."

"Oh, they're not that bad."

But Morgan wasn't so sure. The Bustardo docks and shore were simply rotten with sea lions. Desperate for attention and even the tiniest sorts of nourishment, they barked and clapped and fought to interrupt every thought. *"Odd, odd, odd,"* they barked, splashing the passersby and befouling everyone's conversations and shoes and generally ruining everyone's day. When Al reached into his pocket and held out a piece of hardtack, Morgan jumped between him and the obnoxiously capering swarm of sea lions.

"Kindness won't work," she said firmly. "They're not reasonable. Give them an opening, and they'll overrun you. We don't have that kind of time to waste."

"Odd, odd, odd!" the sea lions clattered, and a few large ones muscled their bulk onto the shore and tried to galumph directly at Al, their beady eyes shining with avarice.

"I didn't think they'd actually come after me," Al said, nervously shoving the hardtack into his pocket and backing away from the oncoming menace.

"They definitely play on your good faith and altruism," Morgan admitted. "That's why the ship is fitted with such heavy chains—so they can't climb aboard and make a nuisance of themselves."

"But they seem so clever—"

Morgan slashed a hand at the sea lion standing on its nose and waggling its tail. "Performative cleverness is all a ruse. Don't fall for it. Keep walking."

They hurried away from the dock, glad to hear the obnoxious calls of the sea lions fading into the distance. At least the loud, offensive things were limited to the foul, chummy waters of the harbor and couldn't invade real life.

"Now that we're out of range, we should find a fishmonger to make sure Otto is well fed," Morgan said, for the otter was still draped around her shoulders and chirping at her every so often to remind her that he would enjoy a little smackerel of mackerel. "Then get ourselves to a Dinny's and see if we can't find out who's behind the Mutae Mercantile Association."

They quickly found a bustling market full of assorted mongers and got Otto a bucket of clams from a clammonger, and a small bucket of oranges for themselves from a fruitmonger, and a smaller bucket of bonbons for later from a bonbonmonger.

"I wonder if all the mongers buy their buckets from a bucketmonger?" Al asked, and that was the moment Morgan knew they would be friends.

They paused to sit on the rim of a bubbling fountain to enjoy their quick repast. Morgan could almost feel the citrus beat back an incipient case of scurvy, and it was good to taste food without the fumes of grog dulling her senses. Otto splashed in the fountain and ate his clams while floating on his back, and Morgan smiled at his adorable antics. She was happy that Tempest was following her dream, but she already missed her friend. At least she still had Al and Otto.

"So what's our angle at Dinny's?" Al asked. "Elf magic? Force? Stealth?"

Morgan wrinkled her nose. "Elf magic is messy, and force would bring the city watchmen pretty quickly. But I don't think we should go in there as customers either." She fiddled with her beard as she considered it. "Because then we'd have to deal with servers, and if experience is any guide, they've been trained to deflect questions about EATUM and ultimately say they don't know anything, which is probably true. We need to see the manager and get him or her to show us some paperwork. So I say stealth."

"Yes! Subterfuge. I like it," Al replied. "What did you have in mind?"

"I think we should pretend we're from the MMA."

"Great! Uh . . . how do we do that?"

"Well, first of all, we probably need to look like we didn't just walk off a pirate ship."

"An excellent point. A bath, then, and clothing that looks mercantile. Very middle management. Wrinkles easily and shows pit stains."

"Hopefully we can find something pre-wrinkled and pre-pit-stained, because we don't have all day." Captain Luc planned to ship out with the tide around sunset.

Al pointed to a large board off to one side of the public square in which they sat. It was plastered with notices and advertisements, and a small throng was clustered in front of it, reading them. "That might tell us where we can find a clothier."

They finished up their oranges, and Morgan checked on Otto. "How are you doing? Still eating?"

He squeaked at her. He'd finished off most of the bucket and only two clams were left. He'd made quite a mess, however, and she and Al had to pick up the empty shells and put them in the bucket after she set aside the two survivors. "We've gotta go. You want to come with us, right?"

Otto squeaked in protest as she stood up, and he put his little otter paws on the two uneaten clams.

"Go ahead and eat them. We'll wait that long."

Otto cracked open the shells with his sharp teeth and sucked out the mollusks inside in a minute. Morgan reached down to pick up the shells, and Otto used the opportunity to scamper up her arm and curl across her shoulders again. He was, of course, soaking wet from the fountain, causing Morgan to cringe a wee bit, but she figured she'd be bathing soon anyway. Being chosen by an otter was, after all, no small thing.

They joined the crowd in front of the board, looking for clothiers but finding mostly dwarvelish-potion vendors claiming that they had the absolute freshest and strongest batches of Ol' Chub's Tubby Nub Elixir for Potent Virility sold in convenient crocks. But there were also several notices advertising handsome purses for the capture or slaying of various criminals and, in one case, a hefty reward for the recovery of a lost lady.

"Oh, badger buns," Morgan cursed.

"What?"

She pointed at a flyer in the lower left corner and whispered, "That one's about me."

Al squinted at the artist's rendering of her likeness, which included long, flowing locks, a dainty dress, and an utterly hairless, ethereal face. "Looks nothing like you."

"I know. I'm glad I kept the beard and lost all the floof."

"Yeah, good call."

Morgan ripped the sheet off the board to study it more closely.

HAVE YOU SEEN THIS LADY FAIR?

THE LADY HARKOVRITA OF BORIX HATH GONE MISSING

STOL'N FROM HER COMFY TOWER BY SOME DASTARD

THE EARL OF BORIX WILL PAY HANDSOMELY FOR

INFORMATION LEADING TO HER SAFE RETURN

SHE MAY OR MAY NOT BE ASLEEP.

"You were stolen?" Al asked. "Uh, pardon me: *stol'n*, which is for some reason more sinister when pronounced as a single syllable?"

"No, I left on my own. My father just can't believe that. He thought I was property to be married as he chose, so of course he thinks I must have been stolen like property. Plus, as far as he knew, I was under a sleeping spell."

Al grinned at her. "And now you are a pirate. Not the career path he would have chosen for you, I'm sure."

"No. I was supposed to be married to Lord Vendel Vas Deference of Taynt, whom I've never even met." She crumpled up the paper and tossed it into the fire upon which a local vendor was roasting hot chestnuts of the non-equine variety.

"And are you happy now? You've defied your elders and you have an uncertain future and few resources, none of the comforts you're used to."

Morgan nodded and smiled. "I do miss pie, but I'm very happy. I'm seeing things I've never seen before. Making new friends who appreciate me for myself rather than for who my father is. And my future's quite certain, as far as I'm concerned: I'm going to save the otters."

"And after that?"

Morgan shrugged. "Turning the rich into the poor through piracy sounds like justice to me. Odds are they got rich through means far more villainous than piracy in the first place. If you knew how most lords and earls got to where they are, you'd need a long weekend with a brain leech."

"No need. I'm well aware. My uncle is a king."

Morgan looked at the elf with concern. "So you ran away too, I take it. What will you do now, Al? I know you were disappointed by the Sn'archivist. Are you going to head back to Proudwood Lighthouse?"

The elf's amusement faded. "I don't ever want to go back. Comfort is a trap. I'd much rather remain free, like you. And I think my disappointment was my own fault. I'd built up this fiction in my head about what the Sn'archivist was, and there was no way he could live up to it. Besides, he might have given us a clue about . . . all this."

"Really?" Morgan folded her arms across her chest. "Do tell."

Al leaned in and spoke softly. "What do you know about the Sn'archivist? Do you believe that he's divinely inspired by Pellanus?"

"I suppose it's possible, although I'm not sure I believe it, especially considering your Grand Huff after meeting him."

"Well, divinity is mysterious. And there's definitely a mystery here. The Sn'archivist just wrote a new book filled with only two words, repeated again and again: *otter balls.*"

"Why?" Morgan asked as Otto screeched in outrage.

"He said those words would save me in my most trying hour. That those were the words that I needed to hear, or was destined to hear, or something. Also, uh . . . there were two more words that he said were important . . ."

Al's eyes glazed over, horror suffusing his features, and Morgan shook him gently by the shoulder. "What is it, Al? Come on, you can tell me, no matter how terrible it is."

Al blinked, then gulped and licked his lips nervously. "This is going to sound ridiculous. I apologize in advance. But it seems we might somehow be saved by . . . my own butt."

"I beg your pardon?"

"Elf butts. Pellanus has supposedly been obsessed with them for decades, and the Sn'archivist has thousands of tomes on the subject. Apparently they're far more important than anyone realized."

"What the Pell . . . ?"

"I don't know," Al said with a shrug. "Like I said, it's a mystery. But perhaps you can now understand my disappointment. I expected knowledge. Enlightenment. Wisdom. And all I got was otter balls and elf butts."

"Right. Lots to unpack there. We'll get to that later. But look, Al, you don't have to go back and be what someone else wants you to be. I mean, you can, or you can choose to do anything else—that's all your decision, which should be made for your own reasons. Are you still willing to go with me to Dinny's?"

"Yes," the elf said, nodding nobly to emphasize his willingness. "We have a mission here. We should get to it."

It took them little time to find a dwarvelish inn and bathhouse: The Divine Suds was adjacent to the market and offered a quick *De-Slime the Grime!* option for sailors such as themselves on limited shore leave with limited funds. The owners cleverly offered basic garb as well so that sailors could get a new pair of trousers or a shirt that didn't bear a thousand stains. Morgan and Al each took advantage of this, consigning their old clothes to be bleached, restriped, and re-sold, and asked where they might find a clothier selling used uni-forms to complete their disguises. They were directed to Madam Merkin's House of Jerkins around the block, and there they found some sober forest-green jerkins made of scratchy, cheap-looking fab-ric with a few lines of fake-gold thread to suggest that they were at least adjacent to wealth if they did not possess it themselves. They agreed that getting the same color and cut would make it seem like they were wearing a company uniform. And, honestly, they couldn't afford much else. Until they hit the loot, Luc said, fickels would be scarce. They would even have to supply their own pit stains.

The nearest Dinny's was just a short walk away; the district near the docks was a bustling area catering to sailors and tourists alike. Morgan smelled the restaurant before she saw it, compelled by the delicious scent of cinnamon buns and crispy bacon. But once Alobartalus showed her the clever, glittering, elven-made urinal cakes hanging from every eave, she understood better the magic she'd been huffing with every breath. Nothing near a fisherman's wharf could smell that good without a lot of help, and Dinny's had its own greasy odor to cover up.

Morgan could see through the large windows that this Dinny's was packed. People shoveled EATUM into their faces, ignorant of what they were really consuming, ignorant of the true cost of it; despite what the menu said, it wasn't free. The sad emptiness of Otter Island had been testament to that. She reached up and gave Otto a reassuring caress, and he purred and went back to sleep. He would hopefully remain so and just resemble an unwashed mink stole, as long as no one looked too closely.

Steeling herself, she said, "Follow my lead," and strode into Dinny's, with Al close behind. A cheerful halfling hostess greeted them with a practiced smile.

"Welcome to Dinny's. Two for lunch?" she said. Her name tag read *Mallorie Butterbuns of the Muffincrumb Butterbunses,* and Morgan really hoped that was her actual name.

"No thank you. We're here to see the manager on a rather important health issue."

Mallorie's smile faded. "Oh. Wait here; I'll go get him."

They waited, and after a couple of minutes a harried man with light-brown skin, an untrimmed mustache, and an atrocious haircut appeared to meet them.

"Yes? I'm the manager. How can I help you?"

"Hello, sir. I'm Verna Veal and this is Ham Hamlin. We are from the MMA, and we're concerned about recent shipments of EATUM you've received. We're afraid some containers may be contaminated."

"Contaminated with what?"

"An infection that causes severe foot sweat, a shriveled tongue, and a dire possibility of intestinal explosion ending in a very sudden death."

Some customers who had come in behind them gasped and walked right out the door, and the manager's eyes flicked between the busy waiting area and Morgan. "Let's go back to my office."

He turned, and Morgan and Al followed close behind. "Have any of your customers reported feeling sick after eating here?" she asked his back.

"No."

"Well, if they died," Al said dryly, "they probably didn't report it because they went home and exploded."

"In my office, please," the manager ground out, tension in his voice. He was very aware that some diners were catching snippets of the conversation and looking uncertainly at their plates.

They walked through the hot and steaming kitchen, past a stack of barrels of EATUM waiting to be used, and into a small office with a desk piled high with receipts, employee schedules, payroll ledgers, and old menus of Dinny's past specials. There were also a couple of locked filing cabinets and a macabre motivational poster hanging on the wall. It was a painting of a tombstone, the name worn away by time but the grass doing quite well around it, and the bottom of the poster was emblazoned with the slogan TAKE HEART. SOMEDAY YOU WON'T HAVE TO MANAGE ANYTHING.

Once the door was closed, the manager rounded on them and crossed his arms defensively. "All right, what's all this, then? You're not the regular health inspectors."

"Yes, they regrettably blew up," Alobartalus snuck in.

But Morgan had a spiel all ready to sling. "Recent shipments to Kakapoh, Cape Gannet, and Bustardo may have been contaminated. Two people in Kakapoh have already died, and we have reports of shriveled tongues in Cape Gannet. We're relieved to hear you haven't had any problems so far, and we'd like to prevent that from happening. We need to examine your shipping manifests for just the past month to see if you received one of the contaminated containers."

The manager nodded, a bit of sweat on his forehead now. "Sure. Sure, I can do that, easy. Haven't even filed them yet." He rifled through the papers on his desk until he said, "Aha!" and snatched one from the pile, presenting it to them with a flourish.

Morgan scanned it, ignoring the shipment numbers and dates and looking only for names and addresses. Success! The EATUM had been shipped by the Mutae Mercantile Association on Mack Guyverr, with a Pellican Postale Service box accepting mail at Banhai in Teabring. Interesting. If one assumed that the mail would be near their place of business, that would put the location of Mack Guyverr somewhere in the Chummy Sea between Mack Enchiis and Banhai, rather than somewhere near Khugas or Sinuicho.

"Who's your sales representative?" Al asked, and Morgan blinked. That was a genius question. It would give them a lead to pursue, at least. She would not have thought to ask that.

The manager frowned. "Don't you know that already?"

"No, we're not connected to sales. We're troubleshooters. We work for the big guy."

The manager's eyes widened. "You work for Angus Otterman? You've met him?"

"Angus Otterman?" Morgan recalled the chewed-up hat they'd found on Otter Island with the letters ANG on a label inside.

"Yes. What's he like?"

Morgan improvised, making an assumption based on Otterman's name and the fact that he was more than willing to kidnap and kill otters to make his fickels. "Terrible," she said. "Fearsome."

"So I've heard!"

Al pounced. "What else have you heard?"

The manager gulped. "Well, uh. Only rumors."

Morgan didn't let it go. "What rumors have you heard *exactly*? And please remember that our report will go back to the inspection division, not to upper management."

"He . . . maybe eats people," the manager almost whispered.

"Maybe?"

"Well, a bit." The manager put his thumb and forefinger close together to illustrate the concept of a smidgen. "Just a little."

"Which people?"

"His employees on the island."

"You've heard he eats just a little bit of his employees? Like, one or two bites?"

"No, I mean, he eats all of a few of them."

Al asked, "Why would he do that?"

The manager shrugged. "I don't know. Maybe they misbehaved? Or they looked delicious or tried to unionize? I sympathize, believe me."

"You do? You want to eat your employees?"

The manager waved his arms. "No, no, that came out wrong. I sympathize with the employees who get eaten. Never mind. They're only rumors and nobody believes that stuff." Desperate to change the subject, he pointed at the shipping manifest. "So, did we get a contaminated shipment?"

"No." Morgan handed the paper back to him. "You're in the clear. Thanks for your cooperation."

"Who's your sales rep again?" Al pressed.

The manager responded without thinking, relieved. "Brenna Mac-Fleshgrinder."

Al and Morgan blinked, exchanging a glance. "Isn't that a troll name?" Al said.

"Well, of course it's a troll. All the sales reps are—hey, wait! You're not really from the MMA, are you? What is this?" The manager's eyes, half dead with dread and the spirit-crushing weight of customer demands before, now glittered with suspicion.

So Morgan kicked him squarely in the groin.

"Oof!" The manager curled in on himself and collapsed. Otto screeched a war cry. Al opened the door and they bolted out of the office, heading for the employee exit.

"Back to the ship?" the elf asked as he ran, huffing and puffing a little.

"Back to the ship," Morgan agreed, grateful for her superior physical fitness. "We have a target now. He employs trolls, kills a lot of otters, and occasionally eats all of some of his employees or possibly some of many of his employees."

"Or so the rumors go."

"We know two out of three are true. So that's reason enough to go after him."

Al chuckled as they exited the filthy, grease-spattered alley behind Dinny's and slowed down. "By Pellanus, that was fun! This is so much better than selling Morningwood rods to tourists. It scratches that elvish itch for mischief while also being useful."

The door burst open behind them, and they whirled to see the manager pointing in their direction. "There they are! Get them!"

Three rather tall and athletic Dinny's employees sprang into action, each of them holding a weapon and each of them bigger than Morgan and Al, and the manager shouted something at their backs, which Morgan didn't catch because Otto screeched in alarm.

"Well, this isn't better," the elf corrected.

"I agree," Morgan said. "I don't want to die behind a Dinny's. Run!"

17.

DISCOVERING THE MARTIAL
APPLICATIONS OF RED VELVET CAKE

Al had grown up being told that elves were superior to humans by most any measure, but the length of his stride and the capacity of his lungs were definitely areas in which he fell short. Unfortunately, the long-legged, EATUM-powered waitstaff of Dinny's had most likely been promised something insanely attractive by the manager, like fair wages or health benefits, if only they caught the two strangers in green jerkins. They were rapidly closing the distance.

Al sighed—or more accurately, wheezed—hating what had to happen next.

"See that alley up ahead?" he panted, flailing a hand in its general direction.

"You mean Obvious Hideout Row?" Morgan asked, squinting to read the sign.

"Yes, that one. Skid in there and hide between the conveniently placed garbage bins."

"How do you know there will be—"

"Because this whole neighborhood reeks of elvish knavery."

As Morgan darted down the artificially slimy-looking alley between two tall buildings, Al reached into a bag on his belt and pulled out a handful of glitter. He hated this trick back home and couldn't understand why elves still found it funny after thousands of years. He'd never used this particular glitter a single time, but now he would join legions of his ancestors in messing with humans in the name of magic, ultimate embarrassment, and possible near-death experiences that would make great stories one day.

Tossing the glitter in the air in his wake, Al followed Morgan and found her waiting, as he'd assumed, between two large garbage bins. As they watched from this handy hiding place, three tall humans in Dinny's uniforms ran directly into the cloud of glitter hanging in the air. One began coughing as if she were choking, one started whooping as if he were having an asthma attack, and one turned red and stopped breathing altogether.

"Are they okay?" Morgan whispered.

"Not really," Al whispered back. "But they were going to kill us."

Morgan tilted her head at him. "You really think they were going to kill us?"

"I don't know! I've never been involved in corporate mustelid espionage before! But as they're all holding EATUM-stained cutlery, I assumed that at least a serious case of sepsis was on the line."

"True. Are they going to die, though?"

The trio had begun to attract quite a crowd as they choked, whooped, and flopped around on the filthy cobbles. The audience seemed to think it was some sort of wrestling bard show and kept throwing coins and shouting, "Give him the chair!"

"They probably won't die, no. Elven glitter doesn't generally last too long. If it did, the king would never fill his cheese larder with bribes. So let's saunter to the end of this alley and join the crowd in whatever shady-looking eating establishment we find on the other side."

"How do you know we're going to find an eating establishment?"

Al stood, stretched his back, and sauntered with expert nonchalance. Morgan joined him, although her saunter looked more like she was dancing in slow motion; she must not've gotten to that part of the pirate manual yet, or at least had not done the practice exercises, Al thought.

"The thing is," he said, "elves like to mess with people. In the Morningwood, there's a predictable pattern for dealing with humans, a mixture of pretending to be the mythic elves of song while being randomly nasty when the humans least expect it. Outside the Morningwood, they tend to drop the mythical pretense and just lean into the random nastiness. It's obvious that this part of the city was masterminded by elves. The layout, the decorating touches, that hole in the wall of the bathhouse that looks so inviting but will probably be full of squirrels or acid leeches. And you can't trust it, can't trust the magic at all, because it's an elaborate farce. But at the same time, if you recognize the magic, you can use it to your advantage."

Up ahead, warm light shone out of thick glass windows, and a sign over a welcoming wooden door read: THE RAMROD INN.

"There it is." Morgan gasped in surprise, which Al's elvish heart enjoyed, much to his dismay.

"Exactly. An inn so conveniently placed that it's bound to be the breeding ground of tempestuous dungeon parties, star-crossed lovers, and raucous pie fights."

Morgan's sword made a threatening sort of rattle against her leather scabbard. "And you think we should go in?"

Al chuckled, pointing at the stone walls now blocking them in on either side and around back.

"I think we have no choice but to go in. That's how ramrodding works. But look at it this way: We're beyond the Dinny's cleavers for now. Might as well have a glass of mead, yarrrr?"

Morgan grinned. "True. What's the point of shore leave if you don't have a pint?" When Otto woke up and chittered winsomely, she added, "And perhaps there will be some clam juice."

Al pushed open the door. The crowd within was loud and tipsy, the floor exactly as sticky as one might expect. Overburdened servers hurried to and fro with platters piled high with meat and totted taters. The clientele ranged from small, tidy gnomes holed up in a corner with a large vat of pudding to an enormous troll stuffed into a booth and thumbing through a stack of *MacMurderclub* and *Watchtrolls* comic books. In between were various collections of humans, dwarves, halflings, and elves, although Al noticed that the elves were wearing hideous caps to hide their pointy ears.

As Al scanned the room for a table, someone shrieked in his ear with no warning, and he spun around, dagger already in hand.

"Morgan! Al! Thank Pellanus!"

Much to his surprise, it was Tempest, who looked like she'd jumped into a lake and been strangled. Her green hair drooping and her black robes sodden and six inches deep in mud, she had a mass of books under one arm and, of all things, an irate flamingo on a bedazzled leash.

"What are you doing here?" Morgan asked, awkwardly hugging her moist friend and earning a harsh flamingo peck in return.

"Did you miss your ride to the castle?" Al asked. "I swear, these elvish pranks . . ."

Tempest looked down, blushing. "No. I got there. I just didn't like what I found."

Morgan winced. "Lawyers?"

Tempest snorted, making her hair fly out. "Didn't even get that far. In between the labyrinthine transportation, the rudeness of the students, and the fact that they wanted me to wear a shirt with a roach on it, I just realized it wasn't the school for me."

Al first heard and then saw a booth empty of human bards, who announced their exit with a peppy tune performed on kazoos, and he led his companions toward it. A weary halfling man cleaned the oiled wood with a paisley handkerchief, and they sat.

"Well, it's not the only school," Morgan began cheerfully. "There's Hillygorny and Batbuttons and—"

Tempest held up her books. "I think I'm going to do mail-away courses. Now that I've got Mingo"—she tried to pat the flamingo, but it upchucked shrimp-speckled white goo onto her hand—"I can learn by correspondence." She smiled warmly at Morgan. "And stay on the ship."

Morgan visibly brightened. Al smiled, too, and wished that he had a friendship like these two women did. He'd never actually met an elf he liked, and the tourists to the lighthouse had come and gone swiftly, staggering away with tubs of Morningwood grease and grumbling about how he wasn't a proper elf at all. The king had ordered Al to bed as many women as possible to spread the elvish seed, but the closest Al had come to seduction at the lighthouse was when an older woman with cataracts had wandered into his upstairs apartment and confused him with a famous human bard named Ned Sheerin.

As Tempest wiped off her hand on a napkin and described her horrific time at Bogtorts, Al knew without a doubt that the school was run by elves as a joke. It stank of their humor and their ill-fated attempt to breed pet flamingos for profit. But Al wasn't going to say that; Tempest felt silly enough as it was, without knowing she'd chosen a school that would likely hand out disappearing diplomas if not turn her into a newt outright.

"I'm glad you'll still be around," he said, at what felt like a polite break in their conversation.

Tempest gave him a warm smile. "Me too," she said.

The waiter arrived to take their drink orders, and Morgan told Tempest about their trip to Dinny's. Tempest made the appropriate noises of horror and victory and scratched Otto behind the ears. Al asked about her journey from the school, and Tempest explained that she'd simply made the most sensible choices heading back to the city proper and had discovered that the parts of Bustardo not recommended by the school were far less annoying.

"And so I went down Auspicious Avenue, and then the road dead-ended into this inn, and I was starving, so here I am," she finished. Al noted that she had entered from a different side of the building than they had, which was good to know. Elves often enjoyed planting fake doors just for the joy of watching humans run headfirst into them.

Soon their drinks arrived, and Tempest ordered a ginormous salad of greens and shredded roots dubbed the "Rabbit Bonanza," while Al and Morgan begged off, having eaten their fill of oranges and bon-bons earlier. Otto, still feeling safe and full from his bucket of clams, sighed contentedly and went back to sleep on Morgan's shoulder.

Tempest was complimenting them on their lovely new jerkins when the door from Obvious Hideout Row burst open and bounced off the wall, startling Otto awake with a squeak. Vic the centaur bar-reled in on unsteady hooves.

"Halp!" Vic shouted, wobbling a little. "Dey wanna eats me! I'm d'lishus an' it's not mah fault!"

"Oh, my gosh," Tempest murmured, trying to hide her face under her hood. "He's drunk. So embarrassing. He doesn't see us, does he?"

The centaur danced farther into the dining space, his hooves slid-ing on the mead-sticky floors. Trembling and wheezing, Vic smacked a dwarf woman in the face with his tail and nearly trod upon a gnome, then spun in circles, apologizing profusely.

"What is he even doing?" Morgan murmured.

But Al could tell something was wrong. He rose and hurried to Vic, grabbing the centaur's flailing hand and patting it.

"Hey, buddy. It's me, Al. What's going on?" he asked softly.

Vic leaned down, his eyes leaping from left to right. "Mah *kinney*. Hoomans tried to steal it! For eating porpoises!"

Al could see that Vic was either very drunk or possibly drugged. "Someone wants to eat porpoises?"

"No no no. Chef wanna eat mah *kinney*. He gimme droogs in mah ohmeal."

"And where is this chef?"

"He dead! Cuzzee sploded. But udder hoomans, Al, they affer me! They all wanner eat mah giblets!"

Al glanced at the open door and around the inn at all the curious faces. "We've got to get out of here," he said, mostly to himself, as Vic kept turning away to offer his heartfelt apologies to people who desperately wanted to get out of his radius before he accidentally stepped on their toes.

"What's up?" Morgan called, and Al hollered back, "We need to leave. Now."

"But I haven't had my Rabbit Bonanza," Tempest protested.

"No time, sorry." He tossed her his bag of remaining fickels—careful not to throw the bags of various elven powders—and soon she and Morgan joined him near Vic, their bill paid and their waiter tipped, for they weren't *that* sort of pirate.

"We're going now, Vic," Al said gently. "Back to the ship, where it's safe."

"Where zits safe," Vic agreed, nodding vigorously.

"What happened to him?" Tempest asked, her face wary.

"From what I can tell, someone tried to drug him and steal his organs."

Tempest's teeth suddenly seemed sharper as she scowled. "They *what?*"

"They're alwaysh trying to steal my lucky arms." Up close, it was easy to see that Vic's pupils were wide and black. Whatever he'd been given, it had to be potent to render a fully grown Clydesdale centaur stallion nearly insensate. These people—they meant business.

As if in punctuation, the door from Obvious Hideout Row swung open again, causing all the hungry halflings to wail in dismay and the gnomes to scoot under their table, pulling their hats down over their eyes. Three imposing humans in Dinny's uniforms burst in, one holding a bloodstained cleaver, one holding a butcher knife covered in bits of gore, and one holding a bread knife that looked like it had seen some rancid butter. Behind them stood the most frightening thing Al could imagine: a pleasant but self-satisfied watchman, aware that he reeked of authority and righteousness.

"That's them!" the cleaver holder cried, pointing at Al and Morgan. "They tried to kill our manager!"

"He threatened us first!" Morgan shouted.

"Why do all theesh people wanner chop up their customers!" Vic yowled, and Al was grateful to see Morgan pull her sword and step in front of Vic.

"Now, see here," the watchman said, because that's what they almost always said as they tried to work through whatever was occurring. "You can't just go around nearly killing managers, even if you want to, and even if they usually deserve it."

A smattering of timid applause went up around the room, mostly among those who looked like managers and were wearing tight cravats cutting into well-fed jowls, glints of terror in their beady eyes suggesting fear that someone might have noticed they were cooperating with business owners to exploit their workers.

"I only kicked him in the nards," Morgan explained. "I never tried to kill him. If I did, he'd be dead—" The door slammed open yet again, interrupting her explanation, and some angry dwarves and humans in white aprons crowded in, pointing at Vic.

"There he is!" a dwarf shouted. "That centaur killed two people at the Knacker Barrel!"

"They desserts it! They drogged me!" Vic shrieked.

"My friend was indeed drugged," Al said, hands up and voice gentle. "He acted in self-defense because they poisoned his food and attempted to harvest his organs without his consent. With your permission, we'll just take him back to our ship and trouble your fair city no more. Call it squaresies."

"That's not how squaresies works!" the Dinny's lady with the bread knife cut in. "Or policing! You can't kick someone in the nards and then beg off!"

"Or murder one of the city's finest chefs and walk away because you were drugged!" the dwarf added.

"I'm afraid they're right," the watchman said, and he did look sorry about it. "We can't have people nard-kicking and chef-killing willy-nilly and then traipsing away. Think of all the almost deaths we'd have on our hands."

"And the *actual* deaths!" the dwarf chimed in. "Let's not forget that centaur killed two people, all right? They're super dead!"

"Since they're already super dead," the watchman said, frowning down at the dwarf, "they can afford to be patient, can't they? The nard-kicked manager of my favorite restaurant needs justice *now*, however, so I hope you'll forgive me, Master Dwarf, for hewing to clear priorities."

"Yes, sir," the dwarf said, looking down as if his beard required sudden inspection.

The watchman shook his head and then turned to Al and the others apologetically. "I'm afraid you'll all need to come with me to the dungeon while we administer justice fairly and as swiftly as possible considering the backlog we have and our staffing shortages. Budget cutbacks, you know; nothing to be done, but we should have you on the docket in a few months."

"Nuh-uh!" Vic said. "I'll cake you firsht."

"Kick me?" The watchman's face purpled and he pointed a finger at the centaur. "Are you threatening me, an officer of the law? How dare you!"

"Hnngh," Vic said, bringing his fists together, and a gorgeously moist three-layered red velvet cake fell from the ceiling directly onto the watchman's head, making his face disappear entirely. "I said *cake* you."

"Oh, that looks so good. I'm so hungry," Tempest moaned.

"Let's get out of here!" Morgan said, gently steering her friend toward the front door. Al likewise gave Vic a little push from behind, and it looked like they might make it. But before they could open the door, the Dinny's employees rallied and screeched their war cries, surging past the caked watchman with their weapons raised and their greasy faces alight with fury.

Morgan met the encrusted butcher knife with her sword, sending sparks and bits of dried EATUM into the air as diners dove under their tables or tapped their feet extra loudly for their bills. Then she delivered a straight kick to the ribs of the wielder, driving him back into the flailing watchman and sending them both to the floor in a mess of red crumbs and cream-cheese frosting. Tempest tugged her flamingo out of the fray and hunched under an empty table. Al allowed himself a brief moment of frustration at that; every good pirate knew that you had to defend your shipmates. That was why he had his dagger drawn in one hand and was poking around in a pocket with his other hand, guarding Morgan's flank from attack. There was no way he was going to simply hide or exit and leave Morgan to fight alone.

Vic spun and kicked the lady with the bread knife into the dwarves behind her, who wanted a piece of him too. He kept mumbling, "Sorry! Sorry!" as he did, and Morgan knocked the cleaver out of the other man's hand and twirled her sword expertly at him. Al was about to engage the fellow with the butcher's knife, who had risen to come back for more, when something smacked him right between the shoulder blades, robbing him of breath and leaving his new green jerkin drenched in what smelled like mustard.

"Sorry!" someone shouted. "I'm not a very good shot!"

"We need to go," Al muttered as Morgan parried a strike of the butcher knife. "With this much chaos, someone's going to get hurt for real, and Vic's still not himself."

"I've never heard him apologize so much," she said, lunging and leaning as she fought off the various blades that hungered for her heart and Vic's hocks.

"You keep them off Vic, and I'll get Tempest."

"I'm here," Tempest said, popping up between them. Al had assumed she was hiding due to terror, but she looked quite pleased with herself and was unencumbered by her hateful flamingo. "I sent Mingo on with a message for Luc, telling him to have his sturdiest gangplank down and be ready to sail."

That made Al smile; he'd been wrong about her. She hadn't been hiding at all. "Clever girl," he said.

Tempest scowled at him. "Intelligent woman," she barked back. "Now, let's go."

Knowing it was, again, a last resort, Al told his friends to hold their breath as he whipped out his bag of powder and blew it in the direction of their foes, causing them all to suddenly fall prey to restricted airways. Tempest led them through the door to the kitchen, past a veritable army of halflings in aprons, and swiped a Rabbit Bonanza off the kitchen pickup area, which might have been hers anyway and which they had actually paid for. Al, firmly clutching Vic's big, meaty hand in his, tugged the centaur along, murmuring the sort of pleasant things one said to horses and children on cough medicine. "Come on, now. Giddyup. This'll be fun. Let's just go this way. Oopsy, that's a big vomit! Right into the soup! They'll taste that later! And here's the nice outdoors."

Once they were outside in an alley—as all kitchen exits everywhere opened into alleys—Al slammed the door and placed a conveniently sized trash barrel under the door handle, hoping that it would hold whatever wheezing, knife-wielding maniacs tried to follow. With Vic wobbling along, moaning about kinneys and lucky arms, they hurried down the dark and twisty alley and onto the main thoroughfare. It had seemed so busy on their way into the city, but now, after the Ramrod Inn, it felt downright pleasant and freeing. The masts and sails of many ships bobbed against the late-afternoon sky, and the crew scrambled toward the docks at the fastest pace they could manage while keeping Vic on four hooves. All his former bravado and rudeness were gone; whatever drugs he'd been given made him pliable, friendly, and almost childlike. He thanked everyone repeatedly, apologized ad nauseam, and somehow kept coming up with fresh sandwich cookies, which he pressed into everyone's hands with tender compliments about their eyes. He gave more than a few to Al.

They were very near the time when Captain Luc had said they'd be sailing—they might even be upon the very hour. Tempest forged the path by shouting, "Watch out! I'm eating salad here," and she did so with gusto and plenty of noise, squirting more than one unwary passerby with the wayward juice of a ripe cherry tomato. Morgan and her sword followed right behind, and Al hurried in the back, herding Vic along as he distributed excess cookies to the local urchin population. Although he kept looking back, Al didn't see any Dinny's uniforms, much less a red-velvet-crumbed watchman or someone turning the terrifying puce of anaphylactic shock. As they stepped onto the docks, he was quite sure they were safe. Qobayne and Queefqueg waited for them by the gangplank, their swords out and ready and their faces wearing Pirate Expression Number 19, the ol' "I'll Stab Ye in the Face," as they waved everyone aboard. Al had never felt so welcome.

Getting Vic up the gangplank was not the easiest job of his life, and they ended up promising him a big vat of drug-free oatmeal if he'd just get onto the ship. Al was the last to embark, and he exhaled a sigh of relief as the gangplank was pulled up and the ship began to sail.

"That was neatly done, me hearrrrties," Captain Luc said. "Sending on the histrrrrionic birrrrd like that. I'll not have some line cook cuttin' out the orrrrgans of me crrrrew. How ye feelin', Vic?"

The centaur tried to puff out his chest but looked more like a toddler who'd eaten a frog. "Wobbledy, Cap'n," he answered.

"That'll do. Get some rrrrest, and Milly Drrrread'll see to that bowl of grrrroats we owe ye." As Vic wandered off to his favorite sleeping corner, the captain fixed Tempest with a beady eye. "So ye've come back, lass?"

She smiled shyly. "If you can use me."

"We can always use cunning hands on *The Puffy Peach*."

"But I still won't perform any healing."

He bobbed his head. "Didn't expect ye to. And Miss Morrrrgan. How was yourrrr time on shorrrre?"

Morgan narrowed her eyes and looked to Al. "We've uncovered more clues about the otters. Have you ever heard of Mack Guyverr? Or Angus Otterman?"

"I have not, but we can ask arrrround as the jourrrrney continues.

I don't like this business, ye see. Them otterrrrs are a pirrrrate's frrrriend. Neverrrr done nothin' mean. Just bein' joyful. We need joy on the sea." He briefly entertained a look of painful, faraway longing, then snapped out of it and directed Feng to walk on.

Feng went to the ship's wheel, where the captain cocked a beady eye at the docks. Down below, a crowd was gathering as the sun dipped toward the horizon, and they were getting a bit shouty and pointing at *The Puffy Peach*. Al saw that one of them was the caked watchman, his features smeared with cream-cheese frosting and a desire for vengeance. Al had no way of knowing if they would be pursued, but he privately bet that Captain Luc was planning for contingencies if they were.

"*Odd, odd, odd!*" the sea lions cried, amassing as they sensed a captive audience already roused to anger. No, Al would not miss Bustardo.

Morgan and Tempest went belowdecks, probably to finish Tempest's extreme salad. After a few moments of standing around on the deck, looking awkward, the flamingo shrieked and fluffed its feathers and followed them.

Since Qobayne had the rest of the crew jumping to various duties, that left Al and Vic some space alone on the deck. Although Al had heard stories about the supposed benefits of centaur giblets, just like he'd heard the stories of unicorn horns and mermaid tails, he'd never seen such ignorance on display—never thought anyone would be cruel enough to attack a centaur in a public restaurant in a civilized town. Before Vic, centaurs had seemed to him like another far-off magical creature, as impossible as a gryphon. But here was Vic, standing eight feet tall, shivering by himself under the yardarm, terrified and alone.

"You okay there, buddy?" Al asked, giving the centaur a friendly pat on the wither.

Vic's flesh shuddered, and he looked over his shoulder and down at the shorter-than-usual elf.

"That was scary," Vic said quietly. "I guesh . . . I guess nobody's ever tried to really hurt me before."

Al nodded. That was indeed a scary feeling. He well remembered the moment an unhappy customer at the lighthouse had straight up punched him in the nose because they'd disliked the way they looked in the Uglification Mirror of St. Uggo. He'd felt surprised and angry and hurt to think that someone would actually cause him injury.

"Yeah, the world can be a scary place. But it's over now. And you've got friends."

Vic sighed, a deep and sad sound, and gently folded his legs until he lay on the deck. Now they were almost eye to eye, although Vic had to have ten times Al's mass.

"Nobody likesh me," Vic said, and Al could tell that although time and exertion had cleared some of the drugs from his system, whatever it was, it was still lowering the centaur's inhibitions.

"I think maybe they don't know you very well yet. You can be . . . a little aggressive."

Vic looked down. "Imma centaur. S'what I'm *s'posed* to do. Be all swole and manly."

Al grinned, loving the feel of the deck swaying under his feet again; the sea changed things for him, and maybe it would change things for Vic too. Al was a different person now that he'd left the lighthouse and given up on the Sn'archivist. He was still learning who that person was, but he liked him better than any other version of himself so far.

"I don't believe in the word *supposed*. I think you can do whatever you want. Out here on the sea . . . well, anything is possible. You don't have to be swole or manly or whatever. You can just be Vic."

"Thosh guys didn't like Vic. They wanted to kill me."

"It wasn't personal."

"Theresh nothing more personal than murder!"

Al had to agree. "I just mean . . . they weren't trying to kill *Vic*. They were stupid bigots trying to kill a random centaur. If they knew you, I bet they wouldn't want to hurt you. And it's sad for them that they won't get that chance."

Vic's eyes, which had always been full of fury and swoleness before now, began to tear up. "You're a real nishe guy, you know that? Even if you're all covered in mustard. Somebody tagged you real good back there." And then Vic was crushing Al in a hug that smelled strongly of horse. And mustard.

"And you make really nice cookies," Al whispered at the end of the hug.

Vic drew away and looked at him, suspicious and angry and terrified all at once.

"I don't . . . there's no . . . no cookies!" Vic growled.

Al held up one he'd stuck in a pocket on their run. "These are delightful. And that cake was perfect, I could tell, even though I never had a bite. You don't have to hide your gift," he said.

But Vic wouldn't meet his eyes. He took the cookie and tossed it overboard. "Yesh, I do."

Al patted Vic's shoulder. "Maybe you won't have to one day, then."

Al walked away and climbed up to the crow's nest, sighing happily. His grin melted away, however, as he looked back at the docks of Bustardo. A rather large and ominous ship was detaching itself from the wharf, unfurling many lengths of canvas, including skysails and moonrakers. The red light of sunset revealed that the mainsail was emblazoned with a stylized gryphon, the insignia of the Pellican Royal Navy. And there were strange dark thunderclouds forming above it in an otherwise clear sky.

"Battle stations!" Captain Luc squawked before Al could say anything. "They be afterrrr us, lads, and they be brrrringin' the wizarrrrd along!"

18.

PELL HATH NO FURY LIKE
A PARROT SCORNED

❧❦❧

Filthy Lucre felt a cold thrill shudder through his cloaca at the sight of that gryphon sail. That was a royal clipper ship, specifically designed to take down pirate ships like *The Puffy Peach*. Very little cargo space but a whole lot of sails and guns. Facing that would be enough excitement on its own—cause for equal measures of dread and drama, the very best of stress cocktails to remind one that living should be full of such stimulation and should not descend into comfort or downy nests or giant vaults filled with sunflower seeds. But there was more: They had a battle wizard on board! He was summoning a bank of gloomy gray storm clouds, touched with magenta and purples as the sun kissed them good night, white strands of electricity combing through them like fingers through poufy hair. Soon he would send the clouds over their ship and strike them with bolts of lightning, setting their ship aflame or punching holes through their hull, dooming them to death by either fire or water. It was a strategy Luc had seen before, but he had never been on the receiving end of it until now. Those Bustardian bastards meant business.

But that particular wizard made Luc's gizzard wither, for he'd seen those exact storm clouds before. Once upon a time—not so long ago, really—Luc had perched on that very shoulder, back when said wizard was young and raw and itching to buck the system. Back when he could only conjure a tiny puff of a cloud. He'd been eager to listen and learn, eager to plunder the juicy cargoes of the rich and redistribute the spoils among the crew and give generously to the holy Cinnamonks, who lived on the fourth Toe Island and ran an orphanage and shelter for the wayward souls of Pell. That's where Luc had found him, in fact. Had *saved* him. And now—Luc's feathers flattened, crushed by hurt feelings.

He remembered well the day he'd visited the Cinnamonk Succor Shelter and met young Ramekin Cloudtalker. A grimy kid with warm brown skin, he'd lost his parents to giants in Corraden who had twisted them into meat pretzels and eaten them with horseradish. Ramekin had no other family, so he'd been shunted down to the Cinnamonk orphanage, where he learned to be grateful for their radical kindness and resentful of an unkind system. He'd worked on the monastery grounds for many years, and when he was all grown up, he had the strongest yet tenderest shoulder to perch on as a result of that manual labor.

Luc adopted him, and soon afterward young Ramekin manifested a talent for summoning storm clouds and lightning; his surname was no mere patronym but a magical heritage. Oh, the coastlines they'd pillaged! The squiffy mushrooms they'd bootlegged! The barrels of grog they'd gulped, the shanties they'd sung, the timbers they'd shivered! The chests of gold and silver they'd taken from greedy merchants and given to the Cinnamonks!

And then they'd met some navy recruiter in Cape Gannet, a pretty woman with a bright smile, and she'd spoken honey-throated promises to Ramekin—lies, really—and corrupted him to the side of government. The side of the establishment. Ramekin abandoned Luc, rejected the anarchy of piracy, and now he was in the navy, protecting the rich friends of the crown, the same people who'd done nothing for Ramekin the orphan. The same people who'd refused to pacify the giants so that kids like Ramekin wouldn't have their parents turned into meat pretzels in the first place. Luc's old friend was looking after *those* interests now, a living betrayal of his younger self. He'd been seduced by the narc side.

And now here they were, facing each other over the sea. Luc's crew had offended the rich people of Bustardo. And said people had turned to the government to protect their fortunes and wounded pride.

So it came to this.

Running was not an option. Even if they could outrun the clipper ship—a highly doubtful scenario—they could never outrun the lightning that Cloudtalker would send against them. There was only one desperate chance at survival: destroying the other ship before those storm clouds could drift above their own sails.

"Come about! Brrrroadside!" Luc ordered, and Feng spun the wheel. "We fight now orrrr we die! Qobayne, get me a rrrrrange-finding shot soonest!"

"Aye, Cap'n!" the boatswain replied.

Boots stomping on the deck and shouts floating in the air ruffled Luc's feathers, but that was only the beginning. Soon there would be the sulfurous stink of gunpowder on fire and humans soiling their britches, the cacophony of explosions and people screaming at the end of their lives. Sinking that clipper as it came at them head-on would be a tall order for even an expert crew, and Luc did not have an expert crew. But maybe some would survive. They were not so far from shore that drowning was a given if they had to abandon ship. And Luc himself could always fly away, so long as lightning didn't take him down. He had no assurance of that, however. This lightning would not be so random as that provided by nature. There was no nature behind it, after all. It would strike more or less where Ramekin Cloudtalker told it to strike. The question was, would he destroy his old ship and everyone on it or merely cripple them and deliver them to the dubious care of the navy, which would most likely throw them in a dungeon for a couple of weeks before executing them in public?

Or . . . perhaps Ramekin didn't know whose ship he threatened? No, that was impossible. He knew this vessel, even if no one had told him that he was after *The Puffy Peach*. He knew every creak of its boards, every booby trap in Luc's cabin, and even where the seeds were stowed. He knew that Luc was aboard. He knew that Luc *knew* that he knew. And still he pushed those storm clouds their way, rumbling with promises of electric death, of sizzling internal organs with white-hot heat until they popped like popcorn. His betrayal could not be more complete.

"Fire!" Qobayne shouted, and a single cannon boomed, and they watched the seas to see where the ball splashed down. It was well short of the clipper ship and off to its port side.

"Load up! The rest of you, angle up ten degrees! Fire on the captain's command!"

Luc closed his eye for the space of three seconds and muttered a prayer to whatever face of Pellanus gave a damn about pirates. He hoped he or she would be more invested in this battle than the side that cared about the Royal Navy.

He opened his eye and cried out, "Firrrre!" and heard the hiss of the fuses before they lit up the gunpowder and the cannonballs boomed out of their orifices. The ship rocked under the collective recoil, and the balls all missed, but they got much closer to the ship than did the original range-finding shot.

"Very good! Reload!" Qobayne said. "Lower five degrees, because they're coming fast! Fire when ready!"

This was good. Qobayne would adjust each shot as needed, trying to get one good hit, maybe two, and that might be enough to let them escape. Get the clipper to take on water and it wouldn't be so fast.

They had to score a hit soon, however. Those storm clouds were starting to drift in their direction. And there, on the prow of the ship, distant but plainly visible, a familiar figure clutched at the air. In the ruddy twilight he was a pinkish phantom, but well could Luke imagine his mouth moving as he cajoled the winds and vapors to do his bidding and deliver death straight ahead.

The rain began to sheet down between the two ships like a dishwater curtain; the cloud bank advanced and thunder growled, low and threatening. Visibility decreased as the sun kept sinking and the clouds and rain darkened the skies.

Two cannons fired, and Qobayne told the others to hold while he watched the splashdown through his spyglass. Distance was correct, but they still missed to either side. He yelled for fine adjustments to the others and told the first two to reload, but then there was a squawk of protest.

"Oi! Where you going, girl? Get back here!" Qobayne barked.

"I have something that can help!" Morgan's voice floated up from the cannon deck.

"It's muscle and gunpowder that can help us now, nothing else! Ye don't abandon your post during battle stations!"

"Trust me!"

"How about ye obey orders or get your arse keelhauled!"

"I promise it will work!"

"Fire!" Qobayne said, and Luc lost what was said next, if anything, as the other two cannons doubled up. One of the shots missed entirely, but the other plunged through the fo'c'sle behind the battle wizard, and that probably meant they'd be taking on water soon if it continued through the hull. A cheer went up on *The Puffy Peach,* for that was a damn lucky shot.

But neither Qobayne nor Morgan was cheering. They were raging at each other, the boatswain trailing behind the young woman as she protested that she had the solution to the problem and the old sailor pointing out that the cannons would do just fine if only she'd stay at her station.

The rain caught up with them and began to soak the deck and the sails. Any bolt of lightning that struck the deck would travel through that moisture and fry a few people here and there.

"We need to take them out now!" Feng said, stating the obvious.

"We need anotherrrr hit, that's most definite," Luc agreed.

And then the human woman Morgan stood before him, cheeks blackened with gunpowder and soot, Qobayne coming up quickly behind, his face purpled with rage and shouting that every single part of her was mutinous rubbish, and through the din she shouted at Luc, holding a gunnysack and a small golden something in her hand.

"Captain, I have a gnomeric firebird!" she said. "Permission to deploy it against the clipper ship?"

Luc flared all his feathers in shock and relief. Where on Pell had she gotten one of those? She answered his question before he could ask.

"My cousin was a pyromaniac and he gave it to me for my sixteenth birthday."

"Perrrrmission given," Luc crowed, "but only against the sails, do ye ken? Not against the hull!" He could not consciously send death directly to Ramekin, but with a set of burning sails, they'd never be able to catch up to *The Puffy Peach*.

"Aye, Cap'n!" Morgan replied.

"Do it now!" As Morgan scurried away, Luc swiveled his head to the right. "Qobayne! Let's deal with herrrr disobedience laterrrr. Sails full! Now we rrrrun! Feng, come about south by southwest!"

Qobayne began to shout new orders, as Luc watched Morgan tinker with the gnomeric construct and whisper instructions to it. He'd only heard tell of these things before, and he hoped it worked or they'd all be lost.

It was fortunate that Feng spun the wheel when he did, for the bolt of lightning that lanced down through the air singed only the topsail as it missed the deck and struck the ocean to starboard, electrocuting any fish or sea lions that might've been swimming nearby. Tendrils of electricity flickered in the clouds as another strike built up, and the air smelled of blackened tuna, but not the good kind.

Queefqueg laughed maniacally and chucked Mort on the shoulder as they jogged to the stern to taunt the battle wizard, in defiance of Qobayne's orders. That was the danger of letting Morgan go unpunished: Others would think it fine to shirk their duties as well. But Luc said nothing, because he was worried about the more important question of whether Morgan could deliver them to safety or not. If she didn't get that firebird away, they were done for. She was fiddling with its tail-feather controls and whispering to it. The eye sockets glowed like orange coals. It belched a sulfurous, crackling affirmative and then took wing in a shower of sparks as terminal flames built within its breast, a forge of phosphoric heat that would burn even in water.

With the firebird in the air, Luc's attention was drawn back to Queefqueg, who was standing near the tiller, shouting imprecations at the clipper ship.

"Ha ha! Missed us, you fool! You empty peapod! You will never! Sink! This! Peeeeeach!"

A bolt of lightning shut Queefqueg up before Luc could. It lanced down and cooked him to a smoking cinder. He tumbled into the sea, a shocked moan of grief from Mort following him into the deep.

Feng also cried out, and Luc felt his pain. Well did he know the abrupt tug of loss, a sudden emptiness where one used to be full, a missing piece of a pie that would never be whole again.

But there was nothing to be done but tell Feng he was sorry. "Look, Feng, and see how ourrrr rrrrevenge begins," he said, extending a wing at the gnomeric firebird, which was simultaneously growing smaller and brighter with distance. "Ourrrr special deliverrrry should serrrrve us well, if it not be shot down."

Two different strikes did indeed try to knock the small firebird out of the sky, each weaker than the one that killed Queefqueg, but they missed, and there was not enough charge built up in the clouds to summon more.

"Yes! It's going to hit!" Luc chortled.

The firebird flew straight into the foresails and erupted in white-hot flames. Once the sails caught and a hole had burned through, the fiery orange edge of it climbing upward, the machine flew on to the mainsail and duplicated the procedure, then onto the mizzenmast and its host of sails, until they were all alight and the crew was scrambling for buckets and rain barrels.

The white clouds churning over *The Puffy Peach* receded, Ramekin wisely recalling them to deal with the fire on his ship, but the gnomeric firebird wasn't done. Not satisfied with lighting all the sails aflame, Morgan had instructed it to fly up near the crow's nest and explode, which it did in a horrific pop of streaking flames. Balls of fire dropped down all over the deck, igniting both wood and sailors.

And then the screaming began.

Already the sails of the clipper ship were shriveling to blackened ashes, and Luc knew he'd won, at least for the moment. But he worried about that last explosion—or, rather, he worried that Ramekin would be hurt by it. He had to know if his old perch was safe.

"Sail on, Feng," he ordered. "Make forrrr Cape Gannet. I'll be back soon. Unless I'm not, and then Qobayne is captain, ye underrrrstand?"

Feng knew better than to argue. "Aye, Captain."

Filthy Lucre launched himself off his current perch in search of his former one. The one who'd melted, rebuilt, and then broken his tiny parrot heart. His plumage was a riot of red and yellow against a canvas of dark sky, clouds of gunsmoke, and sheets of rain. He found Ramekin aflame and rolling on the bowsprit, trying to put out the gnomeric phosphorous fires in his robes when nothing would.

"Rrrramekin! Rrrramekin, why did you do it? Why did you leave me?"

Ramekin gritted his teeth. "Augggh! Come to gloat, have you?"

"No, no, no! I only meant to burrrrn the sails. I didn't intend you to get hurrrrt. I didn't want any of this."

"Yes, you did! You were plotting against me. Keeping me from greatness. Now look what you've done! Arrrrgh . . . !"

"No, *you* did this, Rrrramekin! You should be with me on an endless quest for booty! Instead, you let some rrrrecruiterrrr seduce you to darrrrkness!"

The young man snarled, baring his teeth. "You were always jealous of me! Of my power!"

"No! You werrrre my chosen one! You werrrre supposed to *destrrr-roy* the Rrrroyal Navy, not *join* them! Brrrring balance to the seas, not leave them to capitalists!"

Ramekin's skin popped and hissed as flames licked at his limbs. "I hate you!" he cried.

"You werrrre my perrrrch, Rrrramekin! I loved you!"

The battle wizard made no reply but only screamed as flames consumed him and he tried to summon more rain to extinguish the fire. With a last mournful squawk, Filthy Lucre banked around in the air and returned to *The Puffy Peach,* his feathers pelted by rain, the sky deepening into a dark cobalt as the last sliver of sun sank into the sea.

The Royal Navy would put the Clean Pirate Luc at the very top of their MOST WANTED list now. Reward fickels would skyrocket. He'd be a hero to some pirates for incensing the navy to such measures. But other pirates wouldn't hesitate to turn him in. He might have survived this battle, but there would be no safe harbor for him now. And he was about to sail directly into the most heavily patrolled waters in Pell: the Seven Toe Straits.

Perhaps this resourceful girl Morgan would prove useful there as well. She was the opposite of Ramekin, now that he thought about it: Raised in the highest echelons of privilege and comfort, she now wanted to tear that all down instead of defending it.

It was too bad that her shoulder was too bony yet to serve as a decent perch, and that she was still very raw as a sailor—disobedient too, which had to be dealt with. But shoulders could be built up. And seamanship could be learned.

Yes.

There could be another.

19.

IN A TUREEN AND DEEPLY DISCOMFITED
BY FLOATING TURNIP CHUNKS

Even down below, in her bunk, where Qobayne had sent her as soon as Captain Luc had flown away, Morgan could tell the exact moment that the battle was over. The ship seemed to still, and several voices cried out in triumph. Not the captain's, though, she noted. Her firebird must've worked. But the success, she knew, would be as ephemeral as a moth party around a campfire. The manual had made it very clear what happened to pirate crew who defied their captain during a battle. There would either be many lashes across her back, her wrists bound around the mast, or there would be plank-walking, her component pieces gobbled by sharks and crabs. Either way, the heavy steps headed her way were not going to bring thanks and her flesh would not fare well. She'd have to be taught a lesson, or else her insubordination would spell out mutiny.

Sensing her trepidation, Otto chittered and skittered into a corner. She didn't blame him.

The footsteps turned out to be Feng's, and the captain was perched on his shoulder, his one eye moist and gleaming in the lantern light. "Well, lass. Ye've won us the battle," Luc began, grudgingly. "An' prrrrivately, I'm grrrrateful. But forrrr the sake o' the otherrrrs . . ."

"I have to be punished."

"Rrrright. But that can wait until morning."

Luc flitted down to a chest of drawers and Feng excused himself, clomping up the stairs. The captain regarded Morgan with a sad eye and shifted around on the chest, either out of nervousness or a dislike for the surface.

"Is something else bothering you, Captain?" Morgan ventured.

"Aye. Me hearrrrt is heavy today. That battle wizarrrrd . . . Well, the two of us have a historrrry. And that firrrrebirrrrd ye sent saved *The Puffy Peach* but also ensurrrred we'd neverrrr have a futurrrre togetherrrr."

Luc radiated pain, and Morgan teared up on his behalf. "He's dead?"

"As good as. Unless he's got a heck of a magical healerrrr with him, orrrr possibly a fleet of gnomerrrrric inventorrrrs, therrrre ain't much left of him to piece back togetherrrr. I'll admit to ye, and only because we'rrrre alone, that I'm not quite surrrre how to go on."

Morgan sat, giving her captain her full attention. His feathers were puffed out, his beak clicking nervously, his eye not quite meeting hers.

"The same way anyone does, Captain. One foot in front of the other. Or one flap of the wings. Whichever hurts less." She paused and looked down. "And for what it's worth, I'm sorry."

Luc bobbed his head several times. "No no no no no. Saving us all was the rrrright thing to do. But enforrrrcing ship's discipline is also the rrrright thing to do. Now, go to sleep, if you can. Tomorrrrow morrrrning, be it sunny, you'll take yourrrr punishment. Betterrrr to get all the pain overrrr with quickly."

"Not the plank, then?" Morgan asked, voice trembling.

Luc squawked, almost a laugh. "And waste a fine sailorrrr who saved me ship? Neverrrr!"

He flapped away and up to the deck, and Morgan spent most of the night awake and dreading the next day. The rest of the sailors stayed up awhile to celebrate with an extra cup of grog as their adrenaline ebbed, and when they tumbled belowdecks in the early morning, she feigned sleep so no one would say anything kind or damning.

The next morning, as soon as the sun kissed the sky, she rolled out of her hammock and forced her posture from meekness to a straight back and stubborn chin. For all the times she'd disappointed her father, she'd never felt this bone-deep shame. Perhaps it was because he represented a set of values to which she could never subscribe, and therefore disappointing him was not only inevitable but the proper thing to do. She hated disappointing Luc, though, because she respected him and wanted to be like him someday. But she'd take her licks and endeavor to earn the trust of the crew again. Even if it hurt, even if she would have scars, it would be worth it to stay on *The Puffy Peach*.

As she climbed the ladder to the deck, she was surprised to find fresh blue skies and fluffy white clouds, the oppressive storm clouds fled with the night and presumably the demise of the battle wizard. She took up her day's duty of swabbing and swabbed her heart out. When the other sailors rose, hungover and exhausted, to stare at her, she noted who looked apologetic, who looked avid, and who looked crafty, judging their future mischief based on how her insubordination was punished. When Luc gave him a nod, Qobayne walked to stand, hands clasped and face grim, beside the mast; Luc perched on Feng nearby. Morgan didn't need the captain's nod to know that was where she had to go. Tempest hurried to her side and they wound their arms together, while Al joined them but kept his distance.

"You did the right thing," Tempest assured her in low tones.

Morgan sighed. "Yes, and as you know the law, you know I must be punished."

"But not too horribly," Al added. "We would've died if you hadn't acted. Like, in chunks, nibbled by barracuda. And eventually even smaller chunks, inhaled by whales and filtered through their baleen and possibly honked out as ambergris." The elf shuddered, having grossed himself out.

As they passed by Vic, he clasped Morgan's hand, and when she opened it again, she found a tiny, dainty pastille in striped colors. When she popped it in her mouth, it seemed to have a soporific effect, and her nerves calmed like the sea on a still day.

"Morrrrgan, forrrr insuborrrrdination, you will rrrreceive ten lashes," Luc said, his voice loud and ringing.

She reached Qobayne and held out her wrists. He indicated that she should wrap her arms around the mast, and he bound her wrists together on the other side with rough rope, whispering, "On behalf of the ship, I thank ye," so low she thought she imagined it. Tempest gently pulled up Morgan's new jerkin, exposing her back to the crew. A few sniggered, low and mean, and she remembered that too.

And then she felt the whip on her skin for the first time.

She set her forehead against the weathered wood, clenched her teeth, and accepted the pain. She wouldn't have done anything different. Ten strokes, even and sure. Not shirking, but not excessively deep either. Whatever was in Vic's pastille helped soften the pain.

When the lashes were over, the crew cheered. Not because they reveled in her punishment, but because it was over and she had borne it well. Looking up, she found Qobayne smiling with tears in his eyes and Luc fluffing his feathers in relief. Tempest pulled down her jerkin for her and put a warming hand on her back, and after a moment the pain ebbed out of her completely.

"Tempest?" she asked in wonder.

Tempest looked away, scratching at a dark, raised patch of bark like a scab on her wrist. It was the second such mark on her warm-brown skin.

"I hope it wasn't too horrible," she said.

"It feels fine now," Morgan told her. "Thank you."

But her friend hurried away to her bunk, and Morgan was left feeling loved but confused. What had Tempest just done? For Morgan . . . and to herself?

After that, the crew treated Morgan differently. She felt less like an outsider, more like a real pirate. Old Milly Dread cuffed her on the shoulder and gave her an extra splash of grog. Mort tried to tell her a dirty joke but forgot the punch line and started crying about Frij and Queefqueg instead. Feng dropped a tube of Bimli's Bearded Nation Skin Laceration Maceration near her feet, a popular dwarvelish remedy, and told her to use it thrice daily on her back until it was gone. She was promoted to a slightly bigger cannon. Apparently public ritual embarrassment was tantamount to popularity as a pirate. She should've gotten herself beaten weeks ago.

Her relief wasn't to last, however. Some days later, she awoke to the clabber of the ship's bell as Captain Luc squawked, "All hands on deck! Evasive maneuverrrrs! It's the POPO!"

Morgan yawned and looked over to where Milly Dread was dropping out of her own hammock.

"POPO?" Morgan asked.

Milly spat on the deck, then helpfully rubbed it in with her shoe. "That be the Pellican Ocean Patrol Office, lass. Private navy of the merchant oligarchs, trying to protect their interests from pirates in the Seven Toes since the Royal Navy don't do such a good job on its own. If they get their tidy paws on us, we'll be in the brig, or hangin' from the gibbet! If ye love yer otter and treasure, ye'd best help move the *Peach* around!"

The old woman darted upstairs, spry and vital, and Morgan followed with Tempest and Al. Up top, the deck was a jumble of work, with sailors adjusting sails and generally doing their best to make *The Puffy Peach* move, slick and sure, through the glistening waters.

As no one shouted orders at her, Morgan went straight to the captain, her friends trailing behind her and Vic creeping in to listen.

"Captain, what can we do?" she asked. "Blast holes in their hull?"

Luc squawked irritably and didn't look away from the spyglass Feng held to his eye.

"Shootin' at the POPO's suicide. Speed's the only thing forrrr it, lass. If we can find an island beforrrre the POPO finds us, we can claim sanctuarrrry. They can only take our booty and heads if we'rrrre asea, though sometimes that doesn't stop them. Still, we have no booty to defend, only ourrrr lives. So we shall head to land as fast as possible."

"One of the Toes?" she asked, as she'd always wanted to see the Seven Toe Islands for herself.

But Luc shook his head. "Not close enough. We'll have to hit something small, a barrrr island. Most likely uninhabited. All we need is a bit o' sand."

Morgan joined the crew in following whatever orders Qobayne gave, her heart racing. She considered everything in her Chekkoff's gunnysack but couldn't think of anything that could help the situation like the firebird had. The sails puffed out and the ship cut through the water like an angry parent's words through a playground. An island soon materialized up ahead, and it looked like a veritable paradise, like the Toes Morgan had always dreamt of. Sugary white sand; swaying palm trees; a black volcano rising in the center, sizzling and sighing white smoke over the lush jungle.

As she and Al climbed the rigging to help with the sails, he said, "I've heard of islands like this. Wild places full of stranger dangers. Sometimes they're inhabited by folks who've never left their lands, who don't even know that the rest of Pell exists."

"That doesn't make sense." She shielded her eyes and peered at the swiftly approaching island. "We can't be the first Pellicans to land here. It's not like the island is hiding. It's just across the strait from Cape Gannet. The POPO patrol here."

"They're savages on that island!" Mort called down from the crow's nest, his eyes a mite wild; he'd been drinking a lot, after losing both Frij and Queefqueg. "The ladies wear naught but coconuts over their bubbies, and the men wear fig leaves over their danglies, and they all has bones through their noses! Some of 'em are cannibals even!"

"Uh, that's super ignorant," Morgan said, looking up at the leering man. "You can't just assume that every place that isn't your home-town is weird and backward. Or equate clothing and accessory choices to a lack of civilization."

"I been to islands like that plenty much," Mort shot back, all sniffy. "Weird piercings and everything. So seems to me like *you're* the ig-norant one, Miss Never Been to a Toe Before."

"I only hope they have fresh fruit and no elves," Al said, more privately. "We must be ever vigilant against the twin evils of scurvy and glitter."

Morgan huffed a sigh. "We'll find out soon enough. I'm sure they're just people, like anywhere else."

"Spoken like someone who ain't never met cannibals," Mort growled from overhead.

Things happened quickly after that. *The Puffy Peach* ran aground, which was really more of an abrupt push into the white sand like a ten-year-old belly-flopping into a pile of sugar. Luc ordered the crew off the ship and into the shadows of the trees, urging them to scatter. Morgan zipped down the rope ladder with Tempest and Al and hur-ried across the beach and into the jungle. Poor Vic was left on ship with Qobayne to bribe the POPO, as there was no way to lower the gangplank for him to disembark. Without a dock it was too steep, and Morgan tossed the nervously jigging centaur an encouraging smile and wave as Feng and Luc led the crew deeper into the island's interior.

"Qobayne knows what to do," Luc said as the Pellican cruiser pulled up and let down its anchor. "*That wasn't me, Officerrrr. How fast was I going? The ship isn't mine. Holding it forrrr a frrrriend.* 'Tis an old dance, ye see. No way they can pin anything on us now. But let's go a bit inland, just to be surrrre."

Morgan would've expected the island to be hot and sticky, with mosquitoes everywhere, but it was balmy, with fond breezes and no biting bugs. They soon found a neat trail cut through the heavy trees and ferns, and she ran a finger along the straight, clear slice in a broad leaf. It reminded her of her father's cadre of gardeners who spent their days trimming the hedges into perfectly symmetrical lines.

"This is a pretty well-maintained trail for uncivilized people, eh, Mort?" she said, holding up the leaf.

"Anybody can wield a machete," he scoffed. "They just do it gooder here."

When smooth paving stones appeared, she didn't have to say anything. Mort's jaw was already dropped. The trail became a road, and the road eventually led up to a grand gate set between flawlessly smooth stone walls with attractive seashells set into the mortar. A beautifully hand-painted sign read: WE WELCOME ALL TRAVELERS TO THE CITY OF CLAN NABI.

A guard in flowing red robes opened the gate, bowing. Morgan noted that he wasn't wearing armor—or any weapons. So maybe he was more of an usher than a guard.

"D'ye speak Pellican?" Captain Luc growled.

The man smiled. "Of course. We are people in the world. Welcome, visitors, to the City of Clan Nabi!"

Morgan would've expected someone born in the sunny islands to have darker skin tones, but the guard's skin was as white as hers, covered up by his loose robes and headdress.

"What's this all about, then?" Luc pressed.

But the guard bowed them all in silently, closed the gate behind them, and waved a hand to indicate they should follow him. The city opened up before them like a blossom unfurling, the beautiful clay buildings shining as white as the sands and the roads all paved with shells. There were no huts, no coconut brassieres. The people walking to and fro greeted the pirates with wide, welcoming smiles, bowing, in all manner of dress. Morgan noted flowy robes that appeared to be from Qul, as well as dresses and capes from the cold, wet borders of Borix and everything in between. She didn't see any gnomeric or dwarvelish garb, but she didn't see any gnomes or dwarves either. It was all humans, and they all seemed overjoyed to find a filthy, nervous crew of pirates stalking through their midst.

Morgan had a million questions, but she'd learned her lesson on ship. Only Luc could talk here.

"What's the deal?" Luc asked again, when the guard didn't answer his previous inquiry.

"Clan Nabi welcomes all visitors. I shall take you to meet our queen, long may she reign."

"We don't have anything to trrrrade," Luc warned. "An' we can't pay a hefty docking fee."

The guard laughed. "We put no price on friendship."

Soon they walked up glimmering white steps toward a beautiful casita flying the flags of all earldoms. Morgan glanced nervously to and fro to see if there might be another poster with her face on it, but the art was limited to tasteful murals of flowers and fish and poems written in iambic pentameter about health, wealth, and the importance of regular massage. When she glanced to Mort, the shock in his eyes was at least somewhat gratifying, but she suspected it was mostly because the island conformed to his conception of "civilization" and not his racist expectations.

The guard must've really enjoyed throwing doors open dramatically, as he kept on doing it, and finally they were admitted to a plush royal chamber. They were a shoddy group, huddled there on the fine silk carpet, covered in gunpowder and sweat, but the queen rose from her throne and walked toward them, arms open in welcome. She was a beautiful woman in her forties, probably, with impeccable style. Her gown was tasteful and perfectly matched her jewelry and tiara, and her blue eyes were deep set and soulful. As she stood amidst her finery, she looked very much the jewel in a crown, a bright spot in a flawless mix of patterns and colors designed solely to highlight her beauty.

"I am Queen Hannabelle of Clan Nabi, and I welcome you to our city," she said, her voice slightly accented in a way that made Morgan wish to hear her speak again. "Please join us. Bathe in our hot springs. Sit at our table. Drink of our wine. We are glad you have come."

"Now, wait herrrre," Captain Luc broke in, sounding salty. "I been sailin' the seas a long time, and nobody everrrr issues an invitation without expecting a rrrrepayment of one sorrrrt orrrr anotherrrr. Do ye have eyes on me carrrrgo? Have yerrrr folk already begun to plunderrrr the ship?"

The queen's smile was placid and gently amused. "Oh, no! We get so few visitors, you see. We love news of the outside world. Books and stories. Believe me, Captain: All we want is your company."

"Well, we ain't givin' up the weapons," he hedged.

"We would never expect you to."

"And we ain't stayin' long."

"Oh, I'm sure you won't be with us long."

Someone in the court chuckled at that, and Captain Luc ruffled his feathers and looked around, dissatisfied but stuck. "Aye, well, then. We'll take advantage o' the hospitality, at least until the POPO is done interrrrogatin' me men back on the ship. And then we'll give ye a bit o' grrrrog and set sail."

Queen Hannabelle clapped her hands, and a variety of handsome handmaidens and handmen scurried into the room in matching jerkins and led the sailors away by gender. As for Luc, he flapped a wing at them and said he'd stay with the queen. As Morgan left, she glanced back once and saw Queen Hannabelle indicating that the parrot could take his rest on an elaborate perch.

"I love the architecture here," Morgan said as their handmaiden led her, Tempest, and Milly Dread up hundreds of shell-encrusted stairs to the opening of a cave in the side of the volcano. The handmaiden made no reply.

The stairway was lined with flower baskets and afforded a sublime view of the island and its majestic buildings. Once inside the cave, the girl gesticulated at them, suggesting they disrobe and enjoy the mineral springs heated by the nearby volcano. Milly Dread wasted no time dropping trou and cannonballing into a glowing blue pool.

Morgan was unsettled but also feeling, well, a bit superior. "I hope Mort learned something about making assumptions. This civilization is under better rule than my father's earldom back home."

"I guess. But something is bothering me," Tempest said. "The captain's right. Nobody is this nice. They have to want something."

"Or maybe they *are* that nice. They have so much, everything they could ever want. Except sensible clothing for this climate—did you see that some of them are dressing like they're in Borix instead of a tropical island? But never mind. They must be governed wisely. I didn't see a single hovel or urchin. It must be quite exciting to finally have visitors to shake things up. Our castle was like that—deathly boring. The most exciting thing that happened most years was a pie-eating contest."

"Maybe."

Morgan could tell Tempest felt off too, and why wouldn't she? After the grave error of her attempt at secondary education in Bustardo, she probably would have trouble trusting a good thing. But even an overly suspicious dryad couldn't deny the siren call of a hot bath after weeks on the ship, washing with tepid seawater. Giving her friend a smile of encouragement to show that everything was fine, Morgan slipped out of her clothes and into the pool, her entire body sighing into the heat. There were soaps and unguents and a lovely deep conditioner Morgan applied to her hair and beard, and the handmaiden took turns pulling the women out one by one and scrubbing them thoroughly with oily salts and pumice stones.

"You have such lovely skin," the handmaiden sighed.

"Thanks. Can I wash out my hair now?" Morgan asked.

The handmaiden laughed. "Oh, that won't matter," she said.

"Why not?"

The girl just laughed again, and Morgan decided she wasn't quite right in the head.

Next, Morgan was ushered onto a cushioned stone table and given the best massage of her life. Every muscle was rubbed until it loosened and melted, making her sigh and wish pirate ships kept a muscular masseuse on staff. Up until the moment she felt completely relaxed, she hadn't even realized how stressful her time on ship had been. In the hot pool again, she floated on her back, glad she'd left Otto behind on the ship with Mingo. Otter poop in the sacred pool would've been most embarrassing. Milly Dread had returned from her massage even gassier than usual, and the handmaiden had suggested she soak a bit longer. The old woman said nothing, merely ate the cucumber slices she'd been given to put over her eyes and resumed floating on her back, half asleep.

When it was Tempest's turn for her massage, the handmaiden fussed over the two dark splotches on her arm, and Morgan grew angry with the girl when she saw how embarrassed Tempest was by the attention.

"They won't come off," Tempest said, on the verge of tears. "Please stop trying. I've scrubbed them and plucked them and burned them, but they won't go away. They're just . . . part of me."

"It's a shame, is all," the girl said. "The queen will be most upset."

"That she has some marks on her skin?" Morgan barked. "How is it any of her business?"

The handmaiden dropped Tempest's arm and turned away. "All business here is the queen's business. Please continue to enjoy the waters."

With a small bow, the girl took her scrubs and sprays and pumice stones and soaps and hurried out of the cavern.

"What the Pell was that all about?" Morgan huffed. "I've had servants, and that is not how they're supposed to act."

"It's okay." Tempest sadly rubbed at one of her spots as she stepped back into the pool. "It's just how things are."

"Well, I'm not okay with that. I don't care how pretty their city is and how nice they are in front of the captain; they can't go around insulting us. My father used to talk to me like that, and I didn't get this far from home just to hear—oh!"

Morgan didn't get the chance to continue her diatribe, as her feet were swept out from under her, tugging her head underwater. She barely had time to hold her breath, and then the rushing water was yanking her deep into a hole in the center of the cavern. Flutters of warm skin passed her, and she knew that had to be Tempest and Milly Dread. She could only hope they were holding their breath too and that, whatever was happening, they would soon be able to breathe again. She fought the current, but it was simply too strong. Perhaps this was how the tide affected the island, sucking the bathing pools out to sea, or maybe something had happened with the volcano. All she knew was that it was pitch dark, and she flailed and panicked as her body was sucked through what felt like tubes; then there was a rush of air as she fell and splashed down into water that was shallow enough to stand.

"What happened?" she asked, wiping salt water out of her eyes.

"We got played," Tempest said.

"That was the worst waterslide ever."

Much to her surprise, the new voice belonged to Al, and he sounded more defeated than he ever had so far. When she got her wet hair out of her eyes, she could see why.

Their entire party, naked and scrubbed clean, was in a giant tureen full of hot water and vegetable chunks. Bits of turnip and cubes of onion bobbed against her skin, making Morgan shudder. Under the tureen was a jumble of wood, including what had to be the chopped-up hull or deck of a ship.

"See? See? I told you there'd be cannibals! They's gonner boil us alive!" Mort shouted triumphantly, right before Queen Hannabelle appeared with a flaming torch.

20.

SURROUNDED BY BUTTOCKS MOSTE MOIST AND MEATY

Tempest surveyed the situation with anger thrumming in her sap. The moment the water had sucked her down, she'd known: It was all a trap. The gorgeous beach, the well-kept road, the shining city, the careful scrubbing of flesh, and the dip in what must've been some sort of antibacterial marinade. She'd known something was wrong, but she'd gone along with it and ignored her gut.

Guts, she realized, were always to be trusted.

The moment she saw the queen's smug face and the capacious white bib over her cooking apron, she knew that Mort's triumph at being right regarding the existence of cannibals would most likely end at the edge of a serrated knife. She did a quick head count around the pot to ensure all the sailors were accounted for, carefully avoided looking down at anyone's jiggly danglers, and then hunted around the room for Captain Luc. They were in something halfway between a ritual chamber and a kitchen, which did not bode well. The captain was no longer on his fine perch and was instead confined to a fussy cage in the corner, the door firmly shut as he beat himself against the metal bars.

"This is an outrrrrage!" he shouted. "Ye can't go arrrround eating my crrrrew!"

Queen Hannabelle turned to him and smiled graciously. "Watch me, glitterpigeon," she said.

"Wait!" Morgan called next. "What can we trade you for our release?"

The queen shook her head and held out her arms. "Your flesh. My people are hungry."

"Then maybe hunt like normal people? Or raise a few chickens?" Al said. "I mean, instead of waiting for strangers to come around. Most civilizations have figured this out already."

The fire was high and well-stoked, and the water was getting hotter. Tempest had to doggy-paddle to save her feet from the bottom of the red-hot tureen. She could just see over the edge, and the view was chilling. The people of Clan Nabi were cheerfully preparing for a great feast, raking the coals in a huge oven full of metal racks and greasing what looked like an enormous sausage grinder. Children roasted vegetables and fruits over a grate while wearing bibs with chubby little stick figures of people stamped on them. Tempest hated to admit it, but these people did, in fact, look very happy and sleek and healthy. And like they had no qualms about eating pirates.

"You are not the first visitors to question our ways," Queen Hannabelle said as she sharpened a knife with unnecessary violence right in front of them. *Zip zop. Zip zop.* "But you see, eating nu ham is what has allowed us to flourish. Instead of spending our time moving goats around, growing corn and grain for feed, plucking chickens, and rebuilding big fences, we wait until a ship stops by and gather up our next harvest. We have meat, and we have timber, and we have whatever else is on board. Books and scrolls, magic potions and clothing. It's the most elegantly simple solution to all of life's problems."

"But it's stealing!" Al roared. "And murder!"

The queen stared at him. "You are pirates, are you not? All pirates do is steal and murder."

"We're not really that kind of pirate," he shot back, slightly chastened. "So far, we've just rescued a bunch of otters and tried to save our centaur from kidney thieves."

At that, an excited murmur went up around the crowd.

"A centaur!" Queen Hannabelle's face lit up with lurid glee. "We'll send a contingent out to your ship to collect it. I hear their internal organs are succulent."

"That is so ignorant!" Morgan wailed.

"If it makes you feel better, *your* internal organs are succulent as well," the queen reminded her, resuming her knife-sharpening as several of her people ran out through a grand door, carrying ropes and cleavers and long sausage forks. "In fact, pretty much all internal organs are healthy and delicious, if prepared the right way. Don't even get me started on bone marrow. And brains! Like butter! So good on toast."

"That's it," Tempest muttered to herself, her arms tiring from treading the water. "Queen Hannabelle, have you heard of mad human disease?"

The queen cocked her head. "I have not."

"It's awful. You get it from eating the brains of humans who've eaten sick cows. It drives you insane, and your body pretty much rots around you."

The queen considered this, and the pirates waited with bated breath that actually smelled like bait because they ate a lot of fish.

"Even if you're lying, we can't risk it," the queen finally said, and Tempest exhaled in relief.

"So we won't eat your brains, I suppose. We'll use them for tanning leather. We make really cute water-resistant shoes here." She held out her foot, and Tempest almost complimented her flesh-sandals before she realized her gambit had failed and the Nabi still intended to eat her and her friends.

"Maybe eat one of us at a time?" she offered, hoping a route to escape might present itself later on. "So the meat won't go bad?"

Queen Hannabelle rolled her eyes and shook her head. "Do you think our food hasn't tried to talk us out of dinner before? You're not unique. You're just chatty bacon. We've developed methods to preserve meat with salt, with acid, with smoke. We've spent centuries building our unique culture around nu ham, and I don't think that's going to change because some spotty-wristed girl with limp hair likes to argue."

Tempest took a deep breath, feeling rage bubble up from her burning feet. How dare the queen speak to her that way, insulting her skin and hair, patronizing her while in the process of killing her? Morgan tried to pat her arm in a calming sort of way, but she pulled away. She could feel something happening to her, but she wasn't sure what it was, so she tried to edge away from the others. "Stay back," she whispered to Morgan and Al. "I'm not sure . . . what . . . is going to happen now . . ."

"Don't be so sensitive," the queen said. "It's not personal."

"I told you she was weird about her moles," the handmaiden whispered to the queen, and as they had a private laugh, Tempest felt her hair lift up, her toes and fingers beginning to spread and change.

With a snap like lightning striking, Tempest's arms stretched out in either direction, somehow both flexible and hard, somewhere between a branch and a vine. Leaves sprouted along her limbs, and she reached for the edge of the tureen and lifted herself free of the steaming water. Her toes had shot out like roots, and she used their tendrils to clamber out of the water and stand, dripping, on the stone floor below. She was naked, and yet she wasn't. Rugged brown bark had sprung up to cover her skin like armor. Her hair writhed overhead, a nimbus of branches and leaves.

"I'm not meat anymore," Tempest growled. "So who wants a little fiber in their diet?"

"What—" the queen began, but Tempest reared back and punched her right in the nice white teeth.

Of course, it wasn't a woman who had cracked those canines—it was a dryad in full temper, and the queen flew back, her head turned the wrong way on her neck and her teeth sproinging out like popcorn. Seeing Hannabelle lying on the ground like that, soft and meaty, aroused something Tempest had hoped never to feel, and for just a moment she craved the hot gush of blood.

But no. She would not stoop to the level of Clan Nabi, and she was not yet a willowmaw, and she had friends to save. As the queen's people abandoned their feast preparations to scurry around their broken ruler, Tempest turned to the tureen, wrapped her vine fingers around the hot edges, and pushed it over, spilling her friends and hot water over the floor. The water drained away in a creepily efficient grate, and naked pirates struck the ground and struggled to their feet before plucking up the various barbecuing accoutrements strewn around the room, brandishing them as weapons. Clan Nabi was caught defenseless, nothing but bibs between them and the death they were so accustomed to doling out. It was swiftly apparent they weren't trained in any sort of self-defense, that they had grown all too comfortable and complacent with their cruel ruse, and Tempest soon had Luc out of his cage as the crew demanded—at spatula-point—new garb from their previous captors and cooks. Soon the pirates were dressed in the robes and jerkins the Nabi had taken from past visitors, and the Nabi were naked and tying their bibs over their groins. Only Tempest remained unclothed, clad solely in her hardening bark.

"Arrrre ye okay, lass?" Luc asked, his claws clicking against her woody shoulder.

"I'm not dead," Tempest said, her voice creaking like an old tree in a wind.

"That ain't what I asked."

"I don't know what's happening," she said, her voice as mournful as willows soughing in the wind. "This shouldn't happen . . . until I'm old . . . unless I use my powers . . ."

"Listen up," Luc squawked in her ear. "It's not time. You'rrrre Tempest, a nice lass who swabs a mean deck. You like law books,

220 DELILAH S. DAWSON AND KEVIN HEARNE

you've a fine mind, and you'rrrre kind to yourrrr frrrriends and always stand up for yourrrrself. You'rrrre brrrrave but soft, so just rrrrememberrrr what that feels like: being soft. Think of little grrrreen leaves in sprrrring, aye? Soft bunnies and wee ducklings."

"But I'm so hungry," Tempest moaned, envisioning branches snapping up tender little birds and tucking them into her trunk.

"Then we'll get ye some nice harrrrdtack, or maybe some fish."

"I'm a vegetarian. But I also just really want to eat people."

"Then you'd be as bad as Hannabelle and herrrr Clan Nabi," Luc argued.

Tempest's leaves shook as her branch tendrils reached out for Mort, who was frozen in place, white as the toga he was dressed in.

"Trees are beyond good and bad," Tempest said, her mind half lawyer and half monster.

"Look, you don't want to eat Mort," a new voice broke in. It was Al, standing just out of reach. "Think how terrible he'd taste. A Mort torte? Abort, abort! Nobody wants that."

Laughter burbled up through Tempest's trunk, making her branches quiver. "Mort torte. With a glass of port!" she wheezed.

"You wouldn't want to eat Milly Dread either," Al went on. "Unless you like leather. Probably break a branch on her hide. No Milly Dread bread."

"Or smirky jerky," Tempest giggled, her tendrils backing away from Mort as she considered Milly's edibility.

"And Captain Luc—"

"Leave me out o' this, you!" the bird squawked.

"I bet when you pluck him, he's about the size of a winged rat. And his first name is Filthy. You'd probably get flukes."

"Luc . . . flukes . . ."

"Would make you puke," Al added.

Morgan ventured up, tentative and quiet, and put a hand on Tempest's shoulder. "C'mon, Tempest. You're the nicest person I know. Come back to yourself and let's go save Vic."

Surrounded by her friends, looking into their eyes instead of at their meaty buttocks, Tempest took a deep breath and focused inward, feeling the rough *ticktock* of her heart in its woody cage. She thought of soft things, of sweet things, of friendship and tea and the sea, and she let the anger drain out of her system. Sap pooled around her ankles, and leaves fell from her hair, and bark crumbled away like an especially bad sunburn, and her warm brown skin was soon skin again. Luc fluttered up from her shoulder as she shook off the last of the treeish trappings.

Only her arm showed any change: The scaly parts had grown together, creating a patch of woody bark about the size of a shoe, something that could not be easily overlooked again. She'd been so careful not to use her healing powers that she'd forgotten that rage could end her just as quickly as mercy. Rubbing at the bark, she reminded herself that she'd saved dozens of lives. That it was worth it.

"Oh, no," she muttered. "I forgot. They're still going after Vic and Qobayne!"

"Aye, lass, that they arrrre. Ye done good. But we must now get to *The Puffy Peach* and see what's become o' the grrrand dame."

He was worried about his people too, Tempest realized, even if he couldn't say it outright.

Armed with pokers, forks, machetes, spatulas, and a wayward pineapple corer, the strangely dressed pirates ran out the door that the last batch of Nabi had used. The stone road led back into the city, where dozens of people wearing bibs and carrying silverware cried out in dismay as they passed. The defenseless guard at the gate couldn't stop them, and soon they were barreling through the jungle, well-moisturized and smelling of garlic and oregano but furious at nearly being eaten. Right when the paving ended and the jungle truly became jungle again, a giant hippopotamus burst into their path, grabbed Mort with its curving ivory teeth, and dragged the screaming man away into the heart of the thick green foliage, leaving only splattered plops to mark the trail.

"Mort!" Feng lunged after the hippo, taking a few steps after the fleeing betonkus and waving his spatula.

"It's too late to save him!" Luc shouted to his perch. "We can't fight the beast! We have no rrrreal weapons! On to the ship!"

But Tempest saw Feng trembling under Luc's claws, his face shattering as the last of his three close friends disappeared. First Frij and Queefqueg, and now Mort. Poor Feng. There was no time to comfort the man, however, no time to remind him that perhaps the deaths of his friends could usher in a new era of personal meaning and growth and help him become the man he was meant to be. No time to tell him that loss and tragedy were what shaped a life and gave a person meaning, that such loss might very well spur him to become the hero of his own story.

No, they had to run on, back to the ship, to save what could be saved.

But as they emerged from the forest, they saw the worst thing they could imagine coming from *The Puffy Peach*'s stretch of beach: a plume of smoke.

21.

OUT OF THE FRYING PAN AND
INTO THE CAKE MOLD

Vic pranced in nervous agitation on the deck. It was just him and Qobayne against a POPO ship with its cannons pointed right at them. Thus far his relationship with the boatswain had consisted of Qobayne shouting orders at Vic and Vic failing to do much of anything correctly. His most successful duties had been swabbing the deck and saving people from the sirens by punching them in the face. Qobayne hadn't been particularly impressed by either feat.

The boatswain had a nose one might consider beakish, or a beak that looked noseish. Bold eyebrows forever drawn down made him look like he was scowling even when he wasn't, though Vic was pretty sure he was actually scowling at the moment. He was growling and muttering at the POPO ship as someone on the deck waved flags at them. Vic knew this was supposed to be a way to communicate across the water, but he had no idea what the flashes of color meant. Qobayne could read them, however, and said the flags were semaphores.

Which Vic briefly confused with spermatophores, grossing himself out.

"Won't that be messy?" he asked.

"Shouldn't be. Just says they're sending over a boarding party for inspection," Qobayne replied. "We're to allow it or else."

"Or else what?"

"Or else we get cannonballs through the hull. You can bet the crew they have manning the guns are experienced too."

"What will they do when they get here and realize we have no cargo?"

Qobayne shrugged. "Probably rob us of anything that ain't nailed down. But the captain is aware of that danger. We'll be all right as long as we can make it to one of the Toe ports. We only need to keep the ship in one piece."

"How do we do that?"

"We let them board and rob us."

Vic's hooves began to tap. "Will they kill us?"

Qobayne walked to the rail and spat over the side onto the white sand. "I'm hoping not. It would ruin my day." Vic grunted a half laugh and Qobayne gave him a dry grin. "Har harr," he said. "But with that on the table, are ye ready to fight?"

Vic joined him at the rail. "Absolutely! I can fight. I mean, I've never actually been in a real fight when I wasn't drugged by kidney thieves or punching people in the face for their own safety. But, Boatswain, I have a question."

"What is it?"

"If we fight the boarding party, won't they fire their cannons at us?"

"Aye. And we don't plan to fight them. But they might fire on us anyway."

"Why would they do that? The ship is useless to them if it's full of holes."

Qobayne scratched his cheeks. "Because they're going to want to enter the captain's cabin. And if they do, they probably won't come out alive. He's got it trapped nine ways to Nancy."

"Who's Nancy?"

"Never mind that. It's just an old Qul saying. Anyway. That cabin's gonna be a bone of contention. We have to try to talk them out of goin' in. If things get bad, they'll destroy the ship and we'll be stranded. Or dead."

Vic peered over at the POPO ship. "Is that ship better than *The Puffy Peach*?"

Qobayne took his time considering before he gave an answer. The POPO were lowering a rowboat into the water, and armed men were climbing into it. To Vic's eye they didn't seem any different from pirates. They wore no real uniforms, but there were lots of kerchiefs tied on heads and wide hats with feathers stuck in their bands.

"Well, their ship is longer, has more guns and more sails," Qobayne said, "so it's faster and deadlier. But it has less cargo room. Whether it's better or not would depend on your priorities."

Someone from the POPO boarding party shouted from the rowboat and pointed at the water off the port side. When the rest of the party looked, there were shouts of dismay and alarm.

"What's the matter?" Vic asked. "Is there something in the water?"

"There's always something in the water," Qobayne replied. "This time it looks like . . . yes, see it writhing?"

Vic squinted and saw a churn of slender shapes barely breaking the surface. "What is it? Are they making that noise?" There were strange *glub-glub* noises bubbling up from the area around the rowboat.

"They are. Those are gargling eels, lad."

"Why do they gargle? Is it halitosis?"

"It's part of their filter feeding system. But that's not their preference, ye see—they only filter when they have no other options. They prefer fresh meat, and that rowboat is full of it."

Vic grimaced. "So . . . sharp teeth, then?"

"They'll go through you like a rapier through yogurt."

"Why would anyone stab yogurt? Oh. That's probably another Qul saying."

"You're catching on."

Vic hoped the gargling eels would take care of the boarding party for them, but the eels disappointingly remained in the water while the sailors remained in the boat. Said sailors were from many earldoms, a palette of skin tones from a light beige to dark brown. There were eight of them in the boat, and they rowed up to the starboard side of *The Puffy Peach*, right by the stern in the shallow water, and demanded that a rope ladder be lowered down. Their ship was anchored in the strait and had eight cannons trained on the *Peach*. Qobayne obeyed.

One by one, the POPO climbed aboard to crowd the aft deck, the leader of them last. He was a dour man with light-brown skin and a dark mustache that was twisted and waxed at the ends in a style that Vic associated with villainy. He wore a purple jacket embroidered with gold thread, which didn't quite fit him because his chest was so broad and muscled. His eyes fell on Vic first, perhaps wondering who was more swole. Vic felt the urge to challenge him to an arm-wrestling match but squashed it. Qobayne said they needed to talk their way out of this without violence, and Vic doubted he had the skills for that, so it would be best to let Qobayne do the talking. Swoleness would not save them this time.

Swoleness, Vic was starting to realize, never saved anything.

"Where's the captain?" Villain Mustache asked.

"Not aboard. Out with the crew, seeking provisions. Hoping there's a spring here," Qobayne answered.

The man grinned smugly. "Oh, aye, there's fresh water here. But I doubt your captain and crew will be back. People who walk around the interior of this island tend not to be seen again."

That sounded rather alarming to Vic, but Qobayne seemed undisturbed by it. He was the coolest of Qul people, so Vic did his best to join in the lack of looking worried. They were going to be chill like, uh . . . snow? Vic realized at that very moment that centaurs didn't have any cultural sayings about being calm.

"Our captain is resourceful. How can we help ye, sir? We have no cargo."

"No cargo, eh? You won't mind if we confirm that?"

Qobayne shrugged. "Be my guest. Hatch is open. I wouldn't enter the captain's cabin, though. He traps it whenever he's away."

"We can always send you in first."

"There's nothing I want in there, and then you'd have to deal with oodles of guts exploded all over the place. Sounds like a lot of paperwork."

Villain Mustache grunted. "What's the name of this ship?"

"This be *The Shot Oyster*," Qobayne lied.

"*The Shat Oyster*?"

"Not quite. When one visits a fine seafood establishment, the oyster shot becomes the shot oyster and eventually, it is true, the shat oyster, but our ship is named after the middle stage, when the oyster has entered the belly but not yet exited."

Villain Mustache sniffed and shook his head once as if to indicate he had no taste for clever wordplay. "Search the ship, lads."

"The cabin too?" one of them asked.

"Aye. Two of you go through the cabin."

Qobayne raised a finger. "Good sir, please note that I warned ye and do not hold us responsible for any injuries, explosions, or deaths that may occur."

The man's mustache twitched as he contemplated the ramifications of exploding two of his men and ruining part of the ship he might yet commandeer. "Well, then, did your captain leave you any instructions regarding such a boarding? Some courteous gesture for us, a token of his goodwill?"

"Aye, that he did." Qobayne dropped a hand to his belt and the stuffed bag hanging there—a rather full purse. He worked it loose and tossed it to the Villain Mustache. "I think you'll find him very courteous indeed."

The POPO lackeys paused while the corrupt officer checked the contents of the pouch and grinned. "Belay that last order, lads. No need to search the captain's cabin or the hold."

"Excellent. That's very kind," Qobayne said. "So, if there's nothing else—"

"There is."

"I beg your pardon?"

Villain Mustache pointed straight at Vic. "We've heard about him."

"You have?"

"Aye. This here ship ain't *The Shot Oyster*. It's *The Puffy Peach*, captained by the Clean Pirate Luc, wanted by the Royal Navy. I know because that centaur is wanted for murderin' people in Bustardo. We got a message by flamingo to be on the lookout."

Qobayne snorted. "That's just silly, sir. What's your name, by the way?"

"Captain Kronch."

"Fine. Captain Kronch, how do you know that centaur is the one you're after?"

"The description said he's a muscle-bound Clydesdale. How many other muscle-bound Clydesdales do ye suppose are sailing these waters right now? How many centaurs of any kind are sailing on pirate ships?"

"I wouldn't know since I don't keep records o' such things. But I can assure ye that all Clydesdales have a lot of muscle, so that's not a very good description. And our Vic there hasn't committed any murders."

"Maybe so. But we must take him back to Bustardo just to make sure. There are people there who can identify him."

"I didn't murder anyone!" Vic shouted. "They drugged me and tried to steal one of my kidneys with a knife! I have the right to defend myself!"

"Aha!" Captain Kronch grinned in triumph, white teeth flashing under his waxed mustache. "So you *are* the centaur we're looking for!"

Vic's equine cheeks puckered as he realized his mistake. "I didn't do anything wrong!"

"That's for a judge to decide."

Vic planted his hooves. "I'm not going to see any judge. You all have prejudices against centaurs."

Captain Kronch drew his sword. His sailors also drew their weapons. "Prejudice don't enter into it, lad. This here is a matter of finance. We get a bounty for your head whether you're guilty or not, so you're coming with us. Or at least your head is. And your kidneys."

Vic realized that when someone threatened to take his head or organs, the time for talk was over.

"Gyyaaaaugh!" he shouted, and a high-velocity death scone punched through Captain Kronch's chest. His mustache twitched and his eyes flew wide in surprise and then he fell over backward with a squelchy thump. In the shocked silence that followed, Vic pointed at the other sailors one at a time and spat, "Bundt! Bundt! Bundt!" causing a dense and very heavy Bundt cake to materialize on the sword arm of each. It did not harm them but it did weigh down their arms, freak them out, and make them forget that they were supposed to be subduing Vic.

Maybe they thought—after seeing what happened to their leader—that the Bundt cakes would explode and sever their arms. Or maybe they thought such delightfully aromatic confections should not be possible without an expert pastry chef and hours in a professional kitchen. Or perhaps they were simply befuddled that the cakes had apparently been baked around their arms and they could not remember inserting their limbs through a cake mold. Regardless, they were staring at their arms in surprise and thus were unprepared to be kicked over the stern by the powerful back legs of a desperate centaur. They fell shrieking into the shallows, which were still just deep enough for the gargling eels to feast upon their flesh and have cake for dessert.

Qobayne joined the fray once he realized that there was no going back when you'd put a hole through a man's chest, kicking surprised sailors over the railing and making a few more eels very happy. Unfortunately, the POPO ship also wanted a piece of the action. The first cannon boomed and the ordnance crashed right through the cabin of Captain Luc and out the other side of the ship, plopping onto the beach on the port side of the fo'c'sle.

Mingo the flamingo and Otto the otter had been sunning themselves on the deck above Luc's cabin with no thought for the POPO's cannonballs or the ridiculousness of their own names. With a honk of outrage, Mingo rose in an ungainly heap and flew away into the island's welcoming jungle, refusing to submit to such shenanigans as artillery fire on a nice day. Otto hopped up with a petrified squeak and ran to Qobayne, quickly scaling his frame, wrapping himself about the boatswain's neck, and squeezing his tiny eyes shut.

"We gotta get off the ship," Qobayne said, retrieving his bag of gold from the body of Captain Kronch. "Unless ye can do something to stop their cannons? I mean, Luc said you were some kind of wizard, but I got no idea what the Pell you just did there."

Vic's fingers twitched as he realized he couldn't hide his magic from the boatswain any longer. "I Bundted them," he confessed. "Except the first guy, who got sconed. I don't know about cannons, though. Maybe? I mean, I would need to think of something, because—" Another shot fired and plowed through their second level, and it must have hit a barrel of gunpowder, which ignited and exploded, rocking the ship under their feet and hooves, respectively.

"Never mind!" Qobayne said. "It's over. Now we really gotta get off the ship."

"How?"

The boatswain pointed to the front of *The Puffy Peach*, which was now burning amidships. "Your best bet is a jump into the water. Land on the sand, and you'll snap a leg. Use your Sn'orkel if you must, but I swear the old fishwives' tales say centaurs can swim as well as any horse. Run along the beach. I'll meet you there with the rowboat."

"Then what?"

"Then you think of something to do to those cannons with yer fancy breadstuffs or we're dead meat."

Vic had absolutely no idea what he could do. Centaur swoleboys weren't supposed to be fighting naval battles. It was impossible to punch or kick something a hundred yards away across the water.

"Wait, I mean, how am I—"

But Qobayne was already descending the ladder to the rowboat. "Just do it!" he shouted.

Vic went, hooves clopping on wood, coughing through the cloud of smoke billowing amidships, and hoping the deck boards weren't weakened so much that he would plunge through.

He didn't want to do this. His entire frame shook with warring desires. He didn't want to jump into deep water and drown while being eaten by eels, nor did he want to jump into shallow water and risk breaking his legs, because broken legs on a horse were essentially a death sentence. But he also didn't want to burn alive in the inferno rapidly spreading along the gun deck. There were honestly no good options.

The deck of *The Puffy Peach* rapidly disappeared underneath his hooves, and he whispered a precautionary thank-you to his dam for bearing him, in case he didn't make it. And then his haunches gathered and he leapt, nothing but air between him and the churning blue water.

Splash!

It was immediately chaos as he held his breath, his legs thrashing and his arms pinwheeling. With a soft thud, his back legs struck sand and sank in, then his front legs followed. He tried to open his eyes, but all he could see was bubbling blue and white. And a sinuous purple body. An eel! Without thinking, Vic punched and felt the give of a slippery body, tiny bones crunching like dry spaghetti within.

He had to get to the beach. Which meant he had to see what was above water—before he drowned or met a bigger eel. Bunching his hindquarters, he leapt up until his head broke the surface. He didn't have long to scout for the beach, but he saw it and twisted his body in that direction, taking a huge breath right as his weight plunged him back down. His hooves hit sand again, but at least he was pointed the right way, and he knew what to do, athletically leaping again.

"Whoa," he said as he surfaced, realizing that the combination of weight and buoyancy meant he couldn't swim . . . but he could do a gentle sort of underwater bounding.

He found his rhythm, gained momentum, and was soon leaping out of the waves and onto the sodden sand.

"Ha?" he ventured, uncertain that he'd really made it. "Ha ha!" he added, and then, letting loose his bladder on the beach, he shouted, "Ha haaaaaa! I am literally Pissing Victorious!"

He spotted Qobayne on the starboard side, rowing into the shallows as promised while the POPO continued to fire on *The Puffy Peach*.

"I hope you've thought of something!" the boatswain called. "They're going to get lucky and hit us if we give them enough time!"

Vic hadn't thought of anything. He'd been too busy trying to survive and performing his underwater ballet. He took a few steps into the surf as Qobayne drew near.

"Well, how do cannons work?" he asked.

"Are you serious?"

"Yes. I never learned, because I couldn't get down to the gun deck. And I know the dwarves had their tampoon cannons on deck, but when I helped out, I did more tamping than pooning."

Qobayne sighed but made it quick. "Ye pack the barrel with powder, wadding, and shot, then you light a fuse—really just a vent filled with more powder—and it ignites the powder in the barrel and the shot is propelled—"

"Tell me more about the fuse. Where is that?"

"On top, near the back."

"How do they light it?"

"With a match held at the end of a stick between pincers."

"Okay, let me try something." Vic picked the rearmost cannon, which looked like it was zeroing in on them. He reached out with one hand and then curled his fingers in as he rotated his forearm. "Glehhh!" he said, and Qobayne blinked once before turning around to see what effect this ejaculation had. "Glehhh!" Vic said again, repeating the gesture at the next cannon in line. Neither of them fired, but the next one did. The ball splashed down only a few feet from them, drenching them both and nearly upending the dinghy in the shallows.

"Whatever you're doing, hurry it up!" Qobayne said.

"Glehhh!" Vic shouted. "Glehhh! Glehhh! Glehhh!" Twice more he glehhhed, and the eight cannons remained silent. There were distant shouts of anger and dismay from the POPO ship, though.

"Well done, I suppose," Qobayne said, one side of his mouth curling up into a cautious smile. "What did you do?"

"I filled those fuse-vent-hole thingies with a sugar glaze, like a really thin frosting, you know? Wet and sticky. Can't ignite the gunpowder that way."

Qobayne stared at him for a few seconds, then said, "Well, it saved our buttered biscuits, so that was great. Good job, lad. Now get in."

"You want me in that tiny boat?"

Otto squeaked on Qobayne's shoulder, as incredulous at the prospect as Vic was.

"Yes. Get in and then fold your legs underneath you."

"Why?"

"We're going to go out and take that ship."

Vic hadn't been this confused since the Oatmeal Incident. "What? How? There's only two of us, and I'll never be able to get out of the rowboat!"

"I'm making this up as I go. But we need a ship, Vic. Witness *The Puffy Peach*, currently on fire. Now witness the POPO ship, currently not on fire. One of these will get us off the island, and one will not."

"We can't get off the island if we're dead!"

"Let's not die, then. That's worked out pretty well so far. *Get in.*"

The dinghy was pulled up into the sand, and Vic splashed into the water, grateful that the incoming waves hid his dancing hooves. He couldn't humiliate himself like that time at the gym. But the boat was so *tiny* compared to *The Puffy Peach*. And those gargling eels were still out there. But maybe, Vic reasoned, they were getting full on the POPO men.

The boat tipped and wobbled precariously as he boarded, but it settled down once he'd awkwardly splayed himself in the bottom of it. And why not? It was meant to ferry heavy cargo, after all.

"Oh, shiver me limpets. The ship—it's leaving!" Qobayne said. He gave Vic the sort of look one might give a hero. "Can you stop 'em?"

Vic watched the ship as the sailors pulled in the anchor.

"How? Anything I do would destroy the parts of the ship we need!"

Qobayne's lips twitched. "But sugar melts in time, lad. All we need is somethin' to keep the anchor down right now."

Understanding bloomed, and Vic nodded and smiled. He aimed his fingers at the anchor chain. "Blorgh!" he cried, realizing that nonsense words really helped focus his energy.

The anchor dropped back into the water with a gargantuan fruitcake packed densely around it, and all the sailors grunted and shouted in despair. Fish would nibble the fruitcake off soon enough, but for now the anchor had to weigh nearly twice as much, and even if the POPO could get it up to the deck, it would be far too awkward and gummy to wrangle the thing on board.

Vic's chest puffed out a little. "Aye aye, Boatswain."

Qobayne grinned and considered him as he rowed. "I've been sailing a long time, ye know that, right?"

"I do."

"I've been around. I have seen some shite."

"I have no doubt, Boatswain."

"But I have *never* seen one sailor take out six others with baked goods. Or silence cannons with frosting. Or weigh down an anchor with fruitcake. Nor have I ever rowed in a boat with a centaur. Hey, wait. You've got huge arms. You row."

"I . . . don't think I can move around enough to do that." Rowing in dramatic fashion was exactly the sort of activity that Vic had always imagined would make his buff arms look fantastic, so he regretted denying his boatswain. It felt good, being useful. And Qobayne hadn't said a single negative thing about his magic.

"The point is, lad," Qobayne continued as he took up the oars again, "I want to tell people what I've seen today, and I don't even care if they believe me. I just want to tell the story, y'understand? So we are not going to die. We are going to win. Ye hear me?"

"I do!"

"Good. Now, there's going to be a first mate on that ship acting as captain, and he's not going to be an idiot. He's realized by now that one of us is a wizard. So he's going to be shooting at us soon. You need to look out for guys with muskets on the rails and figure out how to either stop them from shooting or make them miss."

"Got it."

"Then we have to board."

"Yes, about that . . ."

"What is it?"

Vic took a deep breath. He could shoot cake all day, but when it came to admitting his shortcomings, he felt like a colt on his first legs. "There's no way I can pull myself up a rope or climb a ladder. I know I'm swole and I would be great at hefting casks all day, but climbing is not a thing that centaurs can do. I'm going to need he—" The word died in his throat, and he swallowed a few times.

"Heh?" Qobayne asked.

Vic tried again. "Hel—"

"You're gonna need hell? I don't know what that is. Some sort of invigorating cream?"

Vic cleared his throat, looked up, and said the one word he'd sworn he'd never say.

"I'm going to need help."

Qobayne nodded like he already knew that and wasn't at all surprised or disappointed. "That's fine, that's fine; we'll get to that once

I've secured the deck. Now. What can you do to make sure I can take that ship?"

Vic saw a glint of sunlight on metal up ahead. He wiggled his fingers at it and muttered, "Gaooolllph." A gush of hot tea fell on the spot, and someone screamed.

"What was that ye said?"

"I dropped some hot tea on someone's head. They were aiming at us."

"Oh. Right—you take care of that, then. I'll row."

Vic squinted at the POPO ship, considering. "All right, there have to be people manning the cannons, so that's, what, sixteen people minimum there?"

"No. Five people per cannon, so that's forty people at least on the gun deck. The captain probably has another forty on board somewhere, if not more."

"So we're two against eighty? Gaooolllph!" Vic tea-splashed another sniper.

"You're framing it wrong. We're not just two normal lads. We're a wizard and a boatswain. Together we fight crime. And the POPO."

Vic's head spun with a skirling wave of dizziness, and he slumped to the left before lurching back upright.

"Whoa! What was that?" Qobayne said.

"Nothing. I mean, it wasn't me almost fainting! But casting all these spells, it takes energy. I ate a well-balanced breakfast, but I kinda burned through all those calories, and now I'm casting on fumes here. Ah! Gaooolllph!"

Vic's vision swam after he tea-splashed yet another POPO sailor taking aim at them, and he might have blacked out as well, because they were about halfway to the boat and then they were suddenly right next to it and Qobayne was pinching him awake.

"Hey. Vic, wake up. I need one more thing from you."

"Whaaa? Wuzzappinin?"

"I can climb up this anchor chain to get to the deck, but there are plenty of lads up there right now waiting to cut me down. I need you to clear it somehow."

Vic looked up and saw leering faces peering down at them and brandishing swords. "Clear it? You mean . . . knock them overboard?"

Qobayne shrugged. "Or knock them out, kill them, whatever. Then I can probably keep the gun deck contained, as long as their first mate is out o' commission."

"So I take them down and then what? Fritter away my time hanging out with the eels?"

"Look, I promise to get you aboard as soon as possible."

Vic shook his head and steeled himself. "No, listen. I know what to do. I just . . . hope I can."

The boatswain grinned. "Okay, do it. Do it now, before they pour some oil down on us or something."

Vic craned his head back to look at the sky and shot his hands up, fixing his gaze upon a spot above the crow's nest before half-spitting, half-grunting, a major conjuration: "Thurppf! Appfth! Huuunngh!"

Qobayne looked up, expectant, but nothing happened except that the POPO laughed at them. Nothing kept happening, and Vic attributed his shivering innards and swimming consciousness to a lack of strength. To failure. He muttered an apology. "So tired. Woozy. I'm sorry, Qobayne, I guess I just don't have enough juice."

The boatswain pointed up. "What's that, though?"

A rapidly growing dark spot appeared in the sky above the crow's nest. It kept growing and, as it grew nearer, looked to be a boat-shaped silhouette.

"Ha ha! They're coming," Vic said. "I called them and they're coming."

"Who's coming?"

"Fritters. Apple fritters. Heavy slabs of fried dough traveling at high velocity. I'm gonna bury the POPO in donuts."

The POPO had not been looking up, so there was no cry of warning. There were plenty of cries, however, once the fritters started landing. Men were indeed knocked out, for even dough can damage a noggin when traveling at sufficient speed. Some staggered and fell overboard. Most were buried, either conscious or unconscious, in the unrelenting rain of an arcane donut shower.

Qobayne chuckled as he snatched a fritter out of the air after it bounced on the rail and fell toward them at a much more sedate pace. More were plopping into the ocean after similar rebounds. "You're a bloody genius, Vic. But, whoa, eat this. Maybe eat ten. Ye don't look so good."

Vic tried to take the fritter but completely missed. His vision and his muscles didn't appear to work together anymore. And then nothing appeared at all as a cold flutter spiraled through his bulk and he slipped into a hypoglycemic swoon.

22.

LURED INTO THE VELVETY DARK BY A VOICE MOST CLOYING AND MENDACIOUS

Travel, Al had learned, was the great bestower of perspective. When he'd stood at the railing of the Proudwood Lighthouse and stared out at the sea, he'd dreamt of settling down with the Sn'archivist to become best friends and writing companions, forever ensconced in impressive robes daubed with ink and mustard. Once that dream had been dashed to bits, he'd hoped for a pleasant life at sea, swabbing things and climbing nets and eating hardtack spread with mayonnaise while dangling his feet from the crow's nest. But then adventure had struck. Repeatedly. He'd never expected to be nearly boiled alive by royalty with a penchant for barbecue, and only when running back toward the beach had he realized how much *The Puffy Peach* had become home. And now that home was burning like a badly made s'more, and he didn't have a new dream yet.

His current dream, as it was, was going up in smoke faster than a marshmallow. And there wasn't even the consolation of chocolate and graham crackers to soften the blow.

"What do we do?" Al asked, along with everyone else. He looked to Captain Luc first, but seeing the bird gone nearly feral with fear and rage, he next looked to Morgan. She was levelheaded and brave; something about her went cold and calculating whenever danger rang the old doorbell. Just now she was shielding her eyes, staring out at their ship, which was very much on fire and, truth be told, more full of holes than King Thorndwall's favorite moose cheese.

Al knew then that there was no saving *The Puffy Peach*. She would be reduced to ashes, and then spread in the sea like graham cracker crumbs.

"Does anyone see Vic and Qobayne? We can't save the *Peach,* but we can save them," Morgan said. When there was no answer but Luc's mangled squawk, the girl ran toward the ship, and Al followed her, with Tempest on his heels. The rest of the crew was waiting for Luc, but the captain seemed trapped in his emotions; he looked like he was choking on a nut.

As they got close enough to feel the sizzling heat rolling off the *Peach,* Morgan pointed out to sea, where a rowboat bobbed a bit away from the POPO ship.

"I don't get it," Morgan said. "Why aren't the POPO shooting at us? And what is that great lump of a thing sitting in their dinghy?"

As they watched, a figure appeared at the rail of the POPO ship and threw down a rope ladder. He joined the great lump in the dinghy and rowed laboriously toward them. Al pulled his barbecue fork, as did everyone else, but something was clearly amiss. The rower was traveling alone, which wasn't something one did en route to fighting a horde of strangely dressed pirates armed with spatulas on a beach, if one could help it. And as the rower drew closer, Al recognized his back.

"That's Qobayne!" he shouted, pleased to have such excellent eyesight thanks to a lifetime of carrot soup.

The waves eventually pushed Qobayne and the rowboat ashore, where it became clear that the great lump was in fact an unconscious centaur. Everyone gabbled their questions until Captain Luc finally broke through. "What's all this, then?" he barked. "What's happened to the *Peach*?"

Qobayne flapped his tired arms and rubbed at his blisters, not quite able to meet his captain's eye. "'Twas the POPO, sir. They fired on us and hit the powder belowdecks, and the *Peach* went up like a ball o' cat hair. But it's not so bad as it looks."

"Not so bad?" Luc squawked, flapping up off Feng's shoulder to batter Qobayne about the face with his wings. "My ship is on firrrre!"

Qobayne, amazingly, smiled. "Aye, sir, your old ship is. But your new ship ain't." He pointed at the POPO ship. "Sails are in good shape, and there's a crew on the gun deck ready to be recruited or keelhauled. I've got the hatch battened and the cannons silenced."

Luc settled down on Feng's shoulder and ground his beak. "It's too easy, lad. Did the crrrrew not mutiny? Did the captain not choose to go down with his ship?"

Qobayne glanced back at the ship and then to his captain, nibbling his sunburned lip. "It was mostly Vic, sir, if I'm honest. That magic o' his you mentioned. Ain't never seen the like, and he took out most of the crew, but what's left of 'em on the gun deck should be easy to persuade to sign on with us. I got 'em secured just now, an' they're terrified that Vic'll concuss 'em with starchy muffins if they step out o' line."

Luc fluffed his feathers and shook his head. "Ain't norrrrmal, that," he muttered. "Not the magic, I mean—that's a foine thing. But crrrrew shouldn't give up. They eitherrrr fight ye or beg ye. Let's load up and go see why the morrrrally rrrrighteous POPO would so easily consent to join a pirrrrate crew. Must be some kind o' legerrrrde-main."

The entire crew wouldn't fit into the dinghy, of course, especially with Vic taking up so much room, so the first folks across were beefy sorts who could help get Vic aboard, which included Feng. Al and Morgan and Tempest were a bit lacking in the muscle department, so they remained behind, kept an eye out for cannibals vomited forth by the jungle, and waited to board the new ship once Qobayne and the other sailors had rigged a harness to the cargo pulley system to load Vic aboard.

"What can you see?" Morgan asked Al.

He squinted, wishing for his spyglass, which had perished along with his beloved crow's nest. "There's a big mess on deck. Sludgy brown stuff, knee deep. They're tossing it overboard in chunks, along with bodies."

"And no sign of Mingo?" Tempest asked.

She'd been pacing the beach since Qobayne informed her that Mingo had flown off into the jungle once the bombardment of the *Peach* began. Without knowing where Tempest would be, Mingo might never find her again. Al didn't know why she was attached to the cantankerous creature, but he hated to see her in distress.

"No pink that I can see," he told her. "But . . . well, there are worse fates for a flamingo than to be set free in a series of tropical islands, even if he's forever doomed to cry out for mail that will never be delivered."

"I'm just not ready to say goodbye," Tempest murmured, staring off into the jungle, and Morgan put an arm around her shoulders.

"Well, you still have us," she said, and that, at least, made Tempest smile.

Once Vic was safely hoisted onto the POPO ship, Brawny Billy returned to ferry them over in the empty dinghy, and it was a quick enough jaunt. Al was only too glad to board the new vessel, for he was relatively certain that no one on the ship wanted to eat him while wearing a bib. But since Al was a pudgy elf whose asthma had been exacerbated by running through a jungle full of pollen, the actual boarding was a bit of a trial. This wasn't his favorite part of being a pirate, as he didn't like bobbing near a bunch of murderously sharp barnacles while getting thwacked in the face with salt water and clambering up splintery wood as he banged against the ship's hull over a swarming sea full of hungry eating machines, but he had to remind himself: It was still better than the Morningwood. No one had given him a wedgie in ages, nor had he found a sign on his back reading KICKETH ME, rendered in beautiful elvish calligraphy. He would soon find his stride on this new ship, and they'd continue on their quest to find Angus Otterman, whoever he was, and end the EATUM empire, thereby doing real good in the world.

Otto the otter was certainly glad to see Morgan again. He squeaked and leapt from Qobayne's shoulder to hers and chittered at her as he nuzzled her neck. The snap of sails was music to Al's ears, and the new crow's nest looked particularly inviting. As the ship swayed beneath him, he smiled. It felt like home, even if a slightly new home.

"What'll you call her, Captain?" Al asked, gesturing to the deck of the ship.

Luc blinked his single eye and minced side to side on Feng's shoulder, his beak clicking. "*The Pearrrrly Clam*," he finally said. "And may she hold many hidden trrrreasurrrres for the likes o' us."

Al found *The Pearly Clam* an altogether different sort of ship. For one thing, everything smelled like black tea and twists of lemon, and chunks of what appeared to be donuts were all over the place, floating in puddles of brown liquid. For another, Vic wasn't clopping around on the deck; he was awkwardly lying down, only half conscious, cramming apple fritters into his face, one after another, from a small pile of them collected nearby. And for yet another thing, the remaining original crew members were clean, tidy, and utterly silent, quaking in their boots as they watched each new stranger climb up on the deck.

"You therrrre," Luc said to a man in a very nice red coat. "You the firrrrst mate?"

"For now," the man said, his eyes darting everywhere.

"What's yourrrr name?"

"Gorp, sir."

"And yourrrr crrrrew is willing to stay on and submit to my orrrrders?"

"You're the captain, sir? But you're—"

Luc flapped into the man's face, talons spread in fierce rebuke.

"I'm the captain, boy! Clean Captain Luc, also known as Filthy

Lucrrrre! And this is now my ship, rrrrenamed *The Pearrrrly Clam*, and you can show me rrrrespect orrrr walk the plank!"

Luc's crew all raised their fists and shouted, "Luc!" and Al was just a few moments behind, as he hadn't seen this sort of display before. Gorp gulped and gawked at the rest of his crew, men and women from all walks of life, all dressed in shades of red and cream.

"Did you hear that?" the man cried. "This is our captain now, and anyone who doesn't like it can go kiss an eel!"

As no one appeared to want to kiss an eel, Captain Luc merely bobbed his head, steered Feng over to the ship's wheel, and ordered Qobayne to divvy up tasks; Gorp was to be second mate on *The Pearly Clam* going forward, thereby coopting any argument that the new captain disrespected the veteran crew. Gorp's first task was to direct his men in chipping the fruitcake off the anchor, which would keep them too busy to cause trouble.

"You three head down into the hold," the boatswain said to Al, Morgan, and Tempest. "Do a quick inventory of cargo."

"Oh, you don't want to go down there," Gorp said.

"And why is that?" Morgan put her hand on her commandeered cutlass and raised an eyebrow.

"Because it's . . . that is . . . you don't . . ." Gorp had gone as white as a sheet. "Those were standing orders from Captain Kronch."

"Well, the old captain is gone, and the new captain's orders are to do an inventory, so that's what we shall do." Morgan gave the man a nod of daring and headed for the ladder. Tempest followed her, and Al came last.

"Keep a lookout for maps," Morgan said. "We still need to find Mack Guyverr, and I'm sure this POPO captain has confiscated all sorts of atlases and goodies." Otto chittered around her neck, and Al thought he heard fear in that cheerful little voice.

"Don't worry. You're not going to get stuck in the hold again," she told him.

Al stepped from sunlight into the shadow belowdecks. As the

velvety darkness swallowed him whole, all the little hairs on the back of his neck stood at full attention.

"Do you feel that?"

"Feel what?" Morgan asked as she climbed down below him, but the moment her feet hit the boards, her voice went low. "Oh. That."

"That feeling like a slug is climbing down your spine," Tempest added.

"Like it's twenty degrees colder down here and we're knee-deep in penguin vomit, yes." Al snatched a lantern off the wall and held it aloft. The short hall down below had two doors, one to either side.

"Should we split up?" Morgan asked.

"No!" Al and Tempest blurted at the same time, as Otto said, *"Eep!"*

"Ooookay. I guess I'll go first." Morgan held out her hand for the lantern, and Al gladly handed it over. Whatever was happening belowdecks, he had a bad feeling about it.

Al waited to see which door Morgan would choose, and she went left. That room did seem to call to him somehow, as if it had a heartbeat, a pulse. As if it wanted something. As if it yearned. He paused on the threshold.

"Riches beyond measure," a voice whispered from inside the door, but no one said anything about it, so Al hoped it was merely a side effect of the recent stress of nearly being boiled alive and eaten with gravy.

He wanted to stay with his friends and go through the door, but then again, he very much didn't. Ultimately, he had no choice. After seeing Morgan flogged, Al was going to do his best to follow the captain's orders. He had very thin skin that scarred easily, a low tolerance for pain, and a scream that could at best be called high and wobbly and at worst could be described as sounding like a llamataur mating.

Up ahead of him, Morgan crept into the hold, the boards squeaking under her bare feet, as they hadn't bothered to stop the cannibals and ask their shoe sizes before fleeing and were therefore all shoeless. Tempest followed her, and Al followed Tempest. Taking up the rear, sword in hand, he told himself, was a chivalrous duty, such that he could defend the women from the back. But mostly he was just terrified and didn't want to go in the whispering room first.

The hold wasn't much different from their last hold. It was smaller, that was certain, but also longer and contained even more cargo. Looming shadows suggested the usual sorts of things one found under the deck—casks, traveling trunks, and skeletons.

Wait.

Skeletons?

Al looked at the place where he was sure he'd seen two skeletons splayed companionably side by side, but all he saw were two sacks of meal.

"Come closer," someone said. "Look within. All the gold."

"*All* the gold?" Al asked. "Because I don't think that's possible."

Morgan turned to stare at him. "What?"

"I was just responding to that whispering voice."

Morgan and Tempest looked at each other, aghast and pale. "What whispering voice?"

Panic sweat bloomed on Al's back, instantly freezing there. Either he was going crazy or they were, and the odds were that the guy hearing voices was the one with the problem.

"The voice in the back of my head," he said, affecting nonchalance. "Figured the POPO would be up to the gills in gold."

"Maybe," Tempest said. "But this mostly looks like the regular sort of stuff. Bags, casks, skeletons."

"Aha! Skeletons!" Al chortled, pointing.

Morgan put a hand on his shoulder. "Why are you talking about skeletons?"

"B-because Tempest did?"

The women shared an even more horrified and pitying look. "Al, I didn't mention skeletons. I said there were bags, casks, and chests."

"Ha ha. Sure. Of course. Must still have turnips in my ears from that tureen."

Morgan gave him a look—specifically, *the look*, the one that suggests you're going a bit potty and might need to have a snack for your blood sugar and make an appointment with the local healer for some strategic sextopus treatments.

"Al, you're acting really weird. Do you want to go abovedecks?"

Al firmly shook his head. "No way. Captain said to do inventory, and there's a lot to go through. I've got a notebook and pencil, so let's get it over with." He did not mention that he was nearly peeing himself with fear.

They developed a system that worked for Al, because it hinged on him sitting by a lantern and writing things down while the girls poked around the terrifying bounty of the hold. It truly was full of riches, and a life of piracy began to make sense. The pirates stole from the rich men, and then the rich men hired the POPO to take the riches back, and then the POPO most likely kept the riches for themselves and said, *Oh, gosh, those nasty pirates sure are fast!* A cunning system, and one King Thorndwall would admire.

"And that's another cask of grog," Morgan called.

Al looked down to make a hash mark and discovered that instead of the neat notes he was sure he had taken, he had somehow covered the entire sheet of paper with drawings of bones, bloody cutlasses, and skulls wearing pirate hats. The largest of these skulls sported a white beard, and Al had drawn a little speech bubble that said, *I'm going to eat your gizzard!!* complete with two energetic exclamation points.

"One cask of grog," he said, firmly drawing an *X* over the biggest skull. "Nothing else. Nothing creepy, especially. Just normal stuff."

"Over here," someone said. The voice was beautiful and soft, and Al couldn't stop his body from standing and turning to face the darkest corner of the hold. Step by step, his feet walked him over to a dingy chest coated in a fur of cobwebs.

"Let me out," the voice said, a bit desperate, and Al fumbled with the rusty clasps. A soft blue light began to glow from within the chest.

"That's another box of hardtack," Tempest said. "I swear, has no one taught pirates about crackers? Or biscotti? Can they actually enjoy that stuff?" She paused. "Al, where'd you go?"

But Al ignored her as he opened the top of the trunk.

"Al, no!" Tempest yelled. "That looks spelled—"

Much to Al's surprise, he was forcefully flung against the wall, which he slid down, landing roughly on his rump. Tempest and Morgan appeared and knelt beside him, but no one asked him if he was okay this time, because the room was full of that eerie blue glow from the trunk as it swirled around in a cold vortex, rattling chains and sending up gouts of dust and ensuring that no one was okay just now.

"What is it?" Morgan screamed into the whirling ether.

"It's ghosts," answered an unfamiliar voice. "Obviously."

Al's eyes came back into focus as the coiling vapor coalesced into a crew of see-through pirates. Some of them did look a little bit skeletonish, truth be told, and the captain looked very much like Al's sketch, right down to the skull and white beard.

"I am Captain Skullbeard," he said, bones clacking around. "Welcome to my ghost ship."

"Er, beg to differ," Tempest said with an air of apology. "This ship is the property of the Clean Captain Luc. And it's not a ghost ship. As in, it's not ghosty. It's corporeal. Because we are bodies and we're standing on it."

"Nonsense! I am here, and I am a ghost, and the ship has not been taken from me, and thus it remains under my command. A ship belonging to a ghost is a ghost ship. That horrid POPO fellow may have locked us up in this magical trunk and surrounded us with lines of salt, but we're now free, which means we're retaking the ship."

Oddly enough, now that the ghost pirates were free, Al had lost his fear of them. "Just for argument's sake," he said, "can you steer the ship? Since you don't have a body?"

"Well, no," Captain Skullbeard admitted. "But I can still give orders!"

"Okay, but what happens if no one follows those orders?" Tempest ventured.

Captain Skullbeard's visage trembled and became a hideous horror show of rotting flesh and bulging eyes. "Then I'll haunt you!" he screamed. "All day and all night! I'll screech and wail, and—"

"Okay, so that's fun, but let's get back to inventory," Al said. "Bad news is that I was somehow ghost-hypnotized before, so I didn't get an accurate count and we'll have to start over. Good news is that I'm fine now, and, also, this cask of grog is dripping a little in a way that suggests I could—" He cupped a hand under the cask in question and soon raised a handful of grog to his lips. "Oh, yes. Inventory just became a party."

Tempest found extra lanterns, and they were soon grog-tipsy and digging through oodles of loot. Captain Skullbeard and his crew tried all sorts of gambits to get attention, rattling ethereal chains and walking through walls and yanking off their ghost bones to throw at people, but the chill of terror Al had felt had fled. Of all the scary things that could've been in the hold, he was glad it was only some boring old ghosts. Ghosts he could deal with.

As he finished up his tallies, pleased to give Captain Luc the good news, he heard a sad sigh and looked over to find Captain Skullbeard sulking against the wall.

"Chin up," Al said. "It's not so bad. Luc's a good captain, and we're going to have an adventure. And we won't put you back in the trunk if you'll stop being annoying."

"The ocean takes everything from us," Skullbeard said, his voice echoing. "Such is the fleeting nature of life. Everything can disappear in a moment. The fathomless depths claim no prejudice, only souls. We haunt this ship as she haunts us, and one day you, too, will know the embrace of the still, cold water." He shook his transparent fist at Al and shouted, "Crabs will pick the flesh from your bones! Particles of your person will be filtered in the baleens of whales!"

"Auggh! I hate baleens! And you made me lose count," Al said.

When he, Morgan, and Tempest finally took the numbers upstairs to share with Luc, the parrot squawked appreciatively.

"'Tis a verrrritable trrrreasure!" he crowed. "Losing the *Peach* was a blessing in disguise! Extrrrra grrrrog for all! But what's this about ghosts? Why did ye inventorrrry ghosts?"

Al sighed. "Yeah, that's the bad news. I counted thirteen. They're really annoying."

"That's just rude," Skullbeard said, as he was now standing a few feet away, arm bones crossed prissily.

"Aye, well, ship ghosts always arrrre. They can't rrrreally hurrrrt us—only borrrre us."

"I want to go north," Skullbeard whined.

"No. Now shut up," Luc barked, before flying right through Skullbeard's face.

That night, as Al tossed and turned in his new hammock, Captain Skullbeard stood over him, his empty eye sockets dripping with melancholy and possibly ectoplasm.

"Gah! What are you doing? What do you want?" Al cried.

"When ye were coming into the hold, did I overhear the otter woman say you were looking for Mack Guyverr?" the ghost asked craftily.

Al sat up a little. "Yeah, actually. We hear there's an illegal otter-meat abattoir there."

"I can get you there," the captain whispered, then paused dramatically before adding, "for a price."

And then, just when Al wanted the ghost to stick around, he disappeared.

23.

OF GHOSTS AND BARGAINS AND THE JOYS OF MUSUBI

᯽

Filthy Lucre had Feng set a course for Cinnamonk Island, the fourth of the Seven Toes, and had Gorp assign his crew to clean up the cannons that Vic had befouled with frosting. He relayed an offer to them all: Stay on as crew and enjoy a portion of the treasure they were on their way to discover as well as a share of the treasure already in the hold. Or be dropped off on Cinnamonk Island, be paid their due from the POPO, and find work on another ship. They had until docking at the Cinna Monastery to decide, and in that time, Qobayne would work to earn their allegiance. His experience and competence as a boatswain would prove to them that the Clean Pirate Luc was worth following.

Since they were sailing as the POPO in disguise, no one gave them any trouble. Royal Navy ships hailed them and asked by semaphore if they'd seen *The Puffy Peach*, and they lied and responded, WHAT. NO. WHAT IS THAT. NEVER HEARD OF IT. WEIRD. Other pirate ships changed course to avoid them, and merchant ships waved merrily at them as they passed.

Yes, it was good that they had switched to *The Pearly Clam*.

Brawny Billy came over to report good news. "Cap'n, the centaur is awake, an' Milly Dread is feeding him oats and slices of grilled potted meat on a bed of sticky rice."

Feng lit up with excitement. "The ship's galley has musubi?"

"While supplies last," Billy confirmed.

"An' it ain't EATUM?"

Billy shuddered slabbily. "Nah, it's SPUM: Snouts, Pouts, Udders, an' Mushybits. One hundred percent non-otter parts, or your money back."

"Cap'n, can I get in on that?" Feng asked eagerly.

If a parrot could smile, Luc would've done so. Feng had been down in the dumps since losing all three of his friends and had not yet rallied. This was his first smile in days. "Billy, fetch some musubi forrrr Feng, please."

Billy nodded and took his leave, and Luc instructed Feng to head for Vic. They found the centaur on the hoof, with his eyes wide open instead of half closed with exhaustion. Some food and sleep had done him wonders. When they'd first arrived on the new ship, he'd looked like an old feather pillow with hooves.

"Arrrre ye feelin' fine, Vic?" Luc asked.

"Aye, Captain, thank you," the centaur said around a mouthful of musubi.

"Good good good good good," Luc said. "Ye have my thanks as well. I underrrrstand this ship would not be ourrrrs if not forrrr yourrrr aid. Yourrrr passage to Mack Guphinne is amply paid. We will stop therrrre afterrrr we visit Cinnamonk Island."

"Thank you," the centaur said, and for once, he sounded genuine. "I hope you'rrrre prrrroud of what ye did. Ye should be."

The tea wizard puffed up with pride and looked around to see who else might have heard that praise delivered. There was only Al, the short elf, who had just rushed up to them in his bedclothes.

"Yes, good job, Vic," Al huffed, and then executed an elvish salute at Luc. "Captain, the ghost captain Skullbeard says he knows where to find Mack Guyverr. He knows where the otters are being taken!"

"Well, have him tell us, then," Luc said with more patience than he felt.

"I don't know where he is. He said he'd tell us for a price and then he disappeared."

"Rrrrot and rrrruin," Luc muttered in Feng's ear. "These bloody ghosts can eat Brrrrawny Billy's boxerrrrs."

"No, we can't," Captain Skullbeard said, suddenly standing next to Feng and unable to resist the chance to bore a crowd. "We lack digestive systems or any corporeal body. Which is sad, because we can't get smashed on grog or food drunk on musubi. But we can't get scurvy either, so that's good. In fact, an interesting thing about ghost anatomy is—"

"What's yourrrr prrrrice, Skullbeard?" Luc squawked.

"We can get to the price in a moment. First I'd like to know why you've been so dismissive of me and my wishes. This was my ship, after all, once upon a time." His haunting whine set Luc's beak on edge.

"Because ghosts arrrre selfish."

Skullbeard clutched his ghostly jabot. "What?"

"I think ye hearrrrd me just fine with those ectoplasmic earrrrs ye have."

"Aye, I heard ye, I just can't believe I heard right. How can you sit in judgment like that?"

"I've met ghosts like you beforrrre, Skullbearrrrd. Ghost pirrrrates, haunting theirrrr old ships with unfinished business. And I know what that business is."

"Oh, ye do, eh? Please enlighten me, ye daft bird."

"Ye need to give of yourrrrself beforrrre ye can move on."

The ghost snorted out a small green puff of ectoplasm in response. "There's no more of meself to give. I'm a ghost."

"Ye have knowledge to give—useful, unborrrring knowledge—

that will save lives! Therrrre's an awful lot of dying going on at Mack Guyverrrr. The deaths o' innocent otterrrrs. If ye help, ye will be doing the worrrrld a good turrrrn. Make up forrrr all the evil ye did while ye lived. Give us a map, Skullbearrrrd, and I'll take ye to Cinnamonk Island, and the Cinnamonks will send ye to eterrrrnal rrrrest."

The ghost gave a prissy harrumph. "Huh. Ye think I have a heap of evil to carry around? A guilty conscience?"

"I do."

The spectral Skullbeard scoffed. "What about you, then? Are ye not in the same profession? Won't you be a sad ghost parrot some-day?"

Luc ruffled his feathers. "Firrrrst of all, that's an ad hominem at-tack, and it doesn't worrrrk with smarrrrt people. But, no, I won't. I steal from the rrrrich and give to the poorrrr. Filthy Lucrrrre is filthy—I've been awarrrre of that forrrr a long time, and the moni-kerrrr I chose is the Clean Pirrrrate Luc, ye see? My conscience is clearrrr. What doesn't go to paying the crrrrew goes to the Cinna Monasterrrry. Otherrrrwise, how am I differrrrent from the capital-ists? The exploiterrrrs of all people and things? Nay, I seek trrrrea-surrrre to save lives. To give the disadvantaged the same chances to succeed that the prrrrivileged take for grrrranted. And now ye can do the same. Be a blessing unto otherrrrs, be the saviorrrr of otterrrrs, be forrrrgiven—be at peace."

The ghostly Skullbeard sighed in wistful longing at the idea and nearly dissolved. "Give me a chart of the Several Macks, then," he said. "Being ectoplasmic is exhausting."

"Aye. Follow me into the cabin. And thank ye, Al, for brrrrringing this to my attention."

Feng walked Luc into the cabin, which Luc had not yet had time to rearrange to his liking or advantage. It was a dimly lit space that smelled of cheap pipe tobacco and stale beer. Feng rummaged around in drawers until he found a proper map of the Several Macks. He spread it out on the table facing Captain Skullbeard, set a lantern down on top of it, and the ghost raised a luminous, transparent blue hand to gesture at the islands in the Chummy Sea.

"There's not much to the Macks. Nobody living on 'em but the odd hermit or religious zealot because they're so inhospitable."

"I'm awarrrre."

Skullbeard tried to tap the southernmost island and his finger disappeared through the map. He grunted in frustration, raised his finger, and simply pointed at it. "Sail to this cliff face here—the Cliffs of Inanity, do ye know them?"

"Aye."

"From there, ye set a course south by southeast. Ye will see Mack Guyverr's spiral whirlwind soon after ye lose sight of Mack Enchiis on the horizon and before ye see Banhai ahead."

"Perrrrfect. Thank ye, Skullbearrrrd. I will take ye to the Cinna Monasterrrry."

"I wasn't done."

"Oh?"

"Ye can't get through that whirlwind without some aid. It's unnatural, ye see. A dark spell protecting the whole place."

Luc huffed an avian sigh. "How do ye know?"

"We did a couple of cargo runs for the MMA and so we had to know, didn't we? You're right to want that place shut down. It's an island of horrors, probably more so now than when I was alive. So to pierce that spell, ye have to go to Mack Guphinne first and harvest the berries of the ding-gull bushes. Watch out for the ding gulls themselves—they'll fight ye for them and they're territorial. But get yourself a bushel. Ye crush those into a paste, dilute into a wash, and paint your prow and railings with it. That will get ye in past the whirlwind."

"What if we can't find enough o' these ding-gull berrrries?"

"There's plenty, don't worry. Even the old dried ones will work. It's just that they don't grow anywhere else, because they're pretty nasty and no one wants to look at them."

"Rrrright. Anything else?"

The ghost tried and failed to pick up a quill. "They'll let ye dock easy enough on Mack Guyverr. But they're going to want to see a shipping manifest or purchase order as soon as ye step off. If ye don't have one, you're going to be in for a fight."

"How bad of a fight?"

Skullbeard gave an exhausted shrug. "I don't rightly know. I never had to fight them. They have plenty of muscle standing around, though."

But Luc had bigger problems than swole dock boys. "Who cast the spell arrrround the island? Do we need to worrrry about a wiz-arrrrd?"

"No. Word is, it was cast by a powerful witch who was dating the Dread Necromancer Steve at the time. Now she's a marmoset in Songlen."

"What?"

"Hey, magic's a dangerous business. Ain't enough treasure in the world to get me messing around with that stuff. Especially now that I'm dead."

Brawny Billy knocked on the door and entered with a platter piled high with potted-meat musubi, and Luc was gratified by Feng's pleasure and enthusiasm after his days of moping. Food had miraculous power to heal. Skullbeard excused himself while the first mate chowed down, the ghost having no need to eat nor any desire to watch the living indulge, and Luc also noted for the future that the arrival of food might be a half-decent way to banish ghosts.

The Cinnamonks were more into permanent banishment, or "releasing spirits into the ethereal wind," as they called it. Once they landed on the fourth Toe Island, Captain Skullbeard and his crew gladly went to their eternal rest at the ritual behest of the monks, who chanted and gonged and otherwise entertained Pellanus, who, as a result of the entertainment, was inclined to indulge their prayers. Perhaps ghosts bored the gods as much as they bored humans.

Some of the POPO crew chose to leave the ship with their shares of the booty already in the hold, but most chose to remain under Captain Luc's leadership and seek even more treasure in the Several Macks. Everyone from *The Puffy Peach* crew used their shares to purchase new clothing—they hadn't enjoyed proper fits since losing their britches on the island of Clan Nabi and losing their ship to flame. Stripes, buttons, and artistically frayed hems abounded, along with squeaky new boots. Milly Dread took advantage of the bustling port market and restocked the galley with potted meat and rice for more musubi, as well as sacks of oats and other goodies for Vic's voracious appetite; keeping the centaur fed was now understood to be as important as keeping a good supply of gunpowder. Luc had Feng buy up plenty of paint, that the ship might be repainted in a secretive cove of an uncharted island. Qobayne made sure they were well stocked with armaments and repair materials; they'd enjoyed an anonymous run through most of the Seven Toes, but now that some of the POPO crew were leaving, word would get around that the Clean Pirate Luc was at the helm of *The Pearly Clam,* and they could expect more trouble.

After they set sail for the Chummy Sea, Luc left Feng at the wheel and called Morgan into his cabin. "We need to talk about the futurrrre," he said.

It was time to move the girl on to the *real* pirate manual.

24.

STAINED WITH THE REPUGNANT JUICE
OF STICKY, HAIRY BERRIES

*T*he *Pearly Clam* sailed past the last three Toes and toward the Macks swiftly and with surprisingly little trouble. With more crew on board, Tempest was free to return to her studies, and even Captain Luc was supportive, proclaiming that, "Having a lawyerrrr on a POPO ship can only be a good thing. The lass can arrrrgue with anyone what seeks to keep us from ourrrr goal! Orrrr at least keep 'em jawin' and distrrrracted whilst we sneak up with sworrrrds!"

Every day, as she read and made notes, accustomed now to the sway of the deck and the heat of the sun, Tempest rubbed at the brown scaly patch on her wrist and constantly watched the sea for threats. She felt certain that someone would keep them from their goals, that the pirate life was becoming too easy and the crew was due for shenanigans of one sort or another.

But day after day, nothing terrible happened. The sea was calm, the winds fair. No one suspected that the repainted *Pearly Clam* harbored the wanted crew of *The Puffy Peach*. She soon finished all her books and notes and wished Mingo were still around so that she might order her second-year books by mail and be that much closer to a correspondence degree. She asked Luc if they could stop in at a port to do business, but the captain fluffed his yellow feathers and shook his head.

"Not safe," he said, clicking his beak. "We need the element of surrrrprrrrise if we wish to stop this mustelid-killing maniac."

And so Tempest grew cagey and anxious. She would've normally talked about it with Morgan, but Morgan had entered a new stage of mentorship with Captain Luc and now had studies and worries of her own. She practiced giving orders and sometimes even steered the ship as she learned about navigation. Tempest was happy to see her friend coming into her own but very aware that she personally felt left out. She had no aspirations to be a sea captain, and although she enjoyed life on the *Pearly Clam*, it didn't feel like her true calling. When she searched the sea, she often felt as if she were searching for herself. And she kept finding nothing.

Al had obtained a journal in the Cinnamonk Market, and he spent more and more of his time in the crow's nest, writing feverishly and staring at the clouds. When the muse took him, the elf was a madman, up all day and night, scribbling. And when the muse was off shopping for togas or whatever muses did, he was fractious and sleepy and not much fun, muttering about his longing for an affirmation gecko of his own.

Vic, too, was cagey. He'd grown more open about his tea magic but hadn't gained any social skills. The few times Tempest tried to talk to him, he went back into what she considered Swole Mode, like he still thought being tough and brusque was a good way to win friends. He always apologetically slipped her a little cake or cookie as she took her leave, but she felt sad that she couldn't break through the centaur's metaphorical hard candy shell to gain a deeper understanding of the sweet, mushy center within.

By the time the ship neared Mack Guphinne, Tempest was sick of potted meat and desperate for some kind of adventure—well, any kind that didn't involve cannibals, no matter how luxurious their pre-murder bathing practices. She volunteered straight off to march inland to obtain the ding-gull berries, grateful for the chance to walk with her toes in good, rich dirt and run her fingers through wiry grasses and along the waving green leaves of tropical plants. Her skin had dried out, her feet cracked and callused and crusted with salt. The sea, she was beginning to realize, was probably not the best place for a freshwater dryad.

Qobayne led the landing party, and the only other people Tempest knew were Milly Dread and Brawny Billy. The rest of the berry gatherers were new folk, all wearing the red undershirts they'd kept from their POPO days. Most of the crew had stayed behind to fish, sit on the beach, or, in Morgan's case, take a captaining exam. Even Al stayed up in the crow's nest, calling down that he felt like the muse was about to return home with fresh groceries, and Vic apparently had mysterious business of his own on the island and was being laboriously lowered down to the bigger dinghy, using the pulley and harness. As she slogged through the sand toward the jungle, Tempest looked back to *The Pearly Clam,* bobbing merrily in the deep-blue water, and felt quite alone. But as soon as the sand turned to dirt and her toes sank in, she felt more at home than she had in weeks.

"Whot's that say?" one of the red-shirted crew asked, pointing at a sign made of ship boards nailed together and painted with what looked like concentrated bird feces.

"Says *help*," Qobayne said. "These uninhabited islands almost always have this sort o' thing. Some poor critter gets shipwrecked and starts leaving messages to get themselves saved. And then they get saved and leave their trash behind. Rude, if you ask me."

"Come to think of it, I noticed some rocks as we came in, spelling out *SOS.* What's that mean?" Tempest asked.

"*Save our skins,* I think," Milly Dread said, scratching her bum. "Or maybe *send over spaghetti.* Must get pretty hungry, trapped out here. Lovely island, but not much in the way of restaurants."

And she was right. The island was big, by Mack standards, and

Tempest couldn't imagine why no one had settled there, or on any of the Macks. She thought it had much to recommend it, from beautiful vistas to a lush jungle to bountiful plains. Skullbeard had muttered about the ding gulls being too horrific to make it worth bothering, but Skullbeard had said a lot of things, most of them negative. This path, he'd said, would lead directly to a huge field positively fecund with ding-gull berries, and each sailor had a big, clean bucket ready to fill with their bounty. Tempest swung her bucket as she walked, loving the dappled sunshine that filtered through the tropical forest and enjoying the variety of trees grown to maturity and housing what had to be thousands of songbirds. She smiled at their song, and—

"Ahhhh!"

The group stopped, and the jungle went silent.

"What was that?" one of the red shirts asked, his voice tremulous with terror.

"Someone said *ahhhh*, but in fear and surprise rather than physical satisfaction or sudden understanding," Milly Dread explained.

"Wait, where's Marko?"

Qobayne stopped and looked around the group. "Who?"

The red shirt quaked harder. "Marko. He's just a guy?"

"Never heard of him."

"Well, he was with us, but now he's not."

Qobayne looked at the man like he was insane, scanned the dense forest around their trail, and shrugged, seeing nothing in the thick undergrowth. "Let's hope he went off for a pee. Continuing."

The trail seemed well trod and well kept, for a deserted island, and the birds resumed their song, and they passed a sign that said GO AWAY and the loveliest grove of plumeria, and—

"Ahhh!"

"There it is again!" Milly Dread said, cocking her head. "Strange reaction to have on such a lovely walk, isn't it?"

"And now Poloe is gone," the quivering red shirt said. "That's two men missing!"

Qobayne looked at the red shirt in a way that suggested the man was being part of the problem instead of part of the solution.

"I don't recall either o' these men, but if it makes you feel better, we can call for them as we go along so they can rejoin us after their peeing. Or whatever." Hands on hips, he shouted, "Marko! Poloe! Marko! Poloe!"

Milly Dread put her hands over her ears. "Cor, that's annoying! What kind of a fool would walk around shouting like that? Makes my old ears hurt, that does!"

After a few minutes of fruitless shouting, Qobayne shrugged and went quiet. The red shirts were all clustered together now, three of them, and Tempest fell back a little so she didn't have to hear their worried chatter about the obvious dangers of peeing alone. And since she was the last in line, she just so happened to be watching when a huge log swung in from the right to the left, taking a red-shirted lad with it.

"Ahhhhh!" he cried.

"Would you *please*," Milly Dread called from the front, "stop saying that?"

But Tempest stepped forward. "No, the red shirt—what's your name?" She asked the man who had spoken up about Marko and Poloe.

"I'm called Hayu."

"Hayu is right, Milly. His friends are disappearing. A log swung in and smacked a man away. It was tied with vines, and—" Closing one eye, she tracked the log's trajectory. "Yes! There it is! Lodged in that tree, using some sort of contraption. This is a very complex machine."

"Hmm. A man-bashing machine," Milly Dread mused. "That's right marketable, that is."

The group hurried toward the log to find the missing red shirt—

"Oh, no. Not Jimson," Hayu moaned.

—only to find the remains of Jimson as crimson as his shirt, smeared against the trunk of a tree into a tomato paste with chunks of bone in it.

Qobayne looked at what was left of Jimson and stroked his chin. "So the big question is this: Are these old, abandoned booby traps, or is someone actively trying to kill us?"

But Tempest had had enough. "I think the real question is, why are we standing here when someone is killing people with logs? Now, follow me. We've got to stay off this trail." Without waiting to see if Qobayne found this remark dangerously rebellious, she took off running, her berry bucket bouncing.

The others, thankfully, followed her, and she kept their path parallel to the murderous one but zigzagging through the dense foliage. To be honest, she was only able to run a few feet, and then she had to laboriously push through branches and leaves. Brawny Billy, who was silent but deadly, moved ahead of her to clear a path with his machete, giving her a perky grin and a wink over his massive shoulder.

"D'ye think Marko and Poloe are dead?" Hayu asked.

"I would assume so," Milly said. "I mean, live people would pop back out and mention an interesting bug they saw while having a pee, not shout *ahhhh* and disappear forever." And then true horror dawned on her lined face. "Oh, no. They might be ghosts soon. We need to walk faster."

Brawny Billy cut the trail as quickly as his machete allowed, and soon the remaining berry pickers stood on the threshold of a spectacular field of berry bushes. Shielding her eyes from the sun, Tempest scanned the area for the dreaded ding gulls Skullbeard had mentioned. Truth be told, a wide variety of birds should've been feasting there, but the bushes were unburdened with beaky grazers, even though plenty of the fruits dangled from branches in plain view.

The ding-gull berries were plump and ripe if ugly, a wrinkled sort of brownish-purple, like spherical prunes with hairy tufts at one end and splurty squirts of brown juice at the other. Although Tempest had never heard of this type of berry before, she'd imagined stuffing herself with something like blueberries or blackberries until the bones in her lower legs stopped hurting. But the stench of these berries suggested no one would wish to eat them. The crew moved into the field, buckets ready to be filled.

"Ye've got to use your knife to cut them off," Qobayne said, demonstrating by cupping a berry in his hand and sawing at the thick, hairy stem. When it was cut through, he held up the berry and winced. "They're sticky little nuggets too. Be sure to wipe off your hands afterward. Now, let's get this done and get back to the ship. The ding gulls will surely show up soon, if they're as territorial as Skullbeard said." He dropped the apricot-sized berry into his bucket with a meaty plunk and untangled the next hairy stem from the bush.

Tempest dutifully went to her own bush nearby and began sawing. She quickly realized she was not a fan of ding-gull berries. They were unpleasantly tacky and had hideous little bumps that sometimes felt a bit like corn kernels or cashew chunks. But they weren't here to feast, she reminded herself. These berries were the key to saving the otters. Without the juice from many squashed berries, they'd never get through the magic aura protecting Mack Guyverr. She thought about Otto's sweet face and adorable antics; she couldn't let further harm come to the otters. And so she redoubled her efforts and committed herself to having as many ding-gull berries in her bucket as possible, and—

"Ahhhh!"

"Oh, not again!" Milly Dread cried.

But this time, it wasn't some random stranger from the former POPO crew. No, it was Brawny Billy, and there was an arrow sticking out of his belly. A piece of white fabric attached to the arrow was crudely painted with the words PRIVERT PROPERTE.

"Is that true?" Qobayne murmured as Milly Dread tried to help Brawny Billy.

If it had been one of the scrawny red shirts who'd taken the arrow, they could've easily carried him back to the ship, but they didn't call Billy brawny because he was wee. He was a large lad with huge muscles and a sweet smile who was especially good at carrying things.

the vanguard of a hu[ge]
sion of their feeding
horror.

Ding gulls were pr[o]
the cut of their wings
blance ended. Their p[l]
an *a* and only a hint of
eyes. They had dark-
sounded like rusty sa
And their beaks reall[y]
hairy berries that bor[e]
successfully brought h
soon be torn to shreds
The berries weren't wo[rth]
sliced into strips of jer[ky]

"Hold your bucket[s]
food might be all that

It sounded like a be
of, which was nothing
gulls approached, squa
the bucket to make th[e]
saw some of them adj[ust]
was a mess of feather[s]
between beaks, and ta
bucket aloft. Qobayne
the same.

The noise was nigh
gulls that had fed too[k]
merly rusty, scratchy c[r]
berry juices coated thei[r]
their voices. And soon,
their whistles wetted, t
in the field, and Temp
ding gulls. She had ne

Captain Luc sometimes called him the Quickerrrr Pickerrrr Up-perrrr because he could carry a barrel farther and faster than anyone else. And now he was dying on the ground. Another arrow thwacked out of nowhere and stuck in his chest; the tag on this one read WE MEANS IT.

Tempest knelt by Billy's side but could immediately see that there was very little any healer could do for him. Maybe she could—

No. She couldn't. Soon her entire arm would be bark. But perhaps she could use her law knowledge to stop more arrows from being fired.

"This isn't private property!" Tempest shouted. "I checked the atlas before we landed. This island was never claimed. It's part of a public trust held by the king. If you'd like to claim a plot, you'll have to fill out form JNY8675309 and submit it to the King of Pell along with the requisite taxes, but I hear there's a six-year backlog of claims."

After a moment, an arrow thwacked into the ground at Tempest's feet, reading WHOT?

"Exactly what I said. I'm studying to be a lawyer, and while we are well within our rights to pick these berries, the law is very much against you, I'm afraid! Murder is a pretty big deal."

For several minutes, no arrows thwacked, and everyone hovered around Billy, saying unhelpful things like "Where does it hurt?" and "What can I do?" and "Thoughts and prayers."

But then a new figure appeared as if out of nowhere—no. Two figures.

Nearly identical white men, except in age. Handsome, muscled, suntanned, with long, wild, gold-bleached hair and long beards to match and extremely tight, tattered pants torn off mid-shin. One, however, looked like an older copy of the other.

"Who the Pell are you?" Qobayne asked.

"I'm Robin," the older man said in a deep, dramatic voice.

"And I'm Robin's son, Kruso," said the second one in an equally deep, equally dramatic voice.

"And why are you p
think sailors grow on
you think it's worth t

"Three!" Hayu pipe

"Going on four,"
voice, "Not you, of co
of someone else."

"Well, we did hav
grown fingernails, loo

"Which one? We
HELP, which seems co

"Well, HELP does
said in a helpful way. "
Orders from the big g
passing."

"It's public land!"
can't trespass on publi

"Glurk," Brawny B
about to contest the i
She looked down at
sweating, his eyes lost
He pointed a weak fir

"If only we had a h
someone could save h
significant glare.

"Well, I—"

But before Tempe
fears and her destiny,
own righteous path, t
screeching and blood.

The blood was Ro
from behind and its sh
artery. The screech wa
ter of the forest, pursu

---

those ugly birds, which were all happy now and swooping playfully above the field, aggression slaked with their appetites. There must've been some euphoric agent in the berries as well.

Tempest checked on her companions. Their buckets were empty and their arms all ran with streaks of blood and globby brown berry juice, but they were alive, unlike Robin and Kruso.

And unlike Brawny Billy.

At some point during the feeding, he had died of his wounds.

Tempest felt something then that she'd never felt before—a wash of guilt and shame and regret. This kind, foine boy who did nothing but exactly what he was asked, who had leapt before her to cut her path without expecting a word of thanks—a word she'd never given—was now dead. And for no good reason. And she could've stopped it, could've healed him, if only she hadn't been so selfish. She put the bucket down and looked, really looked, at the blood welling around the two arrow shafts stuck in Billy's torso.

Usually, blood made her hungry, made the willowmaw deep in her soul crave flesh.

Now she just felt empty.

"They killed him," Tempest said, but even as the words left her mouth, she knew they weren't true.

She had killed him.

By doing nothing.

Tempest's mouth was dry, her eyes wet, her hands stained red. "We need to get more berries, don't we?" she asked aloud.

"Aye, I think we must," Qobayne answered. "Might be a good idea to do it fast. If they get hungry again, we'll have some defense. And they might let us harvest while they're happy."

"Then let's be about it."

They hurriedly sawed and hacked at the bushes to refill their buckets, all while the ding gulls spiraled above them and filled the air with melodious chimes. Tears coursed down Tempest's cheeks as she realized they were creatures not unlike dryads—by turns terrible to behold and wondrous to witness in the wild. There was a balance to their lives, a darkness and a light that could not be denied, for Tempest had never heard anything so magical in all her days, and it was a more fitting tribute to Brawny Billy than anything she could have said.

When they had filled their buckets and the ding gulls were still happy and airborne, they tried every way they could to move Brawny Billy, but the lad was just too heavy; they couldn't carry him and the ding-gull berries too.

But Tempest wouldn't accept that. The thought of simply leaving him there was intolerable to her. "He's coming back with us for a proper burial. That is all." She handed her bucket of berries to Qobayne and gritted her teeth as her arms lengthened and grew rough bark. Her crewmates scampered ahead as she took her half-tree form and carried Brawny Billy's body over her newly broad shoulder. On the way, they took the path that Billy had hewn with his knife. With every step, Tempest's heart felt heavier and more wooden.

After her time on Mack Guphinne, she knew two things: She couldn't live with herself if she kept letting people get hurt or die just to avoid her own destiny.

And her destiny was going to arrive sooner rather than later.

25.

Up to the Fetlocks in the Viscous Muck of Self-Knowledge

It was seriously hard to maintain one's coolness while being lowered onto a dinghy using a pulley system designed for large barrels of grog and lard. Vic felt pretty stable and cool on land, but in the air he became awkward and unbalanced. It was a dicey business in the best moments, and choppy seas near Mack Guphinne as Vic neared his longtime goal did not make it a best moment. At last, he would find the cure that would expurge his tea magic, leaving him undeniably swole and masculine.

"Quit wiggling!" Feng shouted from the ship.

"I'm not doing it on purpose, bro! My front half weighs more because it has an extra torso on it!"

"Well, stop being that way, then!"

Vic took a deep breath and tried to shop shaking. "That's why I'm here," he whispered to himself.

They finally got him lowered into the dinghy, which didn't make him feel any less wobbly. He immediately clunked down onto his knees to help stabilize the boat, knowing full well the rough wood would skin his shins. Taking up the oars to row, he realized that it was actually good that there were so many things demanding his attention—it kept him from freaking out about what was going to happen once he reached the interior of the island of Mack Guphinne.

Two of the red-shirted POPO sailors had been sent along to help, and they now cowered in the dinghy, appropriately frightened to be trapped near their first centaur. As soon as the boat washed up on sand, Vic stood and leapt out, and the men dragged the boat farther in and looked about the beach.

"So do you want us to go with you, or . . . ?" one man said.

"Or what?" Vic asked.

The man shrugged. "I don't even know what I'm doing here."

Vic felt that more deeply than he was willing to admit.

"I should be back in a few hours," he said.

"We'll be waiting. Unless something eats us."

The red-shirted man said it as if that was something that regularly happened to his cohort.

It felt harder than it should have, walking away from those two random strangers and the boat that had become home after the other boat that had become home had burned to a crisp. Vic was a war of emotions: great purpose and destiny arm-wrestling with mild terror and discomfort. What if the cure he sought on the island was just an old dams' tale? What if he'd spent all this time, exposed his magic to friends and enemies, barely escaped death repeatedly, taken lives, and it was all for nothing?

When he looked back, the two tiny sailors in their red shirts waved nervously, and Vic waved in return. He crested a dune and shielded his eyes against the sun, looking for the right path. He was blinded at first, but soon he saw it: a shimmering ribbon of white sand snaking deep into the jungle, just as the legends said it would. His hooves slid a little on the way down the dune, but the path was solid underneath him, tiny shells crunching pleasurably under his hooves. Lush green foliage arched overhead, and glinting metallic insects buzzed from flower to flower as jewel-like birds flitted to and fro and sang raucously in the trees.

"This isn't so bad," Vic said, conjuring a cup of lavender Olonkh tea with lemon and sipping delicately as he walked through the dappled sunlight.

But of course he had spoken too soon. About an hour in, he grew concerned about the lack of signage and the distance to the temple, which he was certain he should've already reached. He felt the path change under his hooves. The sugary white sand grew dingy and gray and wet, sucking at his bare hooves and making him glad he'd given up horseshoes on the ship. The lush emerald-green foliage slowly curled away and died, making way for graying pricker bushes, sad little weepy trees, and dolorous cattails. The sky went from crystal blue to barnacle gray, and the sun's warmth faded to a clammy kiss of moisture that made Vic's skin twitch. Soon the ground became downright swampy, muddy water sloshing in over the path and leaving nasty splatters on Vic's pasterns. The air smelled of old chowder and mildewed socks.

The path will show itself to the righteous was what Vic had always heard, and he knew he was righteous in multiple ways, but this was ridiculous. At no point had the legends said anything along the lines of *The path will show itself to the righteous and then gradually get rather boggy and make the righteous feel as if perhaps they missed the proper turnoff.* And yet Vic could still see the path just ahead, zigging and zagging among the plants, always looking as if the next patch of white sand and blue skies might be just around the bend. But with each step, it seemed to disappear beneath him in muck.

Still, he trod on. He'd told the men he'd be back in a few hours, assuming an hour's trot up a beautiful path, an hour's soul-searching or whatever, and a quick canter back with his wretched tea magic gone forever, his soul washed clean of mareishness, expunged of pink icing and porcelain saucers and replete with protein shakes and shoulder hair and manly swagger. But it must've been hours already.

Hours of slogging. Hours of exhaustion as he pulled his hooves from sucking mud and plunged them down again into the same. Hours of flicking off horseflies with his tail and rubbing mosquito bites on his guns. Hours and hours of following an enticing path that disappeared the moment he reached it.

He was dying of thirst, but there was no water—

Wait.

Panting, muscles quivering, he conjured up a jumbo latte mug full of iced green tea with honey. Even as he gulped it, he refilled the mug, slurping until his belly was cold and sloshy. Bolstered by the tea, he rubbed his fingers together and produced mounds of his favorite cucumber sandwiches, dainty logs of pillowy white bread with just the right amount of mayo and a sprinkling of salt on top of thinly sliced cukes. It was like eating coolness, and he finished up his repast, eaten on the hoof, with a handful of cake balls, conjured on their own little sticks so he wouldn't get his hands too dirty and risk touching the filthy water below to clean them off.

"That's better!" he said, and looking up, licking his fingers, he found the sandy white trail under his hooves again.

He took to trotting now, enjoying the rise and fall of the trail as it wound through pastures of golden wheat. Birds took flight overhead, dancing and swooping, and he picked up to a canter, arms out, shouting, "I'm king of the world!" and swiftly adding, "But not Pell—ha ha—because we all know that's Goode King Gustave! Please don't sue!"

His canter fell back to a walk, and he stepped off the trail to expunge his bladder of what had to be ten gallons of green tea. The moment his last hoof was off the white-sand path, a cloud passed over the sun, and brown water squelched up around his fetlocks, and cattails brushed his belly, and he bellowed, "Oh, come on!" as he took a mighty pee of annoyance.

It took several long moments, as he was both a horse and a man and a repository of much tea, but when he finally finished, he threw his arms at the sky and shouted, "Is this how it works? I slow down or lose faith or stop, and the trail becomes awful? Because that's not how I was told it worked."

In response, thunder rang out, and rain poured from the now cloud-filled skies as if someone had dumped a very large bucket directly over Vic on purpose.

"Fine. If this is what it takes to reach my goal, then this is what it takes."

He tried to sidestep back to where the path had been, but that path was gone. Up ahead, in a lone sunbeam, an enticing ribbon of white sand waited. He leapt for it and fell, staggering into knee-deep water. His hooves sank in soft mud, the cattails closed around him, and the rain pelted him like a million tiny rocks. He was cold to his bones, lost, farther away from home than he'd ever been. Even the cruelty and violence of the Centaur Pastures was better than this lonely darkness. The sun went down, hidden by clouds, as he struggled through gelid water. A light always seemed to dance ahead, showing flashes of shining white sand, but he never reached it. His head hung. He couldn't lift his arms to conjure food. His tongue grew thick in his mouth, and exhaustion suffused him. He began mumbling to himself, staring down at his equine chest as his body sank in the swamp.

"C'mon, Vic. What's the matter? What's wrong? C'mon, bro. I understand. It's too difficult for you, bro."

And then his hocks were underwater, his hooves icy.

"Vic! You're sinking! Turn around, bro! You have to! Come on! Be swole! Fight against the swampness!"

His man torso strained forward, his muscles taut, urging his horse body to comply. When his horse legs just sank deeper, he smacked his rump, again and again, as he'd seen humans whip horses to a frenzy.

"Horse parts! Please! You're letting the swampness get to you. You have to try. You have to be swole!"

It was almost as if he was being torn in two, as if he didn't control the horse half of himself any longer.

"Come on. For me! You're my butt! You're where I keep most of my organs. Stupid bod! You've gotta move or we'll die! Please!"

Still, his legs seemed so far away, so cold. In a last burst of fury and fear, he broke off a willow whip and smacked his rump with it, hard, screaming, "No! Stupid horse butt!"

And then his rump was underwater. All of him, up to the human nipples. He felt the water creep over his guns, his shoulders, up his throat. But the moment that brown, murky, muddy, slimy water touched his lips, he was done.

"No!" Vic shouted. "That's nasty!"

As if he'd been struck by lightning, his legs straightened beneath him and his hindquarters bunched to action, full of feeling again and quivering with energy. This time, the nervous dancing of his hooves helped loosen the boggish mud. He unleashed a furious tantarella, feeling his nerves fire and his muscles swell with blood. He fought with his arms, plunged his hooves into the muck, struggling to get out.

"I did not come all this way to die in a swamp!" he shouted. "I don't care how gross it is! I don't care if the legends were lies! I'll go back to the ship and just learn how to be magical before I let this dumb bog win! Screw you, you stupid temple!"

Gaining traction, he turned and reared, and—

His front hooves came down on stone.

The swamp was gone. The cattails were gone. The trees were gone. He was in a beautiful circular temple, the aged russet stones overgrown with lush vines. Kindly smiling statues gazed down at him, and a circular hole in the roof showed bright-blue sky. The air smelled of incense and chai, and somewhere nearby, wind chimes clattered on the breeze. Torches lit the shadowed walls, and candles glowed in a limpid pool set among the stones, each light floating in the center of a lily.

"Uh, okay," Vic said, lifting his feet nervously to see if he'd tracked any mud into this sacred space.

"What brings you to the Temple of Woom, my son?"

He expected to see a holy woman in embroidered robes, or perhaps an aged monk, or, in his fondest dreams, a pretty Appaloosa centaur mare with a fondness for mullets. But the high, feminine, musical voice had come from . . .

Was that a chinchilla?

It sat on a tiny stool by the pool, knitting something.

"Who are you?"

"I am the Guardian of the Broken Waters."

"But you're a chinchilla."

"And you're a centaur. Life, uh, finds a way."

Vic shook his head in disbelief, but his vision didn't change. "Am I still dreaming?"

The chinchilla shook her head too, but like he was an idiot. "Of course not. You were never dreaming. You were merely on the path."

"On the path?"

Huffing a sigh, the chinchilla put down her knitting and strode as purposefully as a spherical chinchilla can toward the confused centaur. "Stop asking stupid questions. You know you were on the path. You know the path was a test. The test took you a long darned while, and that's why I'm still knitting instead of getting along with my life. Now. Again, I ask you: Why have you come to the Temple of Woom?"

Vic fidgeted, and sugar cubes clattered from his fists, making him blush fiercely. "I wish to be expunged of my tea magic, that I might be whole and swole."

The chinchilla politely sneezed. "That's not what you want."

Vic gasped and looked down. The chinchilla's teeny hands were on her round hips, and her teeny eyebrows—did chinchillas even have real eyebrows?—were raised in that way that suggested your next answer had better be both truthful and correct.

He cleared his throat. "It *is* what I want, though. I have this magic, see, and my sire says it makes me feminine and weak. So he taught me how to lift, taught me how to act tough, told me that I had to make up for being born this way. So I . . . I don't want to be this way anymore. I don't want the magic."

His answer must've been the wrong one. The annoyed chinchilla stopped to take a dust bath, her teeth grinding, and then looked up at him again.

"Has anyone ever told you you're an idiot?" she said.

"Y-yes?"

"And have you ever bothered to look a little deeper and see if that might be true?"

Vic suddenly felt deeply uncomfortable and fought to hold in his apples. He had never been confronted by a chinchilla before, and he would've preferred to take on an entire gymnasium of swoleboys to being eviscerated by her knowing, beady eyes.

"I figured there would be time for introspection after I came here and got fixed," he finally said, trying to keep a stiff upper lip, though his upper lip was mostly just sweat and snot at this point.

"I thought so. Now come down here so I don't strain my neck. You're very tall."

"Or maybe you're very short."

"You think? Listen, swoleboy. Turning everything around on the other person won't work here in the Woom. Here you've got to get right with yourself. So come on down."

Carefully, Vic kneeled, wincing at the touch of rough rock on his poor, dinghy-scraped knees. Once he was there, the chinchilla tapped the floor between them with a claw.

"Pellish breakfast tea, cream, four sugars, and a biscuit, if you can manage it," she commanded.

Vic conjured it exactly as she liked, and she happily sipped and crunched, her nibbles making an adorable *chick-chick-chick* sound and her round cheeks wobbling like crazy as Vic quietly prepared for a mental breakdown. Finally, when she'd eaten all that a chinchilla could manage, she put a wee paw on his foreleg and looked deep into his eyes.

"I don't think you want to lose your magic, kid. I think you like your magic. Heck, I think you *love* your magic. But your sire's poisoned you, see? He decided he didn't like it, or maybe he's scared of it, or maybe he's jealous, but instead of getting right with himself, he took it out on you. So you grew up being told you were the one with the problem, when *he* was the one with the problem. There's nothing wrong with magic. It's a rare gift. Something to be celebrated. And that you can do it without a wand is even more impressive. You have tremendous power." She sighed sadly, and Vic was about to ask her if she was okay, but she wasn't done.

"So what is it you really want? Deep down in your heart? If your dad didn't exist and there was no one left to impress, what would you want?"

"I don't know."

The chinchilla blew an adorably high-pitched raspberry. "Not good enough. Try again."

Vic closed his eyes and tried to let his heart speak, but his heart had spent many, many years remaining silent. No answer appeared in the darkness of his mind; no words came to his tongue.

"I just . . . I mean . . ."

"That's it. Into the pool."

Vic stood and nearly fell over again thanks to gravity, blood, and centaur biology not playing well together.

"What?"

The chinchilla pointed at the pool. "I was trying to avoid this bit, as it's messy, and you're unwieldy, and I really hate mopping, but you'll just have to do it. March your rump right into the Pool of the Broken Waters and prepare to be reborn."

Vic stepped closer to the pool and looked down into its infinite blackness. The flowers holding the candles all politely drifted to the edges, giving him plenty of room. He dipped in a hoof, and it came back slick with something thick and reddish.

"I don't really think that's hygienic—"

But someone shoved him in. And it wasn't the chinchilla, as she was way too short, and shoving a two-ton centaur anywhere requires some mad muscles.

Vic plunged into the pool, tumbling deep underwater. He felt weightless and frightened, his worst dreams of drowning in dark water coming to pass. There was no purchase, no edge, no soft sandy bottom—just endless floating. But then, after several moments of not dying or even feeling his lungs burn, he opened his eyes.

He was back home in the Centaur Pastures, watching a Clydesdale colt run away from a jeering herd, all wearing baseball caps and mitts. The stallion was still young and gangly, all skinny legs and huge hooves, but he was unmistakably Vic's sire.

"Dad?" he muttered under his breath.

But the scene did not respond.

"Go on, butterfingers!" another stallion called from the herd. "We don't need your kind on our team!"

"Yeah, you're supposed to be the batter, not the maker of batter!"

The younger version of Vic's father galloped away, crying, as Vic watched from somewhere overhead. As the colt skidded to a stop behind a gnarled old tree, Vic saw it: thick yellow glop oozing from his hands.

"It won't stop," the coltish version of his father said, his voice high and unsure. "Why won't it stop?"

Vic looked closer and saw that it was batter. Pancake, by the lumps.

"I wish I was normal," his father said.

And then Vic was tumbling through the red glop again, the tepid liquid washing away the tears that had somehow formed on his cheeks. When he opened his eyes, he was in his home pasture, and he saw his parents curled together in the deep grass.

"Would you look at that!" his mother said, holding up a wobbly cupcake.

His father dashed it out of her hand, and Vic's heart seized in his chest when he saw a foal version of himself, lip quivering as the cupcake hit the ground.

"No son of mine should do such things," his father said gruffly.

"But it was beautiful," his dam said. "It was, my little Pissing Victorious. Beautiful."

His father stood and stamped a plate-sized hoof. "He'll never live up to that name. Don't encourage . . . that." When he galloped away, Vic's mother scooped up the sniffling foal and cradled him to her chest. "He'll come around, love," she said. "You're so special and precious."

"He don't like me," Baby Vic said.

But his mother didn't deny it. She just pulled him closer, and fat tears plopped into his curly hair.

Vic tumbled through the dark water again, and when he opened his eyes, he saw himself standing on the deck of *The Puffy Peach*, smiling, fishing. He had a barrel of caught fish by his side, and as he pulled in one more wriggling silver tarpon, he laughed and tossed it on the deck for Brawny Billy. When he was sure no one was looking, that version of Vic made two teacups filled with tea and clinked them cheerfully, drinking down both before throwing them overboard.

"That's good tea," he said. "Darned good tea. The sea and tea for me!"

The next time Vic opened his eyes, he stood on the reddish stones of the Temple of Woom, slick and wet with red muck, hands in fists. His father stood before him, a hand taller and a good bit more swole.

"Pissing Victoria," his father said with a sneer, putting emphasis on the cruel jab.

"Sucking Fabulous," Vic said, trying to keep his hocks from shaking.

"Are you still making your dainty little tea cakes with their pwetty wittle fwowers?"

Vic's instinct was to put his head down and mumble, "No, sire," as experience had taught him that that was the best way to get through life with his father unscathed. But Vic had been through a lot, and the scenes he'd recently witnessed had enlightened him on parts of his father's own history left undiscussed, and Vic reckoned that his sire had to be at least thirty-two and therefore no longer strong enough to push him around.

So he puffed out his chest, stomped a foot, and said, "Yes, as a matter of fact I am still making tea cakes. Chocolate or pistachio?" He did jazz hands and ended with a beautifully decorated tea cake on each hand, bowing to his father in a mocking sort of way.

"Why can't you be more like your brother, Crapping Fantastic? You disgust me," his father said with a snort, knocking the cakes to the ground.

Vic looked down at them, both broken to show thoughtful layers of filling inside, their pretty sugar-work decorations crushed. Rage flared, but then he felt only . . . pity.

"You just make me sad, sire. Who hurt you? When did you stop using your magic? And doesn't it hurt you to hurt me?"

"You're talking like a mare. Humph. Feelings. Be a stallion."

"I am a stallion, sire. But there are different kinds of stallions."

"No. There can be only one."

His father turned his back and was suddenly clad in black robes that flowed from his human form down over his horse rump to the ground. When he spun around, his face was hidden by a deep cowl, but from it grew a long unicorn horn that lit up a violent, glowing red.

"What is even going on?" Vic asked the darkness.

His father—the robed unicentaur with the fire horn—slashed at him, and Vic leapt back.

"Uh, chinchilla lady? Things got really weird."

But no comment came from the darkness.

Without a word, without a single hoof clomp, the robed unicentaur/dad thing stabbed at him, driving him back, and Vic realized that he, too, had a horn coming out of the center of his forehead, but his was a clear, pure blue—even bigger than his father's—glowing with optimistic energy and self-love, and he reared to strike at his unicentaur/father's heart, and—

Then he realized it was basically the stupidest, most obvious dream metaphor he'd ever experienced, and he shouted out into the void.

"Fine! Fine! I don't want to give up my magic. I just want people to like me."

The moment the words left his mouth, Vic rose, sputtering, from the pool at the center of the Temple of Woom. Slick red liquid sloughed off his coat, leaving a sheen like warm coconut oil. Although the pool had seemed endlessly deep, he was able to step right out of it to stand on the dry stone. The chinchilla lady was grinning a puffy-cheeked grin as she stared up at him.

"There now. Took you long enough. Wasn't so hard, was it?"

"That was completely barmy. I mean, glowing head horns? Robes?"

The chinchilla giggled into her hands. "Look, kid, I don't come up with this stuff. You see what you need to see. And you've been granted your greatest wish."

Vic looked down at his hands, focused, and conjured an exquisite bear claw.

"How do you know?" he asked, gently dropping the bear claw in front of the chinchilla.

She began nibbling it and gave him a tiny thumbs-up. "Well, I already like you, so that's one person. Now, get out of here and—"

"And?" Vic asked, anxious to receive more wisdom.

The chinchilla burped into a fist. "And do whatever you want. You're free. Nothing stopping you. You got your wildest dream, and now you've got to figure out how to go on."

Vic took a nervous step toward the pool. "Maybe I could just go back in and . . . ?"

"Nope. From here on out, you figure it out yourself. But believe me—choices are a lot more fun when they're all your own to make."

With that, she shooed him away, hopping along the stone behind him. Vic turned to wave goodbye, wishing he could stay for a while longer in the peaceful, contented Woom.

But his next step landed on white sand, and then he was on the beach again.

When he approached the dinghy, both of the red shirts were staring at him, agog.

"What, didn't think I'd be back so soon?" Vic asked.

"No, it's just that you're covered in blood," one of the men said.

"Oh, don't mind that." Vic grinned and offered them each a bracing éclair. "Placenta is good for a shiny coat."

26.

STICKY WITH FAILURE GROG
AND DISCOMFITING REALIZATIONS

"Ye got an A," Luc said, pinning his eye on Morgan.

She sighed in relief and went a little boneless, at ease for the first time in weeks. She'd been dreading the PSAT—the Pirate Studies Aptitude Test—and she hadn't been feeling good about her first attempt at the practice test, which Luc had just graded.

"An A? That's great!" she said.

But he shook his head. "No, lass. It ain't. The A is for *Arrrrgh*. Ye wanted a Y for *Yarrrr*! I'm sorrrry to say ye've failed."

Feng placed the test on the scarred wooden desk nailed to the floor of Captain Luc's quarters. Scratched in blood-red ink, it said *50/100* and, again, that word: *Arrrrgh*. Morgan flipped through it and was crushed to see Luc's little red footprints marking Xs—well, actually, Ys—over many of her answers. Her essays ran red with ink blood and white with a few parrot plops. For all that she felt at home on the deck and comfortable performing almost every duty Luc had thrown at her, the intricacies of official piracy were maddeningly . . .

intricate. From the recruitment of crew, to the twisted tax and bribe rules in port, to which flag to use when, to how many weevils were acceptable in hot dog buns, her head felt like a chum bucket swimming with useless answers.

"So what happens now?" she asked quietly.

Luc gave an avian shrug. "It's like anything else, lass. You take yerrrr licks, study what you got wrrrrrong, wait a week, and trrrry again. Oh, and tonight you get a full horrrrn o' grrrrog."

"Getting drunk after an awful disappointment is always fitting," Morgan quoted from the manual, but she didn't sound happy about it. She looked up at Luc and cocked her head. "Captain, have you ever failed the PSAT?"

Luc glanced away, preening the feathers on his back for a moment. "Parrrrots got a long memorrrrry, lass. Just how I'm made. You've a good hand with rrrreal-worrrrld solutions, so I'm surrrrre this was just firrrrst-test jitterrrrs. Don't take it too harrrrd, aye?"

She couldn't stop her shoulders from sinking. "Aye, Captain."

"And don't forrrrget, lass—ye don't need to pass the test to save them otterrrrs. A courrrrrageous hearrrrt is worrrrrth morrrrre than cerrrrtification. Now, go see yourrrr shipmates. Vic and Tempest have both come back, and Feng says they look like they've seen some shite."

Morgan picked up the hateful test, and as soon as she was on the deck, she sadly galumphed to the rail and threw it overboard, watching it sink into the sea before a pod of chattering dolphins arrived to playfully tear it to shreds.

"What was that?" Tempest asked, nudging her gently with a shoulder.

Morgan turned to her friend, and she did indeed look like she'd seen some shite. The brown splotch of tree bark on her arm was much bigger than before, for one thing. But she'd asked Morgan a question, so Morgan started there.

"That was my first PSAT. Practice PSAT, technically."

A dolphin horked and vomited up a red-splattered page, chittering angrily that anyone would serve up such tasteless fare.

"I guess it didn't go so well?"

Morgan looked around the ship, cataloging everything she could've actually gotten right on the test. She knew every knot used. She knew what was in the hold. She knew the names of the crew and the contents of every treasure chest, but that was a drop in the swabbing bucket compared to a world the comparative size of the sea.

"I failed."

Tempest smothered her gasp in a cough and did that thing where people act five times as perky to cover up their horror. "Hey, no big deal! It was only a practice! Now you'll know better! You can take it again! That didn't count! Hey, I'm using way more exclamation points than anyone uses in real life, aren't I? That's so weird!"

"Yeah." Morgan slumped against the rail, and Otto waddled in from somewhere and climbed up to pat her cheek with his paw.

"Anything I can do?" Tempest put her hand on Morgan's arm, and Morgan studied her friend. Tempest looked the same, really, but there was something new there, besides the bark. Morgan couldn't quite put her finger on it.

"No, I just need to feel my emotions right now," she said. "But what about you? You seem . . . different."

Now it was Tempest's turn to look away.

"Something happened on the island. I'm fine, but . . ."

"But?"

Tempest gave her a brave smile, the sort that has nothing to do with happiness or amusement but is intended to be an aegis against pain. "Brawny Billy died and it rattled me."

"Oh, no! I really liked him."

"Me too. And the ding gulls . . . Morgan, they are so terrible and beautiful at the same time. And that's what people say about dryads, you know? Terrible when we're trees, beautiful when we're bipeds. It's given me much to think about."

The ship shuddered under their feet, and both women turned in time to watch the crew undo the pulley straps around Vic's belly and hindquarters. The centaur also looked . . . different. His shoulders were back, his chin was up, and he was actually smiling. And handing out cookies as he thanked the people who'd heaved him up onto the deck. Seeing Morgan and Tempest, he waved and clopped over.

"Where've you been?" Morgan asked, knowing from experience that the only way to get anything out of the centaur was to ask very pointed questions that couldn't be answered with shrugs and *sure, bruh.*

"I made the pilgrimage to the Temple of Woom," Vic said, offering them each a lovely tea cake with a mermaid theme and little gold curlicues of fondant. He conjured a teacup for himself and, for the first time, drank it in full view of the entire ship, without turning his rump and hiding his sipping behind his massive shoulders. He even let his pinky stick out.

"The Temple of Woom? I haven't heard of that. What is it?"

Vic smiled a dreamy, satisfied smile—another very new expression for him. "It's a spiritual experience. The journey there is . . ." He trailed off and his eyes focused on the distance, recalling something, but he resumed his story further along. "And then you get there and . . ." He snorted and leaned down conspiratorially. "Right? And the mystic chinchilla rolls up and says—well, nah. I think it's a very personal thing. I can just tell you that it was good for me."

Morgan and Tempest looked at each other, dumbstruck. It was the most Vic had ever spoken in one go, and he hadn't used the words *bro, bruh, dude,* or *sup* a single time. He looked relaxed and contented, and Morgan bit into the tea cake and nearly exploded with sensory bliss.

"That tea cake is amazing," she enthused after shoving the whole thing in her mouth. "Did you use new ingredients?"

But Vic only smiled and gently patted her shoulder. "The secret ingredient is love. Self-love." He began to walk away and then turned around to hurriedly assure her, "Not in a gross, creepy way. I just learned not to hate myself, and apparently that makes the magic more powerful. Pretty cool, right? Now, let's get sailing and save some otters!"

With that, he headed toward a group of red shirts, whom he relieved of swabbing duty.

"That was a surprise," Tempest said.

Morgan slumped down until her chin was on the ship's railing, wishing she had two dozen of those mermaid tea cakes and a big bottle of wine and could binge-watch some of the more romantic Sharkspeer plays at a festival somewhere. "Maybe I should visit that temple of his. I feel like I need a spiritual experience."

Tempest rubbed the brown spots on her arm with her thumb. "I think that with that sort of thing, you don't so much go to it expecting to be remade. It comes to you when you need it, and you do the work, and then it takes root."

With their centaur on board, the ship set sail. Morgan looked longingly at the now receding island, wondering what had happened to Vic and Tempest there. Mack Guphinne was surely more powerful than it appeared from out here on the ship. And instead of going there and having an adventure, she'd stayed here and failed a test. And now they were sailing away, shortly to bury Brawny Billy at sea. Morgan looked up at the crow's nest, where Al's red hair was billowing in the breeze. Everyone seemed to know where they belonged, except her. She'd been so certain before that test, but now . . .

She'd never failed at anything before.

And it sucked.

"Where are you going?" Tempest asked as Morgan slumped away.

"To retrieve my failure grog and get drunk."

"Do you want company?"

The answer should've been yes, but it was no. Morgan wanted to marinate in her embarrassment and disappointment without anyone studying her, trying to fix her, saying they were sorry, or mentioning that when she got upset, her face got rashy.

"Just take care of Otto for me, okay? I don't want him to see me like this." She handed over her otter and went to find the grog.

As she walked away, she heard Otto chittering nervously.

"I know," Tempest said, as if she understood everything he said. "She *is* starting to look a little rashy."

Alone it was.

⁓≈⁓

The main problem with being really, truly drunk for the first time, Morgan reasoned, or tried to reason, was that everything got wobbly. Right now the ship felt like it was upside down, which was not a problem covered by anything she'd read in any of the pirate manuals.

"Profably get that one wrong on the test too," she muttered to the huge black horn of grog Milly Dread had given her. "Know what I mean, Horny? Wait. S'not a good name. Whassa good name for the chopped-off body parts of goats? Goatly?" She took a deep, comforting swig. "Yeah. You get me, Mister Goatly. We really get along."

The ship was at full speed, which she knew because everything was sloshy. And the sea was being more sloshy than usual, as walking caused her many problems. The floorboards, it seemed, were out to get her. And the crew had so very many questions, like "Hey, are you okay?" And "Where can I get one of those giant dunce caps full of grog?" And "Is that vomit?" That's why she'd flopped down into the hold, where things were nice and dark and quiet. Now it was just her and Goatly.

Or so she thought.

"Young bearded woman, what are you doing?"

Lifting her head, she saw a very stern-looking ghost aiming his ectoplasmic hook right at her.

"Oh, grah! Grossbeard! I mean, Beardskull! I mean . . . hey . . . you," she answered, nearly falling off the chest upon which she was splayed. "Thought you got . . ." Her muddled brain struggled for the right word. What had the Cinnamonks done? "Thought you got some exercise."

"I," the ghostly figure said, drawing itself up firmly, "am clearly not Skullbeard. That boring fool got himself exorcised by those meddling monks. Glad to have him gone from my ship, finally. I am his predecessor, Davey Bones."

"The guy with the locker?"

The ghost, who she now realized was wearing an older version of a pirate's costume, pulled an ornate necklace out of his fluffy jabot and draped it over his sharp hook. "It's a locket, actually. Lovely, is it not?"

The object in question was mostly see-through and slightly dripping with ectoplasm, so she merely nodded and made an appreciative *ooh* noise.

"Failed a PSAT, I assume," the ghost said knowingly, awkwardly squatting on a box nearby as if trying to sit and somewhat failing, as he was incorporeal. "I remember when I failed my first PSAT. I can still taste the grog in my dunce cap."

"S'a goat horn. S'name is Mr. Goatly," she corrected, taking a deep swig.

"No, my dear, I'm afraid that's a dunce cap. Most captains learn to drink deeply from it before they ever earn their hat."

Morgan held out the black cone, saw the truth of it, and nearly dashed the dratted thing against the wall. But . . . grog. So she kept sipping.

"Just wish I knew what I was s'posed to do wif my life," she said, half to herself and half to Mr. Goatly the Dunce Cap and half to the ghost pirate politely picking his nose as he watched her, and she was so deep in her cups that the math made sense. "Didn't wanna marry the Taynt. I mean the Vas Deference. Who's a lord. Or somethin'. Was cursed 'n' hairy 'n' woke up 'n' left. An' now I'm a pirate. Sailor. Thought I was meant to be a captain. But Arrrrgh!"

The ghost startled and stared at her with concern. "What's wrong?"

"S'the grade I got. Arrrgh. Nowhere close to a Yarrr, even if they sound about the same right now. Arrrghyarrr. Yarrrrgh. But if I'm not s'posed to be a pirate, what'm I supposed to be? Prolly not even good enough to save the otters."

Davey stood and paced a bit, but with far more gravitas than

Skullbeard had ever shown. Morgan prepared herself for a lecture on navigation or maybe a whine about the number of spoons in the mess, which Skullbeard had found offensive; as Skullbeard was the first ghost she'd ever met, Morgan assumed they were all boring and pedantic. Instead, this ghost tried to put a hand on her shoulder and make eye contact for an uncomfortable period of time.

"What are you doing?"

"I'm giving you a Look of Great Import," Davey explained.

"Well, blink or somefin. It's uncomfy."

He drew back. "Look here, my lady. Just because you fail at something doesn't mean it's not your destiny. Do you think Pangolini, the great violinist, played perfectly the first time he tried? Do you think Pickleangelo picked up his first paintbrush and created a masterpiece?"

". . . Yes?" she said, knowing she had a 50 percent chance of being right.

"No. Everyone has to wallow in failure for a while. And if you keep at it, you get better. That's what makes great people great. Not that they were born with great talent, but that they stuck with it, kept on with it, even when it got hard." He leaned in so close that Morgan could smell the ghost of failure grog. "I myself was not so great a ghost when I first began. If I'd properly scared off Skullbeard when he was alive, my afterlife would've been far more pleasant."

"But were you a good captain?" she asked.

He raised a ghostly eyebrow. "Well, I'm dead. So probably not. But I was an amazing mime before I lost my hand."

Davey looked like he was about to walk back through the wall, but Morgan suddenly didn't want to be alone.

"Wait! Mr. Beardbones! Skulllocket! Davey!"

The ghost turned around, head cocked. "Yes?"

"Lessay I stick with captaining. How do I know that's what I'm s'posed to do?"

He did the unblinky stare thing again. "There is no 's'posed.' You simply pick something to do. And then you do it until you're not terrible at it. That's the secret. But if you're looking for outside confirmation, you might try visiting the Oracle of Pellanus on Mack Enchiis. Although I have not visited the oracle myself, my predecessor Bluebones did."

"And did th'oracle help him?"

Davey shrugged. "I don't know. He died before I could ask. That's how I got the ship."

The ghost disappeared, and Morgan tried to put down the dunce cap but couldn't figure out how to do so without spilling grog. She felt her will coalesce and at least knew her next step: She would go to see this oracle and find out what the future held. And she wouldn't die doing it either. If there was one thing she knew she didn't want to do, it was to be yet another annoying ghost on *The Pearly Clam*. Holding Mr. Goatly, she did her best to sloshily stomp up to Captain Luc's quarters.

"I want to see the oracle on Mack Enchiis," she said with true captainlike command.

But then she ruined it by exiting in a hurry to yark over the rail.

And that was how, one week later, Morgan came to be standing alone on a black-sand beach, her hands blistered and dry from rowing the smaller dinghy out to the least popular part of the island called Mack Enchiis. It wasn't going to be an easy trip, Luc had told her—and which maybe Davey Bones should've mentioned while giving her a speech she'd mostly forgotten but was sure she'd taken to heart.

First, she had to climb the Cliffs of Inanity, the bottom portions of which looked stark and forbidding until she put her hands on the frayed rope and realized it was super easy to climb, all while adorable puffins flew and danced and sang around her. The tough part was not laughing so hard at their antics that she fell off the rope. Once she'd pulled herself up onto the plateau above, a sign told her to walk the labyrinth, but it was actually one of those labyrinths made of small stones and was very easily traversed. Lastly, she had to answer the

Questions Three to earn the right to cross a bridge, but as it turned out, the questions posed to her by a disconsolate guard were pretty simple.

"What's your game?"

"Dungeons and Flagons."

"If you could pick any nose, whose would you pick?"

"Mine."

"Do you have any hardtack? Because I don't get paid good for guarding this bridge, you know."

"Sure."

Morgan was once again glad that she always carried extra snacks. After that, it was a short jaunt to the crumbling stone temple. As she walked up the path, she wondered if this was how Vic had felt, approaching his Temple of Woom; perhaps, like Dinny's, this was some sort of franchise? She was excited that she might get answers but terrified that they might not be things she wanted to hear. It reminded her of how she'd felt right before opening the PSAT, which was a bad sign. But she was committed, and she would walk through that grand door and discover her future even if it destroyed her.

As she stepped inside, she felt as if she were crossing over from one life into another, as if the next stage might begin within, when she learned her destiny. The soaring ceiling was painted with visions of Pellanus and the myths, and torches burned in sconces, and a bored guy in his twenties sat at a desk.

Morgan did a double take, but that's exactly what she saw. No mystical pool, no fountain, no maidens in long white dresses, no old blind seer with one of those stick things. Not even a knitting chinchilla.

Just an exceedingly normal guy at a desk.

"Can I help you?" he asked, looking up as if she'd interrupted something desperately important, even though he was clearly doing a word search in which he had found exactly one word.

"I am but a humble pilgrim seeking the wisdom of the oracle," she said in the proper sort of mystical, committed tone.

"Okaaaay," the guy said, still staring at her.

A few beats passed before she asked, "So how should I go about doing that?"

"Just ask me whatever."

Morgan looked around for someone else, for some trick—or at least for a visitor's chair, as she'd gone through quite a lot to get here and was excited about the prospect of sitting. But the temple was clearly empty other than the guy at the desk, who was now tapping his finger in a pointed sort of way.

"Uh, okay." She took a deep breath. "What am I supposed to do with my life?"

The guy was now doing that half-squint thing that suggested she was an idiot and he was already bored.

"How the Pell should I know?" he asked.

"Isn't that what oracles do? Tell you the future?"

The guy chuckled and leaned back in his chair, putting his dirty bare feet up on the desk. "Oh, sorry, no. You've got it all wrong. I'm a boracle. And I can only tell you your past."

"How," Morgan asked, trying not to shout, "is that helpful to anyone ever?" But seeing his sneer, the shouting happened anyway. "I was *there* for my past. I lived it!"

"But you didn't understand it. You clearly know nothing about this sort of thing."

"Clearly."

For a long moment, they just stared at each other, arms crossed.

"I can see you doubt my powers," the guy said, nose in the air.

"I'm not seeing you *exhibit* any powers," Morgan shot back.

The guy put his feet down and shifted forward in his chair, steepling his hands on the desk. "Oh, because I'm here to show off for you? Because, what, I'm like an animal in the zoo? Because I'm some dancing monkey?"

"Because I guess this is your job, and you, I don't know, want to do it? Or help people? I mean, I could accept you being cryptic. I was *expecting* cryptic. But rude is uncalled for. Forget it."

"Forget what? I never offered you anything. You clearly have no interest in my work."

"What work? A word search? In which you've only circled *boobs*? What a phony."

As Morgan stomped off toward the door, infuriated with him and with herself for thinking she was going to have some life-changing experience based on a ghost's recommendation based on his dead boss's probable cause of death, she heard the man's chair scoot back.

"Dueling curses," he said.

Morgan turned around slowly. "What did you say?"

She'd expected the man's eyes to be all white, or for a vapor to surround him and lift him into the air, or for there to be some sign of the gods' interference and more-mystical qualities, or at least the creative and humane use of theatrical snakes. But he was just standing behind his desk, leaning aggressively forward on it like he was daring her to ask for a manager, and there was a ketchup stain on his jerkin.

"Dueling curses," he said with a grin of triumph. "The most recent curse put you to sleep. But the first curse? That one set you on the path to being a pirate. The sleeping curse was trying to stop the first curse."

The world tilted under Morgan's feet, or perhaps she wasn't dealing with the elevation well. All of this information was news to her.

"Please tell me more," she said.

The man sat down and interlaced his fingers. "Oh, so now you're interested in what I have to say?"

"I was always interested! But this is the first thing you've actually said that was about me."

"Well, you haven't even asked the first thing about *me*," he snapped. "My name is Roy, in case you were wondering; I'm a pretty good cook, and my favorite color is evergreen."

Morgan's heart was beating like crazy, but she was beginning to see how things were going to go, so she put on her most polite, patient smile. "Well, it's very nice to meet you, Roy. What you just said was really interesting. All I knew was that someone had cursed me to sleep. Is there any way you would use your impressive skills to tell me more about that other curse, the first one?"

Roy preened a little, pleased at her flattery. "What I'm seeing indicates that the first curse was laid at your baby shower. Your mom's ex, some Dark Lord wizard dude named Timmy Fitzherbert, was angry that he wasn't invited to the shower, so he showed up and cursed you. Said that you'd grow up to be a pirate, thereby destroying your father's shipping investments and the chance of a political alliance with some wealthy nobleman in Taynt. And then the second curse was laid to stop the piracy curse."

Morgan finally found her breath to answer. "No. That can't be right. I was there when the second curse was cast. It was because Grinda the Sand Witch was mad that she wasn't invited to my sixteenth birthday party."

Roy sighed and rested his chin in one hand. "Witch, please. Grinda was protecting her own shipping interests and trying to maintain political equilibrium. A bit of advice: Never trust a sand witch." And then, when Morgan stood there agape, he added, "And maybe don't have parties anymore. They don't seem to end well for you. Not that the baby-shower thing was your fault, but still."

"So you're saying . . . I was cursed to be a pirate."

"Yep."

"And the second curse was to stop that, but it's broken. So the only curse I'm currently under is the pirate one."

"Supposedly."

Morgan's head was spinning. All this time, she'd thought becoming a pirate was her first original venture, the very first path she'd chosen for herself. Learning that it was the very path she was cursed to tread was making her brain short-circuit. She'd come here with the hope that the oracle would tell her that she would eventually become a world-class pirate captain, that she'd rule the seas and ensure the safety of every mustelid in Pell. But instead, the future was still nebulous, and the past was more tangled than ever. If she was doomed to be a pirate, why had she failed the stupid PSAT? How could she be bad at the very thing she was cursed to do?

Or . . . wait. Maybe she was meant to be a pirate.

Not a captain. Not a *great* pirate. Not anyone special. Just a regular ol' deck swabber.

Maybe she was supposed to grow old and take over for Milly Dread, doling out grog and hardtack and singing shanties about the supple glutes of dwarvelish tampoonists. Maybe she was destined to take the PSAT again and again and fail every time.

"Thanks," she said, but it was an empty word.

Dropping her gold piece into the bowl on Roy's desk marked PUT GOLD PIECE HERE WHEN DONE; NO CHANGE OFFERED; NONE OF THAT HAVE-A-FICKEL-LEAVE-A-FICKEL SHITE, she headed back out into the balmy afternoon, feeling empty and raw.

"Wait!" Roy called behind her. "One more thing!"

Morgan turned around in the doorway, holding in her tears. "What?"

"I thought you should know that while you were asleep, there was a dead farm boy rolled up in a tapestry in your closet. Decomposing and getting seriously gross."

Morgan stared at Roy. "How is that helpful?"

"Didn't say it was helpful. Just said I knew your past and I thought that bit was interesting, since that farm boy's death eventually led to King Gustave taking the throne. Also, you're looking a bit rashy. Good luck!"

She didn't remember much about the walk back to the ship. Tempest touched her shoulder, and Vic offered her a cake, which she refused, and Al called down a welcome, which she didn't return. And then she curled up in her bunk with Otto and cried.

27.

ON THE DOCK WHERE IT HAPPENS

Alobartalus didn't want to come down from the crow's nest. Not that he was making much progress on his project, but he liked it up there. The sway of it, the sparkling ribbons of sun-kissed foam on the sea winking at him, the creak of boards and the clap and whip of sails and ropes—yeah, no, he actually *loved* it up there. It was like being in the Proudwood Lighthouse without the tourists or the passive-aggressive memos from his uncle, with the added bonus of outstanding tea and cakes from Vic. But he did need to come down and use the part of the poop deck set aside for the actual deed.

And as he did, his elf butt dangling over the sea, he circled back again to the perplexing problem of the Sn'archivist, who was supposedly inspired by Pellanus to write about butts like his, for no discernible reason. Unless Al was to believe the Sn'archivist when he said that elf butts and otter balls would somehow save them in their hour of need.

But Al had so many problems envisioning how this could be true and wondered if it was a failure of his imagination. Supposing that their hour of need would come at Mack Guyverr—a working theory, since that was where there would presumably be otter balls because so many otters were being horribly turned into EATUM for Dinny's—how in Pell would elf butts figure in their salvation? And was the plural significant? Was Al's own butt to be counted among the elf butts of note in this scenario? What if Al was the only elf there? Did that mean Pellanus had inspired a prophecy referring to both of his cheeks as an individual butt, thereby making up the requisite minimum of two for a plural? Was Al's butt, in fact, a Butt of Destiny? A Butt of Action? He felt it was inadequate, if so. And if there were going to be additional elf butts on site at Mack Guyverr, why were the owners of said butts involved in such a shady operation as the processing of otter meat for consumption in greasy diners?

And then he had to doublethink his doubt. His shipmates, after all, were proof that strange destinies happened all the time. Luc was a one-eyed parrot who had somehow become one of the most feared pirate captains of the western seas. Vic was an emotionally scarred swoleboy who could conjure the most exquisite tea and cake out of nothing. Tempest was a dryad learning how to be a lawyer, and Morgan was a proper lady learning how to be a pirate and navigate the hairy rules of beard care. They were all extraordinary beings behaving contrary to expectations. So why, when the moment came, could not his butt perform an extraordinary act of heroism?

He supposed it just didn't feel possible. Al flexed one cheek and then the other experimentally to see if they felt heroic. They did not, but perhaps they would with training. He should practice: *one and two, one and two, one and two.*

"Hey, Al, could you cut that out? It's really distracting." Al swung his head around and saw Feng staring at him from near the wheel, but without the captain perched on his shoulder. "Not that I object to the maintenance of a firm backside, you understand. I encourage it! But maybe you could do that where the crew won't see it and forget what they're supposed to be doing."

Al nearly fell overboard in his haste to pull up his trousers. He was so embarrassed that he couldn't manage a single word of reply.

"Don't worry," Feng said as Al scurried past him toward the ladder to the crow's nest. "I don't think anyone else saw, and I won't say anything about your glute-flexing regimen."

Al gave him a jerky nod, which was one part acknowledgment and one part thanks, and began the climb back up to the crow's nest. How could he even begin to explain what he was doing? That was the very worst part of all this. Without perishing of mortification, he couldn't possibly discuss with anyone the vital role his butt might play in their collective futures. He'd even tried inspecting Otto's nethers once to see if they seemed important and had taken an indignant swipe to the cheek; the otter had avoided him since. He had to figure it out all by his lonesome.

That's why he'd been spending so much time scribbling furiously in his journal. There had to be some secret message hidden in the elf butts—or the otter balls, or both—to make sense of what Pellanus was trying to communicate through the Sn'archivist. He'd filled pages with possible anagrams—which elves did enjoy, as opposed to acronyms—but nothing made sense so far. Why did gods have to be so cryptic and mysterious? One would think that clear communication would be included in the suite of skills that came with omniscience and omnipotence.

Perhaps if he could have hindsight in advance he'd see things more clearly. He had belatedly figured out that Clan Nabi was an anagram for cannibal. The warning had been there all along, hidden in plain sight. He didn't want to be too late figuring out this other puzzle.

He'd no sooner reached the nest and calmed himself by looking at the wondrous Cliffs of Inanity than Qobayne shouted for him to come down again. They were pulling up anchor and heading for Mack Guyverr, and the boatswain required his expertise with knots and sails.

The deck was soon awhirl with activity as sailors leapt to perform the tasks Qobayne set them. Captain Luc was once again on Feng's shoulder by the wheel, and Morgan had emerged from her bunk to help Vic with the sails on the mainmast; Tempest was on the foc's'le, struggling with the spinnaker, so he went forward to help her.

"Sorry," she said. "It's half incompetence and half not wanting to leave. These cliffs are so beautiful."

"They are," Al agreed, admiring the puffins and other seabirds whirling in a gyre above the rocks and diving into the ocean for fish. The small pads of flowers emerging from crevices in the moss-covered rocks shouted in myriad colors to bees that they were, in fact, ready to be pollinated. They were watered by seeps of freshwater and tiny runoff streams from the top, forming a lush vertical garden down to the point where the crash of surf and saltwater spray made their freshwater lives untenable.

"Do you know if anyone owns this land?" Al asked as he tied one tether of the spinnaker to the bowsprit.

"The area around the cliffs is a nature preserve. I think that's what they should do to Mack Guphinne, to ensure that the ding gulls survive. I don't think it should ever be private."

"A nature preserve? Who determines what a nature preserve is?"

"They're created by the king."

"No kidding?" An idea was forming in Al's mind, a way forward for him. He'd figured out after only a few days on the ocean that he never wanted to sell Morningwood rods to tourists again and he was never going back to Proudwood Lighthouse, but he didn't want to be like the half-mad Sn'archivist either, writing down the monotonous words of a deity every day, with only an affirmation gecko to reassure him that he wasn't wasting his life—although he wouldn't turn down a gecko of his own, if one were offered. The pirate's lot was not exactly for him; while he liked the sea fine, the life was rather violent and he did not enjoy being either predator or prey. "Can a nature preserve be formed on land already claimed or owned by someone else?"

Tempest smiled, always glad to talk law. "Of course. The king can do what he wants. He pays for it, of course—he doesn't just steal it—but whoever owns it has to take the crown's offer or nothing."

"That is . . . amazing. How often does the king do this?"

"Not often. I don't think King Gustave has done it yet. He's been busy with other things."

"How would one convince him to do it?" Al asked.

"From what I hear, by offering him a really nice boot. Or some expertly crafted gnomeric oatmeal. But if you mean logistically, you'd need a petition that outlines how such a preserve would be to the vast benefit of Pell. Natural assets must be there, of course, but it would probably help if you can make some economic arguments too. Keep the king's oatmeal coffers filled while doing a good deed, that sort of thing."

Al felt the swell of destiny. "Would you help me craft such a petition? I will compensate you for your time, of course."

Tempest beamed at him. "I think you've already compensated me fairly with all your help on board. You've been doing your work and quite a bit of mine besides. I'm just not good at knots, not that I don't try."

They sat together at the next opportunity and crafted two petitions for nature preserves: one on Mack Guphinne for the ding gulls, and one at the particular place Al had in mind. The language was twisty and regal and strange, and Al felt a rush of warmth for the dryad. Without her knowledge and spirit of giving, what he hoped to do—well, it would not have been possible.

"You're doing a lot of good in the world," Al told her as she crossed the last *T*.

Tempest looked down, almost conflicted. "*We're* doing a lot of good in the world. And it was your idea. I can't wait to see how it all turns out."

"You misspelled *foine*," a ghost said, popping up over Tempest's shoulder, and Al wagged a hand through Davey Bones's chest to shoo the vexing poltergeist away. With the paperwork complete, Al felt a new sort of certainty. Not the sort of certainty the Sn'archivist felt about elf butts, but something on the way there.

At dawn the next day, the whirlwind surrounding Mack Guyverr hove into view and Qobayne supervised the slathering of hard-won ding-gull berry juices on the ship's prow. Al was roped into that duty—literally lowered with a rope around his chest and a mop and bucket in hand to the proper level for swabbing. He was nearly overcome by nausea on several occasions as he worked the foul juices into the wood, painting the crisp white prow a viscous, drippy, lumpy brown.

As they approached the vortex and Al scrubbed at his berry-stained arms with a sponge, Feng relayed orders from Luc. "If this doesn't work, we need to be ready to get out of there! Sails down on my command and then man the oars!"

Al understood the danger. If Skullbeard had steered them wrong—pranked them, whatever—that whirlwind would take hold of their sails and wreck them. They'd need oars to get through or get themselves out, either way. And it was no polite whirlwhind that the witch-who'd-once-dated-the-Dread-Necromancer-Steve-but-was-now-a-marmoset-in-Songlen had conjured. It was a spiraling vortex of leaves, branches, assorted moth bits, and the business cards of insurance agents, the swirling cyclone towering a hundred feet or more into the air, completely obscuring what might be beyond. Anyone not knowing what it was or how to get through it would naturally sail around to avoid getting plastered by the sales slogans of humans who made their living off other people's fear of accidents.

Al thought it probable that all insurance policies sold by the people on the cards would specifically exclude damage by magical vortex.

As they neared, the winds could be felt in advance. Al got splattered by a moth, the body bursting against his cheek like a small gray water balloon.

"Aw, yuck," he said, wiping the goo away. Others suffered similar fates, though Al noticed that Morgan and Tempest only got hit by the business cards of agents who had placed their portraits on them, their dead-eyed faces grinning like a rictus as fat letters exclaimed, *You'll be safe with Allsafe!*

The hull visibly tilted to the right as they got close, and Feng ordered the oars to pull them forward. But once the bowsprit, liberally drenched in ding-gull berry juice, pierced the visible wall of the vortex, the winds calmed and rerouted themselves over the crow's nest, providing a ship-sized window through which they could row in calm water. The island of Mack Guyverr could be seen through it, a small promontory jutting out of the ocean and completely occupied by buildings. There was no verdant jungle teeming with life. It was an industrial site with a shipping bay; several ships were in port, and others were on their way out or in. Feng steered them toward a complicated dock replete with several cranes. They kept on using the oars since the interior of the vortex was like the eye of a hurricane, with no winds to speed their sails.

"Al!" Captain Luc called. "Get up to the nest and tell me what yourrrr elf eyes see."

"Aye, Cap'n!" He scurried up the mast spars to his favorite spot on the ship and looked ahead.

There was a troll on the dock, towering over the humans. The huge, lumbering creature was built out of chiseled muscle and cruelty, which seemed strange until he remembered that the manager at Dinny's had mentioned that his sales rep was a troll named Brenna MacFleshgrinder. Al doubted a sales representative would be waiting for them at the docks, so the MMA must employ multiple trolls.

Stacked six high on the dock were cages full of chittering, crying otters. And there were also two elves in a larger cage, their flowing robes shredded, their lush locks tangled and greasy, their perfect skin marred by smudges of filth. Al did not recognize them, but that was little wonder; he'd not been in the Morningwood for many years. He relayed all this information to his captain but remained at his post, watching the scene below.

Pity for the captives and rage at the captors swelled in Al's breast and then, added to the mix, a stab of revelation: There on the dock were the very otter balls and elf butts the Sn'archivist had foretold! How strange, Al thought, to be a living witness to the fulfillment of divine prophecy, if that's what all this was—and to be aware of it, especially. To recognize that everyone had free will at this moment and yet, somehow, the decisions made and actions taken had been foretold, at least in part, by Pellanus.

But of course Al's primary concern was how they would ever manage to defeat that troll on the dock, because destiny was well and good but nobody had said Al would get out alive.

"You can't spell alive without Al," he told himself, enjoying the wordplay.

And then, suddenly, it came to him. His brain made the kind of intuitive leap one normally makes in the shower or in a dreamlike fugue state after eating dodgy mushrooms. During those long hours in the crow's nest scribbling anagrams in his notebook, he'd come up with one that didn't make any sense until this moment: *Otter balls* could be rearranged to spell *beats troll*! And there was a troll! One they needed to beat, in fact! Standing on the dock in front of many, many otters, some of which must possess balls!

"Whoa," Al breathed. "I cannot wait to see how this plays out."

He climbed down to the deck and reported the numbers and types of potential adversaries in greater detail, being very careful not to say anything weird about his excitement for otter balls.

As *The Pearly Clam* neared the dock, one of the human stevedores— who might also be mercenary fighters—shouted over to them, "Have your paperwork ready as soon as you tie up!"

"Aye aye!" Feng replied.

Captain Luc called Vic over to him and quietly spoke to the centaur as Feng handed over a rolled-up scroll of paper. Morgan stood nearby, her sword strapped on, and Al saw Tempest drift in that direction too. He was ready to join them, when Qobayne ordered him to be ready with the gangplank as soon as they tied up.

"And get the broad, sturdy one for cargo, ye hear?"

"Aye, Boatswain."

He'd need to pair up with someone for that, and Gorp volunteered.

The troll had a huge war hammer in its hand, and the stevedores were all armed with daggers and some with short swords as well. They bunched up on the dock, eyeing the crew with suspicion. Skullbeard had said he'd sailed *The Pearly Clam* in there before, but that had been ages ago, and the ship had been repainted.

The dock, a broad floating number that stretched out for a long way over open water to allow large boats to tie up, led to a quay stacked with barrels of EATUM. Beyond that was a massive stone-and-mortar edifice. Five chimneys belched out greasy smoke, and all the windows were up high, with what looked like sentries watching from shaded balconies. Huge letters made of black stone spelled out MMA on the side. Some smaller buildings with many windows squatted in front of it, and Al ventured that those must be dorms for the workers. On the other side of the island, perhaps, there were pubs and jolly parks and a waterslide, but more likely there was only a giant sluice that dumped blood and offal into the ocean.

As they drew closer, Al examined the faces of the men waiting on the dock, searching for some telltale sign that would mark them as pure evil, the kind of people who would commit environmental atrocities to provide a cheap side dish in a chain of diners, but he found none. No one had tattooed BAD DUDE on their forehead or wore a necklace made of otter feet. They were simply people who looked normal but were apparently willing to sacrifice the future for present profit. Perhaps they didn't even consider themselves monsters. Monsters, in Al's experience, rarely did.

The Pearly Clam fetched up to the dock, and lines were thrown to the stevedores. They tied up and Al lowered the gangplank with Gorp. A human began to ascend once it touched the dock but skipped back when he saw Vic clopping down and merrily shouting at them, waving a scroll. "Behold, my friends! We have a purchase order for EATUM!"

"Stay up there!" the guard shouted. He was a sunburned man, his face leathery and wrinkled, and perhaps an eighth of Vic's size and weight. The centaur simply beamed at him and kept coming.

"Nonsense, I'll bring it to you!"

The troll moved to block the bottom of the ramp, brandishing the hammer and nudging the human aside, and Vic called out a welcome. "Braaah! You are so swole and cut! How much do you lift?"

"Go back," the troll growled.

"Whaaa? There's no going back, bro. Plank is too narrow for me to turn around. Centaurs can't go uphill in reverse. It is known. Just let me turn around down here at the bottom, okay?"

"No." The troll raised his hammer. "Go back!"

Vic twiddled his fingers and made a high-pitched mewling noise, and molten cream-cheese frosting plastered over the troll's eyes. He bellowed and clutched at his face, taking a step back, and then Vic swiftly followed that up by kicking him in the chest with his front hooves. The troll staggered and fell over, knocking a few otter cages off the dock and into the water.

"Charrrrge!" Captain Luc called, and Morgan was first down the plank, now that the way was clear, Otto chirping indignantly on her shoulder. Al and Tempest and a bunch of other sailors followed, and the captain swooped down, raking talons across enemy eyes. But Vic had never stopped. He barreled over some humans, kicked others, and turned around so that when the troll got to his feet, his chest met the full impact of a swole centaur's hindquarters. Vic's hooves clocked him in the sternum, and the troll flew bodily off the dock, plunging into the Chummy Sea with more otter cages.

"Vic, no, the otters!" Morgan cried, and she dove in after them with Otto.

"Hey, wait! The troll's in there too!" Tempest reminded them.

Al knew that Morgan didn't need to worry; trolls did not swim well. Or at all, really. They flailed a bit and sank, their dense bones and musculature dooming them to be picked over by crabs at the bottom of the ocean. Al called for assistance and jumped in after

Morgan to help her save the caged otters. Feng, Tempest, Gorp, and a few red-shirted crew members joined them, and soon they were hauling the cages onto the dock, with Otto screeching encouragement.

With their troll overboard and their smaller numbers overrun with short but feisty pirates in red shirts, the dock crew had no choice but to give up. The stevedores were marched up the gangplank and locked in the ship's brig with Davey Bones, who had prepared a lengthy admonishment. Morgan began freeing the otters, and the chittering critters followed Milly Dread and her bucket of chum up the gangplank, ensuring that they would never become EATUM. Otto, of course, stayed firmly wrapped around Morgan's neck. But Al wondered why the defeat of the troll hadn't involved otter balls at all. It had been centaur hooves that brought them victory, and rather quickly too. Had he misinterpreted the divine message of Pellanus somehow? He looked at his butt in confusion. Even a god of mischief couldn't confuse an elf butt and a centaur butt.

But the victory was fleeting, like the attention span of a two-year-old on a sugar high. A clanging bell at the MMA building suggested reinforcements were on the way. Their assault had been noticed.

"We must make it ashorrrre orrrr they'll have us pinned," Luc said. "Go! Rrrrun to the quay, me hearrrrrties! The fight has just begun!"

"Hey, you, with the cute butt," a smooth voice said to Al. He turned and saw that one of the caged elves was a tall, lithe woman. She had a long, upturned nose and perfectly shaped pointed ears. "You're an elf, right? I can see that big sack of glitter. You seem to be on the right side of the fight, so maybe you could let us out?"

If they'd been almost anything but elves, he would already be working on the lock. But Al had long ago ceased to like or trust his own kind.

"Why are you in a cage?" he asked first.

The other elf, a tall drink of mead with a spade beard, gave him an up-nod. "Because we're part of PITA." As if it was somehow explanatory, he held open his torn robe to show a shirt that said PITA and nothing else of any use. Not even a picture.

"What's up with that?" Al had to ask. "You're saying that like it's an acronym, and elves are really not into acronyms. I'm kind of shocked that you are. Or is it about flatbread? Either way, you're outlaws, aren't you?"

"No! PITA stands for the *Pains in the Arse*," the female elf said. "Or so the humans told us in Cape Gannet when selling us these shirts. We fight for animal rights. They caught us spying on the EATUM operation and confiscated all our glitter and whoopee cushions. And, hooboy, you wouldn't believe what they do here. They kill the otters with—"

"Say no more." Al bashed the lock with his sword a few times, but it didn't seem to do anything. Finally, with a sigh of annoyance, he blew some elvish glitter into the lock and watched it crack open like an egg.

The elves leaped from the cage, shrugged out of their robes to show their PITA shirts, and struck a pose, intoning, "Team PITA!"

"So now what?" Al said. "Can we go? If you're done . . . posing?"

"I vote we follow the parrot riding the centaur," the elf woman said, pointing up ahead. "Those guys really seem to know how to party. And by party, I mean take down this capitalistic paean to greed and unethical meat production."

Al watched all his friends up ahead, weapons out, running toward a phalanx of security guards.

"If that's partying, then let's party," he said.

The other elves shouted, "PITA party!" but Al politely ignored that. And ran.

28.

In the Enemy's Lair and Confronted by a Bevy of Blunderbusses

It was perhaps the strangest moment of Tempest's life so far, and she'd watched her father eat a unicorn once, starting with the end that wasn't pointy. Along with the entire crew of their ship, she was running up the dock toward a dour industrial building of dirty brick, headed directly for a group of brawny men in matching black jerkins emblazoned with the words MAUL SECURITY. She noticed this as if in a dream, as if she'd been standing just behind herself, watching the inevitable occur with no way to affect the outcome. It wasn't real until a beefy fellow in black with cauliflower ears was hacking at her with his sword, at which point she acquired a strange sort of laser focus, merged her dream-self and her watching-self into one body, and felt her lips curl into a bloodthirsty snarl.

So this was a fight.

A real fight.

Not a barroom pie fight, not a friendly pirate skirmish, not being picked off by the swinging logs of madmen on a desert island, but a fight to the death between two groups of people who wanted diametrically opposite things and were determined to win or perish.

Tempest's arms became rock-hard bark, and without really thinking, she threw a forearm up to hack down at the man's biceps before the sword could slice into her soft bits. Both her arms were armored in bark now, hard as a thousand-year-old redwood, and she swung wide and bashed at the fellow's head, surprised and far too delighted to watch it cave in like a ripe melon.

"Bloooood," she cooed to herself.

"What's that?" Morgan called from a little bit away, where she expertly jabbed and parried with her rapier like a normal pirate, not one who was part murdertree.

Tempest forced her tongue back in her mouth and stepped away from the man—oh, dear. The corpse.

"Blood. Food! No, I meant good," she said. "That's it. I said good. As in, it's good that this guy didn't kill me. Need some help?"

Morgan hadn't taken her eyes off her opponent, thank goodness, so she hadn't seen the doom Tempest had so casually wrought.

"I've got it," Morgan said, adding almost under her breath, "or not? Who knows? It's a curse."

Tempest desperately wanted to know more about that odd little addendum, but a fight to the death wasn't a great time for a heart-to-heart with the person who'd become her closest friend since leaving her sisters. She spun around to pummel a security guard harrying Hayu and one of his red-shirted friends, landing a branch across the man's spine and driving him to the ground, where he flailed with his arms but not his legs.

"That's some weapon!" Hayn explained.

"Well, I do have the right to bear arms," she replied.

The Maul Security lads were not as scary as Tempest had first thought—or maybe that was because the deck was stacked in the favor of *The Pearly Clam*. Whereas the dudes in uniform were all human and burly, the pirate crew had a similar number of effective humans with weapons plus a rearing centaur, an angry dryad, Milly

Dread, back from otter duty and armed with a toilet plunger and an elf—no. Three elves now?

Yes, that was what she was seeing. Fighting alongside Al, tossing out sneezing powder from one of his bags and kicking men in the groins, were two far more elfly-looking elves in ragged shirts that said PITA for some reason. Did they sell pitas or were they just militant enthusiasts, Tempest wondered?

But there wasn't much time to think about how young elves could be so easily radicalized by their love of flatbreads, as a new contingent of opponents was pouring out of the dour factory: workers. Dozens of men wearing MMA aprons appeared, holding improvised weapons that nevertheless boded poorly for otters. Sticks, long forks, rakes, pooper-scoopers, and sharp oyster shells hot-glued to broomsticks. Tempest would've been frightened if she'd still been mostly human—and if the workers had looked at all willing to fight. They exited the factory screaming, but the moment they were under the afternoon sun, they went silent and looked up at the sky like they hadn't seen it in years. Knowing how poorly the MMA appeared to treat anything and everything with a pulse, it would not have been a surprise.

"Are you having a stroke?" Tempest asked a man nearby, who clutched a broomstick covered in oyster shells. His eyes were huge, and his mouth flapped open and closed as he watched Vic spray a Maul Security man with tea so hot that his face melted off like a variety of pink crayons.

"Dunno how to fight, missus," he answered, his voice quite tremulous. "But the boss says it must be done, so I suppose . . . ?" He looked back at the factory, turned to Tempest, and batted at her with his broomstick in a halfhearted manner. She snapped it in half with a mighty arm.

"You should find a better job," she said, fighting her instinct to pop off his head and suck out the goo inside as if his neck were a straw.

"S'not a job," he allowed. "S'prison. Penal colony. Work or get tossed into the sea. And the otters, mum." He leaned in conspiratorially, which was a very foolish move. "They got a long memory for revenge."

As if to prove his point, a romp of otters romped out of the doors, blinked at the sunlight, focused on the crowd, squeaked squeaks of rage, and latched on to a variety of men in aprons, squealing and biting their disapproval into tender bits of flesh. Tempest sucked in a breath—well she knew that for all his cuteness, Otto had claws and teeth that could leave their mark. The otters could do a lot of damage once they were out of their cages, and they were going, very specifically, for the workers, most of whom weren't fighting but were instead just hopping around and screaming apologies, their improvised weapons forgotten as the otters spat out chunks of ankle and various pinky fingers.

"Don't hurt the workers," Tempest called to her pirate compatriots; she knew the otters weren't listening. "These men are fighting against their will!"

"Little does that matterrrr to me, lass!" Luc called as he tore off a Maul Security man's ear with his talons. "If they fight us, they be enemies!"

"They're not fighting us, though," Morgan called, dispatching one Maul Security guard and then catching her breath as she sought her next foe.

All the men in black were on the ground, and most of the workmen who hadn't managed to run away were grappling with otters. Tempest was surprised there weren't more fighting men, but then she remembered: This island didn't officially exist, it wasn't on maps, and even if someone did stumble across it, they had to get through the magic barrier. Security wasn't going to be the highest priority for the MMA, because the MMA was set up to be entirely secret and never require defending.

Luc must've come to the same conclusion, as he shouted, "Inside, crrrrew! Onwarrrrd!" And in true Luc fashion, he flapped ahead, leading the pack.

Vic was right behind him, not even sweating from the fight, shoving thick oatmeal cookies into his mouth for energy. Al and his new elf friends were likewise unharmed and on the run, and Morgan appeared by Tempest's side.

"Your arms," she said, gently touching one of Tempest's branches—er, arms. "Does it hurt?"

"They're better for fighting," Tempest explained. "They'll go back to normal once we're safe." Even to her ears, it sounded like the truth. But she knew well enough that that particular truth had an expiration date. One day, possibly soon, they wouldn't go back. With each use of her powers, the brown scaly patch spread farther up her wrist, and that transformation couldn't be reversed. Still, she'd lost Brawny Billy, and she couldn't let the otters or the others in her crew suffer anymore if she could stop it.

Facing no more resistance, they ran into the factory and stopped short. It was not what they were expecting: It was a huge foundry of hissing steam and molten metal. There were no otters at all on the foundry floor; there were cannons being cast and pyramids of shot stacked and waiting to be crated; it was an armory, the fires for the forges producing the belching black smoke they'd seen. The MMA was in the arms business as well. No one was tending the fires at the moment, since the workers had come out to face them.

"There has to be more," Morgan muttered as she led the way across the foundry to double doors on the other side. Once she threw those open, she beheld a vast room like the foundry, but the scene was one of grisly horror. It was so much worse than Tempest had imagined. On the far side were stacks and stacks of drums, lined up on pallets and stamped with the word EATUM—the sheer amount of meat they represented made Tempest's stomach turn. All along the left side were racks of cages full of live otters, sorted by size so that the big ones, the medium ones, and the little ones and babies were all spread out. Many a brown paw reached from one cage toward another, accompanied by soft, desperate mewling. Metal vacuum tubes were affixed at the back of each cage, which sucked out the occupants upon demand and deposited them on a conveyor belt with steep, slick sides that dumped the victims into a giant drum that whirred and clanked like a tornado of blades. The drum had three more tubes leading out of it to lower containers: one deposited hunks of bloody brown fur into a drum, another deposited bones, and the last was a huge vat filled with . . . Gads. Tempest didn't want to look at it, or at the pink-stained conveyor belt that paraded out of it. The entire thing made her sick. At least she could tell it hadn't been designed or built by gnomeric hands—it was a rough thing, ugly and ungraceful, with crooked beads of solder and rusty rivets, no doubt created from scratch in the foundry next door. The walls around the room included various tables, workbenches, aprons, and a variety of terrifying instruments that would've been at home in a butcher's stall. When she turned away toward the otters and their terrified squealing, she could feel her cheeks going cold and wooden and hard with rage.

"Who's in charge here?" she asked, and her voice had the same ancient, soughing tone as her father's last words.

"Whoever it is, I bet they're that way!" Morgan shouted, pointing at a large metal door that read ADMINISTRATION.

"You therrrre!" Luc called to the red shirts of his crew, who always seemed to be hanging a little behind ever since their time on Mack Guphinne. "Rrrrelease the otterrrrs! Herrrrd 'em out o' the gates! Get 'em to the ship, if ye can! Lurrrre 'em with chum if ye must!"

As soon as the cages were open and the otters were streaking out the door, herded and abetted by the red shirts, Vic grasped the handle of the Administration door and heaved it open, his muscles bulging with the effort. Tempest noticed he had Brawny Billy's machete as he held open the heavy door to let the rest of the crew pass through. They were all flush with victory. And why not? They'd bested the dock stevedores, destroyed the Maul Security guards, and cowed the workers—and without losing anyone or taking major damage. All that was left were these mysterious administrators, who would no doubt be cowering behind their desks and shouting for their managers.

The hallway on the other side of the door was all stone, tall and wide and echoing. A reception desk stood empty aside from a small sign that said GLADYS IS AT LUNCH; BACK AT 2-ISH. Smaller doors opened off the hall beyond at regular intervals, their plaques reading SALES or ACCOUNTS PAYABLE or ADVERTISING or OTTER BONE POWDER TEST KITCHEN, which only made Tempest's blood boil to sap. They checked each room but found them all empty, despite the fact that ink was still drying on inventory sheets and someone had made a new pot of coffee in Ye Olde Breake Room. Milly Dread attempted to snag a donut from a pink box, and Luc squawked at her.

"Ye just passed the test kitchen, fool! I'll give ye thrrrree guesses what kind of powderrrr's on that donut."

For the first time ever, Tempest saw Milly Dread put back a piece of food without licking it.

Soon they all stood before the final door, which was the equal of the giant one that had led to the hall. THE BOSS, it read. But when Vic flung it open, they faced a wide set of shallow stairs that climbed up many floors.

"Why do you always have to pass so many levels to get to the big boss?" Milly Dread groaned.

"Because some people always think they're higher up than other people," Qobayne answered her.

"But that just means they've got farther to fall," Tempest finished.

From his perch on Feng's shoulder, a ruffled Captain Luc said, "Speakin' o which. Vic, lad, if ye need to stay behind and guarrrrd ourrrr flank, that would suit. Can't have ye gettin' stuck up therrrre. We need ye back on the ship."

Vic grinned with pride but shook his head. "Thanks but no thanks, Captain. There could still be more guys up there, and if so, you'll need my magic. These steps aren't too steep for me. I'd like to have a talk with this Angus Otterman guy and give him a piece of my hoof in his mind."

With that, Vic tried to leap dramatically up the stairs but found it woefully awkward. He had to sort of dance up, but he kept to the right so everyone else could hurry past him. They didn't hurry too fast, though—everyone was aware that between his swole bulk and his tea magic, he was their finest fighter. So mostly they just slowed down and let Vic lead the way.

The stairs hit a landing and turned, and that's when the first arrow thwacked into play, taking Vic in the shoulder. Six more thwonked harmlessly into the wall.

"Grah!" the centaur cried, throwing both of his arms forward in a veritable tidal wave of hot black tea. Tempest peeked around the corner and saw another dozen Maul Security guards in black armor, bristling with weapons that were currently useless, thanks to the fact that all the men were staggering and screaming things like "My eyes! My eyes!" and "It burns!" and "Where did this white-chocolate cranberry biscotti come from?"

"Vic—" Tempest said, going for the bolt in his shoulder.

He wrenched it out, tossed it on the ground, and shouted, "Don't worry about me. We've got to take those guys down before they get their bows again!" And then he charged up the remaining stairs, hooves slipping everywhere, screaming as he pelted the security guards with bran muffins the size of melons. When he hit the next landing, the men were still too dazed and boiled to do much but stand there flailing as he struck out with fists and hooves, a one-centaur killing machine. By the time Tempest joined him, there was no one left to fight and a heck of a mess for the janitorial crew.

"Be carrrreful now," Luc warned them, flapping overhead. "The closerrrr ye get to the boss, the morrrre dangerrrrous his underrrrlings become!"

As if on cue, just as the pirates had all navigated onto the landing and Vic had moved a bit up the next flight of stairs to make room, seven middle managers in black business jerkins rappelled from the ceiling far above, each one holding that rarest and most coveted weapon, a blunderbuss.

"Now, see here," the lead one said, hopping around a little as he awkwardly stepped out of his harness. "You are trespassing on private property, and since the security guards failed to roust you, I must now command you to leave the premises at once or face legal repercussions." He turned his weapon on each of them, not quite sure whom to aim for, his hand shaking. All of the middle managers' hands were shaking, Tempest noticed. The youngest one had donut crumbs and sprinkles all over his jerkin. There was very little room, after all, since the landings were generous but not designed to harbor so many people. Some of the managers had to perch awkwardly on the stair railings, holding on to their rappelling lines with one hand and their blunderbuss with the other.

Tempest stepped forward, her wooden hands up. "Now, now. Let's not be hasty and go shooting people. Do you have the property deed?"

The man blinked. "The what now?"

"You said it was private property, but I've seen no posted signs, so I'm requesting the property deed. Or any legal papers regarding ownership of this island and proper filing of form MYN1007, which would grant the island's proper sovereign the right to defend his property from aggressive visitors and door-to-door sales-elves."

"Well ... I ... um ... you see ..." the man spluttered.

Tempest gave her calmest smile. "Or perhaps your attorney is present? Or the property manager?"

At that the man rose up on his tiptoes, attempting to look down at Tempest and failing. "I am the head accountant, madam, the senior administrator on staff, and I am ordering you to leave."

"As the captain, I'm disinclined to acquiesce to yourrrr demand," Luc said, flapping his wings from Feng's shoulder and giving the man a steely glare. "Means nope. So you and yourrrr juniorrrr accountants can drrrrop those guns and get out of the way orrrr face the wrrrrath of ourrrr wizarrrrd."

The man looked startled. "You have a wizard? Good gravy. Where is he? What's he want?"

But Vic was ready, and he pelted the man with a fat dollop of crème fraîche right in the face, shouting, "He wants you to get out of the way!" Soon everyone wearing a black work jerkin was fighting a face full of zippy whipped cream, bemoaning the tingle of it in their eyes.

The head accountant's blunderbuss went off, blasting a red shirt in the belly, and a grand mêlée began. The administrators were all blinded by fatty dairy products, allowing the crew to defeat and disarm them with only one other shot popping off and skittering off a stone wall.

"Take these men downstairrrrs and lock them in the cages!" Luc shouted.

Qobayne distributed three blunderbusses to the party of red shirts, who were more than happy to herd the physically unimpressive managers down the stairwell before things got even worse. A sign on the landing pointed the remaining crew up toward their goal. THE BIG BOSS, it said. For a moment nobody moved forward, so Tempest hurried to Vic, put a hand on his wither, and closed her eyes.

"What are you doing?" he asked. "It's warm and tickly."

"We need you whole," she said, feeling the heat flow from her palm and into Vic.

When she pulled away and looked up, the wound in his shoulder was gone. Her arms were still covered in bark, still long like branches and hard as ancient redwood, but now a single leaf bloomed out of her wrist.

"That leaf is pretty," Vic said, considering it. "Thank you for doing that."

She just smiled. "You're welcome. Thanks for taking that arrow for us."

"Oh, it didn't really hurt," he said, and she saw the shadow of his old swoleness for a moment before he shook his head. "Naw, that's a lie. It was the hurtiest thing I've ever felt. But it doesn't hurt at all now, for real."

Morgan looked to Tempest, worry in her eyes. "Are you okay?"

Tempest couldn't tell her the truth, so she nodded.

It was clear Morgan didn't believe her, but she nodded back and asked, "Everybody ready?"

To a one—the original crew of *The Puffy Peach*, Gorp and the bravest of the POPO red shirts, Al and his new elf friends, Tempest and Morgan and Vic—everyone raised their weapon and shouted, "Yeah!" Except Luc, who held no weapon, of course, and who was watching Morgan with a contemplative sort of look.

They climbed the remaining few flights of stairs, ignoring plaques for OTTER SCOUTING and FOUNDRY SALES and EMPLOYEE RESOURCES, which was really just a broom closet, always following the signs pointing up to THE BIG BOSS. Once they reached the door labeled as such at the uppermost floor, Vic grasped the handle, shook his head, said, "Let's do it," threw open the door, and charged outside—onto a sunny rooftop rather than into the lavishly furnished office Tempest had expected.

He'd only gone about ten feet before he took a cannonball right through the middle of his man-gut.

29.

ON A ROOFTOP AND WEAKER
THAN MILKY TEA

❧❦❧

"Oh, man, this is not good. This is intense," Vic said as his legs suddenly folded underneath him like a lawn chair and his horse belly hit the stone.

His head felt pleasantly floaty and numb as compared to his middle, which was somehow both searing hot and very, very cold. His hooves were very far away and had forgotten how to function—they couldn't even dance. His human torso began to wobble, and then he was caught in someone's solid arms, hugged from the front, his face cradled against a bosom that was most definitely not his dam's bosom.

"Sorry," he managed to mutter. "Not objectifying you. This is awkward."

"Shh," she said, whoever she was.

Vic couldn't see so well. He pulled away and looked up and blinked and saw bright-blue sky, for just a moment. They were on the roof of the factory, inside a waist-high stone wall. The sun was shining. Moss and grass grew in the cracks between the stones. It was pretty, even if a battle was raging. There were so many security guards, so many weapons. So much blood.

"Glurgh," somebody said, and a red shirt fell.

Stiff hands pulled Vic's head down, cradled him in shadow, and held him tight.

"I don't feel so good," he murmured into someone's chest, which had started quite soft and squishy but was swiftly becoming hard and rough.

"I know," she whispered back, her voice going raspy.

"Are they gonna eat my kinneys?" he asked, remembering the last time he'd felt this woozy. "They gonner eat me like the otters?" He wanted to panic but couldn't. His heart wouldn't kick up. He felt so sluggish. Just wanted to lie down. To sleep.

"No one is going to eat you," she said. It was his mother, or an angel, or a goddess, or possibly a tree. It was all so confusing. "Just hold still and breathe. And when I let you go, get far, far away from me."

Vic swallowed. He could feel his hooves again. They had gone warm and prickly, like they'd fallen asleep and were now waking up, and the blood was rushing back into all his bits, both equine and man. His tail twitched, and his skin quivered as if he were covered in flies, and his body filled with energy. He was ready to stand, to run, to fight!

The arms that had held him close released him.

"What happened?" he said, standing and stepping back.

But his savior was gone. All he found was a twisted, craggy willow tree with a gaping black hollow in the center, its roots grown into the stone roof and peppered with moss. Oddly, the tree had grown around a black cannonball, which bulged from the trunk, trapped by the rugged bark.

"I told you to ruuuuuuun awaaaaaay from meeeeeeee," the wind seemed to say as it shook the willow's whips, making white buds and tiny green leaves rain down to speckle his glossy brown fur.

Vic looked around, taking stock. He didn't know what had happened after he'd gone through that door, but he knew he was going to make it worthwhile.

"Thank you, whoever you are," he said.

A willow whip caressed his cheek with velvet buds, and another put his fallen machete in his hands.

Whatever had happened, he was ready to fight again.

30.

UNDER THE CHAPEAU PERILOUS

❧

The moment Tempest wrapped her arms around the dying centaur, her whole body began turning to bark, and her hair began to flower, and she cast Morgan one last, longing look, a look full of so many unsaid things about friendship and destiny and doing what's right, about farewells and secret hopes and loving wishes. And then she tilted her head, just a little bit, her last real human movement urging Morgan on into the fight as Tempest gave her greatest gift to the centaur she'd once hated, and the groan from her lips became the deep creak of wood.

And then Tempest, as Morgan knew her, was gone.

Swallowing her sadness and charging into the mêlée was the hardest thing Morgan had ever done, but she did it. She petted Otto where he curled around her neck, hoping he wouldn't get hurt but knowing he wouldn't leave his favorite perch to escape the danger. He patted her cheek and nuzzled in, and that, at least, was some comfort. And then she was in the fight, and she wheeled and spun, parrying and jabbing with her rapier in one hand and her dagger in the other. Maul Security guards fell under her blade, and Luc flew overhead, giving directions and trying to plop on enemies at just the right time. Feng mowed down men with his sword, and Gorp showed himself to be an able fighter as well; Qobayne cried out, wounded, and Milly Dread defended him with her plunger, proving to be deadly with it. But the greatest threat was silently toiling behind the packed crowds of muscle.

"Therrrre, lass!" Luc cried. "You've got to stop the trrrroll at the cannon beforrrre he can shoot again!"

Morgan ducked under a sword's swipe, stabbed a black-clad foot with her dagger, and burst into a run, headed for the cannon that had nearly taken out Vic permanently—until Tempest's ultimate sacrifice. The centaur was now fighting with the strength of ten men and the feet of an elephant and the magic of a really excellent baker, a whirling pinwheel of death and cake, but the troll was yet again attempting to take out the pirates' most powerful fighter with a cannon on the other side of the roof. As Morgan ran by Vic's cinnamon swirl of doom, she nearly got splashed with a rogue geyser of tea, but Vic blocked it with a well-timed scone hurled at a security guard. The wheaty projectile struck the man's nose hard enough to break it with a solid pop and a howl of "Oh, doh!"

"Sorry!" Vic called to Morgan, but she didn't have time to answer.

The troll had loaded up the powder and shot and was now preparing to light the fuse and aim for the centaur yet again. He looked clever for a troll, and instead of the usual fedora, he wore a plaid driving cap that matched his tartan kilt. He was big and gray and bulgy, sort of like a pyramid-shaped rock shoved into the skin of a giant toad. And he saw Morgan coming.

With a snarl, the troll stopped trying to light the cannon's fuse, dropped his match over the wall into the sea, and plucked an umbrella from his belt. But of course it wasn't only an umbrella; it was also a club, because trolls just loved nasty clubs.

"You want to dance, little girl?" he jeered.

"No, I want to fight," Morgan said, rapier and dagger ready, dodging around him as she waited for his attack.

Without another word, he slashed down with his umbrella club, and the fight began in earnest. Morgan danced or twirled away from every not-as-clumsy-as-she'd-hoped thunk of the club, and she soon realized that a rapier wasn't the best instrument for troll fighting. Each time a thrust landed, it was like poking a stone with a twig. The troll grunted, to be sure, but the tip never fully punctured his flesh. There were no telltale leaks of blood. If he'd been anything but a troll, he would've been minced pie by then. Either troll skin was hard as diamonds, or this troll was protected by some sort of magic spell.

"Alobartalus!" Morgan shouted.

"What? That's a weird thing to shout," the troll said. "Is that a spell? Are you a wizard?"

The elf appeared just far enough away to be heard without getting smashed by the troll's club. "What do you need?"

"I think he's protected by magic. Anything you can do about that?"

"I can hear you, you know," the troll muttered, trying to bash in her brains but really just taking out another chunk of rather springy moss in the stone floor as she dodged the killing stroke. "I guess the elf must be the wizard."

Morgan couldn't keep track of Al, but she was fairly certain he ran away, hopefully not for good. It was taking everything she had to fight the troll without getting squashed, and for all her piratical personal fitness, she was getting winded, and the muscles in her arms and legs were on their way to displaying the strength of boiled noodles. The troll could sense it too, and he upped his barrage of club-swiping, grunting and laughing nastily.

Finally Al reappeared, along with the two more elfly elves with the weird fashion sense. They didn't tell Morgan what they were up to, but they were edging around the troll, keeping out of smashing distance, and Al had stuck his hand in that glitter pouch on his belt.

But unlike the elves, Morgan wasn't out of the troll's range. She dove left as a particularly wicked lunge nearly took off her leg; as it was, it grazed her calf and pain exploded there. "Ha!" the troll barked, but Morgan hacked at his fingers before he could follow up. Even if he was mostly impervious, he still didn't like a rap on the knuckles. He recoiled and that gave her just enough time to roll back to her feet, albeit with a limp. The troll swiftly refocused, noting her weakness, and took a step forward. Morgan didn't think she'd be able to dodge another blow.

Suddenly, the two new elves started shouting very rude things at the troll, calling him nasty names like CEO and capitalist and Rando MacCannotfight. They turned and flipped up their PITA shirts, shaking their perfectly shaped rumps at him and thumbing their noses.

"What the huh?" the troll said, and as he focused on the waggling elf bums, Al ran up, catapulted himself off the troll's knee, and smacked him across the slabby cheek, leaving a glittery handprint behind.

As if by magic—because it literally was magic in this case—the troll's skin stopped looking like stone, the color returning to a more trollish green. The troll must have felt the protection draining away, because his eyes dropped to his empty left hand, watching the color change. He snorted furiously like a bull, and Morgan took that chance to slice him across the right arm, which finally yielded the result of a deep cut welling blood and gooey yellow troll fat—and a truly furious troll. Morgan flashed a smile at Al for making the small victory possible, and that split second was all the troll needed to catch up to her. She saw his left hand shoot forward, fingers extended to grab at her throat, and she ducked away as best she could, but she still felt hot, tiny claws rake across her neck as Otto screeched his frustration.

The troll had just ripped the otter away from Morgan's neck.

Her sword lowered, she touched her throat and felt blood there. The troll was grinning with old yellow teeth now, holding Otto firmly by the scruff of his neck.

"Now we're closer to even," he said. "So let's have a chat. Everybody! Stop fighting, or the otter gets it!"

No one really stopped, and the troll's huge fingers cupped Otto's head like he was thinking about twisting it off.

"Stop!" Morgan shouted at the top of her lungs. "Do what he says!"

Morgan's voice carried, loud and commanding. The clatter of swords and thumping of clubs and squawking of one very enraged pirate captain went silent. The only sound was the wind whipping around the willow withes and Otto's furious, terrified shrieking.

The troll sat down on the edge of the wall and gave Morgan an intelligent, knowing smile. With hands both cruel and somehow gentle, he held Otto down and stroked him in a brutal facsimile of what animals actually enjoyed. Otto's eyes met Morgan's, and she realized she'd never come this close to losing someone she loved. Even Tempest was still alive—trapped and changed, but alive.

"Don't hurt him," she warned.

"Well, actually," the troll said, stroking the otter. "You're hardly in the position to bargain."

"It was an order, not a bargain. You don't have to live this way, you know. Whatever Angus Otterman pays you, we'll pay you more. We don't want to hurt anyone; we just want to save the otters."

The troll's hairy eyebrows went up. "The trail of innocent but dead security guards and middle managers you've left on your way here suggests you're perfectly happy to hurt people, whether or not you think you want to. And the otters are free now. So you can go. Walk on out. I'll let you."

Morgan shook her head. "I'm here for Angus Otterman. But I'm guessing, like all villains, he'd cut and run as soon as he was threatened."

The troll smiled and stroked Otto. "Oh, no, Miss Pirate. I'm right here."

No. It couldn't be!

The bottom dropped out of Morgan's belly, and her heart kicked up like Vic's hooves during a lightning storm.

"You're lying," she said. "Angus Otterman isn't a troll name."

The troll chuckled and shook his head. "Oh, and runaway ladies from Borix are the only people allowed to change their names and destinies? That's right, *Lady Harkovrita*. I know who you really are. I read newspapers and periodicals from all over Pell, and there's a hefty reward for your safe return. You'd look better without the beard, by the way, but I'll take you to a proper barber before I send you back to that lordling in Taynt."

"My name is Morgan," she said firmly. "And I like my whiskers, and whatever your name really is, you'd best give me back my otter."

Angus—if that was indeed who this troll was—clutched Otto by the scruff and dangled him over the side of the factory and, Morgan well knew, the jagged, knife-sharp cliffs below.

"I'm a businessman, Harkovrita. I like money. That's why I built my EATUM empire and put considerable investment into hiding our operations. You're not the first person to make the connection between everyone's favorite side dish and what happens here on Mack Guyverr. But you're the first person to care enough to find my secret overground lair. And you're a pirate, which means you haven't told the authorities. Which means you just showed up, furious and self-righteous, ready to take down the bad guy. Is that correct?"

"I don't see how that matters."

"It does matter!" he shouted, slamming a fist into the stone and making Otto squeak. "Because what you're missing, my precious lady, is something every businessman knows about: You have no leverage. If you love otters as much as it seems, you'd do anything to save this one you particularly care for. If I give him back, you kill me or, at best, take me captive. Or try to. So there's literally no reason on earth I would hand him over, is there?" He gave a smug grin and waggled Otto over the abyss again.

Morgan swallowed hard and tore her eyes away from Otto to look around at the rest of her compatriots. Several of their sailors had fallen, some dead and some wounded. Tempest, of course, was still a tree, but she seemed to be aware, listening, waiting. Al and his elf friends were hovering nearby, their shirttails firmly grasped, ready to moon the troll again if necessary.

Across the roof, Vic was standing in the center of a pile of Maul Security guards dripping with tea and studded with panettone. Just to his side was another cannon and a stacked pyramid of cannonballs. Captain Luc sat on the centaur's shoulder, whispering in his ear. Making eye contact with Morgan, Vic gave her a slow, deliberate nod, the sort of nod that suggested that decisions had been made, that chips were about to fall, and that shite was about to go down.

"So what is it you want, then, Mr. Otterman?" she said, trying to stall without letting him see that her hands were shaking.

The troll tipped his hat. "To employ you. You're clearly better fighters than any of my men are—or were. Take over working security for the docks here, and I'll pay you beyond your wildest dreams. There's plenty of free corporate housing, swimming pools, sushi buffets, generous benefits, and paid time off. There's even a water slide on the other side of the island."

Morgan gritted her teeth. "Funny. The workers we met said they were prisoners."

"They are. But you'd be staff. And I won't tell the outside world that I'm harboring a fugitive. You'd be free and safe for the rest of your life. All I ask is that you cease defying me."

"And you'll give Otto back?"

The troll smiled a smile that might've been benevolent if his mouth didn't look like a crater full of hippo fangs with a generous coating of plaque. "As a show of good faith, you have your men put down their swords, and I'll give 'im to you now."

Morgan turned to face the pirates. She gave Luc a nod, and he nodded back and then gave Vic a nod. Vic nodded at Luc and then at Feng and then at Morgan, then again at Qobayne, as they all knew Qobayne hated being left out. Morgan nodded at Al, and then it got very confusing, because they were all just bobbing their heads knowingly at one another when clearly no information had been shared.

She set down her rapier, the others followed suit with their weapons, and she held out a hand. As the troll dropped Otto into her grasp, Morgan stuffed the otter down her shirt and fell to her hands and knees, rolling away, just as Feng picked up and tossed a cannon-ball to Vic, who threw it right at the troll but missed, sending it sailing by his head with an audible *whoosh*. All the pirates leapt out of the way, and only Vic and Angus were left standing, the troll scouting for a better weapon and then, finding none, taking off at a run, right for the centaur. Feng kept tossing cannonballs to Vic so he wouldn't have to work to reload, and the centaur chucked them at the troll as fast as he could. A couple more sailed by the troll, but then one slammed into his gut, making him say, "Ooph," and slow down a bit, allowing Al to run up and toss a handful of elvish glitter in Angus's face.

The troll began sneezing tiny little baby sneezes and turning red and dancing around, and Vic smacked him with a cannonball upside the head, knocking off his hat. Angus stopped and roared, red-faced, before sneezing mightily but tinily. Vic's next cannonball caught him right in the ribs, knocking him over.

"Bowling for trolls!" Vic shouted, giving Morgan a look of intense urging as he recalled the troll's attention and ire to himself.

And that's when Morgan realized it was her turn. She placed Otto on the ground, stood, and ran for the troll as he clambered to his feet, thrusting her rapier right through where she figured a trollish kidney would be, under the ribs. As Morgan yanked the sword out, Angus fell over again, spurting sludgy blood, and she stabbed him on the other side.

"Going to kill you, girl," the troll wheezed between itty-bitty sneezes, on his hands and knees. "Gonna put you through the machine downstairs and separate out your component parts for profits."

"I don't think so," she said. She put a boot on the troll's side and kicked him over, and wounded as he was, he fell like a drunk elephant.

On his back, the troll was a huge mound of flesh, and Morgan didn't want to get too close to those ham hands, which could've squished her to pulp. Vic came to stand by her side, Luc on his shoulder.

"Will ye give him merrrrcy, lass?" Captain Luc asked. "Forrrr although ye've the mind of a captain, you don't have the hearrrrt of a pirrrrate. Ye've neverrr taken a life beforrrre—"

"Are you kidding?" Morgan said, her voice husky with feeling. "I've killed like a dozen guys since we got here, and I don't feel bad about it at all. Because they know that what they're doing is wrong. If it were right, then those barrels would be clearly labeled *Otter Bits* and this island wouldn't be secret and its operations would be aboveboard.

"But, no, these guys come to work every day and watch otters get put in cages and then fed into that deboning machine, and then they watch the barrels get shipped out under the name EATUM for innocent waitstaff to hawk to innocent halfings, and it's all a big lie for money. It's nine kinds of exploitation for self-interest, and that's not the kind of person the world needs walking around. They're sociopaths, or at least jerks who've learned to numb their empathy just so they can amass more money, and that kind of person is the sort who ruins the world and laughs at the suffering of others.

"Perhaps a lady would try to reform him, and perhaps an attorney would prosecute him to the full extent of the law, but me? I'm just a pirate. And this pirate believes some bad guys can't be saved, and shouldn't be."

"So how will you punish this villain, then?" Luc asked in that same ringing tone. "Will ye dispatch a ship to the POPO, and—"

But Morgan just stuck her sword right in the troll's heart and ended his reign of terror.

He died with ululations and a torrent of diarrhea.

31.

IN WHICH THE REAL TREASURE
IS THE ACTUAL TREASURE THEY FOUND
ALONG THE WAY

Al swayed on his feet and held his nose, breathing through his mouth. "Pfauugh! Victory doesn't smell very good," he said, looking at the mess the troll had made.

"Oh! Hey, uh. We won? I guess?" Vic said, looking around for more enemies and spying none. "But where's Tempest? Did she go back for the otters? I lost track of her after she took care of that arrow wound for me."

Morgan looked at the centaur solemnly, and Al felt his throat go tight as Morgan pointed to the huge willow tree with a cannonball embedded in its trunk.

"She was a dryad, Vic. Every time she healed someone—"

Vic swallowed hard. "She grew that brown stuff."

"Bark, yes."

"So she—" Vic choked up.

"She knew it would happen," Morgan said. She stepped a little closer, and the willow branches swayed hungrily toward her. "She always knew."

"But she did it anyway," Vic said, his voice tiny.

"She did, and because of her sacrifice, we won," Morgan asserted. "But we need to finish it. This business needs to end. We can't let someone else come in here and continue Otterman's enterprise. There are going to be more ships delivering otters. There are going to be other ships coming in to collect their ordered EATUM. We need to send Dinny's their final bill."

"Well, yeah, for sure," Vic agreed, "but what about Tempest? I mean . . . she saved my life. Maybe all our lives, in a way. Are we just gonna leave her here? This rooftop isn't exactly a verdant meadow or a lush forest."

Al spoke up. "You can't move her, because she'll eat you if you try."

"Naw, she wouldn't do that. She saved me!"

Shaking his head sadly, Al said, "But that was her last act in her human form. Now she's a carnivorous tree. Standing between us and the exit, I might add."

"So there's nothing we can do?"

"I didn't say that. You can make her human again. You just have to feed her lots of fresh meat."

"Any meat?"

"Any meat, so long as it's fresh. Not those barrels of EATUM."

"No, I would never! That's horrific!" Vic trotted over so that his rear faced the body of Angus Otterman and kicked out, effectively punting the troll toward the trunk of the willow tree. As soon as the body tumbled beneath the canopy, the branches whipped down like so many chelicerae and drew the still-bleeding corpse toward the trunk. The trunk shifted and groaned and the cannonball fell out as Angus Otterman's head and shoulders got shoved in. There weren't any chewing noises but rather some popping and grinding. Everyone had to look away.

"That's a good start," Al allowed. "Now you just have to keep feeding her."

"For how long?".

The elf shrugged and winced a little at the crunching noises. "As long as it takes. I don't think it's ever been quantified. But she's saved many lives during her time as a human, healed many wounds. She has to balance that out in death as a willowmaw before she can walk on two legs again."

Vic blinked, then nodded. "Okay. I can do that. Yeah."

"Excuse me?" Morgan said. "Do what?"

"I'm gonna figure out a way to keep feeding that tree. I mean, if I just walked away from someone who saved my life and left them to starve to death on a lonely rooftop, how could I ever lift my head again and meet anyone's gaze? I mean . . ." He extended his hands. "I owe her. I wouldn't be standing here now, or ever again, without Tempest's help."

"Arrrre ye sayin' ye want to stay on this blasted island, lad?" Captain Luc asked.

"Well, yeah. There's a debt to be paid. I'm gonna pay it, somehow. There has to be a way. I mean . . . if we take over things—I guess we kind of have already—we can take this ruin and make it beautiful again. One day at a time, we right the wrongs. We clean up the mess. We swab the deck."

"Damn right!" Feng said. "I . . . well." He looked at Captain Luc. "I'd like to help him, Captain, if I may. I lost too much at sea. It would be good to help build something great."

"And I," said Gorp. "It's gonna be years before I get the nightmare of that processing plant out of my mind. Best thing I can do is help tear it down and watch those otters we saved sail away with you."

Captain Luc bobbed his head. "Good good good good good! I underrrrstand. Anyone who wishes to stay herrrre may do so. I am no trrrroll who compels someone to worrrrk. But let us move to the otherrrr side of the willow while it is occupied, and then make decisions."

Everyone edged around the willow, which was slowly drawing the body of Angus Otterman into its maw. Al was about to pass by the pile of cannonballs that Vic had used to bring down the troll when an odd detail drew his attention. There was something stamped into the iron, an uneven surface on what was normally a solid sphere of potential destruction. He drew closer and grunted as he picked one up to examine it.

OTTER BALL, it said, and in smaller text underneath, 42# SHOT, and in yet smaller text on the last line, MMA ARTILLERY.

Al looked up with the euphoria of revelation and shouted, "Otter balls beats troll!"

Everyone turned to stare at him, and he realized that he had neglected to inform most of them of the secret prophecy of Pellanus as revealed to the Sn'archivist.

"This is an otter ball," he explained, pointing to it, "because Otterman was trying to be clever, see? Vic hit him with these and it dropped him. And the elf butts were important too—I mean, wow, right? The troll was about to snuff Morgan and then ta-daaa! Elf butts!" Al waved at the two tall elves in PITA shirts. "Theirs, I mean, not mine! Well, uh, maybe you didn't see that because you were busy. But trust me when I say that Otterman was distracted at a crucial moment by the wanton shimmying of their taut, firm buttocks! It gave me the chance to dispel his magic protection so we could bring him down! Which means the Sn'archivist *wasn't* mad, he really *was* divinely inspired by Pellanus, and Pellanus wanted us to end this horror! We're the freewill instruments of divine prophecy, and my dream of visiting the Sn'archivist wasn't actually a waste of time! Isn't that great?"

Al's eyes tracked the many, many faces staring at him as if he were the mad one, and it gradually dawned upon him that he had used entirely too many exclamation points without proper context. Perhaps he had a little Sn'archivist in him, after all.

"Well, look, everyone, I'm a bit excited at the moment and I can explain in calmer, rational tones at a later date on a still night over stale beer, but for now let's just say this happened exactly as it had to happen yet wouldn't have happened at all if it weren't for every single one of you being precisely the person you are. Thank you, sincerely, for being so awesome."

They all seemed to understand that part, at least, and gave him a weak smile for it, and Al noted for future reference that perhaps he should have said that last sentence first and then shut his piehole.

Once they'd all safely edged around the canopy of the new willowmaw, Captain Luc cawed and cleared his avian throat with a trill.

"Beforrrre we leave this rrrrooftop, I want ye all to pause and say a few worrrrds if ye feel like ye should. Otherrrrwise we will assume ye feel the same as those who have things to say now. I will say this: I neverrrr sailed with a drrrryad beforrrre Tempest, and I know I neverrrr will again. That will be a rrrregrrrret of mine until the end of my days. My one eye has seen many a marrrrvelous thing, and of them all, she was one of the best. I will always be honorrrred to say that I once gave herrrr passage and sharrrred a ship's biscuit with herrrr."

Morgan sobbed and said only, "She was my friend. One who didn't care about who I used to be but who cared about who I am now. That is all."

Silence fell until Vic gulped audibly and said, "When we first met, Tempest didn't like me much. And it took me a while to figure out why. But now I know; I get it. And if I could be granted just one wish, I'd like to be able to tell her I'm genuinely sorry for how I behaved, and then I'd leave her alone. I guess that wouldn't be a very good gift, especially in comparison to the one she gave *me*, but I think maybe she would have liked that. I also wish I could conjure up something she'd like to eat now, but cakes and tea aren't going to satisfy a carnivorous tree. So, uh . . ." Vic's lip quivered. "So I'm going to try to be as good a person as she was. She wanted to help people. That's what I'm going to do. And I'm going to start by helping her. And when she's had enough meat that she's able to walk around again, I'm going to welcome her back, and then I'm going to leave her alone and help someone else." He ducked his head and wiped his eyes before continuing. "You never expect the people or the moments that change you forever. You only see them after they happen to you.

338 DELILAH S. DAWSON AND KEVIN HEARNE

So I just want to say it out loud: Tempest changed me for the better. I'm so lucky to have met her. And I am going to do my very best to live up to the person she was. That she *is*, I mean! I am Pissing Victorious, son of Sucking Fabulous and Barfing August, and I swear I will not leave this island until my friend Tempest can walk away from it."

There were some sniffles and sobs after that, as well as a few murmured instances of "The son of what?" but Al joined the rest of the crew in deciding that there was nothing else to be said in memoriam. Tempest's unique gift to him? Well, he would put that into practice soon.

"Rrrright, then," Luc said. "I think we should firrrrst securrrre the island. Then decide how to maintain it. And then we must choose who will go with me to find the trrrreasurrrre and who will stay. I pledge this to ye all now: Those who stay to defend this island frrrrom capitalists—no easy task!—will still get an equal sharrrre. We will come back in a couple of weeks. But I will rrrrequirrrre a crrrrew to accompany me to the island. Let us go below and decide."

The subsequent hours were a whirlwind of activity.

Feng discovered the actual office of Angus Otterman, where documents revealed that he had been born in a wee hamlet of Kolon as Seamus MacThroatpunch. Examination of an address book allowed Feng to compose letters on MMA stationery, informing the owners and regional managers of Dinny's that the production of EATUM would cease immediately and they should not expect their orders to be fulfilled or make any orders in the future; they should, in fact, remove EATUM from their menus on receipt of the letter due to possible contamination.

He and Gorp decided that they would first renegotiate worker shares of the business to distribute profits among them and then continue the foundry side of the MMA business. Al was as surprised as anyone to find that Feng was a genius with numbers and that Gorp knew how to write a heck of a business letter; they were clearly the right crew to stay behind. But they had Vic for muscle too. Anyone who came to Mack Guyverr insisting on being paid for otter flesh, or claiming that they had the right to sell otter flesh, would find themselves carried bodily to a private conference on the rooftop with the big boss to discuss it. There they could argue as long as Tempest would let them.

Leaving many friends behind, Al set sail with Captain Luc, Morgan, Qobayne, a skeleton crew, and a whole lot of otters to seek out treasure near the wee island of Mack Elmorr, located past Mack Ribpe to the north and east of Mack Guyverr. It was a ghostly beach of barren white sand, unremarkable unless one wished to point at it and specifically remark upon its sadness, but off its coast, halfway across the channel to Sinuicho, a tall expanse of rock thrust proudly up from the waves, the pinnacle of some long-forgotten mountain underneath the sea. Coral reefs grew around it, however, and so ships avoided the rock. Off the reefs were kelp forests, and that meant sea urchins and other edible goodies. The otters were encouraged to make their new homes there, and all but Otto left the ship to start a new colony. Luc ordered the anchor to be dropped and they rowed a dinghy out to the reef and waited for low tide. They had to wait a long time.

When the waters finally receded, the reef became obvious. Their boat rested upon it, and they were able to step out and walk around. Luc led Al, Morgan, and a crew with shovels to a small pit of sand that was invisible until the moment they stood before it. But it would've been visible, of course, to someone who could fly and look down at the world from a different point of view.

"Therrrre," Captain Luc said, pointing a wing. "Dig and let us be gone as soon as possible."

Al dug in with gusto. With esprit de corps. With moxie.

They hit something after only a few inches. They hit it again and again, in fact, until they found the edges of it and could dig more judiciously. A half hour's work, and they had excavated enough sand to open a sizable chest.

It was full of gold and silver and jewels and entirely bereft of curses or whiny ghosts.

"Ahh, trrrreasurrrre," Luc boomed. "As I prrrromised ye. Let's get it to the mainland and divide the spoils into sharrrres."

Everyone was smiling and laughing, for here was a moment that lived up to their romanticized fantasies of what life as a pirate was like. Even Morgan, who'd been so serious of late, was grinning, and Al thought he heard her mutter, "All right. Maybe my curse isn't so bad after all."

Back on the mainland again, Morgan, Qobayne, and Captain Luc took the treasure chest to a fence in Sinuicho, while Al went in search of a Pellican Postale Office. Once he found it, he put the documents Tempest had prepared for him in an official-looking pouch and paid the Super Mega Turbo Important rate to have it delivered as soon as possible to King Gustave in Songlen. Al was sure that if his uncle had done anything at all to vex the king in the past, Gustave would approve Al's petition to have Proudwood Lighthouse declared a nature preserve for puffins and otters. It would most likely be settled by the time he sailed back there. And then Al would be the Proudwood P'archivist, able to charge docking fees to those who came to visit the park and to put those monies toward preservation efforts as well as toward a small stipend for himself to live on. He'd never have to sell a single Morningwood rod again. He couldn't wait to toss them all in the sea, in fact, and rebrand the rod grease as an organic puffin unguent.

He was in very high spirits when he returned to the ship and received his share of the treasure. There were plenty of supplies being brought on board, and a few new crew members had been recruited to make the sailing a bit easier. But once everything was stowed and Qobayne announced that they were ready to sail, Captain Luc surprised everyone. He asked for the entire crew to assemble on deck and he spoke to them from atop the ship's wheel.

"I've been a pirrrrate for twenty yearrrs. I've pillaged prrrrivateerrrrs up and down the westerrrrn coast and I've neverrrr been caught. I've done a lot of good forrrr the folks on Cinnamonk Island. I've dealt a lot of death to those who'd opprrrress the poorrrr. And now I finally have found someone who can continue that fine trrrra-dition in my stead. This trrrip has helped a lot of otterrrrs, and we took down the worrrrst capitalist trrrroll I have everrrr seen. And the perrrrson who did most of that worrrrk, who inspirrrred us all, is Morrrrgan. Lads, I'm rrrretirrrring now, and as my last act as yourrrr captain, I am naming Morrrrgan as my rrrreplacement. I give *The Pearrrrly Clam* to herrrr and wish ye all safe sailing, plentiful plun-derrrr, and no hangoverrrrs. She will see that the sharrrres of trrrrrea-surrrre get paid to the crrrrew waiting on Mack Guyverrrr. Rrrrraise a glass of rrrrrum to Captain Morrrrrgan!"

Al was standing right next to Morgan, and he clapped and cheered along with everyone else as her jaw dropped open. He might have been the only one to hear her mumble, "But what about my PSATs?" If Luc heard the question, he gave no indication. Instead, he trilled a few notes, said, "You be good. Bye-bye," and took wing into the har-bor. He circled the main mast once and then pointed himself north-west and flew away.

"Wow," Morgan breathed.

Qobayne stepped near and spoke to Morgan. "Ship's ready to sail on your order, Captain."

Morgan blinked a couple of times and then nodded. "Thank you, Boatswain." She turned to Al and said, "Be my first mate for this journey?"

"Aye," Al said with a grin. "But not forever. I have to return to Proudwood Island, and if you're going that way I'll stick with you until then."

"You're welcome to sail with me whenever and wherever you'd like. Boatswain, let's cast off and head back to Mack Guyverr. We have treasure to distribute and merchants to raid. And we need to turn that island into our base of operations. We're going to own the Chummy Sea."

Qobayne immediately started shouting orders, and *The Pearly Clam* began its first voyage under Captain Morgan—but Al sensed that something was missing.

"Captain, what ephithet will you adopt now that you're making a name for yourself?" he asked her.

Morgan squinted at the horizon as she thought, and then a corner of her mouth quirked up. "Call me," she said, "the Sober Captain Morgan."

Epilogue

ATOP A SHOULDER MOST SUPPLE
AND WELCOMING

⤜❦⤛

Filthy Lucre—no longer the Clean Pirate Luc—spiraled down into Sullenne after a long flight north and asked for directions to the Sullenne Sanctuary for Sulky Critters. The first ten people he asked in the portside market either didn't want to answer him or didn't know. The eleventh person offered him a cracker, and the twelfth gave him a clue.

"I don't know exactly where it is," a fishwife said, "but I hear there's a heckin' lot of mooin' on the northeast side of town outside the walls."

His wings aching and protesting, Luc flapped over most of the city until he found another, smaller market on the northeast side where he could ask around again. Getting directions from a local was much easier, and he could indeed hear a heckin' lot of mooin', and soon he was circling over a fenced paddock full of a wide assortment of creatures that did not normally associate with one another. There were chickens and turtles, raccoons and beavers, cows and camels, and even a Morningwood moose cow with a baby mooselet at her knees. All of these creatures and more were bunched around a figure wearing overalls and carrying a bag of feed, politely waiting their turn to be fed. Or else they were just listening to him talk, for he was talking to them all in the most soothing, friendly voice.

This was the man he'd flown so far to find.

Luc lighted on a fence post and listened in for a while as the man told everyone about his sister, who was still afraid of chickens even though she was dead. The chickens puffed up in pride at this, and the other animals made soft snorts and chitters of amusement. Luc squawked in delight as well, for this man, Morvin, did not even realize that the reason animals liked him so much was that he had a magical gift. They could all understand him.

Morvin's eyes shifted in Luc's direction when he heard the squawk.

"Hello there," he said. "Don't I recognize you? Aren't you the parrot who came into Dinny's to recruit a pirate crew?"

"I am," Luc confirmed.

"Your name was Luc, right? Did you find your treasure?"

"We did. And yourrrr chum, Morrrrgan, is now Captain Morrrrgan. I've rrrretired and given my ship to herrrr."

Morvin's face split into a smile. "No kiddin'? That's great news."

"I see you have also achieved yourrrr ambition."

"I sure did! This is the best heckin' job I've ever had. Turns out there's nothing I like so much as animals that don't belong to Lord Toby, an' they seem to dig me as well. These sulky critters ain't so sulky anymore. Boss likes me because of that and bought me like six pairs of overalls, so I can actually wear clean ones sometimes! Why, these here have hardly any stains at all! I'm feelin' pretty posh about it, but I hope I ain't braggin' too much."

"Not in the least."

The chickens clucked impatiently at him, and Morvin withdrew a handful of corn from the bag and scattered it on the ground for them to peck at.

"So how come you're back here?" he asked Luc. "Is there something you wanted? Are you feelin' heckin' sulky?"

"Not at all. Actually, I'd like perrrrmission to come aboarrrrd, Morrrrvin. I've been thinking that you might be the finest perrrrch in all the land. I can tell ye tales of Pell. I can thrrrrill and delight and frrrrrighten ye out of yourrrr socks. I can even pay the bills. But mostly I want peace, Morrrrvin. I want peace and I think you have plenty of it to sharrrre."

"Well, you can have it if you want it, Luc. I got me a special runnin' right now on peace for the low, low price of free." He tapped his shoulder, inviting Luc to perch on it, and the red-and-yellow expirate, terror of the western seas, a wanted bird in most every earldom, flew eagerly to the indicated spot.

"Ahhh," he sighed, gently squeezing his talons into Morvin's muscled shoulder. "It's as fine as I rrrrememberrrr. So what do ye have planned today, lad?"

"Well, after feedin' all the animals here and swappin' stories with 'em, I was fixin' to try this new restaurant in town that is supposed to have taters you can dress up yourself, as fancy or as plain as you want 'em, no fuss, no judgment. Imagine that, Luc—they just let you have taters your own way! Lotta people think Borix is boring, but I'm gonna have to quietly disagree, because a tater buffet is the most excitin' thing *I* ever heard tell of! Why, they're even s'posed to have a tub of invigorated ham jam just sittin' there—a whole heckin' *tub*, can you believe it? What a time to be alive! So I was thinkin' a starchy repast would suit me darned proper, 'cause there ain't nothin' finer than a deluxe tater. That sound okay to you?"

Luc felt his eye close halfway in contentment, his spirit already salved by this gentle man of modest taterly ambitions. "It sounds perrrrfect."

Epilogue 2

PELLECTRIC BOOGALOO

The squawking pink speck stood out from the dark clouds like a lone boiled shrimp on a black tile floor, and the Sober Captain Morgan put a foot on a pile of rope and squinted.

"Does that bird sound familiar to you?" she asked Qobayne.

"No, Captain," he answered. "But most birds is just feather footballs filled with squawks and slops, one at either end."

They both got misty for a moment. "Not all birds," she replied, and he bowed his head in understanding. Although she'd heard Luc had found his sought-after perch and was busy organizing a rescued avian a cappella group with her old friend Morvin, she missed her erstwhile mentor almost constantly.

The flamingo, for a flamingo it was, landed on the ship in an ungainly heap of tangled pink legs and thrashed around like two umbrellas fighting as the crew gathered around it. An Official Postale Collar around its long neck held a rolled scroll addressed to Captain

Morgan of *The Soggy Biscuit*—for they'd had to rename the ship yet again—and when she unrolled it, she smiled broadly.

> *Your presence is requested at the MMA Foundry*
> *On Mack Guyverr*
> *For a Grande Ribbon-Cutting Ceremony*
> *To Celebrate our Winninge of the*
> *Pell's Best Balls Awarde*
> *(Cannonball Category)*
> *Tea, Biscuits, and Complimentary Cannonballs Wille Be*
> *Served.*
> *P.S. Do not forget the ding-gull berries.*

The date given was a week away, giving them just enough time to get there, if the winds were fair.

When Morgan looked up, Qobayne and the rest of her crew were already grinning.

"We're going, right?" the boatswain asked. It had been a couple of years since they'd taken over the MMA and it was their home base now, but they hadn't been home in four months.

"You bet your Bundt we are," she said. "All hands on deck! We sail east!"

They did indeed find fair winds and calm seas, although there was a small and pathetic squabble with some Ebuk pirates off the coast of Big Potatoe Island. Like all pirates from the foul demesne of Ebuk on that island, they were a cowardly and self-righteous lot, and Morgan's crew sliced through them like a hot knife in ham jam as the pirates shouted at the tops of their lungs about how their doings were fair and hurt no one. Despite their protestations, Morgan found plenty of loot in their hold and happily added it to her ship's rightful bounty, reminding them in no uncertain terms that piracy was not a victimless crime, and she vastly preferred it when Ebuk pirates received their just punishment.

But that petty routing aside, the trip was balmy. When the mail flamingo refused to leave the ship and wouldn't stop nuzzling Otto with its huge, ungainly beak, Morgan began to suspect that it was indeed, against all possible reason, Tempest's long-lost Mingo. Milly Dread took to throwing shrimp at it to make it shut up, but she threw the shrimp in a loving sort of way.

They knew well how to obtain the dreaded ding-gull berries without dying too much, and Morgan's eyes filled with tears as she heard the beasts' chiming songs. They left a tasteful bouquet of flowers on the beach in Brawny Billy's memory and took to washing the ship's prow with the foul juice of the sticky berries. Soon they sailed into the strange vortex surrounding Mack Guyverr, breathing a universal sigh of relief as the magic lifted to reveal the now-gorgeous island hiding within. The factory, once as gray and blocky as a large and particularly unattractive toad, had been repainted white and given those orange, slopey clay roof tiles that made everything feel like a party. The docks were in good repair, and the dockworkers who met the ship were clean and polite and wore flower crowns; not a single Maul Security guard was in sight.

"We have an invitation," Morgan called down to a somewhat familiar man in a red shirt, who held the sort of clipboard that suggested he was very important, or at least thought he was.

"We've been expecting you, of course, Captain," the man called back. "Do you not remember me?"

"Well, of course I remember you . . . buddy!"

"It's Hayu, actually. Formerly of the POPO. Budee works in accounting, with Tsup and Hye."

Morgan smiled brightly to cover the gaffe. "Of course. So good to see you, Hayu. So everything is working out for you here?"

The gangplank was ready, so Morgan walked down to the dock, resplendent in her captain's finery, with a velvet coat, frothy jabot, and a stolen admiral's hat that was big enough for an otter to hide inside, which Otto generally did.

"Everything is well, and we're treated fairly, with no ghosts, which is better than most of us ever expected from life. Please go right on up to the factory. We'll keep watch. They're waiting for you."

Morgan gave a bow, thanked him, and led her crew up the dock, enjoying the certainty that the island's privacy would keep her ship and booty safe. She noticed a few other craft tied up and bobbing gently, but hers was the largest ship, if not the fanciest or schmanciest. A cunning cutter called the *RNS Really Nice Boot* looked both fast and beautifully made, its prow painted gold, and Morgan longed to get her hands on the sleek wheel and see how the quick little ship could maneuver in open water.

The walk up to the factory had once been a rough run up a polluted road with life and death on the line, but now it was an enchanting stroll up a white-sand trail with young palm trees flourishing along either side. The factory's new front door was crafted of gorgeously polished wood with forged-iron fittings, and it read MMA: MACHINERY AND MUNITIONS FOR ANARCHY. Before Morgan could knock, the door flew open, and she was looking directly at a fanny pack.

"Morgan!" Vic bugled, more than a little equine in his excitement. "You came!"

Swole arms embraced her, and her face was crushed against fur as she got a view up his MMA crop top. Surprised but pleased, she returned the hug with an enthusiastic "Mmphrph!"

Pulling away, she gazed up into the face of a Vic she'd never seen before—smiling, open, genuine, unafraid.

"You look well," she said.

"I am well! Feng's new lunchtime yoga program and juice bar have helped me focus on my well-being. Did you know coconut is good for pretty much anything?" He ran a hand through his glistening, wavy mullet. "Even my hair! Even constipation! Even hoof oil! But how are you?"

"Not as good as someone who's harnessed the power of the coconut, but well enough. Business is good. We routed another foul enclave of Ebuk pirates on the way here and have a hold full of booty."

"Ah, booty," another voice said. "One of my favorite words."

Thinking it familiar, Morgan peered behind Vic to see who had spoken.

"Oh, my gosh! Al!" The elf hurried forward for a warm embrace, and Morgan soon realized that she hadn't gotten her requisite number of daily hugs since she became captain of *The Soggy Biscuit* and had to maintain decorum. Al smelled of patchouli and musk, and his red hair had grown long enough to cover the tips of his not-quite-as-pointed-as-he'd-prefer ears. He wore long brown robes, or maybe the robes were a different color but were uniformly coated in brown hair lightly dusted with white and black feathers. He was followed by a circus of puffins.

"Sounds like life is good on the high seas," Al said, helpfully skipping over the how-are-you stage of catching up.

"It is. And how's the lighthouse?"

Al smiled, serene, and showed just a glimmer of elven wisdom. "You must stop by more often. Proudwood Park and Krazy Kritter Sanctuary is flourishing, and King Thorndwall is apoplectic with rage that I'm not capitalizing on it by selling otter grease and puffin sandwiches to the visitors. He told me recently that my father actually was a human farmer, but it wasn't quite the insult he'd hoped, as I kind of love farming puffins. And the Sn'archivist regularly sends me postcards, colleague to colleague. The latest one said simply *mange patties*."

"And you're officially the Proudwood Park's P'archivist?"

"The one and only P'archivist, yeah. I've never been happier."

Morgan's smile was stretching her face to the point of minor discomfort. "I'm really glad it all worked out. Tempest's legal contract must've been aces, if it swayed the king."

"Well, to be fair, y'all," a man's baritone voice said, "the king doesn't require much swaying. His balance isn't actually that great."

The new voice yet again came from behind the smiling Vic, and Morgan peered around him to find a man she'd never seen before outside posters and stamps: Goode King Gustave. He was a little unsteady as he sidled forward, almost as if he hadn't made friends with his sea legs yet, but he wobbled past the centaur and into the open space before the factory's front door, where all the pirates were milling about, curious but pretty ready for something to watch other than tearful reunitings. Morgan had never seen a king before, but she had imagined them as having regal bearing, wearing something that wasn't brown, and picking their nose a good bit less.

The king smiled as he waved in a goofy sort of way and said, "Hi!"

"Yes, your highness?" said one of Morgan's red-shirted crew, bowing low.

"Oh. No. I was just saying hello."

"Yes, your highness?" Another man fell to his knees beside Hye.

"How many of these guys do you have?" Gustave asked, stroking his fuzzy goatee as he stared covetously at Morgan's braided beard. "Because you could all just bow at the same time and get it over with."

Morgan swept her own bow, hat held tightly on with one hand. "Your majesty, these men are called Hye and Hurlo, and my name is Morgan." She left out her full title, knowing she was wanted in more than a few cities. "On behalf of the entire crew"—she looked behind herself and jerked her chin at her crew—"we will now bow together and stop wasting your time being obsequious."

"That's a big word," the king said to Al. "It sounds like it has to do with otters. Does it have to do with otters?"

"It has to do with grrrroveling, sirrrre."

Morgan's heart lifted as she recognized that gravelly growl coming from behind the centaur.

"Luc?"

"Aye, Captain!"

The yellow-and-red parrot appeared as Morvin walked around Vic to sheepishly bob his head.

"If it ain't the lady," Morvin said.

But Morgan was too excited to see Luc, and she had never been more honored than when he bridged the gap between them to land on her shoulder, contemplatively kneading her muscle with his black talons.

"Awww, that's betterrrr!" he enthused. "Gettin' quite supple, lass."

"Well, I did learn from the best."

Otto chittered from Morgan's hat, and she lifted it to let the otter loose.

"I think y'all are messin' with me. It *did* have to do with otters," Gustave said.

But Otto wasn't cavorting around the king. Quick as a shot and squeaking to himself, the otter ran past Vic and anyone else waiting their turn behind him to make an entrance.

"Oh, no," Morgan muttered. "Is there any fish in there that you particularly needed? Because if so, I apologize in advance. It's gonna get messy."

"No fish," Vic said, grinning. "But you might as well come up and see."

Vic turned, and Morgan followed him with Luc on her shoulder, Al by her side, her crew behind her, and the king kind of skipping along with his strange gait in the middle, unworried about being first or last or indeed any sort of protocol, murmuring about tea cakes and how angry his adviser would be when she discovered what he'd done.

"Well, what'd you do?" Milly Dread asked, for she had somehow taken to walking in step with the king as if it were the most natural thing in the world, and their unsteady steps were very similar in stride length.

The king shrugged. "I stole my own ship and set sail to a secret island when I was supposed to be in dance class. That's going to get her goat, know what I mean? She'll be booking a de-stressing session with her wattle masseuse right about now."

"A wattle masseuse! I've heard of those. Is it worth it to go see one?" Milly asked, a hand raised contemplatively to her neck.

Listening to him pace beside the leathery old lady and discuss the various schools of wattle massage in Kolon without shying away from Milly's general aura of chum and oyster juice, Morgan realized he was a very likable king.

They took a familiar path, for all that the factory looked completely different. The otter cages had been torn out, replaced with yoga mats and a juice bar, and the barrels of EATUM were gone, leaving only tidy crates of cannonballs and other piratical munitions. The grand door that had once led to "The Boss" had been taken off its hinges and the hallway beyond painted a cheerful and welcoming lavender. The many offices showed clear signs of use, and Gladys was still apparently at lunch, if the dusty sign was to be believed.

Taking the stairs, they encountered no middle managers dangling from the ceiling or security guards with crossbows, and they soon reached the rooftop. Morgan carefully schooled her face, knowing what she would find on the other side of that door.

Her friend Tempest, the willowmaw.

Beautiful and terrible and bloodthirsty, her maw waiting to snap off a stray arm, her waving branches strong as whips, and all her kindness and intelligence fled.

But what Morgan saw surprised her.

The last time she'd seen Tempest, the dryad had looked like a gnarled old willow with a thick, twisted trunk. But now the willow looked young and supple, with smooth bark. The capacious maw was barely big enough to fit in a finger, much less an entire arm. And it—she—seemed to be smiling. Otto was gamboling at the tree's base, chittering like he'd once done with Tempest in the times when she'd given him a good scratch.

"What happened?" Morgan asked, hurrying ahead to what now looked less like a monster's mouth and more like a woman's amused grin.

"Vic took care of me," the maw said through lips of tender bark. Tempest's voice was as soft as leaves swaying in the wind.

"You can talk!"

"I can. And it's almost time."

"Time for what?"

"Tea."

Vic appeared, holding a teacup full of . . . well, something Morgan didn't want to think too much about. Using a dainty teaspoon, he scooped what appeared to be a flesh smoothie into Tempest's mouth, her dry lips hungrily sucking.

"Uh, that doesn't look like tea," Gustave said, peering into the cup. "That kinda looks like raw meat. Do I even wanna know?"

Vic raised an eyebrow at him. "You do not."

And then it happened.

It started in the branches, which shook and swirled as a golden light shone from Tempest's bark. Her roots pulled up from the rock, and most of her leaves fell to the ground, and the king said, "Oh, wow. That's pretty special. I did something like that once. Did she eat a boot? Because I used to be . . . well . . . different, and then I ate the wrong boot. Or the right boot, I guess. And here I am. Don't tell anyone I told you that."

"What?" Morgan said.

"What?" the king responded. "Hey, I'm gonna go over there now."

The king went a bit away to castigate himself, but Morgan didn't care about kings anymore, because suddenly Tempest was a woman again, on her hands and knees, shivering. Morgan draped her velvet frock coat over her friend and helped her stand, and Vic was laughing and offering her oatmeal cookies, while Al shook his head and muttered, "Mange patties. It's an anagram for *Tempest again*. I'll be danged, that Sn'archivist works in mysterious ways."

"How did this happen?" was all Morgan could say, looking into Tempest's eyes in a way that she'd never thought she would again.

It took Tempest a moment to remember how her mouth worked. "Vic fed me," she finally said. "For however long it was—years?"

The centaur nodded, his lush and healthy mullet gently bobbing on his head.

"And I felt more and more myself with each bite," Tempest continued. "And just a few weeks ago I realized I could speak again, and I told him what would happen, and I asked him to send for you." She looked around at the odd little group, smiling at everyone. "For all of you. And then I asked him to wait to give me the final bite until you'd arrived."

"Pretty rad, right?" Vic asked.

"Verrrry rrrrad," Luc agreed, for all that he sounded like he'd never said the word *rad* before and probably shouldn't ever say it again.

"So why did you guys invite me?" King Gustave asked. "I mean, I came because I needed to get out of the throne room, you know? Not that it's not a swell party, but it seems like you guys are all good friends and I'm just this guy hanging around talking about boots."

"We owe you our thanks," Tempest said, holding out her hands and taking the king's, easy as that. "For Al's Proudwood Park, and for the new MMA contract that's allowed us to transform this place. And for keeping Pell safe and free."

"Oh! And that's the other thing," Gustave said, jumping up and down a bit in a goatlike manner. "I also wanted to thank you for stopping that whole EATUM business. I just . . . really understand why otters wouldn't want to be eaten, you know? I will never eat in a Dinny's again. And the MMA really does make the best cannonballs in Pell."

"We told him MMA stands for *Machinery and Munitions for Authority*," Feng whispered to Morgan. "So he wouldn't know we're pirates who routinely attack Royal Navy ships. I think he missed the sign that says ANARCHY above the door."

"And aren't I supposed to cut some sort of ribbon?" King Gustave wondered aloud. "I know how to use scissors and everything."

Al stepped in smoothly, one hand on the king's back. "We lost the scissors. But could I interest you in a puffin? Or perhaps some elvish magic?"

"No, and no. Way too messy. But can we break into these biscotti?" King Gustave had sauntered over to a long banquet table covered

with the fruits of Vic's magic. Gorgeous tea cakes, mounds of cookies, hands and hands of ladyfingers, and an unwanted pile of crum-
pets waited.

"You're the king, idiot," someone said, a little snippily. "You can eat
whenever you please."

Gustave scowled. "Did you do that thing where you put your ghost
mouth over the food, though? Because stuff doesn't taste as good
when you do that."

At first, Morgan thought the king was talking to himself, offering
further proof that he was barmy if harmless. And then she saw the
ghost standing behind a four-layer cake with a handcrafted willow
tree of modeling chocolate on top. Another ghost appeared on the
ground in front of the first ghost, squatting and pointing at Otto and
the puffins cavorting around the roof.

"Lord Toby, sir, is that some kind of new chicken? 'Cause it followed me under the table with its friends and I feel called out."

The first ghost, a man with a sad little scrub of a beard, looked
down at the new ghost, a woman in a tight rogue's suit. "It is an otter,
Poltro, and those are puffins, and if you ignore the wings, they have
nothing in common with a chicken, outside of being alive. Which we
are not."

"Well, of course I knew that, Lord Toby! Bloody fool I'd be if I
didn't know the difference between alive and dead."

"You didn't know with that crab yesterday," Gustave said, as if
these ghosts were simply normal friends who joined him on strange
outings to odd islands all the time. "You talked to it for like an hour,
and it was definitely dead. I could smell it."

"But I can't smell, you gristly goat! Ain't got nose hairs anymore,
do I? And them puffers look pretty chicken-like, and I'd bet my but-
ternut biscuit they make the grimy, hateful buttfruit."

"Do you," Al began, looking strangely fascinated, "have something
against eggs?"

"Um," Vic gently interrupted, as everyone was crowded around
the refreshments table, starving and salivating but also terrified to eat

during the king's conversation, even one with incorporeal strangers. "Refreshments are served."

The pirates fell upon the food, and Vic had never looked prouder. Many compliments on the victuals rained down from the crew and even the king himself, although the ghost man merely said, "Hmm. Cupcakes. Not as useful in a fight as a day-old baguette, but not bad wizardry, that."

At some point, Morvin dropped his muffin and screeched, and the ghost rogue screeched, and they were soon arguing like siblings because they *were* siblings, and the ghost man began haranguing Morvin for abandoning his landscaping duties, and Al said it was the weirdest party he'd ever been to and he'd once been to a party with the Dread Necromancer Steve.

Daintily holding a shortbread cookie and sipping her tea, Morgan stuck by Tempest's side as various old friends called out their congratulations, and after what felt like forever, the pirates went downstairs to look at the fireworks selection Vic had amassed for their entertainment. Only Morgan, Tempest, Vic, Al, Luc, Morvin, and, oddly, the king and his ghost companions stood on the roof as the sun set picturesquely over the harbor.

"It's been quite an adventure, hasn't it?" Tempest said.

Morgan looked over the wall and down to her ship, which still wore the stains of ding-gull berry juice. She'd come so far from her time in the tower, and she had the beard ring to prove it.

"Definitely an adventure. I never would've guessed that this might be my future."

"Nor mine. I never thought I would be free."

"Me neither. But here we are."

"Yes, here we are."

"With heckin' good cookies," Morvin added, as Luc had returned to his chosen shoulder, and the two women were tearing up and hugging.

Vic sighed happily. "And good friends."

King Gustave raised his teacup, and everyone else did too. "As I'm the king and I can do what I want, I hereby raise a toast. To that lady who used to be a tree!"

"My name is Tempest, your majesty."

"Hey, you wrote the document I had to sign so that kinda elfy-looking guy could raise puffins! My advisor said you had the killer instincts of a shark crossed with a—"

"Chicken?"

"No, Poltro. A shark crossed with something else that was very smart and obviously not a chicken or an egg. Say, Tempest, do you want a job? Our current lawyer is this elf who's always trying to give me a magic wedgie."

Tempest smiled. "It would be an honor. As long as I get good benefits and plenty of time off to sail the seas of Pell."

"Talk to my lawyer about that," the king said.

"Hey, can we finish our cheers soon? Me sister the ghost keeps putting her blue ghost mouth on my cup, and I don't like the ecto-plasmic aftertaste," Morvin complained.

"To Tempest!" Morgan shouted in her best pirate bark.

"To Tempest!" everyone said.

But before they could drink, Tempest added, "And to Vic, for saving me!"

"To Vic!"

Vic raised his glass to Luc. "And to Luc, who got us all here!"

"To Luc!"

"And to Captain Morrrrgan, my finest prrrrotégée!"

"To Morgan!"

"And to the king, because he's such a great guy!" Gustave said out of the side of his mouth.

"To the king!"

"And to Pell," Al added. "Because it's been one Pell of an adventure."

"To Pell!"

After an awkward moment of everyone hoping the cheering was over, they breathed a collective sigh of relief and drank.

The tea tasted like success and also lemons.

"So what happens now?" King Gustave asked, making it kind of weird.

"You're the king. You decide," the peevish ghost Toby muttered.

"Oh, yeah. So I am. I am the king, and I hereby declare . . ." Gustave trailed off, and everyone waited.

"Yes, your highness?" Tempest pressed.

"I declare everyone must live happily ever after."

"But that's impossible!"

King Gustave smiled a goaty smile.

"Nothing's impossible in Pell."

ACKNOWLEDGMENTS

Kevin says: While we must thank all foine people everywhere, we want to especially thank Seattle for literally being there for us as we outlined this novel. During Emerald City Comic Con in 2018, Delilah and I hopped from one sushi place to another as we broke down this story of a bearded lady who wants to save the otters and a centaur swoleboy who eventually realizes he can simply discard the poisonous baggage of toxic masculinity and be super happy afterward. Seattle is a magical place where new ideas are born and yet where many succumb to the siren call of the same old things; it's the perfect inspiration for a cast of characters who look at what society says they're supposed to do and then choose to do better. They're gonna say nope to those tempting siren fish tails.

Thanks to Metal Editor Tricia Narwani and the Del Rey team for shepherding this book to fruition, and to copy editor Kathy Lord for wrangling with our linguistic peccadilloes. Would you believe us, Kathy, if we said we were very sorry for grossing you out with the ding-gull berries but . . . simultaneously delighted?

Immense gratitude to my family for always being everything good.

High fives and super mega turbo thanks to my co-author, Delilah, for uncounted giggles on this journey of poignant silliness. It's not every day you'll find a friend who will let you hook a plot to a prophecy of elf butts and otter balls. I still cannot read "tampoonist" without smiling, and the same can be said for many other passages in the Tales of Pell. Writing these stories with you has been a tremendous privilege and even more affirming than living with an affirmation gecko. Thank you for the laughs, for the friendship, for your unrelenting creativity, and for loving fantasy enough to poke fun at it.

Delilah says: First of all, thanks be to Kevin for always writing his ac-knowledgments first, that I might copy him.

Secondly, yes, many thanks to Seattle. Your foine flavors run through this book, from Spam musubi to rummy grog to the salt tang of Pike's Place Market. Thank you for your flat whites and gluten-free cinnamon rolls in the morning and your flaming tiki drinks at night. This book wouldn't be this book without you.

Nextly, our forever thanks to the entire Del Rey team. You are the wind in our sales (heh heh), and we'd take a tampoon in the chest for any one of ye.

Next nextly, to my family, on whom I often inflicted these chapters with no context to see if they were as funny as I thought they were. Nothing says success like kids laughing so hard they fall off the couch. And to my wonderful husband, Craig, for always acting as my own af-firmation gecko when I need it the most.

High tens and *super mega extra double turbo* thanks to my co-author, Kevin, for asking me to be in an ill-fated fantasy anthology while we were eating airport barbecue at 10 A.M. in the Dallas airport. Some bad decisions were made that day, but not in the realm of dreaming about a book where fantasy tropes were lovingly poked and prodded, along with puns both great and terrible. This series has been such a fantastic jour-ney with you, and I'll forever remember our bar-hopping brainstorming sessions as some of the most lively and fertile creative explosions of my life. It may be time to swab up behind our literary boom-boom, but much like Brawny Billy, it shall live on in fond memories and also as crab food. You're the best, homey!

READ ON FOR AN EXCERPT OF

No Country for Old Gnomes

BY DELILAH S. DAWSON AND
KEVIN HEARNE

The Tales of Pell can be read in any order, so if you
haven't read the other two installments, what are you
waiting for? We're delighted to give you a peek of
No Country for Old Gnomes on the next page, and be
sure to look for *Kill the Farm Boy*, both available now!

"Never trust quotes placed at the beginning of chapters as if they were diamonds of the brain. They were probably written by a halfling expressly for the purpose of deceiving you."

—GNOMER THE GNOMERIAN, in the Fourth Gnomeric Cycle, ∮♭♍-♯♭

In a hole in the ground there lived a family of gnomes. Not a yucky, moist, gross hole filled with worm tails and old chicken bones, nor yet a dusty, crusty, sandy hole entirely lacking modern plumbing and ergonomic seating: It was a gnomehome, and that meant tidiness and comfort.

In this particular moment, however, there was strife. There was, in fact, a Mighty Row. Onni Numminen had finally had enough of his twin brother's ungnomeric antics.

"Offi, you can't wear that thing to the Midsummer Shindig. It's ridiculous."

Offi looked down, the gaslights flashing off his glasses. "Why not? It's a cardigan. All gnomes wear cardigans. And you must admit it's tidy. I'm following all the rules." He tugged his scraggly beard in a way gnomes did when they thought they were getting away with something, which only annoyed Onni more.

"But it's black! With rabid purple bats on it!"

The very sight of the thing nearly made Onni's brain short-circuit.

Tidy sweater, never better! was one of the very first gnomeisms every gnomelet learned in gnomeschool, but it was assumed the sweaters would be in bright colors and feature embroidered ducks, pineapples, or tulips, cheerful symbols of gnomeric togetherness. It was true that Offi had knit himself a finely crafted cardigan, but it was entirely the wrong color. What kind of gnome would wear black? And then he had gone and lovingly embroidered creepy purple bats on it, their eyes made of shiny red buttons. Offi was correct: Technically, there was nothing wrong with it. But it was obvious to anyone with eyes that Offi Numminen wasn't being . . . gnomeric.

And that was the worst thing a gnome could do, outside of stealing pudding or shaving off his or her beard.

"You can't wear it to the shindig," Onni repeated, tugging his own scruffy beard in exasperation. "I won't allow it."

Offi gave him a dark look, in part because that was one of only two looks Offi could give these days, the other being one that said that life was merely a slow trudge toward death and Offi's soul was a black repository for pain.

Onni hated both looks, and gnomes weren't supposed to hate anything, except an untidy sock drawer. And halflings. And anyone who called them "knee-high," since they had their own knees and were appropriately taller than said body parts.

"I can so wear it, and I will, and you don't get to allow me anything. I've tried to be like you, Onni, and where did it get me? Nowhere. Pretending to be happy never made anyone happy. Do you know what it's like, being me, and you being you? Knowing everyone thinks my twin is the poster boy for gnomeric youth? By dinkus, they gave you a medal that straight up says PARAGON OF GNOMERIC YOUTH on it. And I have to stare at it all the time."

He glumly glanced to where the medal hung on a plaque amidst dozens of other medals proudly proclaiming things like EXEMPLAR OF TOGETHERNESS and TIDIEST CARDIGAN and SPIFFIEST HAT and WOW, WHAT A GNOME. And then they both glanced to Offi's identical plaque, which featured only one sad, smallish medal, reading EATS PUDDING WITH MINOR GUSTO.

For once, Onni tried to see things from his brother's point of view.

Onni considered himself a foine boy, and not only because he had three FOINE BOY medals. But he *tried*. He actively wanted to make his parents proud by being the most gnomeric of gnomes. He got along. He spouted the gnomeisms whenever appropriate. He did his best to be round, affable, and clean and to wear only the brightest colors.

Whereas Offi had recently slid into the darkest acceptable colors: navy blue, forest green, and a particularly virulent shade of plum just this side of a bruise. He was appropriately round and clean, but not even a curmudgeonly badger would consider him affable. He was grim. He was dour and even verging on sour. He was, in essence, Not Jolly.

Onni's twin increasingly turned away from people and sought his quiet corner of their father's workshop, where Offi put on his unacceptably greasy work cardigan and tinkered with Old Seppo's broken or forgotten machines. Why, Offi hadn't even gone to the Everybody Goes to This Dance dance! He was destroying Onni's social capital, and that was one thing Onni couldn't abide. So he tried another tactic.

"If you wear that to the Midsummer Shindig, you'll break Mama's heart."

Offi glared. "Mama loves Papa, and he's not the most gnomeric of gnomes."

Onni snorted. "That's different, by dinkus! He's a war hero. They're allowed to get peculiar. And he still wears appropriately bright cardigans. Besides, he's starting to get a reputation in town—you know that. Paranoid, they call him. Just last week at the beard salon, I heard Una Uvulaa call him Crazy Old Seppo."

That finally brought fire to Offi's eyes, a rare third look that appeared to be Characteristically Ungnomeric Rage. "Did she mention he installed one of his Halflings Hate This Heat-Resistant Hatch hatches for her? Because they may talk about him behind his back, but the foine folk of Pavaasik still rely on him to keep their homes safe from halfling firebombs." A flash of worry lit Offi's eyes, and Onni frowned at the shadows around them. By hokum, had his batty twin lined them with soot? They were all . . . soulful.

"It's getting worse, you know," Offi continued. "Pooti Pinkelsen's whole family exploded last week. The halflings' firebombs are getting worse. I heard Papa telling Mama about it. If they'd had one of Papa's hatch covers, they wouldn't have had their giblets blown up. So our love of gadgetry trumps your love of . . . getting along. You can't get along if you're dead."

Onni's hands clenched into fists, and he regretted starting the row. Gnomes were proud of their round stomachs but had little stomach for fighting.

"Look, Offi, gadgetry has its place, but the heart of our strength will always be people. As Mama always says, *Stick together, tough as leather!*"

Offi rolled his eyes, shocking Onni. For all that they were twins, identical down to their blue eyes and golden curls, distinguishable only by Offi's black-rimmed spectacles—which were honestly mostly for show—Onni was quite sure he had never rolled his eyes in such a deliberately rebellious manner. His brother was on dangerous ground.

"Onni, how do you not get it? The halflings are dropping *firebombs* into our *homes*—seemingly just for fun, I might add—and that's not going to stop because everyone wears a nice cardigan and holds hands while singing 'The Get-Along Song.' They tried that once, and everyone blew up! Everyone we know *is blowing up*! My cardigan is not the problem. Father is right. We need weaponry. And not the sort that hurls waistcoats at squirrels to hide their shame. Real machinery, like he built during the Giant Wars."

"Not this again!" Onni moaned.

"Just because you got a B in Trebuchets 101 in gnomeschool, you always look down on machinery!"

"And just because you got a D in Charisma and Charm—"

"The teacher had a natural prejudice against glasses!"

"You had oil on your cardigan!"

"You had . . . er, charm on yours!" Offi tried, pushing up his glasses and glaring at Onni.

"Not this again," Onni moaned.

And that's when they heard the BOOM!

Their eyes met.

"Firebomb!" they said in unison.

"Listen, darlings, onions are wonderful in stews and when grilled really complement a nice steak, but if you walk around smelling like them it's your own fault. Wash your hands after handling them with a bit of salt to get out the stink, then again with soap, and I promise everyone will be happier for it."

—JOOLIA CHYLDE, *The Clever Craft of Corraden Cooking*

All strife disintegrated as the brothers ran for the main hatch. Onni's heart was thumpity-thumping like mad, his brain going to terribly ungnomeric places that involved his beloved mother exploding to bits.

"Do you think—" he began.

"Don't think. Just run," Offi muttered.

They bolted through the tunnels toward the kitchen, but a shadowy shape stepped in front of them, causing Onni to skid to a halt, already drawing his belt knife.

"Die, halfling!" he shouted, lunging forward.

"Good sentiment, bad eyesight," Old Seppo said, neatly blocking the strike. "C'mon, boys. I've got the main hatch sealed, and Mama will meet us outside the lute room."

Without another word, the old gnome took off, running faster than Onni had ever seen him move. As they ran through each section of tunnel, Seppo pulled a hidden lever, and a steel-reinforced door slammed down.

"They got the kitchen?" Offi asked.

"Aye, the dinkuses. That's why Mama and I were eating our pudding in the sewing room. I pity the fool who still thinks a kitchen is a safe place to dine."

They reached the lute room, where Venla Numminen was carefully placing her two most prized lutes into a special carrying case.

"Those halflings won't be looting my lutes," she said with a frown. "Not today."

Onni had never seen his gentle mother so serious. Venla had once been a traveling chanteuse in a popular band called the Magic Morels, and all the album covers of her naked-but-for-the-artistic-placement-of-her-knee-length-hair-and-beard made it easy to forget that she had acted as a nurse during the Giant Wars. Now, faced with firebombs and evacuation of the home she'd lovingly built with Seppo, she embodied calm strength, her orange cardigan perfectly straight and her beard ribbon still neatly tied in a bow.

With the entire family reunited, Seppo opened up a new hatch, one Onni had never seen—not that he tended to notice gadgetry. The tunnel beyond was barely lit by jars of glowing green algae placed at intervals, and four suitcases waited just inside. Seppo pushed one into Onni's chest, and then they were running again, bags in hand. As they passed hidden air vents, he could hear the foul cackle of halfling laughter, far overhead, and smell hints of smoke and sausage. His step faltered, but then he reminded himself: He was a Foine Boy. He was strong, and he would continue to be strong for his family. When he tried to glance back at his twin, he saw that Offi's general woe-is-me-for-I-am-a-tortured-soul-and-I-walk-the-world-alone face had been replaced by a brand-new by-dinkus-this-is-worrisome face. Poor Offi—he just wasn't made for heroics.

The tunnel ended in an empty room, and Onni began to feel the hints of a Grand Panic. But then Offi stepped forward and gave Old Seppo a solemn nod, and together they took hold of some sort of hokum gadgetry affixed to the floor that ran up into the ceiling. It was a mess of gears and cranks and shafts and lube—all that stuff Offi and his father were always talking about; you'd think shafts and lube were the only things in the world sometimes the way they carried on—and now they rammed it up and down, grunting as bits of icky dirt fell down onto their cardigans. It was, Onni realized, some sort of saw, and they were creating their own escape hatch by cutting out a circle of earth. Soon, Seppo pulled yet another lever, and a thick flap of soil and sod levered open to reveal the night sky.

"Where are we?" Onni asked, partially impressed by what his father and brother had achieved and partially terrified of halflings with bombs and also murderous stoats, for gnomes were a smöl people, and the nighttime was considered Quite Dangerous.

"Out beyond the goat pasture," Seppo answered, heaving a ladder into place. "You boys leave your bags with us and head to the barn for the ponies. There'll be sentries, so have your wits about you. Meet us back here when the brouhaha is over. These old bones ain't as bouncy as they used to be."

Onni gazed upon his parents, noting for perhaps the first time that they were indeed becoming whitebeards, and that their eyes were bracketed by a lifetime of smile creases. With the heaviness of the night sky overhead and their home lost forever, they looked wee and old and helpless, and he knew he had to rise to the occasion. He climbed to the top of the ladder and stood on the grass above.

"Mother, Father. Take care," Onni said, injecting nobility into every word as he squinted to the horizon. "We will return."

"By gumballs, what do you think Mama and Papa are going to do?" Offi scoffed, pulling himself to stand beside his twin. "Beat a pudding pan with a stick and say, *Hey, halflings, how's about you lob a foine firebomb me-wards,* or something? Of course they're going to be careful! And what's with all the squinting? Do you need my glasses?"

"No," Onni whispered indignantly as he started for the barn. "I was being heroic."

"Are heroes generally nearsighted?"

Onni's teeth ground together—as if Offi knew anything about heroes! "Come along and shut your pudding hole before the halflings hear us."

The brothers crept toward the barn, and Onni had to admit that his brother's woefully black cardigan was wonderful for sneaking. Up ahead, the goats were bleating and butting heads and ejecting terror pellets as smoke billowed through the barnyard, and this was quite useful, as it covered up the sound of creeping gnomes. The only light came from the moon and the pierced-tin lanterns hanging from the eaves of the barn. Onni saw two halflings standing by the fence, one telling a racist joke as the other picked his nose. Both were turned away from the goats, toward the fire and smoke beyond. Onni wouldn't let himself look at what was left of his home; the sound of cackling and bawdy songs about gnomesplosions and the scent of brauts suggested the halflings were having a by dinkum party and barbecue around the flaming kitchen hatch.

"I see two halflings, but there'll be at least one more," Onni whispered. "In the barn, probably."

"I know that! We took the same How to Be Respectfully Sneaky class. And before you ask, yes, I remember everything they taught us in the Polite but Necessary Stabbing and Smacking About the Face seminar, which we both found so invigorating."

"So this dumb gnome walks into a bar, right?" the racist halfling was saying, in that loud voice people tended to use when telling terrible jokes. "And there's a halfling and a dwarf and a giant, just minding their business, and the bartender says—urghk!"

Which Onni found strange, as he'd never heard anyone say "urghk" before.

Then he saw what had happened: Bulgy Bertram the billy goat had wisely chosen to ram the racist halfling in the crotch, driving him to the ground. While he was there, Bertram finished him off with a concussive head butt.

"Louis, what the—"

The other halfling didn't get to finish his sentence, as a crossbow bolt bloomed from his chest, suggesting that the third, hidden halfling wasn't very good at his job or was perhaps unheroically nearsighted. Now there were two halflings on the ground and being proudly plopped upon by a very self-satisfied goat.

Offi nodded his approval. "I always liked that goat."

"He gave us a couple of shields, didn't he? Let's make use of them," Onni suggested, and Offi nodded in that way the twins had of not needing to talk when picking up racist halflings whose hairy butts would serve as cover.

They squeezed through the fence and darted among the goats to heave the heavy halflings over their shoulders. Onni hated everything about the halfling: He was greasy, reeked of onions and butt musk, and was covered with coarse curly hair that made Onni's neck itch. When he felt something metal bouncing on his back, he realized that the halfling was also wearing the gold medallion of a drub: a Dastardly Rogue Under Bigly-Wicke. The halfling criminal organization had publicly denied being behind the firebombings around Pavaasik.

Onni and Offi ran for the barn door, and they'd almost made it when Onni heard the next thwack of a crossbow. Luckily, the bolt lodged in the rump of the racist halfling, and Onni wouldn't let himself consider how close it had come to his own face. For all that the smöl gnomes, burdened by odiferous halfling flesh, could only run at roughly the speed of an excited tortoise, they were almost to the barn door, and the remaining halfling was in sight.

But then Offi tripped and his dead-halfling shield flopped into the dirt.

Curled into a ball, the unprotected Offi rolled pell-mell toward the halfling assassin, who was hurriedly reloading his crossbow. Onni knew what he had to do. With every ounce of strength in his pudgy body, he threw the racist halfling at the enemy, and then everything seemed to happen in slow motion.

The halfling stepped aside, avoiding Onni's salvo of tossed rogue flesh.

The halfling raised his reloaded crossbow, his hairy finger on the trigger, the bolt aimed for Onni's heart.

But the halfling had forgotten about Offi.

Onni watched, proud and terrified, as his unathletic brother rolled up and swept the halfling's leg, just like they'd learned in their Great Ways to Run Away class.

The halfling went down hard, the crossbow flying from his fingers.

Onni saw an opportunity to employ one of the 37 Methods to Finish Him from that invigorating seminar. He picked up a milking bucket and beaned the third halfling in the noggin, hard enough to knock him unconscious and raise a goose egg on his forehead. With all three enemies dispatched, Onni put out a hand to help up his twin.

"Uh-oh, my foine lad! There's hay on your cardigan," Offi said, voice dripping with irony.

"Make hay while the sun shines, bake hay pudding when it rains!" Onni dutifully recited.

Offi rolled his eyes again, like he was getting used to the forbidden gesture. "Who are you underneath all those memorized sayings, brother? I like you better when you're not spouting gnomeisms."

"And I like you best when you're taking down halfling assassins before they can shoot me," Onni admitted with a smile and open arms, hoping his brother would take the olive branch and stop being so stonking difficult.

It almost worked. Offi accepted the hug, but he didn't relax into the embrace and wiggle, as happy gnomes did. He just gave a dreary sigh.

Then it was back to business. Onni kept watch at the barn door with the crossbow as Offi saddled their four fat little sway-bellied ponies and wrangled the donkey into his harness. Onni had never been more glad to see Puggyrump and Buttertum and Jellybells and Mrs. Wicklebum and their dear little miniature donkey, Happy Mumbletoes. They were so cheerful and pudgy it was impossible for even Offi to grump around them. Soon they were leading the beasts toward the secret hatch where Venla and Seppo waited. Their father claimed the fourth pony as his own. Seppo always said she had once been a fierce war steed, and as his father tied on his bags and mounted the shaggy little beast, Onni almost believed him, for a moment.

They paused outside the barnyard to take one last look at their gnome-home. It was now nothing more than an open hatch filled with flame and billowing black smoke, a ruin surrounded by capering halflings waving sausages on sticks. Their overwhelming arsenal of incendiaries had defeated their father's booby traps. Old Seppo shook his head and held out his hand to Venla for reassurance. She grabbed it and squeezed.

"Listen to them laugh, Venla. That's our pride and sweat they're burning down. Our peace and love and joy."

"No, Seppo. I won't believe that. They can never burn down our peace and love and joy. We carry that with us in the pockets of our cardigans. *Home is where the gnome is.* Let the rogues laugh now. We've already outsmarted them and they haven't a clue. We'll come back when we're ready, and then they won't be laughing."

"No, they won't," he agreed, and he released her hand and turned his mount to the west. The old gnome glowered at the horizon, squinting, his face a web of wrinkles. "When we come back, they'll be dying."

"But where will we go?" Onni asked.

"We'll head to Bruding. Scuttlebutt says there are refugee centers there among the humans and that Lord Ergot won't allow the halflings to cause trouble in his demesne. We'll find our people, regroup, and plan our revenge."

Onni's eyes slid over to his brother's face and saw such sadness there that he felt himself welling up. They were a long way from the Grand Row they'd had earlier, when they'd had nothing more pressing than a silly black cardigan to worry about. Onni looked at his brother's chest, and his mouth fell open as he spotted something by the firelight.

"Offi, your cardigan," he said, pointing to the once-neat sweater with its embroidered bats. "It's ruined. There's . . ."

"Blood on it," Offi finished for him. "Halfling blood."

Looking off to the horizon, properly and heroically squinting, Onni added, "Get your washtub ready, brother. It will be a bloody business when the gnome empire strikes back."

"Whoa," Offi said, with feeling. "You totally just gave me chills."

ABOUT THE AUTHORS

DELILAH S. DAWSON is the author of the *New York Times* bestseller *Star Wars: Phasma*, as well as *Star Wars: Galaxy's Edge: Black Spire*, the Hit series, *Servants of the Storm*, the Blud series, and the Shadow series (written as Lila Bowen and beginning with *Wake of Vultures*). Her comics credits include the creator-owned *Ladycastle*, *Sparrowhawk*, and *Star Pig*, as well as work in the worlds of *Star Wars*, *The X-Files*, *Labyrinth*, *Adventure Time*, *Rick and Morty*, and *Marvel Action Spider-Man*. She lives in Florida with her family and a fat mutt named Merle.

whimsydark.com
Twitter: @DelilahSDawson
Instagram: @delilahsdawson

KEVIN HEARNE hugs trees, pets doggies, and rocks out to heavy metal. He also thinks tacos are a pretty nifty idea. He is the author of The Seven Kennings series and the *New York Times* bestselling series The Iron Druid Chronicles.

kevinhearne.com
Twitter: @KevinHearne
Instagram: @kevinhearne

Please visit talesofpell.com for more.

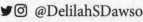